A VALENTINE KISS

The marquis dismounted just as Toby galloped towards him. He gestured to the boy to hold the reins, then strode quickly to Deborah's side. "Are you hurt?"

Too shaken to speak, her breath coming in painful gasps, she slid from the saddle into his waiting arms. For a long moment, she took immense comfort from the feeling of security that engulfed her as she nestled against his broad chest.

Sunderland held her, murmuring soft endearments against her hair. His hand slid down her back, soothing her as he would a skittish filly. "There now, my darling—it is over and you're safe . . . quite safe."

Her heart slowed its frantic beating and a little color returned to her face. Still, she did not move from his embrace. It felt so good to be enveloped in his muscular arms, so right to rest her head against his shoulder, so comforting to feel his hand lightly stroking her back—but it was also very wrong. She tilted her head back slightly, intending to tell him she was unharmed.

As her gaze locked with his, her lips parted slightly, but she stood perfectly still, almost mesmerized by the intensity of his dark eyes.

"Deborah . . ." His voice was whisper soft, almost as soft as the kiss he bestowed on her temple. Then his lips were moving against her mouth.

She closed her eyes. Swept away by a torrent of emotions, she silenced her conscience. No kiss had ever tasted as sweet . . . or as wicked . . .

—from THE VALENTINE'S DAY HUSBAND,
by Carol Quinto

YOU WON'T WANT TO READ
JUST ONE—KATHERINE STONE

A
VALENTINE
BOUQUET

Paula Tanner Girard
Judith A. Lansdowne
Carol Quinto

Zebra Books
Kensington Publishing Corp.

http://www.zebrabooks.com

ZEBRA BOOKS are published by

Kensington Publishing Corp.
850 Third Avenue
New York, NY 10022

First Printing: February, 1997
10 9 8 7 6 5 4 3 2 1

Printed in the United States of America

Contents

Cupid's Legacy

Paula Tanner Girard

One

Delphinia Penn was a handsome young lady—as far as handsome goes—although, she had never paid much attention to what she wore or how she appeared to others. The daughter of a sweet-tempered mother and the devout Wilmot Penn, vicar of the tidy town of Ram's Head, Delphinia never quite fit into the mold of her pious and quite ordinary family. Whereas, in due time, all her obedient brothers and sisters married and started proper families as was expected of them, her parents, acknowledging their raven-haired daughter's difference, allowed her at the age of sixteen to enter the employ, as companion, of the elderly and wealthy Miss Cornelia Cloverseed of Whetstone Manor.

A congenial relationship developed between the two women in spite of their great separation of ages, for they were of nature much alike, tending toward a keen curiosity about life and outspoken to the point of being blunt.

"It is my belief," Miss Cloverseed said more than once, "that much of the world is peopled by shallow and silly muttonheads. Men in particular—in my opinion—lead this group.''

Having met few men, aside from an occasional visitor from outside Norfolk, Delphinia had given no serious consideration to the circumstance that she'd really had little contact with the opposite sex, other than those of her own family and the staff at the manor. Quite unaware that she was doing so, she slowly took this particular view of her employer's as her own.

Now Delphinia had arrived at the age of six-and-twenty never giving any thought that Miss Cloverseed would not be around forever. So it was with some surprise and consternation that one snowy day in December her employer announced, ''Penn, I have decided that it is time for me to die.''

''Stuff and nonsense Miss Cloverseed, do not say so,'' Delphinia said, as she set up the table for their usual after-dinner game of cribbage. ''You are always trying to shock me, and you know you cannot do it.''

''Humph! Can and will if I want to, young lady,'' the old woman said, settling into her chair.

Delphinia had her own opinions on that matter, but something in Miss Cloverseed's tone made her fall silent.

''I am not one to be so insensitive as to disturb everyone's Christmas or forget what joy my servants find in receiving gifts, so I have chosen the day after Boxing Day for my journey into the Other World.''

Miss Cloverseed never mentioned Heaven. She told Delphinia that she thought it sounded quite dull, sitting on clouds all day, playing a harp. Nor did she think that Hades could be much better, although she had been finding the cold creeping into her bones more and more of late and the thought of being warm did have its advantages. No, she always talked to Delphinia of the *many mansions* mentioned in the Bible, as though she were sure they were far away places which she had not traveled to yet. She'd made up her mind that once she'd passed over, her next adventures would be to see all the sights which she'd been deprived of exploring in this lifetime.

"Day after Boxing Day is as good a time as ever. Don't you agree, Penn?"

Delphinia thought the question too absurd to answer.

"Cat got your tongue, *Miss* Penn?"

Quite used to the old lady's tricks of trying to set her off balance before they began their evening sport, it was all Delphinia could do to keep from smiling. "You may choose any day you wish, Miss Cloverseed. Now, start the game or you will be too sleepy to beat me."

The old woman peered over her spectacles. "Hah! Don't you laugh at me, my girl. Day after Boxing Day is the day I choose to begin my new adventure."

Miss Cloverseed had always been a woman of her word, so Delphinia was not really surprised when that was exactly what she did. On the night chosen—after she had won their game of cribbage and had uncustomarily given Delphinia a pat on her cheek—for it was not in her nature to be outwardly affectionate—Miss Cloverseed put on her simplest night rail, did not have her maid put up her hair in rags, as was her custom, said her prayers, and crawled into bed. She went to sleep and that was that.

Since no one from outside the small Norfolk community came regularly to see Miss Cloverseed except her man of business from London, Mr. Temple, or her solicitor, Mr. Bleamish, Delphinia assumed that the elderly lady had no relatives. It was with great amazement that Delphinia found Whetstone Manor literally swarming with Cloverseed bees from all over England for the reading of the will.

Both Mr. Temple and Mr. Bleamish had arrived and sequestered themselves in the library for three days before they called everyone to attend them. The servants lined up along the walls, while the strangers sat about in the finest chairs, staring at each other, twiddling their thumbs or surreptitiously examining all the furniture and paintings adorning the room.

There were some murmurings when Delphinia confiscated Miss Cloverseed's chair, but it seemed almost sacrilegious to her that any of those present should sit in the old woman's favorite spot.

The servants were called up first to hear what their mistress left them. Miss Cloverseed had been a generous employer before she died, and now that she had departed this world, was proving to be a more generous one. One by one her loyal retainers came forward and received ample awards and a kind word about their service. The elderly folks, Brambles, the butler, and Mr. and Mrs. Fidget, the cook and his housekeeper-wife, were left generous pensions enabling them to buy themselves a humble cottage somewhere to spend their waning days in comfort. The younger ones were given excellent references and money enough to tide them over until they found other positions, if they did not wish to remain in the employ of the new owners of Whetstone Manor.

From her own observation of the poor collection of humanity assembled, Delphinia could only praise Miss Cloverseed's judgment, for she was certain most of the staff would seek employment elsewhere.

The Cloverseed clan all sat around smiling and murmuring nonsense, until it came Delphinia's turn.

"Miss Delphinia Penn?" Mr. Bleamish said inquisitively, looking about the room as though he didn't know who she was. When his eyes settled upon her finally, he gave a little smile as if surprised to see her. "You will please stay for the formal reading of the bequeaths."

Delphinia was quite certain that had she been a fly, Miss Cloverseed's relatives would have gladly squashed her where she sat, for all eyes which before had seemed pleasantly obsequious suddenly turned hostile.

More amazing and to the point, Delphinia discovered herself to be the recipient of a deed to a London terrace house, which she never knew existed, and a sizable, though not extravagant stipend, to maintain it.

"Here is the key and the papers of ownership, Miss Penn." Mr. Bleamish gave her hand a little squeeze as he folded her fingers over the key. "I shall be handling your affairs, my dear. If and when you decide to journey to Town, feel free to call upon me for any assistance you may need," he finished with an odd crinkling of his nose.

Delphinia stared unbelievingly at the metal object the plump, little lawyer had dropped into the palm of her hand. It seemed strange that for the ten years Delphinia had been her companion, Miss Cloverseed had never once mentioned that she owned a house in London.

The next half hour went swiftly. All the remainder of Miss Cloverseed's wealth and properties were divided among her kith and kin. When the reading was over, they let out a collective sigh, for they all knew that Miss Penn had been handed the family white elephant; and more than one of them was not adverse to voicing this thought aloud.

However, Delphinia held another opinion altogether, and quite overwhelmed by her good fortune, returned to her room where she found the pretty little maid, Mary, placing a large box on her bed.

"Mr. Bleamish told me to carry this to your room," she said. "Miss Cloverseed wished you to have it."

It was covered with old peeling wallpaper. Inside Delphinia found a silvery-gray, silk dress and a ragged, yellowed piece of foolscap. The message appeared to be part of a poem, but couldn't be read, because it had been torn down the middle. A letter in Miss Cloverseed's handwriting accompanied it.

My dear Penn,

When you read this, I shall probably be riding a camel across the Sahara or taking one of those little dugout boats down the Amazon River. I always wanted to venture into the South American jungles to hear one of those monkeys that they say howls.

I am counting on you to use my London residence to your advantage to visit all the fine institutions of learning I told you about. But that is up to you. I am no longer on your plane of existence to give you advice.

There is however one last request I will ask of you. You have by now opened the box, or else you would not be reading this letter. Knowing your inclination toward the precocious, you will be in London at the first possible opportunity, so I do not have to tell you that is what I want above all else. I know you are not one to rusticate in the country for your entire life. Now this may seem a silly thing to ask—and you know that I am not prone to silliness—but should you receive an invitation to a Valentine ball, you will go. And, you must promise me that you will wear the gown in the box and carry the torn piece of paper.

With regards,
Cornelia Cloverseed

Delphinia brushed away a tear from her cheek. She should have known that Miss Cloverseed was bound to get in the last word. She would miss the fiery old lady, but she was sure that Miss Cloverseed was now doing exactly as she desired, crossing deserts or navigating jungle rivers; and Delphinia doubted that even St. Peter would have the ability—or the courage—to dissuade her former employer from her purpose once she had made up her mind.

A request from Miss Cloverseed was as much as a royal command to Delphinia, and she promised silently to do as she was bid. But knowing it was unlikely that she would ever be asked to a grand ball, she set the box aside and thought no more about it.

In the next few days, Delphinia packed her clothes and the books Miss Cloverseed had given her, made a visit to the vicarage in Ram's Head to inform her parents of her good fortune; and after receiving their most heartfelt blessings, she purchased a ticket for the next mail coach going through Norwich to London.

As Mary helped Delphinia to pack, she seemed quite disconcerted. "How shall you find your way about in the big city, Miss Penn, being a lady alone?"

"My dear girl, do not concern yourself. I have no qualms about traveling by myself. I have sketched a detailed map of London, so there is no possibility of my becoming lost."

"Oh, I don't know, Miss Penn," the maid said, twisting a corner of her apron into a knot. "'Twould be best if you always carry a parasol, and if ever a man approaches you in an ungentlemanly manner, a good bang on his noggin with the metal ferrule should set him in his place in no time at all."

"Stuff and nonsense, Mary! I have never owned a parasol. *Impractical fripperies,* Miss Cloverseed called them. They are only meant to keep off the sun. It is not the sun from which a person needs protection, but the cold rain which drenches one's clothing and makes one quite uncomfortable. I carry my umbrella whenever the skies look threatening."

Delphinia had not thought herself a victim of sentimentality, but seeing the tears glistening in the maid's eyes, she felt a strange constriction in her throat. "I appreciate your concern, Mary, but I cannot think that I shall ever have need to defend my virtue."

"Oh, ma'am, if I may disagree. I saw the way Mr. Bleamish was looking at you."

"I cannot believe it, Mary. I have never been fooled into thinking that I am other than I am—plain. Neither can Mr. Bleamish possibly be interested in the small amount of money I am to receive. So if he acted the fool, it has to be something or someone else who attracted him."

The maid bit her lip and slowly shook her head.

"Do not look so dismayed, Mary. I know your intentions

are well meaning, and if it will make you feel better, I promise I shall carry my umbrella with me at all times—just in case."

She was relieved to see the maid's cheerful smile return.

Delphinia arrived in London two days later. She waited until the coach stopped under the portrait of the beautiful Indian princess Pocahontas on the sign outside the Belle Sauvage Inn on Ludgate Hill before disembarking. She ordered a well-packed hamper of food from the inn's kitchen, then hailed the driver of a hack. "What is your name, young man?"

"Malachi, mum," he said, placing the reins in the hands of the small boy beside him.

"That is a trustworthy name," she commented with a nod. "And your partner?"

Malachi jumped down from the high seat. "My son, Henry," he said proudly. "He's learning the trade."

The child looked to be about ten years old. Delphinia nodded her approval. "Boys do get into trouble if they are left idle." She gave Malachi her direction.

"'Tis not far," he said, hoisting her baggage aboard. "Near the Adelphi on the Strand, a very respectable, older section of town. Viscount Linsey owns the mansion on the right and Lord Noblesse, a baron, the one on the left."

"I am impressed. You seem to know the area well."

"Aye, mum. I plied this section of Londontown me whole life. Know every inch o' it."

"Linsey and Noblesse," she repeated. "Well, I shall let myself be known to my new neighbors as soon as I am established."

"Won't do no good, mum. The old viscount is quite high in the instep, I hear, and don't welcome anyone into his house unless he invites 'em. And Lord and Lady Noblesse only come for the Season."

"I am sorry to hear that," Delphinia said.

"That old house been closed ever since I remember."

"Well, it won't be now," she said. "Drive on, my good man."

The journey took them no more than half an hour. Fascinated, Delphinia stared out the window as they wove in and out of the tangled parade of noisy, bustling humans, animals and vehicles. Much different than the quietude of the Norfolk countryside. She could not deny the excitement which ran through her. When they arrived, she impulsively pushed open the door of the carriage and descended before Malachi had a chance to pull down the step. Pointing with her umbrella, she directed him to place her bags on the stoop, then paid him well and sent him on his way.

Delphinia stood on the sidewalk gazing up at the four storey, vine-covered edifice. The house faced the street bravely, even though it could be no more than ten feet wide, if she reckoned correctly.

"I shall call you Cloverseed House," she said.

If it seemed unproportionately narrow compared to the palatial residences spread out on either side of it, Delphinia did not question as to why. She started up the steps. Thanks to Miss Cloverseed this was hers. It was more than she had ever hoped to have. And if the information she'd gleaned from Malachi was correct, it was within walking distance to many of the places she wished to visit: the museums with their grand lecture halls, libraries stacked with more books than a person could read in a lifetime, and galleries of art from all over the world.

Mr. Gregory Fitch was in the front parlor of Lord Linsey's mansion, searching for a wrench which he'd left behind somewhere in the house the night before. He gave a tug at his already disarrayed cravat, completely unraveling the stylish bow his valet, Davies, had so carefully tied that morning. His patience was wearing thin. If his grandfather, the viscount, would quit interrupting Gregory's experiments so often to come greet guests, he wouldn't be losing his tools all the time. There was a greasy smudge across one cheek, and he wore a rather dirty brown smock which covered him from his neckcloth to the heels of his boots; yet it did not hide the fact that he was a man of good height, strong build, and had a rugged countenance, which more often than he wished, attracted the opposite sex. He preferred much more to work on his gadgets than to fritter away his time doing the pretty. The sad fact that his father had preceded his grandfather in death, and set him up as the next viscount, had not altered Gregory's way of life or deterred him from his path of searching for new and better inventions.

A stern-faced woman in black bombazine and starched apron followed him about as if he were a naughty little boy, straightening the objects he kept displacing. This only added to Gregory's ill-humor.

"Mrs. Mudge are you certain that one of your staff has not seen my wrench?"

"Yes, sir," the housekeeper said, grabbing a Chinese porcelain urn just as it toppled off the table. "Do watch your elbows, Mr. Fitch."

Gregory pulled himself up to his full height, which was well over six feet. "Mrs. Mudge, I consider myself an inventor of no little consequence, as active member of the Royal Institution, founded for the purpose of diffusing knowledge of useful mechanical inventions and the application of science to the common purpose of life, I am dedicated to making the households of the kingdom run in a more efficient manner. It is not my duty to keep them neat."

The housekeeper listened in silence. She had heard the diatribe so many times that she could repeat it from memory.

It was only by pure chance that at that moment, Gregory happened to glance out the front window just as he finished his long-winded speech—which he had the habit of delivering every time he felt he was being held at fault. He was treated to the quite extraordinary sight of a woman hopping out of a hired hack, before the coachman could do his duty of assisting her.

Ordinarily, Gregory Fitch would not have bothered to take a second look at a female dressed in such drab attire: a lack-luster brown pelisse matched by a peculiar bonnet perched sideways on her head. What caught his attention was the way she stood staring up at the residence next door, brandishing a large, black umbrella as though it were a saber, and she a knave spoiling for a duel.

The old house had not been occupied for all of his lifetime and much of his father's as well. If there was a story of some kind behind the long absence of any occupants, his father had known nothing about it, nor did Gregory manage to dig any pertinent information out of his grandfather. He only knew that there had been efforts over the years to buy it, but the viscount's man of business had no luck whatsoever in even getting an answer from its owner, who lived somewhere north of London.

Who was the stranger directing the coachman to carry up her baggage? Gregory moved as close as he could to the pane to get a better look, but unfortunately the woman went charging up the steps, and he could see her no more.

The scolding voice behind him made him jump. "Here is your wrench, Mr. Fitch, wedged behind the cushion on the settle."

Gregory's eyes lit up, forgetting his pique. "Ah," he said, cradling the tool in his hand, "now we can get on with the job. Thank you, Mrs. Mudge." He left the room whistling, his good humor once more in place with the thought of the pipes waiting to be connected in the orangery.

Delphinia climbed the three steps to the faded front door, once painted yellow if she judged correctly. There was no door knocker, although a plate to hold one sat squarely in the middle. She placed the key in the lock, but the door did not give way. She scolded herself for dismissing Malachi before she'd gained admittance to the house. It was quite unfair that God had given the preponderance of physical strength to men. But, thank goodness, *He* had balanced that slight by giving females more sense. She stood back to consider the situation, and Miss Cloverseed's admonition came to her clearly.

God must have given women hips for more than one purpose, considering so many of us had the sense to remain single.

Gathering her resources for an assault, Delphinia heaved all of her weight against the solid paneling. The hinges gave way with a loud groan of protest, the door swung open, and she stepped sharply across the threshold into her new home.

Two

A *whoosh* of stale air greeted Delphinia. Atop the gilded, half-moon table just inside the entrance lay a brass door knocker shaped like an owl, staring up at her with unseeing eyes. Delphinia picked it up, and with great ceremony, secured it to its rightful place on the front door. Now she was ready to receive visitors. Next, she pushed aside the elaborate curtains in the front parlor and tried to open the window. But, alas, it would not budge, so she left the door ajar to freshen the air while she inspected the premises.

Gilded sconces with half-burned candles still in them lined the rooms. One was torn loose from the wall, tilted forward like a soldier falling out of formation. The long parlor was fully furnished and ran back a good thirty feet before meeting the back of a stairwell. The knob on the bannister wobbled as she grasped it. Upstairs plush comforters still covered the beds, green or blue velvet curtains with bobbin fringes and gold swags hung at the windows, satin-covered settees and chests of exotic woods sat about as if the owners would return at any moment. A copy of

Chaucer's *Canterbury Tales,* lay open on a bedside table. It reminded her of Miss Cloverseed's fine library, kept current by an acquaintance in London, Lady Jacomena Dalison, who periodically sent all the latest publications. Delphinia sadly wondered at the fate of that magnificent collection which she'd had to leave behind at Whetstone Manor.

Downstairs once more, she closed the front door and carried her baggage to the rear of the house. Fine china and silver cutlery were set out on a table, as though waiting for the butler to announce dinner.

Every room had a beautiful marble fireplace. Delphinia stuck her hand up one of the chimneys and got a shower of soot and a blackened glove for her effort. The cellar kitchen at the back of the house had a much larger, old-fashioned, brick fireplace. She shivered. Up until now, the exercise had kept her warm. Had there been fuel, she would have lit a fire. Thank goodness, she'd had the foresight to bring the hamper of food and wine from the inn.

Although everything she had seen spoke of genteel splendor, Delphinia began to see flaws. A piece of silk wall-covering peeled from the dining room wall, a broken leg threw a beautiful, black-lacquer escritoire off balance, and dust, cobwebs, and the scent of age hung everywhere. It was plain as a pikestaff that it would take more than a feather duster and a bit of beeswax to put it all in liveable order. She needed painters and plasterers, carpenters and chimney sweeps. But how did she go about finding competent craftsmen when she knew no one in town?

Eventually, she found herself in the yard, a skinny ribbon of dirt and gravel which ran between two, high, vine-covered stone walls to the back gate. A single plane tree dwarfed the old garden house and two iron benches. All that was visible of the neighboring manors were the upper gables and rows of chimneys marching across tiled roofs.

She had no sooner set out to inspect the long narrow garden when a crash, accompanied by a string of deep-throated, unintelligible words, thundered over the wall on her right. Only a male could make such a racket, she surmised. Quite possibly, the man could be Lord Linsey's gardener, and a source of the sort of information she sought about acquiring workmen. However, even after she'd climbed atop one of the benches to check the source, she still could not see over.

Delphinia investigated further and discovered a connecting door behind a thicket of tangled vines. But no amount of pushing or shoving would open it. After more hunting about, she found an old ladder in the garden house and placing this against the wall, climbed high enough to peer over into her neighbor's establishment. Attached to the magnificent stone mansion was the largest greenhouse she had ever seen. It overlooked a wide and perfectly laid out garden, even lovely in its winter slumber.

She called out, but the loud expletives which accompanied the banging and clanging drowned out her appeals for assistance. Delphinia did not let this small challenge stop her. She gathered her skirts and pulled herself onto the top of the wall, where she promptly lost her balance and toppled over onto the other side.

Delphinia picked herself up, brushed off her coat, and opened the back door to the conservatory. A blinding fog engulfed her. Although she could not see past her nose, her hearing was not affected, and she managed to follow the path of the abrasive words to their source. A wide pair of shoulders hunched over a strange machine which was chugging out the deafening cacaphony of metalic and vocal noises.

She boldly tapped him on his back. "My good fellow," she shouted.

The man dropped the two pipes he was attempting to fit together. A geyser of steam shot upwards. The roar which followed was not the response Delphinia expected. The accent was that of a gentleman, but his words were unrepeatable. As he twisted a valve to turn off the steam, two dark eyes glared at her from under a thick lock of auburn hair. "Who the devil are you?"

Delphinia pulled herself up to her full height. "The name is Miss Penn," she said primly.

Gregory wondered why the woman thought he would be the slightest bit interested in this information.

"I have moved in next door."

He studied her more closely. Ah, yes! Now he recognized the plain, brown coat, and the absurd little bonnet, sitting lopsized on her head. The picture in his mind had been incomplete without her umbrella, but more of a puzzle was how had she gotten past Mrs. Mudge.

Delphinia gave him no time for further speculation, for her fascination over the tangle of pipes and valves got the better of her. "What in the world are you doing?"

She watched him wipe his soiled sleeve across his forehead, leaving a black, greasy streak from eye to eye. Delphinia thought it gave him a rather comical look, but she refrained from laughing.

Gregory dusted the dirt off one of the pipes he'd dropped. "Madam, even if I drew pictures, it would be impossible for a female to understand the intricacies of the science that goes into the simplest mechanics."

"Oh, you are not the gardener then?"

"No, madam, I am not." That should have ended the conversation. However, Gregory could never resist the opportunity to explain his experiments even to the family dog if it would stay still long enough. He held the pipe under her nose. "I am attempting to create a more consistent summertime atmosphere, utilizing a water heating system, using steam to heat the orangery. I hope to make it possible to grow more tropical fruits and vegetables the year around than we do at present." Miss Penn did not look impressed.

Delphinia sighed. "More's the pity. I was going to ask if I could hire you to see to my garden in the spring. Well, that can wait, I suppose."

Gregory stopped to glower at her. "I knew I could not expect someone of your sex to comprehend such complicated matters."

Ignoring that statement as unworthy of an answer, Delphinia took out a handkerchief to pat the beads of perspiration collecting on her face. "Well, it does not seem to me that you are doing a very good job of it. You will most likely steam cook the fruit off the trees before they are ripe. Here, let me hold those pipes together while you do whatever you have to do to secure them."

Gregory looked at her. The heat had put a ruddy glow in her cheeks which gave her a certain robust appearance. She was not of the sickly pallor so many of his female acquaintances thought so fashionable. Her eyes were nearly as dark as her hair peeking out from the bonnet, which had now slipped further back on her head. All in all, her countenance, though not displeasing, could have been more acceptable to him if it hadn't been for the firm set of her jaw. She was serious about assisting him. That alone made him decide it best that he didn't say what was on the tip of his tongue. After all, he did need another pair of hands to accomplish his task. Heaven only knew that none of the servants would come near any of his contrivances. "Here, wrap this leather cloth around your gloves before you hold the pipe in case it breaks away."

Delphinia threw herself into the endeavor as she did everything she attempted, and the job was soon finished. "You do seem handy with tools," she said admiringly.

Gregory could not refrain from a little boasting. "I consider myself somewhat proficient in that field."

"Well, I daresay you are, my good man. By the by, you did not tell me your name."

Gregory began to collect his tools. "Fitch, madam. I am—"

Delphinia cut him short. "I am sure your background is adequate, Fitch. What I am proposing is right along those lines. I fear my house is in need of a great deal of repair, and I wish to know how to go about getting it done. Now that I have helped you complete your task, you cannot object to coming next door with me. Certainly, Lord Linsey can spare you for a minute." She turned and walked away from him.

Gregory said a few choice words under his breath, but he could see his fierce glare seemed to have little effect on Miss Penn. He had one of his grandfather's dinner parties to attend in a few hours, and he came to the conclusion that the only way he would be rid of the woman was to accompany her back to her house to see what it was that she wanted done. He could recommend a course of action and be on his way.

To his surprise instead of going toward the front of the house, she headed for the back entrance that led into the garden.

"Come, come, Fitch! Don't dawdle."

Grumbling, Gregory hunched his shoulders against the cold air and made his way to the old gate. It was bolted and the lock so rusted that there was no opening it. He considered himself a considerate man with women, but this one was rubbing his patience thin. "How the deuce did you get in here?"

"I climbed the wall."

"Ladies do not climb walls."

Delphinia pulled at a vine stalk to test its strength. "If you kept your master's gates in better order, it would not have been necessary. Now if you will give me a boost—"

"Oh, lord! Wait!" Gregory groaned, pulling a hammer and chisel from one of the numerous pockets on his smock. He broke the lock and pushed open the heavy door. "Madam," he said, and waited for her to pass in front of him.

"That just proves my employer's point," she said pleasantly.

Gregory raised his brows. "Madam?"

"That men's greatest asset is brawn. If I had been able

to do what you did, I would not have had to climb over the wall."

Gregory would have turned around right then and there and escaped back into his own garden, if it hadn't been for his keen curiosity to see inside the old deserted residence, a burning desire which he'd harbored since he was a child. Dutifully, he followed Miss Penn.

The house did not disappoint him. Unbelievably narrow, it seemed to run on forever. Even though the day was fast fading, the inner rooms were surprisingly well lighted. This was due, he found to an ingenius floorplan of alternating the stairs from one side to the other on each floor. Sunlight penetrated down a deep well from a glass dome on the roof. The carved wood ornamentation, the intricate plasterwork in the cornices around the ceilings of each room, the marble work on the fireplaces exceeded all his expectations and held him spellbound. The paintings alone which hung suspended on decorative cords were worth a fortune. Gregory had supposed the couple who had lived and died here had in some way been inferior to them, for his grandfather had never permitted any of the servants to speak their name. What he was seeing was a treasure trove, as good a quality as anything they had at Linsey House, some of it better. But something was missing.

"Where are your servants?"

"It had not occurred to me that I would need any."

Gregory knew his grandfather had offered a king's ransom for the house. How had this plain-looking woman succeeded in purchasing it whereas his grandfather had not? "You are alone?"

Delphinia watched his eyebrows rise in what she was sure Mary would construe as a menacing way. This was not a time to lose her head. While Fitch was inspecting one of the fireplaces, she looked about for her umbrella. She saw it sitting beside her trunks.

He rose suddenly. "You surely are not expecting to stay here overnight, Miss Penn?"

She decided she'd bungled rather badly by not asking Malachi to wait until she'd inspected the house, but Delphinia was not about to own up to the fact that she'd acted foolheartedly. Her chin rose a full two inches. "I see no reason why I should not. There are beds aplenty, and I am not so simple minded as to have come without food."

"There are a dozen reasons why you should not."

Delphinia picked up her umbrella and held it over her head. He was a big man. Perhaps, Mary had been right.

"I did not mean to frighten you, madam."

She could swear she saw a hint of amusement in his eyes, which made her more determined than ever to stay the night. She lowered the umbrella. "I was not the least bit frightened."

"No, I don't suppose you frighten easily, Miss Penn. I was only going to suggest that if you refuse to leave, I shall see that you have fuel to build a fire in the kitchen. You can sleep on one of the servant's cots."

"I would prefer to stay upstairs. The bedrooms are all made up." She could tell he didn't think much of her suggestion.

"And if the chimney is clogged and the smoke backs up into the room, you will ruin priceless wall-hangings and upholstery."

He was right of course, but Delphinia was not about to admit to having made an error in judgement. She looked out the window and threw the conversation in another direction. "It is getting dark."

"Very well, madam. If you are determined to stay, I shall send a man over with a bucket of coal."

"I will not let a stranger in. You fetch it."

He did not seem happy with that suggestion, but the comment she saw forming died on his lips. "And Fitch, you had best hurry if you are going to get a fire started before it is completely black outside."

Gregory turned on his heels and took off in long strides

toward the gate. His mumblings were audible even over the wall and well into the orangery.

While he was gone, Delphinia found some candles and was wondering how to light them, when Fitch returned with a bucket of coal, kindling and a tinder box.

She followed him down to the kitchen.

"Thank you, Fitch. You are certain that you won't get in trouble with Lord Linsey for bringing me these things?"

"Not at all. I do have some free time which I can call my own."

"Oh, that is good to hear," she said. "Then I will not be remiss in hiring you to see to the repairs on the house. When can you start?"

Delphinia could see he was overwhelmed by her offer for he didn't say a word, just stared at her, speechless. "You need not think I shall cheat you, Fitch. I shall inquire of my solicitor what is a fair fee."

"Do you always order everybody about, Miss Penn?"

Delphinia looked at him puzzled. "Why, I never order anybody about. Men think nothing of saying their piece, but when a woman makes a statement, she is accused of *ordering about*. It just shows how oppressed women are."

Gregory choked. "I cannot imagine you taking orders from anyone, Miss Penn."

"You are wrong, Fitch. Everybody who is acquainted with me knows I am quite amiable. I always considered seriously anything my former employer suggested. I trusted her judgement."

"What if the suggestion had come from a male, Miss Penn?"

"She told me that gentlemen seldom make sensible decisions."

"Then you cannot possibly want me to do your repairs."

"I believe she was speaking of the aristocracy, Fitch. They keep the common man down as well as they do their women. You should be able to rise on your own merits."

His smile was a bit strained. "And how do you propose I do that, madam?"

"If you can add to your consequence by supplementing your income, during your free time, you should be able to do so without reprimand. Do not sell yourself cheap, Fitch. The middle class is rising in England. You can be a part of it, if you strive to better yourself."

"Don't you believe that the aristocracy will see that as a threat, Miss Penn?"

Delphinia was not quite sure Fitch saw the capabilities she was trying to awaken in him. "Be bold! Broaden you horizons, Fitch. There is more to the world than the viscount's orangery. Tinkering with exploding pipes is not only dangerous, but will get you nowhere in the scheme of things."

Gregory shook his head as though waking from a blow. He bowed. "Thank you for the advice, madam, but I prefer to *tinker* with my pipes, if you don't mind. Good night, Miss Penn."

He was gone before Delphinia knew it. Stubborn man! He didn't *understand* at all. He seemed bright enough, and she was sure there was potential there, but he was wasting it.

When Gregory gained the house, he took the steps two at a time to reach his apartments. "Hurry, Davies," he called, ripping off the canvas smock. "There is little time to change my clothes before Grandfather's guests arrive."

"Yes, sir," the valet said. "We were looking for you. I have laid out your wardrobe and there is hot water for a quick wash. I believe the Earl of Podwalling is already here with the countess and their daughter."

There would be others, Gregory knew. There always were. A string of young ladies paraded in front of him. His grandfather could not be more obvious in his intent. Lord save him from silly women. He should have set Miss

Penn straight as to who he really was, before he'd found himself so deeply involved. But the temptation to see inside *that* house had been too strong. The fine craftsmanship he'd seen was beyond his wildest imagination. She'd probably employ some clumsy dolt who would ruin the beautiful woodwork or chip the intricate cornices. He couldn't let that happen. His only recourse would be to personally see that top artisans were sent around. That would keep the inquisitive woman out of his hair, and he could get on with his real work.

"Are you ready, Mr. Fitch?"

Gregory jerked to attention. "What, ho? Oh, yes, Davies. I do believe I was woolgathering." Gregory stared vacantly over the servant's shoulder. He wished he could see more of the house next door. A whole house with no modern pipe work, no kitchen stoves, roasters or broilers. What he wouldn't give to be able to run water pipes into Miss Penn's house.

Grandfather, the old curmudgeon, was adamant against his modernizing their antiquated mansion. He'd only been given permission to fiddle around in the orangery. But now! Gregory pounded his fist into his hand. "By George, Davies! I cannot let such an opportunity pass me by. I must think of some way to bring it to pass."

Davies stood holding up his master's evening jacket. "What is that, sir?"

"Why to put into practice some of Count von Rumford's theories. His inventions of kitchen stoves, roaster and boilers have not only revolutionized the heating systems of America and England, but old Boney invited him to the Continent as well."

Davies knew better than to interrupt his master's lectures when he was in one of his *moods*, but time was passing. He tapped gently on one of the broad shoulders.

Gregory automatically raised his arms, and his valet slipped on the coat. A few minutes later, Davies with a smile of satisfaction, saw his master off to dinner, dressed to the eyes in the latest fashion. There wasn't a handsomer young man in all of London, he was sure.

The following day, a bit to the north, nearer Covent Garden, Lady Jacomena Dalison stood in her library with her housekeeper. Holding a paper in her hand, she spoke to the gray-haired woman opening several crates stacked around them.

"Well, Butterworth. The books I sent to Whetstone Manor have now come back to me."

"Oh, dear, does that mean—?"

"Yes, I daresay it does. This is a letter from Cornelia Cloverseed written to me just before she died."

The rotund, little woman wiped her eyes with the corner of her apron.

"No need to be a watering pot, Butterworth. Miss Cloverseed says she planned it all. She was after all getting on in years. Formidable old gel, though. Never met anyone just like her. Saw her first in northern Africa when I was trying to get onto one of those nasty, humped beasts which they make you ride to the pyramids. Spent an exciting adventure with her, exploring ancient ruins and sailing the Nile. We've corresponded ever since."

Lady Jacomena read on silently for a few minutes before continuing. "She says she is returning all of the books I sent, except the ones she gave to her companion, Miss Penn."

Mrs. Butterworth smiled. "She was always mentioning that young lady in her letters."

"Right you are, Butterworth. Miss Cloverseed says she has given over her old house off the Strand to Miss Penn. She encloses her address. I believe that is the same street on which Lord Linsey and Lord Noblesse have residences. Those houses were built prior to the Adams' terrace palaces. Strange that I did not realize there was another house. I wonder why Miss Cloverseed never mentioned it? Well, it does not matter, Butterworth. The important news is that Miss Cloverseed's Miss Penn is coming to Town."

"Is she now? Miss Cloverseed always wrote she was sharp as a tack."

"Well, wc shall soon see how clever she is, shall we not?"

"Ye'll be inviting her here to some of yer gatherings?"

"Of course, Butterworth. How else can we look her over? But first, we will allow her and her staff to settle in. Then, I shall send around an invitation to one of my *conversations*. Miss Cloverseed wants me to use my influence to see that she gets letters of admittance to certain institutions, too. Especially those which the men are so persnickety about keeping to themselves. I am a member of The Society of Arts in the Adelphi, so that will be no problem. At least one such establishment recognizes the fairer sex's intelligence." Lady Jacomena held the letter out at arms length and raised her brows.

"Is there something more, milady?"

"Only an odd request which I shall have to decipher a bit more. Something about a Valentine ball. I must admit, Butterworth, the old gel has whetted my curiosity. Mayhaps, the winter season will not be so dull after all."

Three

The following morning, Delphinia awakened to find a fresh bucket of coal sitting beside the cellar entrance, a pile of cut wood and a barrel of water. How they got there without her hearing anything was beyond her imagination. She and Miss Cloverseed were always up with the birds. Exhaustion could be the only case she could plead for being a slug-a-bed.

The coals in the hearth from the night before were still red, and she had no sooner rekindled a fire than she heard a knock at the front door. Were tradesmen already gathering on her stoop to hawk their wares? Remembering Mary's caution, Delphinia took her umbrella with her to open the door.

Three people huddled on the stoop, wrapped, hatted, and gloved against the morning chill.

"Brambles!" she exclaimed. "Mr. and Mrs. Fidget!"

The tall, gangly, butler, the rotund cook, and his wife stood with expectation in their eyes.

Mr. Fidget spoke first. "We talked it over among ourselves, Miss Penn. We have worked almost all of our lives, and we cannot stop now. Miss Cloverseed may not be with us any longer, but we felt that coming here to be with you will be like not losing her at all."

"So we pooled our money and here we are to stay," Brambles interjected.

Mrs. Fidget nodded. "That is, if you will have us."

Delphinia held out her hands. "Of course I will have you. Oh, you don't know how gladly! You could not be more welcome. I am certain Miss Cloverseed would be as delighted as I am that you have come."

"Our baggage is in the carriage," Mr. Fidget said. "The driver told us he knew exactly where you lived."

Malachi stood at the curb already unloading their belongings, a wide grin splitting his face.

While the men went back to help Malachi, Mrs. Fidget stepped into the house and looked about her. "My, oh, my!" she said. Then with a smile which belied her horrified exclamation, she sketched a path though the dust on the table with her finger, and flicked a cobweb from the mirror. "What a mess! We shall have it tidy in no time at all, Miss Penn. You see if we don't."

It would take a heart of stone not to have been moved by the housekeeper's joy, but, alas, Delphinia already knew that the house needed far more of a rally than the dear, elderly people could give it. She immediately called for a consultation. She included Malachi in the discussion, and it was he who suggested the most practical solution. He kept his equipage at the nearby mewes, he said, and offered the exclusive services of his hack. His niece, Toddy, was seeking employment as a housemaid, and Henry could become houseboy and run errands. An unanimous vote was soon reached to accept his sensible offer.

"So it is settled," Delphinia said with finality. "Brambles and Mr. and Mrs. Fidget will move in. Malachi, you will bring Toddy and Henry to the house each morning, and have your carriage at my beck and call."

No sooner had Malachi and his son left to fetch Toddy, and the trio of upper servants had taken their bags to their rooms, then there came another knock. Since she was the only one available, Delphinia hurried to the front of the house and opened the door herself. A dapper little gentleman stood upon the step, twirling his mustache with one hand, his cane with the other, whistling.

He handed her his card. "Would you tell your mistress that Yohann Brielson, decorator, is here to inspect the premises for alterations."

Out of habit, Delphinia was about to tell him that she would announce him to Miss Cloverseed when she remembered, with a peculiar feeling of pride of ownership, that . . . "I am the mistress of this house, sir."

With skepticism written all over his face, Mr. Brielson stepped back to take measure of her, then the narrow house. "We have just delivered a restored painting next door at Lord Linsey's, and I was asked to stop by to see what needed to be done." He bowed. "Your servant, madam."

"Miss Penn will do," Delphinia said. "Come in."

Once over the threshold, Mr. Brielson's attitude took a direct about face. He ran from room to room, upstairs and downstairs, his gaze hungrily taking in the neo-classical style: the pastel ceilings, the white decorations, the gilded furniture. "Oh, my dear, Miss Penn . . . my dear, Miss Penn. I see the Adams brothers' touch everywhere. We shall restore everything. My artisans shall begin to arrive tomorrow, and I shall personally see to the work."

An hour later, Delphinia watched the natty, little gentleman make his departure. She had to hand it to Fitch. How he had persuaded Mr. Brielson into taking on the renovation of her house, she did not know, but she was willing to give credit where credit was due. Fitch, for all his humble beginnings, was proving to have more bottom than she thought. She would tell him so the next time she heard him in the orangery.

Two days later, Delphinia set out to see the city. Now that Brambles and Mr. and Mrs. Fidget were on the front lines, she was certain that Mr. Brielson's army of chimney sweeps, carpenters, masons, plasters and bricklayers would be kept on track. Armed with her maps and umbrella, Delphinia saw no reason to delay her explorations any longer. She made herself ready to depart as soon as Malachi delivered Henry and Toddy to the house.

Gregory Fitch was next door preparing to undertake an invigorating walk to the Royal Institution in Albemarle Street. He hoped to arrive early to work in the basement laboratory before all the visitors began their noisy intrusion at ten o'clock to see the displays. At least, he thought it a good idea until he espied Miss Penn leaving her own front door at the very same time. Whatever was the woman doing rising at such an unfashionable hour, let alone leaving her house alone? As a whole, he found females a dull lot. However, he'd already ascertained that Miss Penn was not one of your ordinary, commonplace females. Why this should concern him, he couldn't imagine, nevertheless, a niggling uneasiness persisted.

Botheration! If he waited for her to depart, the delay could very well set him back, and he'd promised to meet Dudley and Snifferton at White's for lunch. Now he wished he hadn't. The two did nothing but fritter away their time talking drivel. If they had not been schoolfellows at Eton, he would not give them the time of day.

Gregory took another look out the window. Miss Penn was about to get into the carriage, but had stopped to query a tradesman carrying in a ladder. Another tactic had to be taken. He quickly reversed his direction and made his exit from the rear of the mansion. He was halfway to the stables gates when a splendid idea leaped into his head. If Miss Penn were absent—and he knew she was, because he'd just seen her leave—he could pop over next door and see how the renovations were coming along.

He introduced himself at the back door to an amiable fellow, who resembled a gingerbread man engulfed in a flour-smeared smock with a tall, white chef's hat riding pecariously atop his head. "I am Fidget, the cook," the man said, taking him to be one of Mr. Brielson's helpers. "Do come in, but I hope you will excuse me, for I am busy."

While Mr. Fidget mixed some batter, Gregory came back to the kitchen and poked about a bit, figuring where he could bring pipes in for hot water and measuring to see if he could fit one of the new modern stoves into a corner of the large fireplace. This brought them to a discussion on the need of getting the well cleaned out in the yard. Gregory promised to see that workmen were sent over immediately. As soon as this was done, Mrs. Fidget appeared and insisted he sit for a cup of coffee and some muffins, which her husband had just finished baking.

Half hour later, when he made to leave, Gregory noticed, for the first time, that he'd gotten his boots muddy crossing the yard, and had dropped some pieces of muffin down the front of his shirt. This necessitated a return to his apartments for Davies to fit him out in fresh clothes. It would not do to go to White's with crumbs on his vest.

With a sigh, the valet pulled a pair of pliers and a measuring tape from the pocket of the soiled waistcoat, and placed them on the top of the chest of drawers. Taking out a blue coat and brushing it off, he admonished, "Please try not to get any grease on this one, sir. The sleeve of your gray superfine was completely ruined when you last visited the laboratory.''

"It was not grease, Davies. It was some chemicals Sir Jameson was mixing. I leaned too close to the mortar and my cuff, I fear, dipped into the concoction. But I shall be more careful in the future. I promise.''

The valet's expression did not hold much hope in that confirmation.

As Davies gave his master's cravat a final twist, Gregory saw the clock. A great deal more time had sped by than he'd realized. If he were to meet his chums at the club, there was no point in going to the laboratory. "I am afraid, Davies, that I will not be going to the Institution after all. I shall have to schedule my research for another day.''

Delphinia found Malachi to be a singular source of information and gossip. He did disapprove, however, when Delphinia asked to be set down outside St. Paul's Cathedral at the top of Ludgate Hill, so that she could walk her way home. She missed her long treks across the Norfolk countryside, she told him. But this argument did not hold sway, and Malachi stubbornly clung to his opinion that she would not be safe. A heated discussion ensued, until they reached a compromise. She would walk, and he would follow in the carriage.

On this particular day, while others all around her were loudly complaining about the chill and casting wary glances at the threatening skies, Delphinia thought it a perfect day for walking. A brisk pace took her past the drapers' and mercers' shops to Fleet Street. Here she found herself succumbing to the seductive displays in the windows of the enumerable booksellers, and throwing practicality to the wind, bought a selection of volumes: poetry, treatises on new excavations in Greece, and her first foray into the gothic world of Mrs. Radcliffe. By now, hunger pains announced it was mealtime, and she found a small pastry shop off a little narrow pass.

With a bit of mischievious humor, Delphinia proceeded to enter the alley, knowing that Malachi most likely was having a fit, because his carriage would not be able to follow after her. But she took her time nonetheless and even had a sweet bun wrapped by the confectioner to mollify him. The look of relief on his face twenty minutes later, when she emerged unscathed, did make her feel a bit contrite. She handed him his treat, and after giving over her package of books, she continued down the Strand toward Somerset House.

Before Delphinia could open her umbrella, the storm hit, and she was swept up by the crowd rushing to get out of the rain. Before she knew it, she found herself inside a large building where room after room opened up into the other. Large posters attached to marble pillars proclaimed it to be a student watercolor exhibit.

Her coat was drenched and the rim of her bonnet droopy, but Delphinia was too taken with the colorful display for her to pay attention to her disarray. Miss Cloverseed's fine collection of art had raised in her an appreciation for man's ability to interpret nature's color and beauty. She had wandered through several rooms, when, there, as big as life—she could not mistake those broad shoulders—stood Fitch, looking utterly bored to death. It was plain to see that he was quite out of his element. She raised her umbrella to signal him. "Oh, Fitch!" she called loudly, making her way to his side.

He bowed stiffly. "Miss Penn."

"I have wondered why I had not heard you in the orangery of late, Fitch. I wanted to thank you for sending Mr. Brielson to me. How you snared him, I do not know. But after all, if you felt that you were not up to doing the job yourself, at least you sent the best."

He glanced back over his shoulder, as if looking for

someone, then returned his attention to her. "The work has been satisfactory then."

"Oh, very."

"Good. Good," he repeated.

If Fitch seemed to be having trouble making conversation, Delphinia had no such problem. "I am glad to see that you have so readily taken my advice to better yourself, Fitch, but I did not mean at the expense of your livelihood," Delphinia said.

"I assure you, Miss Penn, my livelihood is not in any danger."

"If you say so, Fitch."

Gregory gave a bark of laughter.

Dephinia pursed her lips. "It is not a laughing matter, Fitch, and I am willing to help you any way I can. If at any time you wish a part-time position, I am sure that I can find something that you can do. There is always the garden in the springtime, if you wish to give it a try. You never know but that you may take to it."

He made a little choking sound. "If you will excuse me, Miss Penn. My friends are signaling me to join them."

Delphinia followed his gaze. She had thought him to be alone, but now, two men and three ladies were rapidly making their way toward them. The young men held their greatcoats over their arms. She wagered that the rest of their attire, trousers, jackets and waistcoats, contained every color of the rainbow. The women chose to keep their wraps on in the cool exhibition hall. Delphinia had to admit, they presented a far prettier sight in their lovely fur-lined capes and wide-brimmed bonnets, than the young peacocks. However, their giggling gave their true nature away.

"I do not say this lightly, Fitch, but your companions seem a bit flighty."

"You profess to be a good judge of character, Miss Penn?"

"I believe I am, Fitch, and I say that with no false pride."

"Then, I suggest you leave the choice of my friends to me."

"As you will."

"I will, Miss Penn."

"Just be aware that I have warned you."

He blinked. "I am sure your party is wondering where you are, Miss Penn."

"Oh, I am not here with anyone."

"Do not tell me you are alone."

"I thought I just did. I said that 'I am not here with anyone.' It is all one and the same."

"'Tis not done, Miss Penn."

"Well, it must be *done*, because I just *did*. Good bye, Fitch."

He bowed once more and turned to leave.

Delphinia did have to admit, Fitch looked quite fetching in his dark blue coat and gray trousers. Others could very well take him for a member of the beau monde, it they did not know his background. There were no limits to what some men would do to acquire town bronze, but at least he was making an effort. She would give him that. His clothes had to have cost him a pretty penny. She only hoped he was not putting himself in debt.

"Remember, my offer still stands if you want to take me up on it," she called after him.

He paused a moment, then stiffened his back and stalked away. She could tell the women were asking him questions about her, for she heard the one who slipped her hand up under his arm ask, "Wherever did you find that drenched muskrat, darling?"

Delphinia was not without a sense of humor, and it took only one glance down at herself to realize that she could very well be taken for a creature who had just crawled out of the river. Only she was not a river animal, and the dampness was beginning to make itself felt. She quickly made her way out of the building and hurried toward the carriage.

"It is time to go home, Malachi."

Mrs. Fidget met Delphinia as soon as she came in the house, and with the proper "Tch, tch," took her wet wraps. "A missive arrived while you were gone, Miss Penn. Brambles put it in the salver here on the table, so you wouldn't overlook it."

Delphinia picked up the packet and turned it over to reveal the mark of a crest in the wax.

Mrs. Fidget peeked over her shoulder as Delphinia broke the seal, revealing several sheets of paper. "Looks important, don't it?" she said expectantly.

"It's from Lady Jacomena Dalison. She says I am to come to a gathering at her town house two weeks from Friday. How very kind of her. I shall send Henry over with my acceptance tomorrow. She says she has received Miss Cloverseed's book collection from Whetstone Manor, and that she has included letters of introduction to some of the institutions and galleries. That is so that I can attend meetings and lectures," Delphinia explained.

Mrs. Fidget slapped her forehead with the palm of her hand. "Your mentioning lectures reminded me—I forgot to tell you, dear, that right after you left this morning, a talkative young man called at the rear door and asked if he could see how the alterations was going. I believe he said his name was Fitch."

"He is an employee of Lord Linsey's. I believe he fancies himself a handyman, but I doubt his abilities in that line, for he turned me down when I asked him to do my repairs. I rather think that Fitch has more ambitious plans for himself. I saw him at an art exhibition this afternoon."

"The dear boy did not appear to me to be the type who would be interested in painting. He seemed more at home in the kitchen, and kept poking his nose into the fireplace and measuring the back wall."

"You may have the right of it, Mrs. Fidget," Delphinia agreed, picturing the large hands turning valves and bending pipes. "I do not think him suited to be an artist."

"He seemed so interested in how Mr. Fidget baked his biscuits and pies, perhaps he would like to be a good cook."

"I tried to give him a more practical view of his possibilities. I do hope he is not aspiring to an occupation ill-suited to him."

"Oh, my, Miss Penn, I forgot to tell you that he did see to getting the well cleaned out."

"Many don't know where their true talents lie, do they, Mrs. Fidget?"

"Well, he didn't seem to give a fig that his boots got muddied. I had to scrub the floor after he left."

"I observed his companions at the art exhibit. They seemed overly frivolous for someone of such an abrupt nature."

"Abrupt?" said Mrs. Fidget. "Why, I thought him to be most pleasant."

Delphinia stared at her in amazement. "Then we cannot be speaking of the same person. It has to be another Fitch—there may be a brother. I have four, if you remember, so I know all about brothers."

The housekeeper thought a moment. "Why, that is true. No telling how many Fitches there may be. I shall ask him if he comes round again."

"I am sorry, madam, but the public is not admitted into the exhibition rooms until ten o'clock."

Delphinia had targeted the Royal Institution for her excursion the following day, and she would not be turned aside now. She shook out her umbrella and began to fold it. "My good man, only a fool would expect me to stand out here for another hour in this pouring rain and catch my death. I was told that your museum houses an astounding mineralogical display gathered by the reknowned Professor Humphrey Davy, as well as an extensive library of rare and valuable historical and scientific works."

"But . . . but, madam, we are not ready for visitors yet," the man sputtered.

Gregory, gowned in his brown smock, chose that very moment to cross the hall at the back of the rotunda, heading for the stairwell to the basement. The husky, and yes, dictatorial timbre of an all too familiar voice struck him like a rod of steel. He ducked his head and hunched his shoulders—too late.

"Fitch! Ho, there, Fitch!" Delphinia called, waving her gargantuan umbrella over her head.

Never taking his eyes off the umbrella, the doorman asked hesitantly. "Madam is acquainted with the gentleman?"

"Oh, my, yes, indeed!" Delphinia said with great fervor.

Fitch looked about for an avenue of escape, but Miss Penn had already pushed past the startled porter and was marching toward him. "Imagine running into you again so soon, Fitch. Are you working here?"

Gregory glowered with every effort he could muster to frighten her.

"That was my intent, Miss Penn, until I was disrupted."

The harried doorman caught up to them. "I tried to explain to her that we are not open to the public for another hour."

"And I tried to *explain to him* that it is foolish to leave me standing outside in the cold when I could very well be viewing the splendid displays inside. Does he think I will absconde with the library?"

Gregory shook his head. "That's all right, Albert. I will be responsible for the lady."

"As you say, sir." The man looked skeptical, but nodded, and scurried away.

Delphinia turned to Gregory and raised an eyebrow. "Well, Fitch, I am truly astounded. An art exhibition, and now, to find you working here."

"Do you have nothing more interesting to do but follow me about, Miss Penn?"

She totally ignored his setdown. "I must commend you, Fitch. You have more ambition than I gave you credit for. If I had known you were trying to fill two positions, I would not have thought to impose another on you."

Gregory weighed his alternatives. No matter how he looked at it, he was stuck with her for the next hour, and he had not known her long enough to know her motives for following him. He decided to keep his true identity to himself and try to discourage anymore contact. "You will have to come with me, I suppose, Miss Penn. We cannot have you rattling around up here by yourself."

"No, I suppose not." Delphinia said, attempting to match him step for step.

Gregory grinned wickedly and lengthened his strides. She practically had to run to keep up with him. "I probably need not ask. You are unaccompanied."

"My coachman is enough for me," she said, taking a deep breath, but not losing one step.

"It is just not done in polite society, madam. I told you that once before."

"You and others seem bent on repeating that silly rule. Men do not require an escort. Why should a woman?"

"Do as you please, Miss Penn. I know that you will anyway, but don't blame me when you are assaulted and dragged down a back alley."

"That does not speak well for your sex, does it, Fitch?"

Gregory quickened his pace, but she wouldn't give up. The woman was unbelievable.

When they reached the bottom of the stairs, Gregory unlocked a door and entered a room filled with large, covered vats, tubing running in strange configurations, and containers of bubbling liquids. No one seemed to be about.

Delphinia picked up a beaker, its peculiar greenish contents, bubbling. "Do you clean all this, Fitch?"

Gregory's eyes grew round. He snatched the bottle from her hand, and as he plopped it down on the table, green drops splashed on his sleeve. "Is nothing safe from your meddling, Miss Penn?"

"I was not going to break it."

A peculiar odor rose in the air, and fascinated, they watched the fabric covering his arm sizzle and curl up.

Gregory frantically rolled up the sleeve of his smock. Thank God, he'd remembered to remove his jacket beforehand, or Davies would have his head for ruining another. He should have left her outside in the cold.

"Miss Penn, would you care to accompany me into the next room? I think it will be safer if I show you uncombustable items. There we have stoves, boilers and even a drip coffeepot invented by Rumford."

"Count von Rumford, the physicist?"

He looked at her peculiarly. "How do you know of the count?"

"Count von Rumford spoke at the museum in Norwich, and my employer and I went to hear his lecture. She had become acquainted with him on a trip to America, before he became Sir Benjamin Thompson. He was born in Massachusetts, I believe, but because he was a spy for England in the scuffle with our colonies, he had to return to the land of his ancestors. Do not think that because I come from a small town in Norfolk that I am uneducated, Fitch."

"Indeed?" Gregory felt a sudden rise in spirits, and completely forgetting he was speaking to a woman, went into one of his lengthy lectures. He pointed to one of the exhibits. "Here is a sample of one of the first double boilers Rumford invented . . . and he was working with heating water with steam, you know."

"I am impressed, Fitch! Now I see what you were trying

to do in Lord Linsey's orangery. You are trying to duplicate the count's steam machine, aren't you?"

A peculiar gleam came into Gregory's eyes. "If I can heat the water in the orangery, I could run the pipes into the mansion and . . ."

". . . and Lord Linsey will have heated water right in his house," she finished. "How clever of you, Fitch.

Gregory scowled. *"Could have* hot water, Miss Penn. The old curmudgeon's thinking is antiquated. He wants to keep everything as it is—or was. He refuses to let me run pipes into the mansion."

"Do not speak ill of your benefactor, Fitch."

He snorted. The truth of the matter was that Grandfather fought any changes he wanted to make.

"I never read them, but I know that my employer had a great many old books and manuscripts . . . books about engineering in the ancient world."

Gregory's eyes lit up at the mention of the books. "Really? Where are they now?"

"She sent her library to a friend in London, Lady Jacomena Dalison. You don't know how thankful I am for that. I am afraid to think of how her collection would have been wasted had it been intrusted to her relatives."

Gregory was staring off into space, the oddest expression on his face.

"Fitch, did you hear a word I said?"

"I heard you, Miss Penn."

"Well, you looked as if your mind was a million miles away."

"Actually only a mile or so away, Miss Penn." *Lady Jacomena of Covent Garden. The bluestocking.* Gregory was still musing over what he had just heard, when a man appeared from behind a tall glassed display-cupboard at the far end of the room. He waved an arm.

"I do believe that man is signaling you, Fitch."

"That man, Miss Penn, happens to be Sir Jameson Penbrooke, professor of chemistry at Oxford—" Gregory was

about to tell her that the baronet had also been a pupil of Rumford's, when a bell clanged loudly from above, cutting off his last words.

The man was jumping up and down, waving both arms. Delphinia started for the door. "That must be the opening of the Institution, Fitch," she whispered. "You should get back to your chores. Sir Jameson seems terribly upset, and it will not do for you to lose your job here. You are learning a lot—so don't make a hash of it."

Gregory, who could not find his tongue until she was out the door, suddenly snapped back to life. "What is it, Sir Jameson?"

"Some mischiefmaker got into the laboratory and spilled my beaker!"

Gregory rolled the cuff on his sleeve a bit higher to conceal the telltale burns. "It was probably a mouse."

"By Jove! Do you think so? What can be done about the pesky creatures?"

"Perhaps, you can invent a better mousetrap."

"Oh, that is a splendid idea, Fitch. That is not quite up my alley, but I shall give it some thought."

Although she stayed until visitors' hours were over, Delphinia did not get to see all that she wished to at the Institution. Not at all. One day was quite insufficient to savor everything it offered. She realized that now. She would just have to come back another time.

As she climbed into the carriage, Fitch's rebuke came back loud and clear. *It just is not done in polite society, madam.* She didn't know why his words should bother her when no one else's had. She was too mature to need a chaperone, but a companion of about her own age, or older, would be to her liking. Someone like Miss Cloverseed. Someone to share her excursions—someone with whom she could converse intelligently. So it was not a matter of propriety which drove Delphinia to make her decision. It was loneliness.

"Malachi, do you know of a registry office which may still be open at this hour?"

"There is one only a few minutes from here, Miss Penn."

"Then take me there at once."

Four

The registry office was dark, cold and smelled of anxiety. Women: thin, fat, old, young and inbetween, huddled in their winter coats along the wooden benches lining either side. Delphinia's gaze swept along the ranks to the far end of the room.

"What is your name?" the woman barked.

"Miss Delphinia Penn."

The woman's face looked rather like a raisincake with a nose stuck on the front. She was dressed in black, perched on a stool behind a high, bleak desk, a stack of papers before her. She pointed her quill pen at Delphinia. "What was your last employment?"

"I was companion for ten years to Miss Cornelia Cloverseed of Whetstone Manor, Norfolk."

"Your reason for leaving?"

"She died."

"Be seated. It is almost time to close. If I don't get to you in the next hour you will have to come back tomorrow."

It was on the tip of Delphinia's tongue to tell her that she was there to hire, not be hired, when the door to an inner room opened and a wisp of a girl came out giggling, a paper clutched in her hand.

Raisincake called a name. Another woman scurried in.

Delphinia did not want a silly young thing that couldn't finish a sentence without giggling. Considering herself a good judge of character, she decided to sit and observe before making her pick. *Then,* she would inform the sergeant-at-arms that she was there as an employer.

She settled in beside a little brown sparrow, who was huddled so low that Delphinia nearly overlooked her until she felt her shiver.

"I'm sorry," the sparrow said. Brown eyes looked up from under the simple hat. "I should have put on my warmer coat, this morning . . . Delphinia. That is what you said, was it not? That is a lovely name."

Delphinia nodded. Now that she was aware of the woman, Delphinia observed her more closely. The hair peeking out from under her bonnet was almost totally gray with a hint of blondness. The lines of age around her eyes betrayed the youthfulness of her gentle voice and speech. Her porcelain skin was flawless, but the pale, pinched cheeks bespoke of someone too long enclosed indoors. Threadbare as her coat was, it was clean and shiny and of a good fabric. No matter what she said, Delphinia doubted she had another. The tiny almost invisible stitches on her silk gloves showed she was adept with a needle, an art for which Delphinia generously admitted she had no aptitude. For that reason she was quick to admire anyone who obviously excelled in such.

The brown eyes were also observing Delphinia. "My name is Harriet. Harriet Snow."

"Have you been here long, Mrs. Snow?"

"It is *Miss* Snow," she said softly. "I have come every day for three weeks now."

Delphinia gasped. "And you have not found employment?"

"They placed me as a milliner's assistant, to sew lace

and ribbons on hats, but it did not work out. My employer said that I was too slow. I could not keep up with the girls."

"Well, I think that is grossly unfair to expect you to do so at your age."

"She did say my work was without fault, but that did not fadge with her. She said she had to turn out a great number of hats to make a profit."

"Well, I am sure you will find something else."

Harriet looked back down at her hands. "I am afraid I am ill-equiped to do much that is useful." she said apologetically.

Delphinia took another, longer look at Harriet. "What brought you to such a state? I can see you were not born to drudge."

"My only brother died in the Peninsula. I had kept house for him for fifteen years after our parents died. He was not cut out to be a farmer, and we went terribly in debt. He thought if he took what money we had and bought himself a commission, he would be able to pay the mortgage. But after he was killed I could not afford to keep it any longer, and had to let it go. I acquired a position with a family of means in Middlesex as governess, but they soon found that I could not keep up with five small children and was dismissed. I foolishly thought that if I came to London I could surely find employment as a music teacher or seamstress. I already told you what happened with the latter."

While they had been conversing, several more women passed through the thick door into the inner sanctum. Some came out smiling, others crying. Delphinia heard a sigh and looked down.

"You see," Harriet mused, "it is the fresh, young things whom they hire. I cannot blame them. They can do twice the work."

"That is outrageous!" Delphinia said, giving the floor such a thumping with the metal tip of her umbrella that all eyes in the room looked her way. "I find that disgracefully

unfair, Miss Snow. They do not educate women to have
worthwhile employment, then expect them to survive
somehow when disaster strikes. Now, I am in the position
to offer you a job. What say you? Would you care to work
for me?"

Delphinia could not imagine what caused Harriet to do
so, but she gave a little cry and slithered off her seat onto
the floor. Soon a crowd gathered around the crumpled
figure. Delphinia took Harriet's hand and felt her brow.
A quick appraisal of the situation told her that the frail
woman had only fainted. No one was really doing anything
of any use, so Delphinia prodded them away with her
umbrella and sent one of the more sensible-looking girls
to fetch Malachi.

Together they got her into the carriage. Once they
reached Cloverseed House, Delphinia had Harriet carried
to her chambers and laid upon her bed. Some of Mrs.
Fidget's hot tisane tea revived her.

As soon as Delphinia saw a bit of color seep into Harriet's
face, she asked, "When did you last eat?"

"Two days ago," Harriet said apologetically.

Mrs. Fidget threw up her hands and hurried from the
room. Delphinia knew that a tray of food would soon make
an appearance.

"My offer still stands," Delphinia said. "I need a companion. There are *some* people who believe that I am in
dire danger of being ravished at every turn. One of your
responsibilities will be to accompany me. I will need you
to mend my clothes, and perhaps sew a few frocks more
suitable for the city. As soon as we know that you are well,
I shall see that you have a warmer wardrobe. I take it you
play the piano?"

Harriet nodded.

"I play badly, so in the evenings, I may ask you to fill
the house with music while I read. I think that several of
the novels I have just purchased would be better read with
accompaniment in the background."

Harriet broke down crying, or at least, Delphinia thought she was crying.

She looked at the frail little woman in dismay. "You believe that is too much to expect of you?"

Harriet removed her hands from her face. Laughter shined in her eyes. "Oh, my dear Miss Penn. I shall be delighted to work for you."

"Delphinia will do," she said hoarsely, trying not to betray her pleasure on hearing Harriet's decision. It was then that Delphinia uncovered a hidden truth about herself. She had tended to Miss Cloverseed for ten years, and her death left a great void in her life. More precisely put, she needed someone to care for—and Harriet Snow needed a protector. It was as simple as that.

"Well, well," she said, sounding quite pleased with herself, "Miss Snow is moving in to stay." Delphinia told Mrs. Fidget to prepare another bedroom. Then she sent Malachi to fetch Harriet's belongings from her former lodgings, which, as Delphinia supposed, were very few. A more extensive shopping trip was needed to outfit Harriet than she previously thought.

When Delphinia made up her mind to do something, she did it with a vengance—or more properly stated, with determination, for vengefulness was not part of her nature. She looked forward to indulging Harriet; dressing her in dainty dresses and pretty bonnets which Delphinia knew she would never wear herself. There are some women who are made for Belgium laces on their gowns and velvet ribbons in their hair, and some who are not.

As soon as Harriet was well enough, Delphinia took her in tow to plunder every shop along Oxford and Bond Streets. Silks, chintzes and muslins of all colors were displayed in fine folds in high windows. Then on to find shoe and slipper shops, milliners, gloves, fur muffs and fancy undergarments.

Delphinia wasn't quite sure how Harriet managed it, but her childlike enthusiasm was so catching and her suggestions spoken so softly, that Delphinia didn't even know that she was being manuevered, until she found herself in possession of a far more extensive wardrobe than she had any intention of buying. Harriet was amazing. Fragile, little Harriet, who looked as if a light breeze would blow her away, even badgered a dressmaker to set aside her other consignments to complete two outfits before Lady Jacomena's gathering, which was only a few days away.

Lady Jacomena, bluestocking nonpareil, still a remarkably handsome woman, her blue eyes flashing, approached Delphinia. "I am glad you could come, Miss Penn. I take it you are enjoying yourself. I heard you taking Sir Henry down a peg or two on his opinions of the divine right of kings."

"I had a very good teacher," Delphinia said. "I feel that I am surrounded by a roomful of Miss Cloverseeds," she said happily.

Lady Jacomena nodded her approval. "I can see you measure up to your mentor's high opinions of you. Never take when you can give."

Delphinia and Harriet had been at Dalison Hall no more than fifteen minutes before they'd been introduced to well over a dozen notables; professors, writers, musicians, artists, statesmen, all quite eager to speak on their own subject of expertise. Delphinia had not realized how starved she was for a good sparring partner. She'd been afraid Harriet's gentle nature would be overwhelmed by the sparks flying back and forth among the participants, but there was one elderly gentleman in particular who claimed her attention almost immediately.

It was more of a surprise to Delphinia to find herself somewhat of an attraction when there were so many more stylishly dressed ladies in the room. In a moment of weakness, she had permitted Harriet to talk her into a very fashionable afternoon dress in a startling shade of blue. A wool pelisse trimmed in gold and a wide-brimmed hat with a military flavor completed the ensemble. It certainly was not the sort of outfit she would have chosen for herself.

Lady Jacomena tapped Delphinia on the arm with her cane. "Now, I am sure you want to see where I have put Miss Cloverseed's book collection."

"I most certainly do, Lady Jacomena," Delphinia said, looking speculatively about the parlor for Harriet.

With relief, Delphinia spied her standing on the other side of the room, a lovely vision in gray, a pink scarf around her neck, which put a pleasant rather youthful glow in her face. Harriet was listening intently to the tall, slender, middle-aged man who punctuated every sentence by jabbing his finger in the air above his head.

Lady Jacomena followed her gaze. "Your little friend, Miss Snow, seems quite content to listen to Ashbourne Medley prose on about his latest composition. Come!" she ordered, pointing with her cane in the direction of the hallway. "I shall show you to the library."

A moment later, Jacomena stood in the two-leveled book room. "You will find Miss Cloverseed's collection starts on the shelves just beyond Caesar's bust. I like to keep things alphabetical. Stay as long as you wish," Lady Jacomena said, closing the door behind her with a bang.

Delphinia was alone, or so she thought, until an enormous head of dark-red hair loomed over the railing above.

"Good, heavens! Fitch! What in the world are you doing up there? Or need I ask?"

The truth of the matter was that Gregory had been in the front parlor when Delphinia had arrived earlier with a woman he didn't recognize. He'd managed to escape to the library before Miss Penn saw him and could give him her *"Ho Fitch!"* salute. But he'd not failed to notice—and he didn't know why it should upset him—that she was soon surrounded by several of his notable acquaintances:

Lord Devers, the antiquarian, Miles Stootbury, portrait artist, and the Honorable Peter Grimshaw, historian. She seemed to be arguing with them immediately—and smiling all the while she was doing it. But what else could one expect of Miss Penn?

"If you must know, I was looking for those writings on ancient engineering you said Lady Jacomena had acquired."

"And you thought to get at them, you would find employment here as well? You are a card, Fitch."

Gregory had always considered himself to be of a serious nature, and it hurt him that anyone—especially Miss Penn—should not see him in that light. He tried desperately to decide which of the three brilliant set-downs he'd conjured up would be the most unsettling to her. But while he glared at her from the balcony, his thoughts became confused. There appeared to be something different about Miss Penn this afternoon, but he couldn't quite put his finger on what it was. In the meantime all three of his smart retorts completely left his mind.

"The books are not up there in the clouds, Fitch."

With a deliberately heavy step, he clumped down the circular staircase.

"If you don't know how a library is set up, don't be embarrassed to say so. I will show you."

It was too much. "Good God, madam! I will not have you showing me how to find a book."

Delphinia ignored his outburst. "You are being stubborn, Fitch."

"I am not being stubborn," he protested loudly.

Delphinia put her finger to her lips. "Shh! If you insist on bellowing like a bull, someone will hear you and put you out."

He was a big man and when he pulled himself to his full height, he towered over her. "I am a rational man, Miss Penn. I never bellow."

It was an extraordinary performance, obviously meant

to intimidate her, but Delphinia was not to be intimidated. She turned her back to him and began surveying the shelves. "Lady Jacomena said they were here somewhere . . . right after Caesar."

"I heard her, Miss Penn."

"I am glad that your hearing is so acute, Fitch. I have wondered about it at times." Delphinia ran her finger up and down the shelves. "Ah, here they are," she said, picking up one book and then another. Finally, after several minutes, she picked up a rolled sheet of papyrus. "I believe these are what we were looking for."

Gregory, his upset completely erased by the sight of the treasure, eagerly reached around her and removed another. He carried the scroll to a table where he carefully unrolled it. His eyes lit up. "Look, here, Miss Penn!"

Not realizing that he did so, he grabbed her arm and pulled her to his side. Delphinia determined not to let his nearness unsettle her. Heads together they studied the scrolls for well over an hour. "That looks like a man running on a wheel," she said, pointing.

He straightened up and peered down at her. "Very good, Miss Penn. That is because it *is* a man running on a wheel."

"You need not be sarcastic, Fitch. What does it mean?"

"Ah, Miss Penn is admitting she does not know everything," Gregory said to no one in particular.

"Well, I would say it is a very foolish thing to do. He isn't going to go far running in one place."

"My theory, Miss Penn, is *that* is an example of a screw pump. See the slant of the wheel? See how the cylinder resembles a sea-shell?"

"Never!" said Delphinia with her usual conviction.

"Miss Penn," Gregory answered with the forced patience one would have with a child, "the steam engine was in existence hundreds of years before Christ."

"Now, I know you are really bamming me, Fitch. The steam engine was only invented a century ago to pump the water out of the coal mines."

Gregory was back at the shelves going over the titles of Miss Cloverseed's books, but not before she saw his lips turn into a wicked grin. He pulled out a thick book, and upon opening it, began making a humming noise—a very monotonous sound—which drowned out any words she tried to say. Oh, he was an annoying man.

"Ahah! Ahah! Here we are!" he said enthusiastically, slapping the book down beside the scroll and pinpointing the drawing with his finger. "There and there and there! I knew I had seen it before."

"What in the world is all the racket?" Lady Jacomena barked from the hallway. "It sounds like Bedlam in here. Miss Penn, your companion, Miss Snow is looking for you. Your carriage has arrived." With no more ado, Lady Jacomena left.

"Well, well, Miss Penn. I see you took my advice and acquired someone to chaperon you," Gregory said, sounding full of male superiority.

"It was not your suggestion entirely, Fitch. I had planned to do it all along."

Delphinia glanced at the floor clock. She stared, unbelieving. "Good heavens! I have been in here nearly two hours," she exclaimed, hurriedly replacing the scrolls.

Gregory called just as she reached the door. "Oh, Miss Penn!"

There was something in his voice which made Delphinia pause.

"Have you ever been to the British Museum?"

"Not yet."

"Then, you may like to know that there is a new exhibit of early Greek and Roman terracotta jars being shown there now. I thought perhaps you . . . that is . . . you and your companion might find some of them to be of great interest. Tuesday is a good day to go."

Delphinia cleared her throat. "Thank you, Fitch. Miss Snow may very well like to see the exhibit."

After she had gone, Gregory scratched his head. Dash

it! Why did he tell her that? Tuesday was the day he'd planned on working at the museum.

Early the next morning, Gregory watched Delphinia go out with her Miss Snow, and thought it safe for him to slip over next door to see how the renovations were progressing. Mr. and Mrs. Fidget had become quite used to the earnest young man's appearances and soon gave no never mind to his comings and goings. It was almost as if he had become a fixture, poking about the cellar walls, peeking into the front rooms to admire the newly painted ceiling, or test the sturdiness of the stairway bannisters. If it seemed strange that he always turned up just as Miss Penn had taken her leave, they did not say so.

Their conversations always followed the same pattern. He would apologize for interrupting, then ask, "May I just take a look around to see how things go on?"

"Of course," they always replied.

"'Tis unfortunate that Miss Penn left," Mrs. Fidget would say.

"Yes, isn't it?" he would answer. "Well, I will take my peek and, perhaps, I will catch her up later."

So it was on this particular day that Gregory was snooping about the house, when Delphinia's unexpected return caught him off guard. Looking for someplace to hide before she spied him, he ducked into the cupboard under the stair. He hoped that she would soon leave again, but to his dismay, the unpredictable Miss Penn sat down in the front parlor and proceeded to discuss some upcoming excursion with Miss Snow. They were still there twenty minutes later when he heard Brambles answer the front door. The air was beginning to close in on Gregory, but if he came out, what possible excuse could he give for being found hiding under her stairs? There was nothing for him to do but to suffer it out in his scrunched up, miserable position, knees drawn up under his chin.

In the meantime, Gregory heard Brambles admit a man whose voice was unfamiliar to him. "Miss Penn asked me to stop by."

"Mr. Bleamish, I am glad you could come," Delphinia said, with far more enthusiasm than Gregory liked. She introduced him to Miss Snow and asked him to sit down.

Gregory eased open the cupboard door a wee crack. The portly gentleman who came into his line of view had just raised his quizzing glass to study the magnificent French Empire clock on the mantel. Right off, Gregory did not like him. Although the man made all the right moves and said all the polite things in addressing Delphinia, his admiration of his surroundings was all too transparent.

"Miss Penn, not as your solicitor, but as a friend, may I have a word with you privately?"

"There is nothing you can say to me that my companion cannot hear, Mr. Bleamish."

"Bravo!" Gregory said under his breath from inside the cupboard.

"I can repair to the next room, dear," Harriet said shyly. "I shall only be a breath away."

"Well, all right," Delphinia agreed.

"No!" hissed Gregory. "It's not done, Miss Penn. Can't you see what the rascal is up to?"

Delphinia cocked her head to one side. "Did you say something, Mr. Bleamish?"

"Not yet, Miss Penn." His gaze ran around the ornate gilded mirror over the marble fireplace.

Harriet was no sooner out of sight than Mr. Bleamish hopped to the settee beside Delphinia, which wasn't a great distance, considering the narrow confines of the room. He brought his wandering gaze around to her to have a good look—or perhaps *ogle* would be a better word. "Oh, my dear Miss Penn. What have you done to yourself? You seem . . . well, different," he sputtered. "The London air must be doing wonders for you."

"That is balderdash and you know it, Mr. Bleamish."

"No! No! No! It is that lovely dress. Ruffles and laces become you, my dear."

Gregory pressed his eye closer to the crack in the door. That was it! Her clothes! That was what was different about Miss Penn at Lady Jacomena's gathering. Why had he not realized it before?

"I am as I always was, Mr. Bleamish," Delphinia said. Which wasn't exactly true. Harriet's ridiculous insistence on her putting the silly lace around her throat and framing her face with those tiny curls made her feel . . . well, Delphinia wasn't exactly sure how she felt. But if the way Mr. Bleamish was staring at her bosom was anything to judge by, she wasn't certain that she liked the change.

Beads of perspiration broke out on the solicitor's forehead. "No, no!" he protested. "I have always held you in the highest regard, Miss Penn. That is . . . I have always thought you extremely attractive."

"You can cut the flummery, Mr. Bleamish. It is something else you want. And I am not interested in helping you acquire it."

Mr. Bleamish had the courtesy to turn red. "Well, I thought it worth a try."

"Nothing ventured, nothing gained," Delphinia replied.

He shrugged and wiped his face with his handkerchief. "Have you ever given any thought to marrying, Miss Penn?"

"Why should any woman of independent means think of such a thing?" Delphinia expounded. "To be at the beck and call of a person who always has to have his way? And all males do, don't they?"

Delphinia was sure she heard a smothered snort nearby, but dismissed it as a sneeze from one of the workmen abovestairs.

The solicitor made one more attempt to press his suit. "Oh, Miss Penn, *all* men are not like that."

"Admit it, Bleamish. Men are selfish creatures who wish to be pampered. I think it best if you stick to being my solicitor." She sat back and folded her hands in her lap. "I called you here to tell you that I have told my decorator, Mr. Brielson, to send his bills to you for payment. Now, if you will excuse us, I plan on taking my companion to the Tower Zoo today. So if there is no other business you wish to discuss with me, we shall say goodbye. Goodbye, Mr. Bleamish."

Gregory let out a sigh of relief. Thank God, the interview was over. He had been about to call the man out. As soon as he heard Miss Penn tell Brambles that she and Miss Snow were leaving, he waited a few minutes, then crawled stiffly from his hiding place and hurried home. Grandfather was having another one of his dinner parties tonight.

"You wanted to see me, Grandfather?"

"Come here, boy. Straighten your cravat. What is wrong with that valet of yours?"

The summons had come so quickly and unexpectedly at eight o'clock the next morning that Davies had nearly had apoplexy trying to make Gregory presentable.

"Can you explain your rackety entrance at dinner last night? You were tardy, you had straw on your shoes, and got grease on Lady Winningham's gloves when you addressed her."

"Before coming to join the party, I had to go back to the orangery to check on a loose joint that was leaking steam this afternoon."

"You are a raspcallion, my boy," the viscount scolded, trying to suppress a smile. "You will probably take a wrench to your wedding bed . . . and I don't mean wench."

Gregory looked shocked. "I would not think of such a slibberslabber thing, Grandfather. But I hope my wife will understand the importance of my inventions."

"Women are not machines, my boy. You cannot turn

them off and on when you want peace and quiet, unfortunately."

"Of course not, Grandfather, but my work means a great deal to me."

"I don't know why you cannot do *nothing* like the rest of the Fitch men have always done. But that is neither here nor there. That isn't why I called you."

Gregory had a sinking feeling that he knew what was coming.

"It is time you married and had an heir."

There it was in a neat little package. "If I am not mistaken, you waited until you were a lot older than I to marry and have my father."

"If your father had lived it would be different. I will be ninety years old on my next birthday," the viscount said.

"You should have had more children."

"Hah! Not if you'd known your grandmother," he mumbled.

"You don't make the married state sound too attractive."

"I was romantic once—all came to nonsense."

"Then why did you marry Grandmother?"

"I didn't have a say in the matter. At least, I'm giving you the option of choosing your own wife."

"I have not found a woman I could stand to live with the rest of my life."

"You don't have to live with her. All you have to do is produce a son. Now—you have been presented to some of the most eligible gels in England, either by me or their mamas. If you'd get your nose out of those blasted machines you would see what a bargain you are getting. I want to see my great-grandchildren before I die."

"You'll probably live to be a hundred."

"Humph! I shall have to live twice that long at the rate you are dragging your feet. But why are we even talking such nonsense?"

"I did not bring up the subject, sir."

"None of your lip, young man. Now get out of here and

start thinking which one of those lovely ladies you are going to ask to marry you."

At that moment, Gregory would promise anything to escape his grandfather's scold. "Yes, sir," he said, backing toward the door. "I shall think seriously on the matter."

"See that you do," the viscount called after him. "Or I warn you that if you don't act soon, I shall have to take more drastic measures. Is that clear?"

"As a bell," Gregory said, leaving as quickly as he could.

Five

"Oh, you don't mean it. Tickets to the British Museum?" Harriet exclaimed as she sat down at the breakfast table.

"Brambles said the missive just arrived by messenger." Delphinia turned the packet upside down and gave it a shake. "But there is no accompanying letter nor signature."

"Lady Jacomena has sent us so many vouchers already. I suppose she is the one who sent them."

"Yes, she must have done."

"What day are they for?"

"Tuesday," Delphinia replied.

"Why, that is today."

Delphinia felt her face grow uncomfortably warm. "Now isn't that a coincidence! Someone only recently mentioned that Tuesday was an excellent day for viewing the new Greek and Roman terracotta exhibit," she said, even surprising herself at her reluctance to mention who that *someone* was.

Her encounters with Fitch had been at such odd places and such odd times, that there had been no occasion for her companion to be introduced to him. Fortunately for Delphinia, Harriet didn't seem to catch her hesitation for she was rattling on about her fervent desire to see the Rosetta Stone.

"Our only plans for today were to visit the shoemaker's in Bond Street and to look for gloves, weren't they?" Harriet said eagerly. "Surely we can do that another time."

"You are right," Delphinia agreed. "The museum, it is. I will send Henry with a note to Mr. Solebender cancelling the appointment to pick up our silk slippers."

So, with high expectations, the ladies completed their meal, donned their winter apparel, and set out in the carriage.

"You do know where the British Museum is, don't you Malachi?"

"Aye, mum, the old Montagu House in Bloomsbury. I used to carry a lot of visitors to the museum. Have you there in the shake of a lamb's tail. You have tickets?"

"Of course, we have tickets, Malachi." Delphinia said, patting her reticule.

"What time is your appointment?

Delphinia pulled out the tickets. "There is no time specified."

"I don't know if you can get in, then, mum. They be very strict on rules there. When you apply you have to state your name, address and the exact time you wish to visit. You may only have the vouchers that allow you to make an appointment for a viewing. That may be weeks away."

Delphinia stuffed the tickets back into her reticule. "Well, we will see about that, Malachi. Miss Snow and I have already canceled our other plans for this afternoon. It would be very inconvenient for us to come another time, and I intend on telling them that at the museum."

The driver didn't try to hide his smile. "I'm sure you will persuade them, Miss Penn."

"Don't worry, Malachi. I feel I am justified in this matter. Drive on."

They had no sooner been set down outside Montagu House, and Delphinia had started toward the entrance, when she heard a man's voice calling a greeting behind them.

"Miss Snow!"

"Mr. Medley!"

Delphinia glanced back over her shoulder. The gentleman from Lady Jacomena's gathering caught up to Harriet.

"I received a ticket to the museum in the morning post."

"We also," Harriet said, a blush coloring her cheeks, as she hurried to catch up to Delphinia. "We gather we owe our debt to Lady Jacomena."

Mr. Medley, showing no intentions of being left behind, hurried along beside Harriet. "By Jove! That must be it."

"You remember Mr. Ashbourne Medley, do you not, my dear?" Harriet asked, as she caught up to Delphinia.

Delphinia nodded.

Mr. Medley tipped his hat to her, but his gaze didn't leave Harriet's face. "Is this your first visit to the museum, Miss Snow?"

"Oh, yes," Harriet replied so quickly that she even astounded Delphinia into momentary silence. "I do hope I get to view the Rosetta Stone."

"Then, that is my wish also, my dear Miss Snow," he said. "But it is so difficult to obtain tickets with this showing of the terracotta, you know. I have made enumerable visits to the museum and find that even at the dullest of times, the crowds are herded through like cattle. A ticket holder is supposed to be allowed an hour in each department, but I am afraid to say that on my last visit we were given no more than thirty minutes to see the entire museum."

"Why that is terrible," Delphinia said. "That is no way to see such an important institution."

"No indeed," Mr. Medley said. "It would take thirty days just to get the feel of the place."

"Then why don't they enlarge it?"

"There is talk of doing just that," Mr. Medley said,

queueing up at the door. "But for now, I am afraid we can expect to be placed in groups of ten and taken through by a conductor."

Delphinia had no such wishes, and promptly told the porter that they refused to be treated like beasts of the field. Although she fell short of coming to fisticuffs, she had to admit that she did state her objections in a rather forceful voice.

The wide-eyed man looked at their tickets and promptly summoned the director. The director, took one look and promptly called for a conductor. A bright young man, all spit and polish, answered the call and with a polite bow asked them to follow him down the corridor. Outside a door, he came to a stop. "Here we are. The Antiquities Room," the young man said. "There are some scientists doing research inside, and we just ask that you do not disturb them at their work. This department won't be opened to the public for another two hours. You are welcome to look around." He closed the door, shutting them inside a room so jammed full of immense stones, marble columns, and bits and pieces of statues, that there was barely room to manuever between them. Two bearded men carrying magnifying glasses, passed by without saying a word.

"Well, well, how extraordinary," Mr. Medley said, raising his quizzing glass to his eye. "How glad I am to have met up with you ladies. It would have been terribly dull doing the room by myself."

"We all are fortunate to have such an influential benefactor as Lady Jacomena," Delphinia said.

"Would you like for me to show you the Rosetta Stone, Miss Snow? I know exactly where it is situated. The Greek and Roman exhibit is over there," Mr. Medley said to Delphinia, pointing in the opposite direction.

Harriet looked apprehensively at Delphinia. "Oh, would you mind, dear? You are welcome to come too."

"Forgive me my manners, Miss Penn. I did not mean

to imply . . ." Mr. Medley stammered, his face turning a splendid pink that nearly matched Harriet's.

"I know you didn't, Mr. Medley," Delphinia said. "I will be quite satisfied, browsing about by myself. I am sure no one will ravish me among the Greek terracotta—unless, of course, the Minotaur is hiding in one of of the jars ready to pounce upon me."

From the shocked expression on Mr. Medley's face, Delphinia reckoned the man had missed the point of her little jest altogether. With a second assurance that she would be all right, Mr. Medley and Harriet went on their way. Delphinia had no sooner watched the couple disappear around an enormous Egyptian temple frieze than she heard a husky, "Psst!" behind her. It sounded peculiarly like one of Fitch's boilers giving off steam—only to her surprise, it turned out to be the man himself.

"Miss Penn! Over here," he hissed, motioning to her from behind a tall Ionic column.

Delphinia looked at him suspiciously. Either Fitch was a very enterprising chap, grasping opportunities to better himself, or he was not what he appeared to be. "I suppose you somehow managed to talk Lady Jacomena into obtaining a ticket for yourself."

Gregory looked all innocence. "Her ladyship knows of my keen interest in seeing the terracotta. You didn't seem to have much trouble gaining entrance."

"It took only a little diplomacy at the door."

"I was out in the hall, Miss Penn. I heard the altercation."

"It was not an altercation, Fitch. It was merely a difference of opinion which was quickly cleared up."

"And you think your opinion took precedence over the matter, I presume."

"Of course, Fitch. I was in the right."

Gregory shook his head. "No doubt, Miss Penn. While you are here, would you like to see the jars which I spoke of at Lady Jacomena's?"

"The ones which you said would interest me?"

"The very same," Gregory said, squatting on his haunches in front of a tall terracotta jar. "They have paintings on them representing everyday life in ancient times. This one is an illustration of a work scene from the sixth century B.C. You will have to get down here to see it, Miss Penn."

It was just like a man not to take into consideration that the crippling fashions women were forced to wear were not going to enable her to take the same position that he had done. Nonetheless, Delphinia was not about to be denied getting a closer view of the drawings. She propped her umbrella against a pillar. Then with a little manuevering, she lowered herself to her hands and knees and faced the jar.

"Do you see that it is the same as in the scroll?"

"Why so it is, Fitch! The man on the wheel."

His brows raised and lowered several times, which she supposed to be an attempt to give her a menacing setdown. "I hate to say, *I told you so*, Miss Penn, but this is a Greek vase from the sixth century B.C."

Delphinia was not taken in by his theatrics. "You were right. It is a water pump," she said cheerfully.

Exhibiting a puzzled expression, Gregory looked as though the wind had gone out of his sails. "You are admitting that I am right, Miss Penn?"

Delphinia reveled in his confusion. "If you must know, I paid Lady Jacomena's library a second visit the day after her gathering and discovered some very interesting facts in her books. For instance, Hero of Alexandria had already invented a steam machine by the fourth century B.C."

Gregory sat back on his haunches and studied her.

His gaze had a strange effect on Delphinia, and she turned her attention back to the jar. "Now, quit glaring at me and show me more of what you have discovered."

"I was not glaring," Gregory said, but he quickly fell forward upon his hands, and shoulder to shoulder, they circled the jar on their knees. "Not many people are willing to listen to my theories, Miss Penn. I cannot imagine why."

"That's probably what Hero said, Fitch, when he was trying to find an easier way for people to pull water from a well."

Gregory was so happy he could barely contain it. "Do you think so, Miss Penn? I had not quite thought of it in that way." Suddenly, he sniffed the air. "Are you wearing perfume, Miss Penn?"

He was looking at her in such a strange way that Delphinia was ashamed to say she blushed. "That is Harriet's doing," she said. "A momentary weakness on my part. It is a ridiculous habit women get into."

The slight smile on Gregory's face refutted that statement.

Delphinia tried to ignore the disturbing awareness she was feeling at that moment, and edged over to the next jar. "Might I confess to you, Fitch, that I am finding the examination of the antiquities far more stimulating than painting. I believe you are too. I notice a distinct difference of interest between what I observed of you at the art exhibit, and what you are now showing here at the museum. I do not think you are suited to a life with a brush and pallet."

Gregory sidled along with her until they were in front of a Roman frieze. "No, I don't think I am, Miss Penn."

Delphinia sighed. "I am glad to hear that you agree, Fitch. I am certain you would not be happy following that occupation."

"And what do you suggest that I do, Miss Penn?"

"Steam power is becoming all the thing now, isn't it? I am certain that ships propelled by steam engines would be far more reliable than those depending upon the whims of the wind. Don't deny it. I have noticed your interest in that field."

"You are very astute, Miss Penn."

"I have also noted that you seem to like to get your hands dirty."

Something akin to guilt crossed Gregory's expression.

"Don't be embarrassed, Fitch. I have four brothers, so I am aware of those things. Two of them have become very successful farmers. One has become a clerk for a local squire, and the other has followed my father's calling and gone into the church. You can guess which ones liked to get their hands dirty. Now I want you to know that I would never tell someone else what to do," Delphinia said.

"I am sure you wouldn't, Miss Penn."

"Do not interrupt, Fitch. With your interest in the steam engine, I think something in the Royal Navy or ship building would bring in a better living than remaining a laborer in a greenhouse."

From the way his jaw was twitching Delphinia could see that Fitch was seriously considering her suggestions.

"Have you been to the Mediterranean, Fitch? Of course, you haven't. Now, I would like to travel. I can put down my interest in seeing foreign lands to my former employer's influence. She was there, you see, searching out much of the ancient world: Constantinople, Athens, Cairo. She filled my head with tales of bloodthirsty battles and derring do."

Gregory observed her in silence for a moment.

"Now that I have the means, and when Boney is put away for good, perhaps I shall follow the path of Jason on his pursuit of the Golden Fleece. Wouldn't it be wonderful, Fitch? Miss Snow would come of course. That would make it quite proper, don't you think?"

"Yes, Miss Penn, I think that someday you will do just as you say you will."

Suddenly, as if from nowhere, two pairs of expensive ladies' walking boots appeared on the floor alongside Delphinia's and Gregory's fingertips.

"Oh, I say! Disgraceful!" came a harsh accusation from somewhere over their heads.

"And in full view of everyone," answered a squeakier voice.

Delphinia did not look up. She and Fitch must have presented a ridiculous sight, on their knees, nose to nose, peering at two thousand year old relics. "Do you suppose that if we don't move they will think us mushrooms which have grown up through the cracks in the floor, and go away?" she said, coming as near as she had ever done to giggling.

"I do not know, Miss Penn. I only know that if I stay in this position a moment longer my back will break and my knees will be permanently imprinted by a Roman emperor's tiles."

"Then I suggest we stand up," Delphinia said.

"You will stay where you are, Miss Penn," he hissed in such a menacing way that Delphinia was somehow reminded of a shark. His hand upon her head persuaded her. She stayed. He rose.

Gregory bowed. "Lady Tewilliger. Mrs. Browne. How nice to see you. Are you having a pleasant tour?"

"Oh, my word! Oh, my word! It *is* you, isn't it?"

"I never thought I was anybody else, Lady Tewilliger," Gregory said, his hand still planted firmly on the top of Delphinia's head. "If I am not mistaken, I believe that is your group going out the door. Is it not? You don't want to be left behind, I am sure."

For a moment, the ladies hesitated, then chose to chase after their companions.

"I told you so, Minerva," Mrs. Browne scolded, as they hustled away. "I warned Lady Winningham about his character, but she would not listen."

"Hurry, Persimmonie! If we become separated from our conductor, they will put us out."

Only after the two women were out of sight did Gregory take his hand off Delphinia's head.

Delphinia sat back on her heels. "I am afraid you are in deep trouble, Fitch."

"I?" barked Gregory, looking at her in disbelief.

"Don't deny it, Fitch. Those women recognized you,

didn't they? My suspicions are rising that you did not come to the museum as a guest at all. You snuck in somehow. I am also beginning to suspect that you are not employed in these places which I find you in."

Gregory grinned. "I do not deny it, Miss Penn."

"Do not get me wrong, Fitch. I admire your search for knowledge, but I advise you to mend your ways on how you obtain it. I would not trust those two women not to go straight to the authorities."

"I doubt they will do such a despicable thing, Miss Penn."

"Well, when you find yourself in prison remember that I warned you. Now, I do believe it is time for me to look for my friends," Delphinia said, struggling to rise.

Gregory's lips twitched as he helped her up and watched her hurry off to join Miss Snow and Medley.

"Do not take the consequences lightly, Fitch. Jail is not a pleasant place, especially for those who cannot afford the better accommodations," she threw back over her shoulder.

Gregory saw Ashbourne Medley standing with Miss Snow. He was glad he'd thought of Medley when he'd arranged for the tickets. He reckoned that if he was right about what he'd seen at Lady Jacomena's, and the composer was as attracted to the older woman as he thought, the man would attach himself to her. Gregory had wanted to have Miss Penn to himself. She was always so sure she knew everything. He'd wanted to see the look on her face when he proved her wrong about the water pump and the steam engines being of an earlier date. But she'd surprised him by admitting he was right. It began to place Miss Penn in a different light.

The appearance of Lady Tewilliger and Mrs. Browne was another matter. There were no worse tittletattlers in all of London. They would have a field day with the *on-dit* of having caught the future Lord Linsey with some lightskirt on the floor of the British Museum. Right when he'd promised his grandfather to start seriously thinking of a bride. Keeping his hand on Miss Penn's head had been the only way he could think of to keep the old gossips from seeing her face. It seemed like the most reasonable thing in the world to want to protect her, and he wasn't sure why. Gregory sat down on a section of a Roman wall and tried to sort things out in his mind.

Delphinia found Harriet and Mr. Medley waiting for her at the door.

Harriet raised her hands to her cheeks. "Oh, my dear, whatever have you done to your new coat? It looks as though it's been walked on."

"I dropped it," Delphinia said, smiling. She wondered what Harriet would say if she told her she was in it when it hit the floor.

"Well, I suppose Mrs. Fidget will know what to do to get out those stains. Come now. Ashbourne has been nice enough to say he would see us to our carriage."

Rain was falling when they left Cloverseed House the next morning, and rain continued to fall all the while they shopped along Bond Street. Delphinia and Harriet had collected their silk slippers, and made a trip to the drapers for more muslin. It was Delphinia who suggested a visit to the Royal Institution in Albemarle Street when it was obvious that the steady downpour made a ride in Hyde Park out of the question.

They arrived at the Institution about two o'clock in the afternoon.

Delphinia took Harriet to see the basement exhibit of household inventions. She had talked about the exhibit in such depth, that Harriet insisted that was the first place she wanted to go. However, Delphinia soon tired of seeing the same objects over again and excused herself to visit Professor Davy's mineralogical collection on the first floor.

"Take all the time you need, Harriet," Delphinia said.

"Let us say that we meet at the entrance to the library at four o'clock. Remember we have tickets to the theater tonight, and I told Mr. Fidget that we would have an early dinner."

However, good intentions aside, Delphinia did not make it to Professor Davy's exhibit. As she passed the lecture room, clapping broke out. Even throaty "Hurrahs!" and "Bravos!" were audible through the closed doors. Evidently the lecture of the day was of some great interest because she realized she was only one of a few stragglers in the foyer. Another burst of applause was too much for even Delphinia to ignore, and she made to go into the semi-circular lecture room.

The porter barred her way. "I am sorry, madam, but the hall is full. The lecture is nearly over, but you may still be able to find a seat in the gallery," he said, indicating a stairway.

Delphinia had not thought to check the board at the front of the Institution announcing the subject of the talk, but the lecturer had to be of some importance to have filled the nine hundred main floor seats. She climbed to the second level and quietly found a place at the back of the gallery. The speaker was a large man who stood with his back to the audience and was pointing a long stick at a large display board. There was something familiar about the broad shoulders, and it was not until he turned around that she caught her breath. Fitch! Delphinia had to admit something very peculiar happened to her then—a sort of tightening in her chest and a shortness of breath. Contrary to how she might make it sound if she spoke of it, it was a pleasant sensation, chilling and warming her all at the same time.

He had on his dark blue coat and gray trousers which she'd first seen him in at the art exhibit. His mop of auburn hair bobbed up and down as he walked. His neckcloth had come unraveled, he waved his arms, he roared, he marched back and forth across the platform like a lion on the prowl. In short, he was magnificent.

My goodness! Who would have thought Fitch would take her advice to better himself to such limits. Delphinia was too stunned to make sense out of one word that he spoke. In ten minutes, it was over, and the crowd was passing out of the lecture hall.

It took her several minutes to make her way down from the balcony. As she was herded past the open doors of the hall, she saw Fitch up on the platform, engulfed in a sea of wellwishers. Even waving her umbrella in the air did not gain his attention. The ever-faithful Harriet was waiting for her at the entrance to the library. Still in a daze, Delphinia let herself be led to the carriage like a puppy on a leash.

Here she had accused Fitch of not taking his calling seriously. It was a pity he had not seen her, but she would be sure to let him know how proud she was of him when next she had a chance.

But Gregory *had* noticed. Good lord! Who could miss that enormous black sword perilously waving over the heads of the crowd? That made grave doubts begin to form in his mind. Was Miss Penn stalking him? He had to admit to a certain disappointment. He had begun to think of her as an Original: someone who was really interested in what he was doing, what he was thinking, and not in pursuit of his future title and fortune. But, was she just more cunning than the other predators? Was that the reason she had acquired the house next to his grandfather's? Wisdom told him that it would be better if he kept her at a distance in the future.

Gregory dropped his smock on the floor outside the viscount's chambers, then roughed his fingers through his hair before entering. Being called into his lordship's presence twice in one week did not bode well for anything. "Did you want to see me again, Grandfather?"

Lord Linsey, his back to Gregory, stood with his nose pressed against the front window, straining to see something down on the street. "Mrs. Mudge informed me that a woman has moved into the residence next door. Do you know anything about that?"

"I believe someone mentioned a Miss Penn, sir."

"Never heard of her . . . don't give a fig who she is . . . nor do I care to know how she came to get her hooks into that property. Even if she is the Queen of Sheba, you're not to have anything to do with anyone who lives there. Do you understand me?"

"No, I don't, sir. I do not have a problem with keeping my distance from the woman in that house, but why are you so perturbed because you can't have that sliver of a building?"

The viscount continued to stare out the window. "None of your business! That isn't why I asked you to attend me."

"I was afraid of that," Gregory said.

"Don't get cocky with me, young man. I want to know what steps you have taken to snare a wife."

"You only spoke to me a few days ago about that, Grandfather."

The viscount swung around. "I suppose that means you have done nothing to make a match?"

Gregory raised his eyes to the ceiling and shrugged.

Lord Linsey's gaze took in his handsome grandson; the lock of hair hanging over one eye and the shirt tail sticking out from under the waistcoat. "Good God! Look at you!" he rasped, throwing up his hands. "What do females see in you? No matter how sloppily you dress or what here-and-therian behavior you show them, they keep coming back."

This time Gregory tried to look as if he were sufficiently contrite. That didn't work either. "Well, how was I to know that Papa was not going to step into your shoes before me. I expected him to be around another thirty years, at least.''

"What has that to do with anything, young man? I'm tired of spending endless, dull dinners with such nincompoops as that pompous Podwalling and his dribble of a countess just so they can dangle their daughters before you.''

"So am I, sir.''

"Then do your duty and pick one of them from the pack and move her in here. Then, I can wash my hands of running this place.''

"I assure you that I shall make a concerted effort to find a wife during this year's Season,'' he said facetiously.

"You're too late.''

A sinking feeling in Gregory's stomach wiped the grin from his face.

"It is nearly time for my dratted Valentine ball. That is what I wanted to talk to you about.''

"Why? You've never asked for my opinion before.''

"I'm not asking. I'm telling. You will pick your bride at the ball.''

"No disrepect to you, sir, but if it has become such a burden, why not cancel the whole affair?'' Gregory suggested hopefully.

"Can't do that. The Linsey Valentine Ball is the highlight of the winter activities for the *beau monde,* ever since the first Lord Linsey started it. Sentimental fool. We can't break a family tradition.''

"Why not?''

"Because it's always been a Fitch tradition, that once it is started, we cannot break a tradition.''

"Oh,'' said Gregory, "I was never aware of that rule.''

"That is because I just made it up. It will keep you from trying to wriggle out of your obligations. How are you coming along with your Valentine poem?''

"You know that any attempts on my part in the past to prose romantic have been abysmal.''

"I agree. Your efforts always sound like a dry scientific dissertation, but you know the rules. Everyone has to bring one, or they can't get into the ball. How would it look if a Fitch broke one of his own rules?"

"Well, it would be a relief to me if I could."

"For heaven's sakes, Gregory. That attitude is what has forced me to issue this ultimatum."

"Why is it I don't want to hear what you have to say next?"

"Don't try to distract me, young man. This year, you will make your choice of a bride by the time the clock strikes midnight. That is the hour when I read the poems and give a prize for the best one. This year, I'll hold yours until last. I will make it appear so touching that I shall ask the poet to come forward. Of course, I shall show great surprise when I find that my own grandson is the author. Then I shall say that the message is so personal, that I am going to let you present it to the woman it was intended for. You will, then, give it to the gel you've chosen to be your wife."

Seeing Gregory's horrified expression, the viscount smiled justifiably. "At least, I am giving you a chance to choose your own fate. That is more than I had."

"What if I don't like any of the ladies whom you present?"

"Don't look so Friday-faced. I have taken steps to guarantee that the hall will be filled with the most eligible debutantes in England—that is, if they aren't beautiful, their papas are plump in the pockets."

"How can you say that you know that many young ladies, sir? Your list is ancient and half the people on it died years ago. The ones you keep asking to dinner are daughters or granddaughters of your cronies from your clubs."

The viscount narrowed his eyes and tapped his forehead with his finger. "Hah! Let me tell you, young man, this brain is not flying loose in the belfry yet. I am not so dumb as to not realize that those who have eligible daughters of

their own are not going to be of any help at all. So I asked
Westmorland's daughter, Lady Jersey, to send me a list
of the debutantes who are deemed socially acceptable at
Almack's. That should cover the fighting field, don't you
think?''

"You are a clever one, Grandfather," Gregory laughed,
in spite of himself, while all the time his mind raced about
to think of some way he could avoid the inevitable.

The viscount looked quite pleased as he expostulated
on his battle plans. "This year the prize will be you and
your poem—so make it a good one."

"You know that would take a miracle."

"Give it no nevermind. I shall choose yours as the best
anyway—just make it halfway decent—pledge your undy-
ing devotion and all that sort of thing."

"But it will be a bare-faced lie and you know it. Besides,
it will be breaking with tradition if you choose mine. It
will be as terrible as ever, and you are the one who said
we Fitches can never break with tradition."

"Don't be so old-fashioned, Gregory. Modernize your
thinking. You cannot stay in the past forever. Fix your eyes
on the future."

Gregory snapped his mouth shut before he looked like
a trout out of water.

"That's better, my boy. Off with you now, and start
writing that sonnet for your valentine. Cupid's legacy must
be fulfilled."

Six

The sun had barely been up an hour when Gregory saw Miss Penn boldly coming up the orangery path toward him. It didn't take her long to cover the distance; too short a time for him to escape. Why hadn't he installed a new lock on the gate?

"Well done, Fitch! I didn't think you had it in you."

He stared back at her blankly.

"The lecture, Fitch. The lecture at the Royal Institution. I was there yesterday, but you didn't see me."

"I saw you, Miss Penn."

"Then why didn't you wave? If I had known, I would have addressed you."

Gregory's curiosity warred against his promise to himself that he would see no more of her. He didn't know why he wanted to hear her opinion, but he did. "You enjoyed it?"

"I am afraid I arrived late and only caught the tail end of your lecture. But I am certain the mice in the walls and the doves in the bell tower heard every word you spoke."

He wasn't quite sure that was what he wanted to hear, but he took it for a compliment.

Delphinia watched him check a length of pipe which ran between the lemon trees. "However, Fitch, there are a few things on which I feel compelled to comment. Hold your shoulders back when you walk, and don't hunch over the lectern. You do not want to look like a gorilla, now, do you? But those things can be improved with a little effort on your part."

Gregory pulled himself up to his full height and shouted over the rumblings of his machines, which Delphinia had noticed were becoming increasingly volitile. "Is there anything more that you wish to say to further shatter my self-esteem?"

It was a splendid performance. "You need not take it in such poor spirit, Fitch."

"Do you have to argue with everything I say, Miss Penn?"

"I am not arguing with you. I am just trying to catch you up on a few minor errors."

Gregory pointed a pair of pliers at her. "You are nosy, Miss Penn, and you are a busybody. You tell me how to order my life. You tell me what friends I should choose, and now, you tell me how I should stand and deliver my speeches."

"Merely suggestions, Fitch."

Gregory thought that she had seemed the least likely woman he'd ever met capable of playing feminine tricks. Therefore, he'd carelessly let his defenses slip. No more. "Go away, Miss Penn."

"Oh, come now, Fitch. You men only like to be told you are clever, not that you have any flaws. Now admit it."

The glare he cast her way was clearly meant to send her fleeing, but she stood her ground. "You are trying to provoke me, Fitch, and I will not . . . will not . . ." Delphinia searched for the right barb.

"You think I am trying to bait *you*. Hah! Just like a woman to blame the man. How singularly self-centered you females are, Miss Penn—to think yourselves so alluring that no male could possibly refrain from succumbing to your wiles." He wanted to throw in Mr. Bleamish as an example of her wanton ways, but supposed that would only open him up to accusations of eavesdropping.

Delphinia decided the leaky pipes had to be what were making Fitch so testy. "If you would let me help, the job could be finished more quickly."

Gregory threw up his hands. "I don't believe this. I am experiencing inadequate heat transfer. I have loose joints leaking steam, and I am losing pressure. I don't need suggestions on how to run my experiments. Especially from you, Miss Penn."

Delphinia gave a snort. If he hadn't been in such a high dudgeon she would have quizzed him—in jest of course—about his *loose joints,* but at that moment Fitch didn't seem in a mood to appreciate anything of a humorous nature. "Don't be so pigheaded, Fitch. Why do you men think you can do everything by yourselves, then you are surprised when your plans blow up in your faces?"

"I wish you would not use that analogy, Miss Penn," Gregory said, leaning over to check another pipe bordering the ferns. "Wait! I think I have it, Miss Penn." His discovery of a possible solution completely wiped out any annoyance at her meddling. "Now, I know what I was doing wrong."

It was getting very hot. Delphinia walked over where she could get a better look at the Fitch's wheezing contrivance. "Surely there is something I can do to help."

"No! It is too dangerous."

"How dangerous can it be to turn a crank?"

"There are no cranks, Miss Penn. It takes boilers, valves, pistons and cylinders to make a steam machine, but you cannot be expected to understand such things.

"Come, now, Fitch. If it is so dangerous, why are you not afraid?"

"Because, I know what I am doing. I read the pressure gauge a few minutes ago, and it was holding steady," Gregory said.

"You mean this little arrow which is dancing back and forth?" Delphinia said.

Gregory swung around. The machine began to rumble and shake, then roared to life. "Oh, my God! Watch out, Miss Penn!"

Delphinia only knew that just at the moment Fitch lunged, their world exploded and clouds of steam engulfed them.

Gregory searched through the mist. "Miss Penn? Where are you, Miss Penn?" There was a strange desperation in the timbre of his voice.

The fog began to dissipate.

She was on the ground; Delphinia knew that much. Fitch was kneeling over her, calling her name. "Miss Penn?"

Somehow her face came to be cradled in the crook of his shoulder.

"Oh, my dear Miss Penn," he kept repeating, his lips only inches from hers. His hands ran down her body and back up again, before the strong pair of arms pulled her tightly to his chest. She was not sure, but it felt very much like he was kissing the top of her head. "Oh, my dear, Delphinia."

It was the first time he'd used her given name. Delphinia could not explain the delicious feelings rushing through her. She kept her eyes shut to savor the moment. Besides, she feared if Fitch knew that she was conscious, he'd drop her back onto the path right then and there.

He attempted to scoop her up off the ground, which Delphinia had to admit was no easy matter. For although he was a powerfully built man, she was no fragile, skinny creature. Somehow he managed to carry her to a bench without dropping her. It could have been said that she helped a bit by putting her arms around his neck. However the minute passed, for as soon as she opened her eyes, his voice returned to its normal, irascible tone.

"How could you do such an addlepatted thing?"

"If you are only going to blame me for what happened,

I think I shall go back to my house right now," Delphinia said, attempting to rise. She promptly pitched forward, and would have fallen on her face if he had not caught her.

Delphinia's world had become a hazy gray again, and she permitted herself the warm luxury of letting her head rest upon his chest one precious minute more.

Now just as the explosion took place, Davies had been on his way to the orangery to remind Gregory that he had an engagement at the theater that evening. Although the faithful valet could barely make out the tip of his own nose, he fought his way through the haze, and was greatly relieved when he found his master all in one piece. However, he wasn't so sure as to the state of the woman lying limply in his arms.

"Do you wish me to cancel your engagement with Lord Ramsey's party tonight, Mr. Fitch?" he asked apprehensively.

Mr. Fitch? Delphinia digested that for a moment, then peeked at the pattern-saint gentleman's gentleman standing before them. *All was not as it seemed.*

Gregory, unaware of the grim thoughts passing through the head pressed against his shoulder, addressed his valet. "No, Davies. As soon as I have seen the lady home, I shall come back to clean up this mess. I don't want any of the servants touching my equipment. Then, I'll be up to my chambers. Have a tub of hot water ready and my evening clothes set out for me. I am committed to dine at Watier's first."

During his seven years service to Mr. Fitch, Davies had been subjected to all sorts of unexpected and remarkable escapades by his master, but this seemed to be out and away the most extraordinary. Although many a young lady had thrown herself at his master's head, Davies had never known him to have an assignation in the orangery before. The woman in his arms appeared quite dazed, and that gave the servant some concern. "Do you wish me to assist you, sir?"

Gregory kept his arm tightly around Dephinia. "If you would open the gate in the west wall, Davies. I can manage beyond that."

Suddenly there was a rustling among the ferns and lemon trees behind them.

"And, Davies . . ." he shouted, loud enough for every plant in the greenhouse to hear, "I want the staff to know that no word of this is to reach his lordship! Is that understood?"

The rustling stopped.

Davies was tempted to smile as he scanned the foliage in the large building. "Yes, sir? I am certain that no one will tell him."

"Good. I would hate to have to explain to Grandfather what this is all about."

"Yes, sir, his lordship would be most displeased."

If it was unusual for Delphinia to find herself short on words for so long a time, she put that matter down to her numbness of heart and spirit. The vagabond had deceived her. She could think of no quick repartee, nor indeed did she feel like sparring with someone who had just broken her trust. She allowed herself to be assisted to the back of Cloverseed House, where she listened to *Mr.* Fitch explain to the Fidgets how she'd met with an accident. He promised to summon his physician as soon as he returned home. Mrs. Fidget and Harriet put her to bed and told her that was where she was to stay until told otherwise.

Not without some objection, Delphinia finally accepted the fact that she was to be held prisoner in her own house. "If you are not going to allow me to go out this afternoon, I wish to see Malachi when he comes with the carriage."

By the time the coachman appeared, Delphinia was not in the mood to mince words "Do you know a man named *Mr.* Fitch?"

"But, of course, Miss Penn. Mr. Gregory Fitch. He is

your neighbor, the next Lord Linsey. His grandfather, the present viscount, is considered somewhat of a stay-at-home, but Mr. Fitch goes about town quite regularly. I am surprised that you have not seen him.''

What an odious joke *Mr.* Fitch had played on her, deceiving her into thinking he was no more than a common laborer. Miss Cloverseed had been right. Men—especially men of the *haute ton*—lured unsuspecting maidens into their dens and then assaulted them. It was all Delphinia could do to remain civil, because names such as: blackguard, scoundrel, and rascally yeaforsooth knave, kept popping into her head.

"Thank you, Malachi. That will be all."

The minute the man left, Delphinia was tempted to fall back on her pillow in a swoon; but she knew that she would do a very poor job of play-acting the wounded dove. There was only one rational course to take. *Stay away from Mr. Fitch.* If she never saw the rogue again in her lifetime, the better she would be for it.

Later that day Lady Jacomena came to call. Delphinia received the woman in her bedchamber where her ladyship immediately exclaimed concern over her young friend's condition. Assured that the doctor had said it was no more than what a day of rest wouldn't cure, Lady Jacomena launched into the purpose for her visit. "You met Gregory Fitch at my gathering."

Delphinia was sure her ladyship didn't want to hear her opinion of Mr. Fitch at that moment.

"I suppose you are aware of the Valentine ball his grandfather Lord Linsey gives each February?"

Dephinia shook her head.

"Well, since you do not, I will tell you. It is considered to be the highlight of the winter season by the *ton*. Foolishness, I call it. Pure theatrics. I don't see why Linsey has the affair, other than it is has been done for generations and people get stuck in a pattern and can't get out. I cannot imagine the old stick-in-the-mud having a romantic bone in his body. I only go because of the viscount's friendship with my late father, the Duke of Hammerfield."

"I can see no reason for that to concern me," Delphinia said.

"It does. I always ask someone to accompany me. This year I am taking you."

Delphinia's eyes grew round. She had not anticipated such a circumstance arising. "Oh, but . . ."

Lady Jacomena raised her hand. "No need to thank me. For whatever it is worth, you will have a chance to meet the cream of the *ton*. Everybody of the first stare will be there, silly cabbages that they are."

Delphinia was shaking her head vigorously when she saw the words appear as plain as if they were written in the air in front of her eyes: *Should you receive an invitation to a Valentine ball, you will go!* She had forgotten Miss Cloverseed's letter. "Oh, my goodness!" Delphinia exclaimed aloud.

"I thought you'd like the idea, my dear. That is settled then," Lady Jacomena said. "By-the-by there is one other nonsensical stipulation. To be admitted to the ball, everyone must bring a Valentine poem. My housekeeper Butterworth always writes something for me. Linsey reads the silly things just before midnight and gives a prize to the one he thinks is the best. I know it is short notice, but I am sure you can find something to wear."

You must promise me that you will wear the gown in the box and carry the torn piece of paper.

Delphinia's eyes narrowed. Something was going on and she could not quite put her finger on what it was.

If Lady Jacomena felt herself in anyway discomfited at being studied so intensely, she showed no outward sign, and reached for her cane. "I loathe receiving lines so I always wait to go an hour after the dancing has started.

My coach will be outside to fetch you at ten o'clock on Thursday night.''

"But, your ladyship, it is right next door.''

"Twaddle! Can't have you walking into Linsey Terrace like a common snippet off the street. We will make our entrance under the front portico like everyone else.'' She rose and signaled to her footman who stood ready at the door to assist her down the stairs. "Until Thursday. Good day, Miss Penn.''

The Valentine Ball had been in progress for nearly four hours when Lord Linsey commenced to read the poems. He now stood on the dais at the end of the ballroom, waving Delphinia's torn sheet of paper in the air. "Who dared to bring this miserable scrap of gibberish? Whoever you are, I want to see you in my study immediately. Until I catch the cuplrit who perpetrated this farce, I will have all the doors in the mansion locked and let no one out.'' With that the viscount tossed the bundle of Valentines into the air while the congregation ran about trying to catch them. As they *oohed* and *ahhed,* their host mowed a path through the crowd and out of the room. His grandson's offering was still tucked into the viscount's waistcoat pocket and he'd not even gotten to read it. This disappointment doubled Lord Linsey's wrath.

Delphinia did go to the ball—not in the beautiful amber sarcenet Harriet had picked out for her—but as she had promised the deceased Miss Cloverseed—in the old-fashioned gray silk: full skirt, lacy bodice, high collar and all. But no one, not even the soft-spoken Harriet could persuade her to add pads or wear a hoop under the voluminous skirts.

Without being aware of it, Delphinia had begun—with Harriet's influence—to be much more aware of miladies' fashions; and she realized the gown she wore was definitely not in the first style of elegance.

"I am not a fashionable string bean as it is, Harriet. My bosom and hips surely do not call for further enhancement."

By now, Harriet was used to her employer's plain speaking. "The gown is quite unusual I vow, but you look lovely in it," Harriet assured her as she piled Delphinia's lusterous black hair into a curly crown atop her head.

"You need not try to flatter me, Harriet. I look like a large gray cloud and you know it."

Harriet retied the ribbon around Delphinia's small waist, knowing it was useless to argue.

Delphinia did not bother to look at herself in the cheval mirror, for she'd found early in her life that it never improved her spirits to do so. "I am sorry you will have to spend the evening alone," she said, pulling on her gloves.

Harriet colored prettily. "I thought that since you were going to be gone all evening, it would be all right to accept Ashbourne's invitation to dinner and the theatre."

"Well, well, Harriet," Delphinia said wholeheartedly, "so it has come to that has it? Then I shall go to the ball content in knowing that you will be happily occupied."

As soon as Lady Jacomena and she had entered Linsey Terrace and handed over their poems to the doorman, her ladyship said she wanted to sit down. Delphinia cleared the way to an alcove off the dance floor with a cushioned settee and surrounded by potted ferns.

Lady Jacomena chorkled. "I see the eagle-eyed Lord Devers has already seen you, Miss Penn, and if I am not mistaken that is young Peter Grimshaw forging his way through the crowd. There will most likely be several people here tonight whom you met at my gathering, for they are high in the instep enough for even a high stickler like Lord Linsey. Take my word, you will not lack for admirers tonight, my dear. Now I plan to sit down and you can fetch

me when it is time to go home." No sooner had her
ladyship settled into the chair than she fell fast asleep.

Delphinia was contemplating the fact that she had never
learned to dance anything beyond a few country reels, and
if she were to keep from disgracing herself, she must avoid
being asked to stand up with anyone. She watched Lord
Devers closing in from the left and Peter Grimshaw rapidly
approaching from the middle, and if that were not enough
to persuade her to want to disappear, her gaze caught
another figure bearing in from the right, with a very determined gleam in his eyes. Mr. Fitch! Delphinia kept her
wits about her. She quickly circled behind the potted ferns
and made her escape down a corridor.

However, her ordeal with Mr. Fitch had not ended and
she found herself playing a game of cat and mouse with
him all evening, until the viscount announced that it was
time to read the Valentine poems. She watched his lordship
throw the cards and letters into the air and stomp across
the dance floor. Now after nearly an entire evening of
dodging Mr. Fitch, Delphihia slipped from where she'd
been hiding in the musicians' gallery above the ballroom,
and headed in the direction the viscount had taken. She
was no coward and had no intensions of allowing any guest
to suffer for her folly. She would face the viscount. "Oh,
Miss Cloverseed," Delphinia said aloud. "I wonder if you
know what havoc you have set loose."

Delphinia approached the room into which the viscount
had disappeared. An elegantly clad footman opened the
door and stepped aside for her to enter.

Gregory watched his beloved Delphinia heading for the
lion's den. Although he'd taken up pursuing her relent-
lessly from the moment he spied her earlier in the evening,
she'd managed to avoid him. His mind was still in a quandry
over the explosion in the orangery; torn between his suspicions that Miss Penn's motives were the same as all the

husband-seeking females and the feelings he'd had after he thought she was injured. The explosion must have addled his brain. From the moment his grandfather had forbidden him to have anything to do with Miss Penn, he found that she was the only person with whom he wanted most to be.

He hadn't seen Delphinia until the ball was well under way. She couldn't have come through the receiving line or he would have seen her, so she must have snuck in some other way. That only left the back gate—which Gregory once again chastised himself for not locking it.

Whatever did the foolish girl think she was doing, crashing the ball? He had to get her out of the house before his grandfather saw her and caused a scandal. Gregory took off in hot pursuit. But when Miss Penn was *there* he was *here.* And when he managed to get through the crush to *there,* she was *nowhere* to be seen. He began to think her a gray apparition appearing and disappearing at will. But the more Miss Penn eluded him, the more his blood raced and the more determined he became to rescue her from suffering one of his grandfather's setdowns. A punishment Gregory knew all too well, for he still felt like a naughty little schoolboy every time the viscount scolded him.

Until Gregory saw her following his grandfather, he thought he'd lost her completely. He picked up his pace and arrived at the door of the study, out of breath. However there was now the problem of getting the footman out of the way. "Thomas," Gregory said, "I believe you are needed in the ballroom. His lordship's little scenario has caused no little excitement and I think more wine would appease our guests."

As soon as the servant hurried off, Gregory pressed himself to the wall outside the study to try to hear what was being said inside.

Delphinia stood before Lord Linsey. He was not nearly as imposing as she had imagined him to be, for he was short of stature for a man—his gray eyes being on a level with hers. No, it was not his height, but his deep rumbling voice—which closely resembled another member of the family—which gave him his commanding presence.

The viscount stared at her.

Delphinia stared back. "Your lordship wished to see me?"

Lord Linsey narrowed his eyes in order to see her better in the dim light. "Who are you and where did you come from?"

"My name is Miss Delphinia Penn and I come from the town of Ram's Head in Norfolk."

"I've heard your name, not the town's. It must be very insignificant."

"I had never heard of Linsey Terrace either before I moved to London, but I would not think to presume it insignificant before I had seen it."

"You are snippety, young lady. How did you get in here?"

"I am the guest of Lady Jacomena Dalison."

"Dash it! Should have known that bluestocking would be behind something like this. Did she put you up to wearing that gown and bringing this?" he asked, waving the torn paper in front of her face.

"She did not, my lord. I am to blame."

Grumbling, the viscount glanced toward the hallway and cocked his head to one side as if listening.

Delphinia would not be cowed. "Do you want me to tell you about it or are you going to do nothing but mumble and grumble all night?"

She thought she saw a twinkle in the viscount's eyes, but she put it down to the flickering of the candlelight. "You are a snippety young lady."

"You just said that, your lordship. Are you going to keep repeating yourself or do you want to hear what I have to say?"

He grinned openly and pointed to a chair. "I do indeed, Miss Penn. Be seated."

So Delphinia told him about Miss Cloverseed, about her

inheritance, and about moving to London. She did not tell him however of her numerous encounters with his grandson, the imposter, Mr. Gregory Fitch.

He studied her intensely. "Do you have any idea what those words meant on that piece of paper?"

"How could I? I am not stupid, but it was only half a poem."

"No, I see that you are not stupid, Miss Penn. Far from it. But first, there is something I must do before you leave." The viscount stood and turned to the door. "Gregory!" he bellowed. "Quit lurking about in the shadows and come in here."

Gregory lost his balance and stumbled into the room.

Seven

Gregory grabbed the door frame to gain his balance. "You wish to see me, Grandfather?"

As long as their voices were raised, he'd had no trouble hearing what his grandfather and Miss Penn said, but as their conversation settled into low murmurs he'd had to strain to hear what they were saying.

"Yes, I want to speak to you. This is Miss Penn. Miss Penn, may I present my grandson, Gregory Fitch."

Gregory bowed. Delphinia inclined her head.

"Miss Penn is leaving," Lord Linsey said. With a great deal of interest he watched Delphinia raise her chin and sail past his grandson. He watched his grandson watch her go. Then with a shake of his head, the viscount crossed to a large desk. Taking a ring of keys from the copper bowl on top of his desk, he opened the middle drawer, took off the lid of a small inlaid box and removed a scrap of paper. "Sit down," he said, "I think it is time I told you the story about the house next door."

"Certainly, Grandfather," Gregory said, finding it hard to hide his excitement. *Was his curiosity finally going to be satisfied?*

The old man placed the two scraps of paper side by side on the desk. "On Valentine's Day sixty-five years ago two lovers were to pledge their troth by melding two halves of a poem."

Gregory leaned forward. "Those pieces of paper?"

The viscount pushed them across the desk. "The same. The meeting was to be in the orangery behind this very house. The rendezvous did not take place, because the young man never appeared. Instead he married according to parental pressure, and the young lady who had been deemed an unsuitable attachment for the young nobleman, withdrew from Town, and he never saw her again."

Gregory looked at his grandfather with amazement. "You, Grandfather? I cannot believe it."

The viscount harrumphed. "Oh, I sowed my wild oats in my day, my boy. Do not think I didn't, but this was different. Miss Cloverseed was that young woman. Her father was a rich merchant, a cit. Not at all the thing to have for neighbors.

"When my father and his brother heard that three lots on the Strand with room for three palatial residences were to be put up for sale, they immediately bought the two unsold lots and started to build the present establishments. It was not until later that they discovered the middle section was owned by Mr. Cloverseed. Well, your great-grandfather and your uncle were not going to put up with such nonsense and schemed to get Cloverseed's land. They knew nothing of business, but they were both gamblers, so slowly by stealth more than skill, they stole his land away from him."

Gregory shook his head. "I cannot believe that Mr. Cloverseed could be so easily deceived into selling his land."

"Mr. Cloverseed was indeed a very astute businessman and had acquired a vast fortune. But flattered by the attention of two highborn neighbors-to-be, he was persuaded to gamble. However before they could take the entire lot, Mr. Cloverseed came to his senses. He had less than twelve feet of property left on which to build; but build he did and moved his wife and young daughter in. I was forbidden to speak to anyone from that house."

"You told me the same thing."

"And, it is obvious to see you paid no more attention to the order than I did," the viscount said, with a grin.

Gregory pondered that a moment. "That explains the strange shape of the house, but how did you become involved with the daughter?"

"Her name was Cornelia. She was a beautiful, spirited young lady. I must confess that I was drawn by her laughter—there was so little of it in our house—and I would spy upon her over the brick wall. Then one day she appeared in the orangery. That surprised me because although all the garden walls have gates in them, ours was always kept locked."

Gregory guffawed. "Don't tell me. She climbed over the wall."

Lord Linsey eyes lit up and the years seemed to fall away from his face. "How did you guess? To tell the truth, I did not know what to make of her at first, but she soon captured my heart and we started to see each other. I began to leave the gate open and she would sneak into the orangery when no one was about. I have never met anyone like Cornelia—and thought I never would again—until I laid eyes on Miss Penn. Oh, they look nothing alike, but the dress she wore was my favorite and the one I had ask Cornelia to wear that night. And when Miss Penn spoke, I closed my eyes and heard Cornelia speaking.

"We agreed to meet at midnight. Even though the daughter of a cit would not be welcomed at the ball, we wrote our own Valentine poem, pledging our love for one another. Then we tore it, each taking a half. That way if anyone found the sonnet, it would make no sense to them, don't you see? We decided that the Valentine Ball was always such a crush that no one would miss me until it was too late for them to do anything about it. We had thought eloping quite an exciting idea and had even talked of running off to America or the West Indies. Cornelia had the blunt to take us.''

"Why didn't you go?''

"She was the adventurous one. I contemplated the outcome. I might lose my title, I would be going to a foreign land where no one knew the importance of my family—but to tell the truth, the thought of having to toil for a living frightened me more. In the end, I cried off and never made the rendezvous.'' The viscount slapped his hand down on the desk. "Sentimentality aside, my ultimatum still stands. What are you going to do about choosing your future wife tonight?''

Gregory cleared his throat. "Sir, . . . about that.''

The viscount rolled his eyes and addressed his remarks to the ceiling. "Wherever you are, Cornelia, 'tis a fine legacy you left your protégée Miss Penn.''

"What did you say, Grandfather?''

"I said you are a nodcock, Gregory. Don't play the fool as I once did. I realize how humdrum my life has been. Your grandmother was a fine woman, good breeding, but dashedly dull. Never really knew her. Produced one son together—your father. Dull like his mother. Liven things up, my boy. Do the unexpected.''

"I thought you hated my experiments. You complained enough about them.''

"Nonsense! Messy, I admit. You look messy most of the time, too, and I thought perhaps a wife would make you more presentable. But now I wonder if that's the important thing. Bye-the-by, I meant to tell you how well you looked tonight. Your cravat is still tied. What happened? Perhaps there is hope for you after all.''

Gregory looked as surprised as his grandfather to find that it was true. The oriental that Davies had tied was still intact.

The viscount grinned. "I think life would not have been as boring if . . . but that is past. I see now what I have lost out on all these years, and what I might have had. Go after her, my boy. You have my blessing . . . and my sympathy. Well, go on! Go on!''

Gregory started for the door.

"Wait!"

Gregory skidded to a halt.

His grandfather dug in his pocket and pulled out the folded sheet of paper. "Here is your Valentine poem. You can read it to your sweetheart yourself."

"Keep it, Grandfather. If Cupid is on my side, I don't think I will be needing it." Gregory charged out of the room, knocking over a three-legged globe stand as he ran.

"Ah, well," sighed the viscount. "I might as well read it myself to see if Gregory's composition has improved over last year's." Lord Linsey unfolded the paper and held it up to the candle on his desk. He let out a whoop. The page was blank.

Gregory found Delphinia in the orangery where he knew he would. She was standing against a partitioning wall between the peach trees and the pineapples. He saw her quickly rub her cheeks, trying to hide the fact that she'd been crying. Gregory ran his fingers through his hair. Grandfather had said for the first time that he looked well enough and he hoped his flattery had not been all false.

He cleared his throat. "Don't run away from me, Delphinia." She looked as if that was exactly what she was contemplating, so he placed his hands on the wall on either side of her head to prevent her from doing so. "Grandfather told me a very interesting story about your house, the orangery, and the poem. Would you like to hear it? We can sit down on the bench."

His use of her given name had not escaped her. It made her all the more suspicious. "I prefer to stand, thank you. I think better on my feet."

"What I have in mind does not take a great deal of

thinking." Gregory would wonder later what impulse came over him at that moment—a sort of insanity perhaps—he had only meant to tell her about his grandfather and Miss Cloverseed. That is, in the beginning. Later he planned on telling her how much he had come to hold her in high regard. Instead he pulled Delphinia into his arms and kissed her passionately.

When he finally took time to catch his breath, she eyed him warily, but didn't try to pull away. "Do you plan to keep me prisoner forever, *Mr.* Fitch?"

"If I must to get you to listen to me. Now if you promise not to run away, I shall lower my arms." But he did not let go of her. "Don't you think that under the circumstances you can call me Gregory?"

"Humph," she said, wishing he would kiss her again. "After the flimflam you pulled on me, I should not even be speaking to you."

Gregory lifted her chin with his finger. "Ah, Miss Penn, you are losing track of what happened. If you remember correctly it was you who made the assumption that I was the gardener. I should be the one to be affronted."

"There may be some truth in that, Fitch. But it was you who led me on."

At least she was back to calling him just plain *Fitch*. That was an encouraging sign. "Aren't you curious to find out what Grandfather told me?"

She remained silent, which Gregory knew for Delphinia was a rare occurance, and disturbed him more than if she had railed at him. He decided to take the chance however, and cautiously removed one hand and then the other from the wall. He'd been dangerously close to kissing her again. "Well?" he said.

Her inquisitive nature once more getting the better of her, Delphinia nodded, and taking his hand pulled him over to the bench. She listened closely as Gregory recounted the viscount's story. "Then Lord Linsey and Miss

Cloverseed were not only going to pledge their troth, but were planning on running away together?" she asked.

"Yes, until Grandfather turned chicken-hearted."

"All men are."

"Not all men, my dear Delphinia. I think he paid quite dearly for that decision."

He was doing it again, calling her by her given name and gazing at her with a strange intensity. It was more than she could stand. "It is quite warm in here, Fitch."

"Gregory," he corrected.

"Gregory or Fitch," she said, "it is still getting very warm."

"Thanks to my steam machine," he said, letting a little bit of pride sneak into his voice.

"I do not believe it is the machine that is making me feel this way."

He put his arm around her. "And how do you feel?"

"Like this," Delphinia cried, pulling his face down to hers and kissing him squarely on his mouth.

Gregory held her away from him. "You know, Miss Penn, now that I have been thoroughly compromised you realize that you must marry me or my reputation will be ruined."

"Your grandfather would never accept me."

"We already have his blessing."

"You mean you came out here planning on . . . doing this?"

"I confess, I did not know if it would work. That is why I let you seduce me."

"You are incorrigible."

He grinned. "Do you know how beautiful you are when you are riled, Delphinia?"

"I am disappointed in you, Fitch. I thought you of all men were above that sort of flummery."

"To prove to you that I can be as romantic as other men, I even brought a Valentine poem to the party."

"That I will not believe until I hold it in my hand."

Gregory ran his finger inside his collar, loosening his

neckcloth. "Unfortunately if you remember, Grandfather tossed the Valentines in the air when he discovered your torn poem."

"That is a pity. I would have liked to have read it."

Gregory hoped his grandfather had tossed the paper away. "That will not be necessary, but I have been giving the matter of my attachment to you some thought."

Delphinia was hoping he felt something stronger than *attachment,* because she now realized her sentiments ran far deeper. She drew in a deep breath. "Fitch! I want to know how you truly feel about me."

"Must I spell it out?" He held up his hands in surrender. "All right. If you want to hear the bare truth, I am enamored with you. I think I fell madly in love the first time I saw you."

"In the orangery?"

"No. The day I saw you raise that enormous black umbrella and charge up the steps to your new home."

After Delphinia had kissed him again, she said. "You know, I think Lady Jacomena had the right of it when she said—" Delphinia's eyes grew rounder. "Oh, my goodness! I forgot about Lady Jacomena."

"I do not think you have to worry about her ladyship. I have an idea that she had more to do with this than we know. Now I believe it is time for us to go inform Grandfather that his Valentine Ball has been a success."

"Gregory."

"Yes?"

"Before we go in, do you think you can kiss me again? I did not know that I would find it so pleasant."

"Miss Penn, I do not believe that would be wise at this moment."

She wondered what had caused him to switch back to a more formal address, but something in the tone of his voice persuaded her not to question why, and she did likewise. "I agree, Fitch. Perhaps after we are married, inbetween your lectures and experiments, we will find more time to . . ."

Gregory placed his finger over her lips. "Miss Penn, don't you know that you are driving me wild?" Then he took her in his arms and kissed her soundly.

ABOUT THE AUTHOR

Paula Tanner Girard lives with her family in Maitland, Florida. She is the author of three Zebra regency romances: *Lord Wakeford's Gold Watch*, *Charade Of Hearts* and *A Father For Christmas*. Paula loves to hear from her readers and you may write to her c/o Zebra Books or P.O. Box 941982, Maitland, FL 32794-1982. Please include a self-addressed stamped envelope if you wish a response.

The Valentine Victorious

Judith A. Lansdowne

To Jody with love

One

The Earl of Wheldon cursed roundly as a torrent of rain spewed from the clouds above and pummeled down upon his new beaver hat. Demme, but it was miserable weather! And it was frigid too! And he must certainly have been out of his mind to have sent the traveling coach ahead and driven his curricle instead. Beside him his valet, Tucker, cursed as well, though he did so a bit more quietly. Carley, the tiny tiger at the rear, merely closed his eyes and clung to his perch in miserable resignation.

"I have not been so wet since I fell into the Serpentine," grumbled Wheldon. "Well, there's nothing for it but to halt at the next inn, Tuck. We cannot continue on in this downpour or we shall all be drowned, men and horses alike."

"Yes, my lord," replied Tucker pulling his surtout tighter around him.

"How is Fearless doing? Not frightened is she?" asked the earl as he concentrated on holding his horses to the high ground.

"She has burrowed down into my waistcoat, your lordship," sighed Tucker, "and is fast asleep. I am not wet quite as deep as my waistcoat—yet."

"Yes, yes, I hear you, Tuck. It will not be much longer. There is an inn just around the next turn."

Wheldon urged his horses to a faster pace, fearing to push them into a run on the boggy road but impatient to be inside in warm, dry clothes by a blazing fire. "I retract that statement," he sighed bleakly as they rounded the turn. "There *once* was an inn around the turn. Now there are ashes. I expect we must needs push on to Fairfax's. Buck up, Tucker, it is not as far as Averdon's. Fairfax will not be expecting us, but he'll put us up for the night."

"Yes, my lord," sighed Tucker with obvious patience and then sneezed. "Do we know precisely where Lord Fairfax lives, my lord?"

"Not precisely," grinned Wheldon, his damp anger dissolved by the long-suffering expression upon his valet's face. "But I shall discover the place. Not to worry."

"No, my lord," breathed Tucker and shivered.

At the end of another hour Wheldon did at last discover the drive to Fairfax House and brought the little curricle up it at a spanking pace. "I shall drive around to the stables and rouse the grooms, Tucker," the earl shouted through the increasing noise of the storm. "They will not have heard us approach and I cannot leave the horses standing a moment in this downpour. Go and knock the butler up for me, eh? I shall leave Carley at the stables along with the horses."

"Yes, my lord," agreed Tucker. He climbed gingerly from the curricle, one hand carefully adjusting a bit of a lump near his stomach, snatched his lordship's portmanteau and his own from the boot and hurried up the steps to the front entrance.

In his pantry the Fairfax's butler did not hear Tucker's knocking for the longest time. Since the household was expecting no one and the insistent banging mixed admirably with the thunder, it took Dashell a good three minutes to come to the conclusion that there was, indeed, someone at the front entrance. When at last he made his way into the entry hall and opened the door, Dashell stared coldly down his nose. "And you are . . ." he droned, glaring at the bedraggled personage who stood, dripping, before him.

"Mr. Tucker," responded that personage, pushing past the butler and depositing two soggy portmanteaux upon the checkered tile of the Fairfax's front hall. "Valet to his lordship, The Earl of Wheldon. No, do not close that door because his lordship will be running toward it from the stables at top speed even as we speak. That is, of course, if there are grooms in your stables capable of tucking his lordship's horses away properly for the night. It will take him a while longer if he must do the thing himself."

"Dashell, I thought I heard knocking," proclaimed a sweetly husky voice from the top of the staircase. "Oh," the young woman said on a tiny breath, the nearly drowned figure of Mr. Tucker making itself plain to her. "Whatever has happened?" And she hurried down the stairs in a most energetic fashion. "Has there been some accident? Dashell, do close the door, you are letting all the weather in." And with that she took the door handle into her own hand and slammed it closed.

Kachunck! The sound came immediately and being so near was quite distinguishable from the thunder. Tucker groaned, a vision of his lordship charging full speed splat into the huge oak door vivid in his mind.

Dashell's haughty demeanor dissipated at once into one of horror at the pained expression upon Tucker's face. "Was that him?" asked the butler fearfully.

"I expect so," sighed Tucker. "Hard to stop abruptly with the rain making everything so slick. I should open it again at once if I were you."

Dashell stepped past the young woman who had slammed the door and opened it again to find a perfect mountain of a gentleman standing wet, muddy and disturbingly dazed before him, blood flowing briskly from between the fingers of the hand he held tenderly over his nose.

"Well, how on earth was I to know?" murmured Miss Fairfax in tortured accents. "There was a gentleman in the hall. Why should there be another? And besides, Thomas, you never said you were expecting anyone."

Thomas, Viscount Fairfax, leaned back into the well-worn depths of his wing chair and groaned. "Wheldon, of all people, Annie! Now he will most likely refuse even to look at The Valentine."

"He has come to look at The Valentine?"

"He has come to buy The Valentine, I hope."

"Oh dear! Thomas, are you certain? No one has ever wished to buy The Valentine, not even when we tried expressly to sell him."

"Indeed, but if there is one gentleman in all of England who would buy The Valentine, it is Wheldon. He is not so easily intimidated, m'dear, as a sensible man would be and not so readily put off by bared teeth and rolling eyes and flailing hooves. Besides, Annie, it is not a simple thing for a gentleman like Wheldon to find a beast equal to his weight and still swift and agile upon the hunting field. And his own Anglaise is coming up on thirteen summers, so Wheldon grows desperate for another mount."

"Well, of all things! To sell The Valentine! What wonderful news that will be for our stablehands!"

"Yes, and Wheldon will go as high as fifteen hundred for the rascal, too. That, Annie, is splendid news for you."

"And I had to slam the door in the gentleman's face," murmured Anne. "Oh, I do hope he is not terribly high in the instep and does not take it as a personal affront. Well, but I must go and tell Mama and Constance that we have an important guest and warn them to be extremely pleasant to the gentleman," she said with a wide smile. "I am certain he will forgive my clumsiness, Thomas, once he has laid his eyes upon Constance."

Miss Anne Fairfax's news was met with wide eyes in the Gold Saloon. "The Earl of Wheldon here?" gasped her mama, hastily setting aside her needlework. "Dear me, Anne, why does Dashell not show him up? Constance, straighten your gown, darling, and go to the pianoforte. You always look so lovely at the pianoforte. Anne, ring the bell. Mrs. Danson must be told at once. He is too late for dinner but he will certainly require substantial refreshments. As I recall, his papa was always in need of substantial refreshments."

"No, no, do calm yourself, Mama. The earl has gone directly to the guest chambers," offered Anne giving her Mama a calming hug. "Apparently he drove his curricle and came near to drowning in this downpour. And he had a—a slight accident as well. As a result he does not feel quite up to snuff. I doubt we shall see the gentleman at all this evening."

"Well, and is that not exactly like the Raynes!" declared the dowager viscountess with a frowning countenance.

"What is exactly like the Raynes, Mama?" asked Constance, who had settled upon the piano bench as her mama had requested and looked quite as delicate and beautiful as a porcelain shepherdess.

"To drive his curricle in the pouring rain and to have an accident besides. Anyone with a bit of sense would have known better than to do so."

"Known better than to drive a curricle or known better than to have an accident?" Anne asked, smiling.

"Both!" declared her mama. "And why did he not send word we were to expect him? That is just like the Raynes as well."

"Because we were not to expect him," offered Lord Fairfax as he entered the saloon. "You look very pretty, Constance, poised there before the pianoforte. Why not play us a tune, m'dear?"

"Thomas, do not be a ninny," sighed his mama. "You know perfectly well that Constance cannot play. Do you mean to tell me that Wheldon has arrived on our doorstep without in the least intending to do so?"

"No, Mama. He was on his way to the Duke of Averdon's. Invited for the hunting, you know. He thought to put up at The King's Inn tonight and then send to see if he might call upon us. But The King's Inn has burnt to the ground."

"Well, of course it has burnt to the ground," replied his mama in exasperation. "It caught on fire, Thomas."

"Yes, Mama. At any rate, Wheldon thought we might put him up, you know, since he wished to call upon us anyway. You do not mind, do you, Mama?"

"As if I would turn an earl from my door," sighed the dowager. "Well, we shall breakfast *en famille* in the morning room and Constance, you will wear your new morning dress, that lovely willow green with the quilling. It will give you an opportunity to practice, my dear."

Constance flushed as she took her Mama's meaning.

"Only think of it as experience for your come-out, Constance," Anne grinned. "He has not come, after all, to scrutinize you, dear sister. He has come to look at The Valentine."

"Oh!" cried Constance glancing joyfully up at her brother. "Do you mean to say that you have found someone who wishes to buy The Valentine, Thomas? How perfectly marvelous!"

Tucker, clean and dry from a hurried bath, was seriously leering at his lordship's nose as that gentleman stood in his shirt sleeves before the looking-glass attempting to comb his damp curls into something resembling a hair style.

"It is not broken, Tuck," mumbled his lordship. "I remember how it feels to have it broken. Fetch me a neckcloth. I ought at least go down and do the pretty to Lady Fairfax."

"Yes, my lord," sighed Tucker.

"Yes, and I ought to apologize to Fairfax's sister as well. That was Fairfax's sister who slammed the door in my face, was it not?"

"Yes, my lord, but it is she, I think, ought to apologize to you."

"Actually?"

"Yes, my lord. I am aware that you are generally in the wrong in such mishaps, but in this one you were not."

"Still, I expect I shall be the one to do the apologizing, Tuck. That is just the way it is with women. You know so yourself. No matter who is in the wrong, it is always the gentleman who must beg pardon."

Tucker, having spent a large portion of his life in the same household as Wheldon, nodded in agreement. Of course, thought Tucker, watching his lordship tie his cravat into an acceptable American, Brookhaven is overrun with females. They rule the roost.

Wheldon turned from the looking-glass and Tucker helped him into a dark claret coat of conservative cut which just missed the height of fashion through the absence of a row of large brass buttons, these being replaced by smaller, plain black ones which matched a most conservative line of braiding on the coat collar and cuffs. "Where's Fearless?" the earl asked, shooting his cuffs into a more comfortable position. "She ain't lost, Tucker?"

"No, my lord. She is right there under the counterpane."

"Where?"

"That lump, sir, there."

"Are you certain, Tuck?" grinned the earl. "You know how she is. One moment she is a lump and the next there is merely air where she used to be."

Tucker moved hurriedly to the bed and patted his hand

down upon the lump in the counterpane which flattened without the least resistance.

"Not to worry," Wheldon chuckled at the panic that mounted to his valet's eyes. "The door is not open, so she ain't slipped out of the chambers."

Tucker groaned.

"What, Tuck? The door is not open."

"Not this door, my lord, but there is another off the dressing room that leads into the corridor."

Wheldon strolled hastily into the dressing room. "It's closed, Tuck. She is in here somewhere."

"But it was open, my lord, when the bath water was brought up."

"No," murmured Wheldon, with a shake of his blond curls, "she is here somewhere. She cannot possibly have gone wandering off about the house. I absolutely refuse to consider that possibility."

"Heeellllppppp! Ooh, git away from me! Git away! Heelllppppp!" The cry itself was ear-piercing and Wheldon, with Tucker on his heels, dove for the door to the hallway.

At the head of the staircase a little maid with the ruffles from an enormous mobcap nearly hiding her face was attempting at one and the same time to balance an armful of linen, climb up onto the landing rail and shoo a most astounding creature away from the folds of her skirt. "Oh, sir, please help me, please!" she cried as Wheldon hurried toward her. "It is the biggest, ugliest rat whatever walked the face o' the earth! An' it be intendin' to dine upon me!"

"No, no, m'dear, she is not a rat," drawled Wheldon in the coolest tone he could muster as he lowered himself to his knees and snapped his fingers at the creature.

Ordinarily Fearless would have gone directly to the gentleman, but she was most curious about this new place and she was reluctant to surrender to his will when she'd been running free such a short time. She turned her little masked face to stare at him innocently and chuckled.

"No, Fearless, come here at once. Do not you go backing up. You will fall right through the gaps in the rail posts," Wheldon muttered. He snapped his fingers again, more forcefully, and Fearless showed signs of thinking to obey him, but at that moment a veritable symphony of feet came pounding up the staircase and sent the animal scurrying at full speed straight past Wheldon and down the long corridor behind him. Wheldon spun on his knees, made a grab for the ferret, missed, got his long legs in a tangle, and stretched his length abruptly across the floral carpeting. Tucker watched the creature scurry directly through his legs, dove after it, and met the carpeting sharply as well.

Dashell came to a halt upon the landing and stared nonplussed at the two men on the floor and the frightened little maid huddled against the rail.

"Whatever is going on?" asked a sweetly husky voice and Miss Fairfax swept past Dashell to view the scene with her own eyes. "Gracious," she murmured as the veritable mountain of Wheldon rose up from the floor and went to assist his valet to his feet as well. "Whatever are you doing, my lord? Jenny, why did you scream? What has happened?"

Wheldon, who would have done better to keep his lips firmly together, could not manage to do so and broke into a dazzlingly innocent smile. It was a smile his mother and all ten of his sisters would have found immediately suspect. But Anne had never seen it before and it bewitched her on the instant.

"Oh, ma'am," breathed the little maid, still balancing her load of linen, "I were attacked by the most gigantical rat and these two gentlemen came to save me!"

"A rat?" asked Anne in disbelief.

"You do not have cats loose in the house, do you, Miss Fairfax?" queried Wheldon, still smiling innocently.

"No, but we shall acquire some immediately," responded Anne. "A rat right here in the second floor hallway! And it came after you, you say, Jenny?"

"Aye, Miss Fairfax. Came scampering right up to me. Trying to bite my—my limb—I have no doubt."

"Well, no, actually she was merely wishing to scramble under your skirts, my dear," offered Wheldon. "She is used to playing about under draperies and my sisters' skirts and, oh, old dresses hanging in armoires and the like."

"Am I to take it that this rat belongs to you, Wheldon?" asked Lord Fairfax peering around his sister and his butler.

"Yes, but she ain't a rat, Fairfax—sorry, Miss Fairfax— I mean, she is not a rat. She is a ferret and she has gone off to explore, I fear. But since there are no cats wandering about, she is not likely to cause much trouble. She will come back to my chambers when she has satisfied her curiosity. I am sorry, Miss Fairfax, for causing so much trouble."

Anne pondered the smiling face, the gloriously sparkling blue eyes, the golden curls that scattered across his smooth, impressive brow and said not a word. How had she failed to notice at once how handsome this giant was? And why had his magnificent stature not impressed her more at their first meeting? Of course, when Dashell had opened the door to him he had been bent quite awkwardly with his hand covering his nose and a good deal of blood dripping between his fingers. Perhaps it had been the excitement of that moment had prevented her from fully appreciating this Lord Wheldon.

"Miss Fairfax? Miss Fairfax? I said I am sorry to be such a bother," repeated Wheldon, his smile never faltering. "I hope you will forgive me."

"What? Oh! Oh! You are no bother at all, my lord. It is I should seek your forgiveness."

"You should?" asked Wheldon, clearly astounded.

"Indeed, for slamming the door in your face. Thank goodness your nose has ceased to bleed."

"Yes, thank goodness for that," chuckled Wheldon.

"Shall we go downstairs? I should like very much to be presented to your mother and your sister. I do remember correctly, do I not, Fairfax? You have two sisters?"

"Yes, two," nodded the viscount with a thoughtful gleam in his hazel eyes. "This is Anne and the other is Constance. We did not expect it, Wheldon, after your soaking and all, but we'd be delighted to have you join us for the remainder of the evening."

Wheldon, upon entering the Gold Saloon, bowed quite properly before Lady Fairfax.

"Oh, dear!" she gasped. "You are larger than your father!"

"So they tell me, my lady," agreed Wheldon seriously though Anne noticed that his lips quivered precariously upward. "My lady mother has requested that I give you her regards and hopes that she will see you in London for the Season, ma'am."

"Your mother goes to London for the Season?"

"Yes, ma'am. She means to fire off my sister, Cecily, this spring. Cecily will be eighteen in March."

"But she did never introduce any of the others, Wheldon," accused Lady Fairfax with confusion writ large across her countenance. "Why your mother has not been to London since the day she married your father."

"No, ma'am," acknowledged the earl, "but my father has been dead five years and she feels it safe to go to town at last."

"Safe?" asked Anne, tiny pangs of curiosity rising within her as she took a chair beside her mama.

"Indeed, safe from all the reverberations of my papa's foibles and follies. Mama thinks Papa's unfortunate adventures to have been forgotten by this time."

Lady Fairfax stared up at him most upset and one small, gloved hand went to fiddle nervously with the gold locket 'round her neck. "Well, well, perhaps you had better warn her, Lord Wheldon, that your father's memory lives on as does your grandfather's."

The suppressed laughter that flitted about the earl's lips and glistened in the deep blue of his eyes came near to bursting out into the room, Anne noted, and he had to take a very deep breath and clear his throat twice before he said another word. When at last he did speak, the words came in a crisp, cool, unconcerned voice that any Corinthian would have envied. "I have attempted to warn her, ma'am, but she says I am as dicked in the nob as either of them and my observations cannot possibly be relied upon. Besides, I think she means to brave it regardless, Lady Fairfax, for the last thing she said was that if she waits any longer it will be my whimsicalities that will keep her freezing her feet in Yorkshire."

Wheldon turned to be introduced to the lovely Constance who curtsied prettily before him and then he took a seat in the wing chair that Fairfax and Dashell had hastily fetched from the library. "You have gone out of your way, Fairfax," grinned the earl. "Were you afraid I should break the other chairs?"

"Merely wished you to feel snug, Wheldon," grinned the viscount. "Attempting to get on your good side, you know, so that you will look kindly upon The Valentine in the morning. You do still wish to see The Valentine, do you not?"

Two

"Can you believe that he has ten sisters?" giggled Constance, setting her candle upon the bedside table and slipping into bed beside Anne for a warm coze. "And himself the only boy! What a household, Annie, and how difficult for his mama too, for she must find husbands for them all!"

"That, I think, cannot be quite so difficult as keeping the earl, himself, fed," gurgled Anne in response.

"Oh! When I saw all that Mama requested Mrs. Danson to send up, I thought surely Mama had lost her mind. And he ate every bit of it! We were lucky to get a tidbit apiece!"

"Yes, but he was most polite about it," grinned Anne. "He inquired over and over again if we did not wish to have a bit of this or a taste of that."

"I would not have dared take more than my tea and a piece of bread and butter," Constance laughed, "not when Mama kept throwing me such speaking glances. She was so afraid there would not be enough."

"There almost was not enough," laughed Anne. "Every plate and platter went back to the kitchen empty. And truly, you ought to have accompanied us. I thought Mrs. Danson would swoon on the instant when Lord Wheldon appeared in her kitchen and praised her cooking to the skies. Oh, Constance, he has won an admirer for life in Mrs. Danson!"

"And in you, I think," Constance offered quietly but with a wide smile.

"Yes, well, he is a splendid gentleman, and most amusing, and he does have the most glorious curls I have ever seen."

"And the very bluest eyes," murmured Constance, "which studied you intently throughout the evening. He is smitten by you, Annie."

Anne gasped, her great brown eyes widening, her lips parting, one hand going to cover her mouth in horror. "H-how can you say so?" she sputtered after a long pause. "You know that cannot be true, Constance. You are the beauty in the family and the one all the gentlemen look upon with favor."

"Not, I think, this gentleman. He did not once look at me with anything more than a good-humored smile, but I saw how he looked at you when he thought you would not notice, Annie."

"How did he look?"

Constance giggled. "Hungry, dear sister."

Long after Constance had slipped from between the sheets and padded back to her own chambers, Anne lay staring up at the wooden canopy above her bed. She knew that Constance had not intended to upset her, but upset her she surely had done.

Most certainly Constance is mistaken, Anne thought. Lord Wheldon could not have looked at me in such a way. With Constance sitting right there before him, he could not have spared me a second glance. No, she was merely teasing me and that is all. Surely she depends upon my knowing that there is nothing about me attractive to a gentleman—except for the Reverend Mr. Cranshaw.

Anne frowned. The Reverend Mr. Cranshaw had been the topic of conversation quite often of late between herself and her brother, Thomas. That gentleman had, in fact, spoken to Thomas about such things as marriage settlements and dowries and had intimated that he might well be thinking to pay his addresses to Anne. And Thomas had attempted to warn him off. Thomas despised the Reverend Mr. Cranshaw.

Why can he not understand, Anne thought grimly, that if the Reverend Mr. Cranshaw does not offer for me and I do not accept, then I shall be forced to live out my life as a spinster? There is no other gentleman who has ever taken the least interest in me, and I am already twenty. Thomas will be saddled with me for the rest of his life.

One lone teardrop formed in the corner of Anne's eye, and she wiped it away with the back of her hand. "I will not," she whispered into the darkness, "feel sorry for myself. I am a very lucky person. I have Mama and Thomas and Constance who all love me and even if I am plain and fat and have big ugly cow eyes and hair as straight as a fence post—and the same color too!—that does not matter. Because once you know you are ugly, you have only to shrug your shoulders and get on with all the other things that life offers you."

Anne bit at her lower lip and turned on to her side plumping up the feathers in her pillow along the way. She prayed quietly into the night, blessing her mama and Thomas and Constance and murmuring a short prayer as well for the Earl of Wheldon and his mama and all ten of his sisters, though not by name.

Wheldon blew again, three times softly, upon the little tin whistle, then stuffed it under his pillow, crossed his arms over his chest and stared at the ceiling above him. Not that he could see it, that intricately painted ceiling. His candle had gutted well over an hour ago and obviously

Fearless was not going to answer to her whistle and what he ought to do was, he ought to close his eyes and go to sleep. And he would, too, as soon as he had decided what he was going to do about Miss Anne Fairfax.

Aubrey Edward Rayne, Earl of Wheldon, had not been raised amongst a veritable gaggle of sisters for nothing. He had been dragged to every modiste's shop in York. He had become intimate with the machinations of silk mercers, milliners, linen-drapers, hairdressers, haberdashers and corsetiers. He had come to know every plot and quite likely every character ever to appear in a Minerva novel and he could, in the blink of an eye, tell how much of her appearance a young lady owed to nature and how much to the rouge pot, the roman balsam and the Oil of Jasmin. And he had learned, too, how to recognize when a gentleman had developed a mere infatuation for someone of the fairer sex and when a gentleman had truly lost his heart. "And in one fatal stroke," he whispered into the night, "I have lost my whole bloody heart! Devil take it, but I ought to have driven straight on to Averdon's! I would even now be heart-whole and fast asleep."

He knew, of course, that all of the Fairfaxes had thought his attention would be immediately drawn to the younger of the ladies. And Constance was very pretty. Almost as pretty as his sister Clara. Indeed, they had in common the same slight figures and glowing hazel eyes, though Miss Constance's hair was a fiery chestnut and Clara's a honey-blond. But neither of them could compare in the least to Miss Anne. From the moment he had caught sight of her peering up at him, mystified, as the blood flowed down between his fingers, he had known without a doubt that she was the young lady he wished to marry.

She had the body of a Juno, tall and rounded and enticing, and the voice of a Siren, husky and sweet. And it had only encouraged him the more when Tucker had explained that Miss Anne had been the one to slam the door shut in his face. What a powerful slam it had been!

One truly worthy of the wife of a Wheldon! Why, his mama would be proud to welcome such a treasure for a daughter-in-law. And he would make Miss Anne Fairfax her daughter-in-law, too. Although, that was going to prove a bit of a problem. He could hardly go downstairs and offer for Miss Fairfax the first thing before breakfast and then pack her up and carry her off to Yorkshire in his curricle. Wheldon had enough sisters to absolutely know that that would prove a disaster. Ladies required courting. They were invariably opposed to being swept off their feet, no matter how much in favor of it the heroines of their novels claimed to be.

Wheldon closed his eyes and visions of Anne rose to meet him. If only, he thought tossing about, if only she does not think me a great gawking clunch. "I am a great gawking clunch," he mumbled, "but please, God, do not let Miss Anne Fairfax think that I am—at least not until after I have won her heart."

"'Tis the biggest bo-kicker I ever seed, guv'nor, a reg'lar nip-nasty," declared Wheldon's tiger excitedly as he met the earl at the stable entrance. "Tried ta eat me 'e did!"

"No, Carley, eat you? Truly?" laughed Wheldon. "Would they not give him anything good for breakfast?"

Carley's vaguely seraphic visage squinted up at the earl suspiciously.

"Miss Fairfax, Lord Fairfax," grinned Wheldon, "may I present Master Carley Witt, horse dealer extraordinaire, who also condescends to pose as my tiger. Say how do you do, Carley."

The excited little boy, whom Anne judged to be no older than ten, bowed extravagantly. "How do," he grinned. "Ye ain't goin' to get no saddle upon that un, guv'nor," he cried then, "I betcha a palace to a prison ye ain't!"

"Oh, you do, do you? Well, I do not have a palace, Carley,

so it will need to be a smaller bet. Possibly a cartwheel to a sixpence.''

"Yer on, guv'nor," grinned the urchin who even Wheldon's livery could not transform into anything other than a mischievous imp. "They bin tryin' ta saddle the bugger since I got up this mornin' an' ain't done it yet."

"Yes, but I am a completely different matter," drawled the earl with a wink at Fairfax. "I am more his size, m'lad."

"Oh no ye ain't!" declared Carley knowingly. "Ain't nobody 'is size, not even you, guv'nor!"

"Well, where is this beast, Fairfax? You keep him well-hidden for such a monster as Carley thinks him."

"In the box stall at the rear," Lord Fairfax answered with a worried glance at his sister. "And he is not so vicious as your tiger thinks him, Wheldon, I assure you."

"Oh, no," added Anne with a most virtuous smile at Wheldon. "The Valentine is simply a bit high-strung. Thomas's grooms do not know precisely how to handle him."

With Carley skipping eagerly ahead chanting "I'm gittin' me a cartwheel; I'm gittin' me a cartwheel," the three strolled to the rear of the building and halted before the door to The Valentine's stall just as a saddle came crashing out, followed in short order by Fairfax's head groom who slammed the bottom of the door shut behind him.

"Trouble, Morgan?" asked Fairfax innocently.

"Oh, no sir," responded the groom. "No trouble, yer lordship. Testy he be this morning, is all. Missin' his exercise, I expect. Fresh he be an' up to mischief."

Wheldon leaned upon the bottom half of the stall door and peered in at the villain who according to Carley was more than a match for all of the stablehands and definitely a match for the earl himself. Inside the stall a pair of huge brown eyes glared defiantly back at him. "Well, and good day to you, sir," murmured the earl softly. "And what a fine bit of blood you appear to be."

"Pshaw," giggled Carley, "he be talkin' ta 'im like he

were civ'lised. The guv'nor's gonna git 'isself bit, he's gonna. That 'un don't likes no talkin'.''

Anne watched closely as the earl's knowing gaze roamed over the strawberry roan. It was not that The Valentine was not a fine horse. His bloodlines were impeccable. He was healthy and nobly built. His only drawback was that he was seventeen hands and powerful and he knew it. But Lord Wheldon was tall and powerful as well and perhaps, perhaps The Valentine would notice *that*.

"I say, Fairfax," drawled the earl without taking his gaze from the animal, "how many men has he eaten over the years?"

"Merely six," replied Thomas with a wry smile.

"Six? Not twenty-six?"

"We do not think to feed our stablehands to him all that often, Wheldon. He truly is a prime bit of blood and certainly up to your weight."

"Indeed. Up to my weight and beyond it, I think. He is broken to the saddle is he not, Fairfax? Someone has ridden him?"

"My father," offered Anne the moment she saw hesitation in her brother's face. "My father was used to ride The Valentine from time to time."

"From time to time, Miss Fairfax? And did your father hunt?"

"Yes, and a fine hunter The Valentine was, too. He flew to the head of the chase, soared over all obstacles without a moment's hesitation. A regular flying leaper. There is not another fox hunter like him in all of England, I assure you."

"Oh, I can see there could not possibly be another like him, Miss Fairfax," replied Wheldon turning to grin down at her. "But while he was flying and soaring and leaping, was your father still upon his back is what I wish to know."

Miss Fairfax blushed and Wheldon's heart stuttered. By gawd, if the bloody horse had been swaybacked and had had three broken legs he would have bought it only because she wished him to do so. But he had spent every moment as he dressed this morning pondering how best to give himself *entreé* into the Fairfax establishment a few more times without frightening the girl by abruptly paying her court. His size intimidated every lady he had ever met. To undertake a campaign to win Miss Fairfax's hand before she grew accustomed to the sight of him would prove a dismal failure. So, he would use the purchase of this horse as his excuse for several visits. He would buy The Valentine, but not until Miss Fairfax had become accustomed to the sight of himself.

"Tell me, Fairfax," he drawled, turning his attention to Anne's brother, "if he is such a good hunter, why do you wish to sell the beast?"

"Well, to tell the truth, Wheldon, I had not actually thought of selling him until Rossland spoke to me and mentioned you were thinking of putting your Anglaise out to pasture. There are not many gentlemen ride as heavy as you, you know, and there are not many horses equal to the—ah—"

"Load. Yes, that's true enough. Well, apparently your men have gotten bit and bridle in place. Hand me the saddle, eh, and I shall attempt to take the rascal out and try his paces. Carley, hand your sixpence to Lord Fairfax," Wheldon grinned, taking the saddle. He then fished about in his own pocket and produced a shiny gold cartwheel. "You are holding the stakes, Fairfax. And I warn you, if that horse comes crashing out of there with a saddle secured to his back—no matter that I lie trampled upon the floor— the money is mine. Is that not correct, Carley? The bet is to saddle him, not to survive the doing of it?"

"Aye, guv'nor," giggled Carley.

"Indeed. So you must just stuff the money into one of my pockets, Fairfax, whether I am sensible or not, because Carley is going to lose his sixpence, of that I assure you." The earl then entered the box stall and paused to close both the top and bottom of the stall door behind him.

"That ain't fair," grumbled Carley. "I wanta see 'im do't."

"Well, but perhaps his lordship means to keep his way of getting The Valentine saddled a secret," smiled Anne, longing to tousle the little boy's bright red locks.

"Naw, miss, I din't mean I wanted ta see how 'e got 'im saddled, cuz 'e ain't goin' ta do't. I meant as 'ow I wanted ta see that big bo-kicker squish 'is lor'ship's pretendshons."

Anne smiled tentatively, but Thomas burst into whoops. For the longest time no sound but the staccato clatter of hooves upon the floorboards and a quiet murmuring came from inside the closed stall. And then a bruising double whomp shook the side walls and made Anne and Thomas and even Carley jump. Wheldon's laughter echoed out at them next, followed by an impassioned whinny, a curse, a general stomping and clattering and a cry of "Enough, you ninny, you've drawn blood!"

"Thomas, you must go to his aid," Anne gasped.

"To whose, m'dear," chuckled Fairfax, "The Valentine's or Wheldon's?"

"Well, if you will do nothing, I certainly shall," scowled Anne. "You know very well what a considerable handful The Valentine can be when he is in bad humor."

"Aye, my guv'nor, too," nodded Carley soberly. "I hope as how that bit o' bone don't go turnin' 'is nibs up sour."

Anne had just reached for the latch when the door opened from the inside and Wheldon led the big strawberry roan from the stall. He winked at Anne and held out his hand toward Fairfax. Fairfax, glancing around the earl to the little tiger, made a great show of producing the cartwheel and sixpence and placing them onto Wheldon's palm.

"And let that be a lesson to you, Carley. Never bet against a Wheldon," drawled the earl coolly.

"Ye got the saddle on, but I don' see ye a sittin' in it," challenged the boy with green eyes gleaming. "Double er nothin' ye cain't stay aboard pas' the first fence."

"No," replied the earl abruptly.

"Ye're feared ye'll lose," taunted Carley with a toss of his head. "Ye're feared ye'll lose."

"No," responded Wheldon, stuffing the coins into his pocket and starting toward the stable yard. Laughing he snatched his wiggling tiger up by the waist of his breeches and carried him along. "I am afraid you don't have another sixpence to stake, my man. In fact, I know you have not."

"Oh, my goodness, he did bite you!" exclaimed Anne as she noted a smear of blood across the seat of Carley's breeches.

"No, Miss Fairfax, he did not."

"But I heard you say he had drawn blood, and there is certainly blood! We must go back to the house so that I may look to your hand."

"No, Miss Fairfax," repeated Wheldon, noting that her tone was one of authority and not of panic, and treasuring the thought that this proved she was a perfect goddess and not some simpering little miss. "The beast was not so fortuitous as to have gotten a taste of me. I simply withdrew my hand rather hastily from his vicinity and managed to scrape it against some boards. It was enough to tear my glove and draw a bit of blood is all."

Fairfax's stablehands, having heard The Valentine was to be ridden, gathered in the yard to watch as the earl mounted the animal. For the barest moment everyone present thought how magnificent the two looked together, and then The Valentine swung his head around and lunged for Wheldon's knee and Wheldon, in response, tugged on the opposite rein and touched his spurs to the horse's sides, and they were most abruptly off in the direction of the western acres.

Two hours later Fairfax and Morgan rode out in search of them while another of the men hooked a team to the farm wagon in the event that the long-overdue earl should require to be carried home. Anne and Constance had mounted as well, and now rode off in the opposite direction of their brother and the groom. "What could possibly have happened?" queried Constance.

"What could have happened?" replied Anne anxiously. "Why anything could have happened, Constance. We sent the poor gentleman out upon the back of a demon without the least warning. Why even now he might be lying dead at the foot of some treacherous hedgerow. You know how The Valentine loves to leap. And he gives not the least thought to whether there is a rider upon his back or not. And he does never so much as slow from a gallop to take a hazard."

"Yes, but that is exactly what makes him a good hunter," mused Constance. "And since the earl often rides to hounds will he not expect The Valentine to do exactly as he does?"

"Well, yes, but The Valentine does it with such vengeance!" exclaimed Anne looking about her for any sign of horse or rider. "And he is so ill-humored besides. I daresay if Lord Wheldon did take a spill The Valentine will have soared back over the obstacle again just to trample upon him for having fallen off. Oh, Constance, neither Thomas nor I said one word to warn him! It was despicable of us. We wanted so much to sell the dastardly beast that we did not once think of Lord Wheldon's safety."

"I cannot think why you should do such a thing," said Constance. "I mean, not warn the gentleman."

"Because if he thought The Valentine to be uncontrollable, Constance, he would not buy him," explained Anne in exasperated tones. "And if Lord Wheldon does not buy him, it will be years before anyone else appears who might be interested."

"Yes, but—"

"Thomas said the earl would go as high as fifteen hundred, Constance. That is quite beyond anything we could have hoped."

"F-fifteen hundred? For a—a horse?"

"Indeed."

"Oh, but Annie, that is wonderful!" exclaimed her sister. "That will make you a splendid dowry. Certainly it is just what Papa hoped when he gave you The Valentine. And the Reverend Mr. Cranshaw, knowing of Papa's reverses just before his death, will be heartily surprised. I am sure he does not expect a dowry so large as fifteen hundred pounds! He will be most pleased when he learns of it and will be certain to offer for you."

"Yes," sighed Anne. "I only hope it does not turn out to be the price of Lord Wheldon's life. Oh, Constance, what have I done? I have endangered a perfect stranger in the hope to purchase my own security. For shame! If the gentleman is found dead I ought to be led straight to the gallows."

Three

The gentleman was not dead, however. At that precise moment he was balanced precariously, mud-streaked and weary, upon an outcropping of rock and reaching gingerly into a small cavern that lay almost hidden behind a leafless blackberry bush. "Do be quiet, you reprobate," he mumbled at the gelding who whinnied just beneath his perch. "I know you do not approve, but we cannot turn our backs upon orphans, no matter who they are. M'sister Charlotte would never forgive us. Ah, now I've got you," he added with a satisfied smile, and tugged a ball of fur from the den, tucking it snugly away inside his riding coat. "I do believe you're the last." Reaching once more into the cavern and feeling carefully about, he discovered nothing more and so began to climb carefully down from his perch, one arm cradling his mewling, wiggling burden. He was merely five feet from the bottom of the outcropping when galloping hooves and high-pitched shouts caused him to divert his attention and he missed his footing and slid upon the seat of his breeches, amidst a shower of gravel and twigs, the rest of the way to the bottom. He landed with tooth-clacking jar, but the arm protecting the burden beneath his coat had remained stubbornly in place and the mewling and wiggling continued unabated.

Wheldon thought to rise at once as he recognized the two riders pounding toward him, but he had landed in a most awkward position from which it would take the use of both arms to gain his feet without pitching forward upon his nose, and besides, he had the most terrible foreboding that the seat of his breeches was no longer of a piece.

"Lord Wheldon! What has happened?" exclaimed Anne excitedly, tugging her mount to a halt. "What has The Valentine done to you? However did he pitch you up upon that outcropping? Or did he chase you there? He is wont to charge after people once he has tossed them. Oh, I knew it to be the case, and I did not give you the least warning! Valentine, you are a beast and a villain," she threw over her shoulder at the strawberry roan as she slid from her saddle and hurried to the earl. "Constance, gather up The Valentine's reins, do, so he does not run off."

Wheldon's eyes sparkled with admiration. Miss Fairfax's hat had gone aflying and her hairpins as well, loosing a thick mane of dark brown hair that glinted with red and gold in the sunlight as it cloaked the shoulders of her chocolate brown riding habit and swung mischievously about pink cheeks flushed with exercise and excitement. And her eyes—those earnest, enormous, empathetic deep brown eyes! Wheldon longed to bestow a lingering kiss upon the lid of each of them as she knelt down beside him. And then he would sit back and watch them widen in charming innocence, agog.

Which will not happen, he told himself determinedly. If I lay one kiss upon her, she will push me away and I'll hit my head on a rock and fall senseless and forego any chance to explain myself and she will think me a libertine and a fool to boot.

"Your arm," Anne murmured, touching that limb tenderly with both hands. "Why do you hold it to your chest so gingerly? It is broken. I know it. I shall make a sling for it promptly and when we get you home, we shall have Dr. Mackinnes to fix it properly."

Wheldon had an overwhelming urge to see Miss Fairfax lift the hem of her habit and attempt to tear a piece of her petticoat free to make him a sling, but his conscience would not allow of it. "No, Miss Fairfax, do not," he murmured. "My arm is not broken. I am merely a bit bruised."

"But you do not move your arm at all, Lord Wheldon, even now," provided Constance, stepping forward with the reins of all three horses safe in her hand. "Do not be shy, sir. Annie is most competent in an emergency."

"Yes, well, there is a sort of emergency," offered Wheldon quietly, a smile stealing across his lips and rising to light his eyes to an even more impressive shade of blue.

He is truly the most beautiful man I have ever seen, thought Anne. And he is besotted with Constance. Just see how he smiles at her slightest word. Anne felt a most disturbing ache in the region of her stomach but could not imagine its cause. For a moment she wished herself as slim and dainty as her younger sister, but she immediately called herself to order. I have lost my cap, and my hair has come undone, and I am all windblown and wretchedly disheveled from galloping across the countryside, she told herself with some vehemence. I was far from appealing when we set out and I am even more so at this moment. And I have not the least business to be wishing for things that can never be.

"I have orphans under my coat," sighed Wheldon. "If I move my arm, they shall all fall out."

"Orphans?" asked Anne and Constance at once.

"Yes, well, not children, of course." Wheldon, his face reddening, produced one tiny ball of reddish-brown fur for their inspection."

"Oh, a kitten!" cried Constance with a clap of her hands.

"Not quite, ' said the earl with an embarrassed smile.

"A fox!" exclaimed Anne.

"Actually, five foxes."

"Five? You have four more in your coat, Lord Wheldon?"

"Uh-huh."

"Well, gracious me! And to think that when Thomas told us that you were a bang-up fox hunter, pluck to the backbone, with more bottom than sense, I thought he referred to your riding to hounds, not to your climbing rocks stealing babes from their den." Anne intended to sound most serious, but her lips twitched and she could not keep the betraying laughter from her eyes.

"I am not stealing them, Miss Fairfax," protested the earl chuckling. "There are two foxes lying dead in that gully over there, caught in a quick run-off yesterday and drowned, I expect. And one of them obviously a female with nurslings. M'sister Charlotte would never have forgiven me if I had not at least looked for the wretched little things."

"And what will you do with them, sir, now you have found them?" asked Anne with a lift of her eyebrow.

"Raise them I expect, though I shall be the laughingstock of Averdon's house party, you may believe me. Once the others discover that I have a pack of foxes in my room, I shall not hear the end of it."

"No, I expect not," laughed Anne, giving way at the martyred look Wheldon assumed. "I expect you cannot gain your feet from such a position with those rascals in your coat, either. Give them to me, my lord, so that you can rise."

Wheldon fished the rest of the kits from his coat and gave them over. "Would you mind turning around?" he asked quietly.

"Turning around?" asked Constance.

"Yes."

"But why?" asked Anne, staring bemusedly down at the furballs in her hands.

"Well, ah, because I have—that is to say—*must* I tell you? Cannot you just turn away without needing an explanation?"

"We can," mused Anne with a gleam of devilment in her eyes, "but now we are terribly curious, are we not, Constance?"

"Oh, terribly," agreed her sister with an equally devilish grin. "In fact, now I do not expect we shall turn away for even so much as the blink of an eye. Unless, of course, you confide in us the reason for such measures, my lord."

Wheldon could not withstand the demons of humor that flashed in both sets of sisterly eyes and he laughed outright at himself. "It is because I have the greatest suspicion that I have torn a hole in the seat of my breeches," he laughed, "and I cannot possibly rise and mount with such imps as you watching me."

"Oh," giggled Anne. "Well, then we shall turn about, shall we not, Constance?"

"Indeed," giggled Constance. "And you will tell us when you are properly mounted, my lord."

Both young ladies faced away from him, still giggling and heard a small shower of rocks as he gained his feet. Wheldon slipped The Valentine's reins from Constance's hand and led the horse off to the other side of the outcropping. In a moment he had returned, astride, with his hunting coat tied by its arms around his waist and a portion of it under him upon the saddle. He took the kits from each of them and tucked them competently inside his waistcoat.

Both girls led their mounts to the outcropping, thinking to find a rock to use as a mounting block, but they found none, all of them being far too low or too high. "I do hesitate to ask it of you," smiled Anne, leading her horse up beside Wheldon, "because it will mean rearranging the foxes again—"

"What will?"

"Helping us to mount, my lord."

"Oh, is that all. I wondered what you were about playing amongst the rocks. Here—take these wretched things. Now lead your horse up beside me, Miss Fairfax. Yes, just there." In one sweeping movement The Earl of Wheldon's arms came down around Anne and lifted her without the least fuss into her saddle. Anne sat breathless, clutching the wiggling kits to her bosom. How had he done it? It was trick enough to lift a featherweight like Constance into her saddle, as he was doing now, without dismounting, but to lift such an ungainly creature as herself! A most unseemly blush stained Anne's cheeks. In that one thoughtless moment Wheldon had made her feel more dainty and ladylike than she had ever felt before.

Tucker was nonplussed. His lordship's riding breeches were beyond salvation, his lordship's riding coat was in a like state and now, besides that wretched ferret who even at this moment chuckled up at him from the floor, his lordship must insist upon carrying a box of foxes with him to the Averdon's. What a frightful sight they should make sweeping up the grand entrance to Hunkapillar in a muddied curricle, his lordship dressed for dinner instead of driving and himself balancing a box of tiny foxes upon his knees and with a wretched ferret stuffed inside his waistcoat. Well, but it would not be the first time that his lordship had deigned to make a spectacle of himself. That was one of the drawbacks of being valet to the Earl of Wheldon. He was a Rayne and the Raynes were oblivious of their consequence.

But at least, Tucker thought, he is not as lunatic as was his father and I shall never be forced to explain why *he* was caught cavorting naked amongst the bushes in Green Park, a situation which Simms laments to this very day. The thought of Simms, who had valeted Wheldon's papa through years of stupefying chaos and amazing mayhem, brought a slow smile to Tucker's lips. For all that the old earl had been a hellion and a bedlamite, Simms had remained loyal and steadfast and had supported his gentleman at all times. "And so I shall do with his lordship," nodded Tucker determinedly. "I promised Simms precisely that when I accepted the position and I shall not go back upon my word."

"What, Tuck?" asked his lordship wandering into the chambers scrubbed and polished.

"Nothing, my lord. I shall not be able to save your breeches and your riding coat will never be thoroughly presentable again."

"Well, but the remainder of our baggage is even now at Hunkapillar, Tucker. It is not as if I shall have nothing else to wear. Am I packed?"

"Indeed, your lordship. The portmanteaux have been carried down to the front hall and even now the grooms are hitching up the curricle. You are not taking the horse?"

"No, Tuck. Not just yet. I must ponder over such a heavy decision."

Tucker's eyebrows rose in surprise. His lordship seldom pondered over anything, and never the buying of cattle.

"Yes, Tuck, I can see you understand the seriousness of such a purchase," drawled Wheldon, fiddling with his cravat. "I am much afraid it shall require a second visit here, perhaps even a third and a fourth. He is quite a beast, you know. Most unmanageable."

Tucker's eyebrows rose even higher. There was not a horse in all creation that the Earl of Wheldon could not manage.

"I know exactly what you are thinking, Tucker, but I fear I have met my match in The Valentine."

"Never, sir," murmured Tucker. "I do not believe it."

"You don't?"

"No, my lord."

"Well, but Fairfax does. And the horse *is* a handful.

Fetch my driving coat, will you, Tuck? I shall bring Fearless and the foxes down, and we'll be off directly.''

"Of course, the driving coat!" exclaimed Tucker in such thankful tones that Wheldon could not help but laugh.

"You have been worrying needlessly again, have you not, Tuck? Well, *I* shall look exceeding silly conveying a box of foxes to a hunting party, but at least my driving coat will cover my evening clothes so none of the other valets will have reason to criticize *you*. And I shall wear the thing direct to my chambers and keep Fearless tucked safely in a pocket so *you* shan't be embarrassed if she pokes her head out before Averdon's butler.''

"Well, I did not think he would," sighed Anne as the sound of the earl's curricle faded away. "It was a deal too much to hope for, Thomas. The Valentine tossed him, he told you?"

"Yes," murmured Fairfax, sitting upon the edge of a high-backed chair across from his sister, his forearms resting upon his knees and his hands twined tensely together. "I am so very sorry, Annie, to have raised your hopes. But I was certain he would buy the beast. The Valentine rubbed him off against a fence as well, he said. And—and he bit him into the bargain.''

"At least the gentleman is not dead," sighed Anne. "I care not a bit for the money, Thomas. I had the most terrible visions of the earl lying cold and still somewhere and nothing would be worth that. I expect we shall never sell The Valentine, but then, we never thought we might until Lord Wheldon made an appearance and raised our hopes. No, we shall go along as we always have done and not despair. Surely we have enough money to continue on quite comfortably and to give Constance a season in town. That investment will ensure that our little sister is well-provided for and perhaps will add a bit to your coffers as well if the marriage settlement is respectable."

"But what if Constance cannot develop a fondness for a gentleman of fortune? What if she should lose her heart to a—a veritable pauper?"

"Then we shall contrive to muddle through, my dear. You know we shall. We have done exceedingly well so far. Mama is not even aware how much Papa lost in the Funds. You are a wonderful manager, Thomas, and have kept us all splendidly."

"Yes, but I had hoped, you know, for you to have a dowry, Annie. Then you might whistle that ass, Cranshaw, down the wind and look about for a gentleman more worthy of you."

Anne felt tears rising at her brother's words, but blinked them away immediately. "The Reverend Mr. Cranshaw is not an ass, Thomas, and why you persist in naming him so I cannot understand. He is a worthy gentleman of high principles."

"Principles shrinciples," grumbled Fairfax. "You can do better than that self-righteous prig, Annie, even without a dowry, and so I tell you. It is just that—well—fifteen hundred pounds would be something."

"Yes, it would be something," agreed Anne, thinking that the Reverend Mr. Cranshaw would literally leap at the chance to marry her if he knew of it. And I would accept his offer, too, she thought sadly. I am all of twenty and I cannot let Thomas go on supporting me forever. He cannot even think to marry with Mama and Constance and I all on his hands.

"Of course, he never said he would not buy The Valentine," Fairfax interrupted her thoughts. "He said that he should like to think about it."

"To—to think about it?"

"Yes. I thought, you know, that he was just declining politely, but perhaps not. Perhaps he meant exactly what he said. Though I would not be thinking about buying the animal if The Valentine had tossed me and rubbed me off against a fence and bitten me."

"No, he was just declining politely."

"But he did ask if he might ride over from Averdon's and perhaps try The Valentine out again in a few days."

"He did? He actually did?"

"Yes. Do you know, Annie, I think we are falling into despair prematurely. Wheldon is not an ordinary gentleman."

"None of the Raynes are ordinary," declared the dowager viscountess as she and Constance entered the Gold Saloon. "Extraordinary the lot of them—well, perhaps not the girls. I have never met the girls."

"I think the earl is most handsome," observed Constance, seating herself upon a lyre-backed chair and taking up her embroidery. "And he has a wonderful smile."

Fairfax observed the speaking look his youngest sister bestowed upon him, but he could not decipher the meaning of it.

"Yes, but he has windmills in his head quite like his papa," replied the dowager. "What will he do with a nest of foxes?"

"Have them for dinner?" chuckled Fairfax.

"Oh, my goodness, no. They are not at all eatable. I do hope there is someone at Averdon's to stop him. If I had known that was his intention I should have urged Dashell to deprive him of them at once. He will make himself ill."

"I was merely joking, Mama," Fairfax explained patiently.

"He intends to raise them, Mama," offered Anne, thinking of the beguiling little balls of fur. "He said his sister— Charlotte, I think—would expect him to do so."

"Well, there," sighed her mama. "The girls have windmills in their heads as well. That is clear evidence of it. What can his sister expect to do with them once they are raised? Put them in charge of the chickens?"

She will keep them for pets, Anne thought dreamily, remembering the conversation she had had with the earl as they rode back to the house. She went to stare, unseeing, out one of the saloon windows. And in the summer Charlotte will stroll across the meadows with little foxes gamboling and frolicking in the tall grass at her feet. How wonderful it must be to live at Brookhaven where apparently such things are acceptable and taken in stride. It must be like living in the midst of a fairy tale.

Wheldon was wishing he lived in the midst of a fairy tale, but was quite certain he did not as he made his bows to the dowager Duchess of Averdon, her daughter-in-law, Catherine, and a number of ladies and gentlemen who had all heard of his arrival with a box of foxes and a ferret peeking from his coat pocket and most of whom were eager to tease him about it.

"I shall wring Charlotte's neck," he muttered after the tenth facetious observation upon his prowess as a hunter of suckling foxes.

"No, do not," laughed Averdon. "Charlotte is much too precious to have her neck wrung, Aubrey. Give her a year or two and she will have some devoted swain to do her will in everything and you may put him in charge of orphans."

"Give her a year or two, and she will have moved from foxes and pigeons and rabbits and ravens to real children and any likely beau will stay far away from her."

"Never," declared Averdon. "She is much too pretty and too sweet. She is an angel."

"Charlotte?"

"Indeed, and well you know it, too. I have been in love with that chit since she was four. Had she been born ten years earlier, she might well be my wife instead of Catherine. Speaking of which," inserted Averdon neatly, "do I understand that you spent the night at Fairfax's and had the privilege to meet Miss Constance?''

"And Miss Anne.''

"Yes, but Constance is the beauty, is she not?''

"Well, gads, Lynn, they are your neighbors. Do you mean to tell me that you don't know one from the other?''

"Of course I know one from the other. Been having an awkward time of it, the Fairfaxes. The old viscount lost a fortune in the Funds shortly before he died. Young Fairfax has had to retrench these last two years.''

"Fairfax is strapped?''

Wheldon asked the question with such startled fervor and such a look that the duke took a step backward to be certain he was seeing properly. I am, he thought. Well, bedemmed, the giant has developed a sudden intense interest in the Fairfaxes. Could it be little Miss Constance's doing?

The present Duke of Averdon had been hoping the past five years for his magnificent cousin to develop a *tendre* for someone—anyone—and the possibility that it had finally come to pass set his heart to leaping joyfully. If only Miss Constance could be made to develop a *tendre* in return; if only she could be made aware of Aubrey's noble sentiments, his grand humor, and his subtle tenderness; if only she could be urged to look past his cousin's intimidating size and see the splendid soul within!

"What's put you in such deep thought, Duke?'' Wheldon asked with a slight frown. "Or are you gone to sleep on me standing up? I did not think myself quite that dull.''

"What? No! No, you are not in the least dull, cuz. How could you be? You have foxes ensconced in one of my bedchambers and a ferret no doubt haunting my kitchen. You have my other guests all sharpening their wit upon you and my servants giggling belowstairs. And now you've fallen in love with one of my neighbors. No, you are not dull at all, merely mystifying.''

Wheldon's lips parted to protest his cousin's last assertion, but closed again without uttering a word.

"You are then!" the duke grinned. "You are in love!"

"Yes, I expect it does no good to lie about the thing, but I hope you will not make an *on-dit* of it, Lynn, because chances are she is not the least bit interested in me."

Four

It had come out of the blue and had sent Thomas into throes of ecstasy—an invitation from the Duke of Averdon to join the hunt. Certainly the hand-written message had been intended to lay to rest the vague enmity that had existed between the former duke and her papa, Anne thought, as she sat her mount beside Constance upon the hillside gazing down upon the hunt as it streamed out below her.

Join us tomorrow, Fairfax. I shall provide a mount, the missive had read. Which meant, Anne divined, that Averdon was aware that Thomas had had to sell all of his hunters in order to retrench. And it had indeed been a great kindness, because not only was Thomas without any hunters except The Valentine, but he had also been forced to drop his subscription with the local pack and Thomas did so love to hunt. And now he rode below them, upon one of Averdon's own hunters, in the wake of the duke's own pack.

"After these past three years, Thomas must think he has died and gone to heaven," grinned Anne.

"Indeed," nodded Constance. "It was exceedingly kind

of the duke to think of him. Look, Annie, there is Lord Wheldon. Oh, what a magnificent sight he is upon that great black. And it is a true black, too, I believe."

"That will be Anglaise. Thomas said the earl had had his horse brought down in easy stages from Yorkshire," replied Anne, her eyes fairly glued to the easily distinguishable figure of Wheldon as he fairly flew over a rasper barely ten seconds behind the pack. She had had the earl in sight from the moment they had gained the top of the hill. Surely none of the other riders were so agile and dauntless in their pursuit. Already she had watched him take a bullfinch, two hedgerows and a wall with gulleys on either side, all at full gallop and without the least hesitation. No one could hold the ground beside him for any length of time. He was a veritable Nonesuch upon the field. She held her breath as the pack switched back in a tight turn and the earl's Anglaise spun on the instant, rising onto its hind legs and pawing at the air then thrusting forward into the midst of the baying dogs and leaping over the high gate to the Fallingham's east field.

"Most certainly Lord Wheldon will have the brush," declared Constance. "He and his mount are almost as fleet and wiley as the fox. Oh, but whatever is he doing?"

Anne blinked disbelievingly as the pack took another harrowing turn and charged toward the narrow stream at the boundary of Fairfax and Fallingham land but the Earl of Wheldon and his mount shot off to the left in the direction of the hill from which she and Constance watched. In a moment a second rider did likewise, his horse galloping wildly after Wheldon.

"Why he is coming straight at us, Annie!" Constance exclaimed. "And there is another gentleman follows. I do not think for one moment that the fox has come this way. The dogs have all gone toward the stream."

The sight of Anglaise and his rider pushing upward toward them at slightly less than full speed was some what intimidating and Anne and Constance both backed their mounts without even thinking to do so. And then the earl was before them, hatless and breathless and smiling such a large smile that they could not help but smile back.

"Morning, Miss Fairfax, Miss Constance," Wheldon managed between breaths. "Are you enjoying the spectacle?"

"Immensely," replied Anne, "but I feel I should point out, my lord, that the fox has run down toward the stream and you have ridden up the hill."

"Exactly what I wished to point out," panted a laughing Averdon as he drew his mount to a halt beside the earl. "Good day to you, Miss Fairfax, Miss Constance. You have saved Wheldon's reputation, you know, by being here."

"Saved his reputation, your grace?" asked Constance with a shy smile.

"Indeed. Had he kept going, he would needs have been first at the treeing and he could not possibly have done that."

"Whyever not?"

"Well, because when one is raising an entire pack of foxes, allowing them to suckle milk from one's own gloves, and putting them to sleep upon one's own coverlet, one can hardly go out and throw one of their cousins to the dogs. But since you've drawn him off, he'll not be in on the kill and have a perfect excuse for it too."

"You are filling their minds with balderdash," drawled Wheldon, attempting to comb his curls out of his face with his fingers. "To say true, Miss Fairfax, I spied you upon this hill and thought it would be a good opportunity to ask whether I might come to look at The Valentine tomorrow and bring this wretched cousin of mine along so that I might get his opinion."

"Well, well, of course you may, my lord," sputtered Anne in surprise. "But you might just have easily asked Thomas."

"He did ask your brother," provided Averdon with a peculiar gleam in his eyes, "just before we started the hunt.

What? Did you forget, Aubrey? I heard you ask him myself, and heard him tell you to come ahead.''

Wheldon wished for just the briefest of moments to strangle his wretched cousin who was proving to be particularly irritating, but he thought better of it and instead asked if the ladies were tired of watching the hunt. "If you are, I should be pleased to escort you home, Miss Fairfax.''

"We should be pleased to escort you *both* home,'' Averdon inserted the correction neatly. ''But I warn you, if you allow Aubrey anywhere near the kitchen after the ride he has had, your larder will be sadly depleted.''

So, thought Averdon, it is not the beautiful Miss Constance has caught my cousin's eye, but the elder Miss Fairfax. Unless, of course, Aubrey is attempting to boondoggle me. But no, I rather think not. Aubrey is not so conniving. Still, he was conniving enough to get me to invite Fairfax to join the hunt just to please that gentleman's sisters. *And* there is some sort of scheme afoot concerning this horse of Fairfax's, too. Perhaps Aubrey has learned a bit of guile, though I still take leave to doubt it. If the great clunch has truly lost his heart to one of these young women, I must speak to Mama and Catherine about it at once. They will know how to help him over the hurdles. ''I say, Wheldon, if we are to escort these young ladies home, we might just as well look at the horse now, no?''

The earl eyed his cousin with the most exasperated look. ''Yes,'' he muttered, ''I expect that makes sense.''

''I wish you will not buy The Valentine,'' Anne murmured so quietly that Wheldon was not certain he had heard her aright.

''But I thought you wished to sell him, Miss Fairfax?''

They were proceeding back to the house at a walk, and Anne could not help but feel honored that this splendid horseman had chosen to ride beside her. And he *had* chosen to ride beside her, too. It was the most amazing thing. He had actually brought his Anglaise up beside her own Maria and left the Duke of Averdon to fall back with

Constance. But perhaps it was merely because he was too shy to speak to such a beauty as Constance. Yes, that must be it, decided Anne with tiny nod.

"We do wish to sell the horse," she said softly, "but he is so unmanageable! Sometimes he will listen to me, but no one else. And often he will not listen to me either. Thomas told me all that The Valentine did to you on your ride. I cannot understand why you should want to see the beast ever again."

Wheldon lowered his gaze to stare uneasily at the reins in his hand. He had not planned on Fairfax telling the tale of The Valentine's indiscretions to Miss Anne. She must certainly think him less than a bruising rider to have been tossed and wiped off and bitten all in one afternoon.

"I could not bear it if you came to harm because of The Valentine," Anne said. "I would never forgive myself."

Wheldon looked at her from beneath slightly lowered lids, and in a moment the engaging grin that every one of his sisters knew meant that he had done some mischief overwhelmed his countenance and overwhelmed Anne as well.

Oh, he is the most angelic gentleman I have ever met. He is so—so—innocent, Anne thought. We were villains indeed, Thomas and I, to hope to cozen him into buying that dratted gelding.

I should not have exaggerated quite so heavily about that dratted gelding, thought Wheldon, focussing the full force of his grin upon Miss Fairfax. Now how am I to convince her that I am perfectly capable of handling him? Which I am, he told himself. Perfectly capable. I think.

"The Valentine is a bit headstrong," Wheldon nodded. "But Anglaise has a mind of his own as well. Do you not, my lad?"

"Oh, no," replied Anne with a shake of her head, her jockey cap slipping just the merest bit to the left. "I cannot believe it. Anglaise is a fine horse and very prettily behaved and the most splendid jumper."

"And very old," laughed Wheldon. "And wishing his jumping days were fewer and farther between. But he is headstrong all the same and has come me acropper a number times through the years."

The four arrived in the stable yard to spy a freshly-painted brown and yellow gig. "The Reverend Mr. Cranshaw is paying a call!" exclaimed Constance. "Come, Annie, we must pay him our respects."

"Indeed," nodded Anne. "Will you join us, my lord?" she asked just to be polite, "and you, of course, your grace."

Averdon's eyes sought some hint of what Wheldon wished him to answer and saw the earl nod without the slightest hesitation. "We would be pleased," the duke responded on the instant. "But only if you are certain Lady Fairfax will not think us barbarians to enter her drawing room in all our dirt."

"Oh, no, Mama will not mind at all," offered Constance blithely. "She will be honored that you stepped in to greet her."

Anne was not quite so certain. Both gentlemen were muddied and windblown and Lady Fairfax might well wish them not to set foot upon her carpeting or enter her drawing room smelling of the stables. But Averdon was a duke, of course, and Wheldon an earl, and even Mama would not tell them to leave once they had entered.

"Anne, my dear," the Reverend Mr. Cranshaw droned, rising as the little party entered the room. "And Miss Constance."

"Good day, Mr. Cranshaw," smiled Constance charmingly. "We have brought company with us, Mama."

Anne, my dear? thought Wheldon, taking note of the extreme informality. His clear blue eyes went immediately to the gentleman dressed quite properly for a morning call in a double-breasted morning coat of bottle green, clinging breeches of dove gray kerseymere, a fashionable cream waistcoat with a small stripe of gray and shining Hessians with elegant tassles. The vicar's neckcloth was tied in a perfect Mathematical, his hair cut in a precise Brutus, and his shirt collars crisp and high and pristine white.

With some misgiving Wheldon followed in Averdon's wake, doing the pretty to Lady Fairfax and bowing politely to Cranshaw. Anne, my dear? he thought again. Had the man said Constance, my dear, as well? No, he had not. He had called that young woman Miss Constance. Wheldon's heart dropped to the verimost toes of his scuffed and totally unfashionable top boots. Why, they did not even have the new white tops to them, his boots. He wore them because they were comfortable in the field, but they had been comfortable in the field for well over a year and looked it, too. And his cravat, he knew, had loosened and his shirt collars were almost nonexistent and his hair was much too long and had been tossed about wildly by the wind from the instant his hat had blown away going over the first hurdle.

And the damnable man is not a great gawking clunch, neither, Wheldon thought with the most overwhelming ache of inferiority as he took the ancient wing chair to which Lady Fairfax motioned him and watched the Reverend Mr. Cranshaw settle down upon the delightful chintz-covered sofa next to Anne.

Averdon had all he could do to keep from chuckling at the myriad humors that succeeded each other upon his cousin's face. Truthfully, he had never in all their years together seen Aubrey brought to such a state. It *is* the elder Miss Fairfax who has claimed his heart, the duke concluded triumphantly. I knew the great clunch could not be attempting to mislead me. His expression changes with every word Miss Anne says in response to Cranshaw's platitudes.

And the Reverend Mr. Cranshaw was filled with platitudes. And his conversation was self-aggrandizing and self-congratulatory and overflowing with the most regal and condescending sentiments. "Not that I wish to boast," he was saying as the tea tray was carried in, "but had I not inserted myself into the midst of the controversy, that young man would be terrorizing the countryside this very day."

"I beg leave to doubt that," murmured Averdon as Anne began to pour out. "The boy is merely six, you know, Cranshaw, barely old enough to terrorize a pussycat. And I do think treating him like some hardened sinner and having him soundly beaten before all the parish was quite uncalled for."

"Spare the rod, your grace," droned the Reverend Mr. Cranshaw. "Why, he refused to hear a word that was said to him and ran about the village doing whatever he liked whenever he liked, paying not the least heed to anyone. He pays heed now, let me tell you."

Cranshaw accepted his tea from Anne's hand letting his fingers touch hers just the slightest bit, which slightest bit Wheldon noted immediately. "A six-year-old?" the earl asked, burying his jealousy of Cranshaw's uncensured gesture beneath curiosity about the child everyone apparently knew but himself. "And his parents cannot control him?"

"He has no parents, my lord. He is an orphan, a resident of the asylum. I am considering indenturing the boy to Mr. Hoage."

Anne, who at that very moment was in the act of passing a cup of tea across the small table into Wheldon's hands, started at Cranshaw's words, juggled the cup and saucer and sent hot tea spilling over the earl's gloveless hand. Caught by surprise and in serious, sudden pain, Wheldon leapt to his feet cracking his shin against the table which held the tea tray and sending tea pot, cakes and short-breads plummeting to Lady Fairfax's prized Turkish carpeting as the remaining tea in his cup flooded down over the front of his own breeches.

"Oh, oh, I am so very sorry," gasped Anne, grabbing for a napkin and attempting to wipe the tea from his hand and dab it from his breeches at one and the same time. Lady Fairfax gasped as well and buried her face in her hands at the pitiful sight of her carpet; Averdon hurried to the bellpull and Constance and the Reverend Mr. Cranshaw sat staring with wide-open mouths.

"No, it is I who am sorry, Miss Fairfax," mumbled Wheldon, taking the napkin from her shaking hand and dabbing at his own breeches. "But I think I shall go and find some cold water if you will pardon me."

"Oh, cold water. Of course. You must come with me at once to the kitchen. Dashell," she said with a most embarrassed look in her eye as that stalwart appeared in the doorway. "Will you fetch someone to clean up this mess, please? I have been most clumsy."

"Indeed, miss," responded Dashell, hurrying off down the hall just as the duke, himself, sank to his knees with a handful of linen napkins in an effort to stem the tide of flowing tea.

"Go, Wheldon," Averdon urged with the most peculiar gleam in his eyes. "Miss Fairfax, do take him to the kitchen so that he may immerse his burns in cold water or I shall have the deuce of a time getting him to sit a horse so that we can ride home."

"Yes, yes, of course," replied Anne, seizing Wheldon's arm and leading him from the room.

"Do get up, your grace," Lady Fairfax sighed, as she took her hands from her eyes and spied her guest upon his knees. "Dukes do not crawl about upon the carpeting soaking up tea. The servants will see to it."

"Yes, ma'am," agreed that gentleman. "But I can see how fond you are of this elegant carpet and I hoped to mitigate the damage as much as possible."

"Does his mama have any carpets left at all?" queried Lady Fairfax mournfully.

"Oh, Mama, that is unfair," protested Constance, at last

come out of her shock and bending to pick a number of cakes from the floor. "It was Annie poured the tea upon his hand that made him jump up."

"Yes, but there is so very much of him that jumps up at one time," sighed Lady Fairfax. "The vicar would never have knocked everything from the table. I daresay you would not have done so either, your grace."

"No, ma'am, I daresay I might not have done, but then I am not as powerfully built as Aubrey."

"No, neither so broad nor so tall nor so ungainly," Lady Fairfax replied with a most despairing look. "You must forgive us, Mr. Cranshaw, for our little accident. You are not injured?"

"No, my lady, not in the least," replied that worthy with an ill-disguised look of disgust at the mess at his feet.

In the kitchen, Mrs. Danson was pumping water over a number of thick towels, wringing them out and placing them into Wheldon's hands.

"I have got the butter," Anne announced, placing a large crock upon the kitchen table. "Give me your wrist, sir," she ordered, and taking Wheldon's hand into her own, patted it dry with a towel and rubbed a handful of butter over it and the back of his hand.

"Now, give his lordship the rest of the butter, my girl, and begone with you," ordered Mrs. Danson. "And you, my lord—take yourself into Dashell's pantry and spread that butter liberally where it will do you the most good."

Wheldon, whose embarrassment had by this time disappeared, shook his golden curls and chuckled. "I think that had best wait until I take me back to Hunkapillar, ma'am."

"Nonsense," declared Anne, who had refused to begone, "it will not do you the least bit of good if you wait that long. And I shall ask Dashell to fetch you a pair of Thomas' breeches to wear home."

"I think not," replied Wheldon.

"Papa's then."

"I think not," put in Mrs. Danson. "There is not a pair of breeches in this house will fit him, Miss Anne."

"No," agreed Wheldon.

"But that is no excuse," continued Mrs. Danson with a stern look, "not to apply the butter directly. Now off with you."

Wheldon, his thighs still throbbing from the scalding he had taken, though his hand and wrist felt a good deal better, shrugged his broad shoulders and slipped into the butler's pantry closing the door behind him. In a matter of minutes the door opened again and he returned walking very oddly, but feeling a deal better. He placed the butter crock back on the table and looked down at Anne quite seriously where she stood beside the oven. "What was it startled you?" he asked. "Who is Mr. Hoage?"

"Oh!" gasped Anne, remembering suddenly what had initiated the entire incident. "He is the undertaker! How could anyone think to indenture that poor little tyke to an undertaker? It is not as if Ethan is a monster. Why he is not near so impertinent as your own tiger. He is only little and curious and full of energy. I did not even go to services on Sunday because I knew what they planned to do to the child. But I do wish I had gone. I wish I had been brave enough to go and to stand right up in front of everyone and stop them. But the Reverend Mr. Cranshaw is so certain he is right, you know, and everyone respects him."

"Not everyone," mumbled Mrs. Danson busily slicing bread and cheese.

"Well, not Thomas, but everyone in the village, and Mama, and Constance."

Wheldon, coming to stand at the kitchen table, gratefully accepted the bread and cheese and glass of ale Mrs. Danson layed before him. "I thank you with all my heart," he said to her, grinning widely. "Obviously, I did not miss my tea, but none of it seemed to reach my stomach. Am I to understand, Miss Fairfax, that you do not wish this child to be indentured to Mr. Hoage?''

"Oh, most certainly not! If only—but I am afraid Thomas cannot afford to hire one more servant, not even such a small boy. And it is perfectly clear that Ethan cannot remain on the parish, because the entire parish is set against him.''

Wheldon's path was thus made perfectly clear to him. "I rather think," he drawled, "that I ought to be going, Miss Fairfax. If you would be kind enough to ask Averdon to join me in the yard? We shall return tomorrow to decide upon The Valentine, I think. I am not particularly up to an attempt to put him through his paces at the moment.''

"Of course you are not," agreed Anne. Nor is he up to facing Mama and Mr. Cranshaw after I have embarrassed him so either, she added silently. "I do hope your ride back to Hunkapillar will not prove too uncomfortable, my lord. I will say my farewells now then, and send his grace down to you.''

Five

"Well, the way I see it, Mama," explained Averdon sitting forward in his chair, his arms resting upon his knees, "Aubrey has fallen in love with Miss Fairfax."

"No!" exclaimed the dowager duchess.

"Yes. Head over heels. Which is why he badgered me into inviting Fairfax on the hunt, of course. And why I have determined that we must set aside whatever stupid quarrel exists between our families. What stupid quarrel does exist between our families, Mama? I asked Fairfax about it, but he had no idea."

"I cannot quite remember, my dear. It was between your father and the old viscount and not even clear to me at the time. Of course we shall set it aside."

"Good, because I cannot for the life of me see how Wheldon is going to win the lady if the only excuse he has to see her is the purchase of her brother's hunter."

"Surely he does not need a reason, Lynn, to pay the girl a morning call," smiled his wife beside him.

"Yes, he does," inserted the dowager duchess with a swiftness that impressed even her son. "Aubrey is not one

We'd Like to Invite You to Subscribe to Zebra's Regency Romance Book Club and Give You a Gift of 4 Free Books as Your Introduction! *(Worth $19.96!)*

I f you're a Regency lover, imagine the joy of getting 4 FREE Zebra Regency Romances and then the chance to have these lovely stories delivered to your home each month at the lowest prices available! Well, that's our offer to you and here's how you benefit by becoming a Zebra Home Subscription Service subscriber:

- 4 FREE Introductory Regency Romances are delivered to your doorstep
- 4 BRAND NEW Regencies are then delivered each month (usually before they're available in bookstores)
- Subscribers save almost $4.00 every month
- Home delivery is always FREE
- You also receive a FREE monthly newsletter, *Zebra/Pinnacle Romance News* which features author profiles, contests, subscriber benefits, book previews and more
- No risks or obligations...in other words you can cancel whenever you wish with no questions asked

Join the thousands of readers who enjoy the savings and convenience offered to Regency Romance subscribers. After your initial introductory shipment, you receive 4 brand-new Zebra Regency Romances each month to examine for 10 days. Then, if you decide to keep the books, you'll pay the preferred subscriber's price of just $4.00 per title. That's only $16.00 for all 4 books and there's never an extra charge for shipping and handling.

It's a no-lose proposition, so return the FREE BOOK CERTIFICATE today!

of your town beaux, Catherine, and would look a perfect ninny dressed to the nines standing upon the Fairfaxes' doorstep with a tiny posy clutched in one of those enormous hands, and even sillier perched upon the edge of a sopha attempting to whisper prissy little compliments to the gel under the watchful eyes of Ermentrude Fairfax."

"Well, yes, now that I think of it," agreed the duchess with a grin. "I have grown so accustomed to Aubrey that I am rarely ever amazed at his size, but I was overcome when first you introduced us."

"Yes, and besides, Catherine," murmured Averdon, "it is not the pretty little Constance who has assaulted his heart but the elder Miss Fairfax. And she is quite unused to beaux, I think. The Reverend Mr. Cranshaw pays her attentions, but none of the other gentlemen in the neighborhood. I doubt she would know how to answer a beau's compliments. She has had no practice in the art of flirtation. But Aubrey is determined to appear upon her doorstep as often as possible. That much is obvious to me. I was thinking to urge him to make free of our greenhouses. He might look odd with a posy in his own hand but that is not to say he might not send her something delightful with his card attached."

"Indeed," agreed his mama. "You shall take him out to Desmond and let the two of them discuss it. It is still winter, however, so there will be few of the flowers in bloom."

Averdon nodded. "And I thought, you know, that perhaps we might somehow include Miss Fairfax in our own activities. With the house party and all, I mean, it will not seem too forward if we were to invite her to dinner or—"

"Or a ball!" exclaimed his wife enthusiastically.

"A ball, Catherine?"

"Oh, yes. It will be perfect. Just a tiny ball, Lynn, with merely our present guests and a few of the neighbors—"

Averdon shook his head in playful exasperation. "It will

not be tiny at all, Catherine, and well you know it. With the gentlemen come to hunt and their wives and daughters, we've near twenty guests now. And if we are to include the neighbors, the numbers will swell considerably because you cannot invite Lady Fallingham without you invite Lady Delby, *et cetera, et cetera.*"

"But it would be such fun, Lynn. And it will give all of the ladies something to do. We shall set one group to decorating and another to planning the menu for a late supper and a third to addressing invitations."

"A costume ball!" exclaimed the dowager abruptly.

"A costume ball, Mama?"

"Yes, that will set even the gentlemen to work. We shall open our attics and encourage our guests to put together costumes from our own trunks. And our neighbors and their guests—everyone hereabout has guests during the hunting season and they must be included in our invitations—will do the same. That will entertain us all immensely. And I shall enclose a special note to the Fairfaxes inviting them to make use of our attics. Because they will not find anything to fit Miss Fairfax in their own, I assure you. But I know where lies the perfect costume for her!"

The second invitation arrived from Hunkapillar in the hands of the Duke of Averdon himself. He presented it with a flourish and a wide smile into the hands of a fluttering Lady Fairfax, expressed a fond hope that she and her son and daughters would attend, and assured her that although Constance had not yet made her come-out, it would be of no consequence for it was to be a small affair with only his house guests and a few neighbors in attendance. He then took himself off to the stables where Wheldon and Fairfax and The Valentine awaited his presence.

"Mama, what is it?" asked Anne as her mother rushed into the morning room waving the elegantly engraved invitation card.

"I was upon the stairs," replied her mother, "when Dashell went to answer the door. And who should be on the other side of it but the Duke of Averdon. And I thought, you know, that I ought to go down, since he could see quite well that I had spied him. And he bowed most conde-scendingly and presented me with this."

"But what is it, Mama?" asked Constance, setting aside a copy of *La Belle Assemblée* as her mother and Anne both came to sit upon the sopha near her.

"An invitation, my dear. For all of us. To attend a cos-tume ball at Hunkapillar."

"Truly, Mama? A ball?"

"Well, a very small ball, I think, for his grace assured me that it would not be at all improper for you to attend, Constance. He says it will be composed only of his house guests and a few of his neighbors."

"When is it to be, Mama?" Constance was grinning from ear to ear. She had never once been to a ball, not even to an assembly.

"Well, that is just the thing. It is to be on St. Valentine's Day, which is barely a se'enight away. And it is to be a costume ball and we are to make free of Hunkapillar's attics to provide ourselves with costumes if we please to do so!"

Anne smiled rather distractedly at their obvious excite-ment but she found she could not become excited herself. She had been to a number of assemblies and knew well what torture it was to sit forgotten amongst the chaperones as all the other young ladies danced past. Well, perhaps not *all* the other young ladies, because Miss Desdemona Cocksbury was short and stubby and had freckles besides, so she did not generally take the floor more than twice and that upon her brother's arm. And Lady Margaret Fall-ingham often sat out a number of sets, though Anne could not understand why. Apparently the gentlemen of the neighborhood were not fond of young ladies who rode to hounds with more prowess than themselves. "Are we to attend then, Mama," she asked quietly, strolling across the room to stand before the windows which were at this early hour ablaze with sunlight.

"I rather think we must, Anne, dear," replied her parent. "The invitation comes from the dowager duchess and the present duchess combined and is signed by both of them. It would be a sad affront should we not attend, especially since his grace has gone out of his way to re-establish a friendship between our two houses."

"Why did we never go to Hunkapillar, Mama?" asked Constance, curious.

"Gracious, I do not in the least remember. Some nonsense between your papa and the old duke. Something about a horse or a field or a carriage. It has slipped my mind completely."

Anne's gaze was drawn to the stable doors as they opened wide and she watched intently as old Morgan led The Valentine out into the yard. Following them came Thomas in deep conversation with the Duke of Averdon and the Earl of Wheldon. Was Lord Wheldon actually going to attempt to ride that villain again? She could not believe it. Yet, The Valentine was saddled.

"I think I shall go for a stroll, Mama," Anne murmured, and in less than two minutes she was sweeping through the kitchen door buttoning her pelisse as she went.

"Annie," greeted her brother as she rounded the corner of the house into the stable yard. "Lord Wheldon has returned."

"Good morning, Miss Fairfax," smiled the earl most charmingly.

"Good morning, Miss Fairfax," echoed the duke, with the most peculiar gleam in his eye, much like the one Annie had noted the afternoon previous. "Wheldon, are you riding or not? He looks a brute."

"No, not a brute," murmured Wheldon, stepping up to stroke The Valentine's nose. The horse side-stepped and took a nip at him in appreciation.

"You, sir," declared the earl in chuckling tones, "are a

genuine bo-kicker, exactly as Carley said, not to be trusted for a moment."

Anne held her breath as Lord Wheldon slipped his foot into the stirrup. The Valentine sidled nervously. The earl swung himself into the saddle. The Valentine spun in a circle and reared on his hind legs pawing at the air. And then man and horse were disappearing around the corner of the house at top speed.

"'Zounds!" Averdon exclaimed, excusing himself and mounting his own hack. In an instant he too had disappeared from view.

"Oh, Thomas," sighed Anne, taking her brother's arm, "that dratted horse has run away with Lord Wheldon again."

"Well, but the duke is after them, Annie. We must just hope that The Valentine does not go tossing Wheldon off again because Wheldon is quite determined to have the beast, but not, I think, if he is tossed and bitten and scraped off a second time."

"He is quite stubborn, is he not?"

"Who? The Valentine or Wheldon?"

"Lord Wheldon."

"Quite stubborn and that is what we must depend upon. If he can out-stubborn The Valentine we will have your dowry and he will have a horse well-fit to replace this magnificent fellow here." Thomas reached up to stroke Anglaise's nose as the horse stood waiting patiently where his master had left him. "Did you see this trooper upon the field yesterday, Annie? Was he not the most splendid specimen of all? I could not take my eyes from Wheldon and this animal so long as they were anywhere in sight."

The Duke of Averdon could not take his eyes from Wheldon and The Valentine as he raced behind them, either. The wretched beast was doing its best to unseat his powerful cousin. And odds are, Averdon thought, that Aubrey will go flying any time now. So the duke was not surprised when the pair ahead of him reached the banks of the stream that marked the southern boundary of Fairfax land and The Valentine came to an abrupt halt, sending the earl soaring over his head and into the water. If Wheldon had not stood up promptly, gasping and laughing and shaking himself like some great sheepdog Averdon might have worried, but as it was he brought his hack up next to The Valentine, seized the dangling reins, and fell into whoops of laughter.

"Enough, Duke," chuckled Wheldon sloshing his way back to dry land, "you are encouraging that rascal no end."

"Actually, cuz," chortled Averdon, "I do not think he craves encouragement. Apparently he does quite nicely without."

"Apparently," laughed Wheldon. "You, sir, are the most mischievous bit of blood and bone I have ever come upon," he added, taking The Valentine's reins from Averdon and grinning up at the horse. "But I warn you, Val, I am going to be the victor and you the vanquished sooner or later. Have you some sugar in one of your pockets, Lynn? I did have some, but for some odd reason, it appears to have dissolved."

This sent Averdon into whoops again. He reached into a pocket and produced an apple. "It is all I have, Aubrey, though I do think that rewarding that rapscallion for tossing you into a stream is the wrong tack."

"Yes, and he will most likely attempt to bite my hand along with the apple, but it won't make the least difference because I am going to ride him and drip all over him so he shall be wet as well, which will no more than serve him right."

"Perhaps you ought to join me on Mirage and lead that beast back to the stable."

"No."

"But we are going directly back to the stable."

"No."

"Come, Aubrey, we must. You cannot ride about the country in February soaking wet. You know you cannot. You will take a chill and succumb to an inflammation of the lungs and your mama will have my head for it."

"I expect you are correct," sighed Wheldon looking about him. "You have not seen my hat, have you, Lynn?"

"Indeed. I saw it sink slowly to the bottom of the stream. And do not go wading out after it. If you've not another with you, I shall lend you one of my own."

"But that's the third hat I've lost in three days. Tucker will have palpitations."

"We will go into Tilby and buy you three more, then."

"Well, I had planned on riding into Tilby now."

"You had?"

"Uh-huh," offered Wheldon distractedly stroking The Valentine's withers. "That is Cranshaw's parish, is it not?"

"Well, yes, but why—"

"I mean to go and fetch that boy."

"Ethan?" Averdon's jaw dropped in complete surprise.

"Yes, the lad you were speaking of yesterday."

"Fetch him and take him where?"

"Why to Hunkapillar, Lynn. I can hardly take him to Brookhaven until I return there myself. You will not mind having the boy about for a week or two. I shall see that Tucker and Carley look after him." With a deal of circumspection, Wheldon inserted his foot into the stirrup and swung up onto The Valentine's back. The Valentine swung his head around and took a nip at the earl's knee. Wheldon moved his knee out of reach and shoved at the big horse's head. "Do give over, you wretched animal," he grumbled. "You are not like to be rid of me no matter how ill-mannered you pretend to be, and that's a fact."

Anne could not believe her eyes, nor could she keep from giggling. Thomas Fairfax had covered his desk with newspaper and spread a goodly number of bank notes out upon it to dry. "Why are they all soggy?" she asked, eyeing her brother with glee.

"Because The Valentine tossed him into the stream and the notes were in his pocket. He must have squeezed a full pint of water from them before he counted them out to me. Fifteen hundred pounds, Annie, drying right there before you."

"I cannot believe it. Why would he buy a horse who had just tossed him into a stream?"

"Who cares, Annie? The fact is that he has bought the beast and seemed very happy to do so. How he and The Valentine will settle their differences I have not the least idea, but Wheldon is as determined to make a manageable hunter of him as The Valentine is determined not be managed. And now, my dear, you have a proper dowry. Are you not pleased, Annie? You will not need to consider Cranshaw for a moment longer. We shall find you a proper husband now that Wheldon's largesse as provided some incentive. Cranshaw will no longer be the only gentleman knocking upon our door."

Anne's smile dimmed as she fingered one of the notes. Now, though, the Earl of Wheldon would not be knocking upon their door. He had no reason to visit Fairfax House ever again. But I will see him one more time, she told herself, at the Averdon's ball. And perhaps, she thought, I will accompany Mama and Constance to London for the Season. Now that I have a dowry, perhaps Mama will consider that I might attract a London gentleman. And she will not like to chaperone Constance everywhere. I shall offer to do so whenever she wishes. A chaperon need not dress so fashionably as Constance must, so it will not cost so very much more for me to accompany them. And perhaps, she added with the most appalling emptiness inside her, perhaps I will chance to see Lord Wheldon at some function while we are there.

"Annie? What is it?" asked Fairfax quietly. "You are

looking quite woebegone. I thought the money would cheer you.''

"Oh, but it does, Thomas. It is merely that—Thomas, we need not tell Mama and Constance right at this very moment, need we? They will neither of them notice that The Valentine is gone.''

"Well, I expect we might keep it a secret between us for a while, Annie. But I do not understand why you wish to do so.''

"Well, because Mama will boast of it to the Reverend Mr. Cranshaw, you see. And then he will have all the more reason to petition me. And—I do wish to marry someone, Thomas. And if no one else will offer for me, then it must be him. I dare not turn away my only chance. But I would so like to have a bit more time. Oh, I am not making any sense at all,'' she mumbled, noting the perplexed frown upon her brother's face. "My mind is all a jumble.''

"He be a cryin' an' a wailin' away ta beat the devil, guv'nor, an' I ain't agoin' ta be in charge of no baby what is afeared of 'orses,'' declared Carley roundly, glaring defiantly up into his employer's face as they stood outside the Averdon's kitchen door.

"Are you certain the boy is afraid of the horses, Carley? He may simply be afraid of you,'' teased Wheldon.

"Naw, 'e ain't afeared of me, guv'nor. I ain't hit 'im nor nothin'. But I'm agoin' ta hit 'im if 'e don't stop 'is wailin'.''

"No, you are not,'' murmured Wheldon, putting a hand on his tiger's shoulder and strolling toward the stables. "You do not remember, Carley, how you cried when first you came to live with me, but I do.''

"I niver did!''

"Yes, because you did not want to be a tiger at all. You wanted most adamantly to wander the streets of York picking pockets just as you had always done. But you could not continue to do that because the Watch had caught you and put you in gaol."

"Well, an' it were only 'cause I were stupid an' little an' din't know no better," grumbled Carley.

"And now you are old and know everything."

"Aye."

Wheldon chuckled. He had borrowed Averdon's closed carriage and driven into Tilby with every expectation of rescuing Miss Fairfax's orphan, and he had made a proper spectacle of himself attempting to do so, too. The truth was, he had not expected the boy to be so very small. Even when he had knelt down beside the tyke to assure him that he was not a giant determined to carry him away to make his bread, he had towered over little Ethan. In the end, he had simply signed the papers at the parish house, tucked the loudly protesting child under one arm, and carried him into the coach. Had anyone heard the ruckus Ethan had made for the entire ride back to Hunkapillar, they would surely have thought that Wheldon was murdering the boy. Luckily, the roads had been empty of vehicles and they had made the journey with only John Coachman privy to Ethan's shrieks.

It was John Coachman who met them at the stable doors, his hands over his ears and shaking his greying head, his eyes lit with amusement. He accompanied the earl to the tack room, sent Carley off, closed the door soundly behind the little tiger, and poured them each a cup of coffee. "Fierce storm a'blowin' upstairs, m'lord, and like to get worse afore it gets better."

"Yes, so I hear, John. Carley says he is afraid of the horses."

"Ain't no horses up there."

"No, but perhaps he thinks they will climb the stairs and come after him. He *is* terribly little. And how anyone could find him such a devil as to take a stick to him, I cannot for the life of me understand."

"'Twas not a stick, m'lord, but a belt, and I were that

close to seizin' it out o' the vicar's hand meself. But that ain't done, ye know. Not by the likes o' me.''

"Yes, and the duke was not there nor Fairfax, but why did not one of the other gentlemen stop it?''

"On accounta they seed nothin' wrong in't, m'lord. 'Twas just punishment is how they figgered.''

"But just punishment for what? What did the boy do?''

"Why, he stole a sheet from Mrs. Gideon's line an' made a tent o' it, and stole a tart from Mrs. Dailey's kitchen to be his rations, and lit a fire with old Mr. Bagley's flints an' pretended ta be a soldier in a camp, m'lord. An' when the vicar caught 'im and took 'im back to the asylum, he called the Reverend Mr. Cranshaw a bad name an' bit 'im, m'lord. That, I think, be what stuck in the reverend's craw.''

"Undoubtedly something did,'' sighed Wheldon. "Well, Ethan may bite me all he wishes, although he will need to share that privilege with The Valentine. And I am sure I have heard a great many more bad names than the tyke can know, so that will not prove too great a problem. And he cannot be near as much a nodcock as Carley was used to be. I must only find some way to calm him down, eh, John?''

"An' soon,'' nodded that worthy with a smile.

"Right now,'' nodded Wheldon in return and rising, set his cup aside and went in search of the wailing Ethan.

Six

Constance and Lady Fairfax were in the attic searching out costumes for the Averdon's ball and Thomas had gone to join the hunt at Hunkapillar and Dashell had been called off to deal with a crisis amongst the few remaining members of the household staff, which was how Anne came to be opening the front door when the knock sounded upon it. For the longest moment she stared unbelievingly, unable to say a word. The Earl of Wheldon in proper morning dress, Hessians gleaming and a new beaver planted firmly but rakishly upon his curls, peered at her from behind an enormous pot of greenery. At his side, scrubbed and polished and dressed in nankeen breeches and a tail coat, one hand holding tightly to the earl's pocket, stood little Ethan.

"Lord Wheldon," breathed Anne after a seemingly endless time. "Will you come in?"

"I expected you to be Dashell," drawled the earl with an attempt at nonchalance.

"But I am not, you see."

"No."

"Will you come in regardless?"

"Yes, certainly. Ah, this is for you, Miss Fairfax."

"For me?"

"It is a—a pear tree."

"A pear tree?"

"I wished to bring you something, but all the flowers looked so—small. And I thought, you know, that this looked more the thing—but if you cannot like—"

"It is lovely," giggled Anne, separating two of the branches to see him more clearly. "Would you like to set it down, sir?"

"Where?"

"Upstairs in the morning room, perhaps? It will be sure to get enough light there and will look quite—quite elegant—before the long windows. Can you carry it so far?"

"Indeed, Miss Fairfax, if only you will lead the way."

The picture of Lord Wheldon, nearly obscured by greenery, ascending the staircase with a little person firmly attached to his pocket was not one to be forgotten. Anne set it firmly in her heart and vowed to treasure it forever. No matter how unhappy I may become now and then, I shall always have this to remember and to bring a smile to my face, she thought with the tenderest of emotions. But why is he bringing me a pear tree? I thought never to see him again until the ball.

"There," sighed Wheldon as they reached the morning room and he set the pear tree in the place Anne chose. "Ethan, doff your cap if you please."

"But you gots yours on, lor'ship."

"I do? I do. Pardon me, Miss Fairfax," sputtered the earl, hastily removing his hat and setting it upon a cricket table. He then removed Ethan's cap and set it atop the high crown of his beaver, which made the little boy laugh.

"You do know Ethan, I believe, Miss Fairfax."

"Yes, that is to say, we have never been formally introduced, my lord. How comes he to be with you?"

"I have hired him, Miss Fairfax," replied the earl attempting to loose the child's grip upon his pocket.

"Will you not sit down, my lord?" asked Anne, a blush staining her cheeks. Has he done this for me? she wondered. Has he taken Ethan in because I was so upset over him?

"I would be pleased to sit if I can unstick myself from this urchin. Yesterday afternoon he was frightened to death of me because he thought I was a giant and meant to eat him for supper and today he will not let me out of his sight—nor let go of me neither. Ethan," he drawled then, peering down his perfectly straight aristocratic nose, "if you set my pocket free and sit down properly in that window seat, just there, I shall put Fearless directly into your hands."

Like magic the child released him and scrambled up on to the window seat. Wheldon reached into his other pocket and lifted a yawning ferret into the light. She hung limply across his palm, exquisitely formed little feet dangling to either side. "I count on you, Ethan, to watch her and not let her get into trouble," Wheldon intoned soberly. "That is part of your job remember."

"Yessirlor'ship," replied the boy in tones equally as sober.

"Very well then. I shall trust you to do your job properly," nodded the earl, placing the ferret into Ethan's lap.

"Watching your ferret is his job?" asked Anne, sitting so that Wheldon might take a seat.

"Not all of his job. He has more to do."

"What?"

"Well, he must feed her and the foxes, and pet them all, and help to keep them clean and play with them too. It is a great responsibility. Tucker and I cannot do it all, you know. We are both much too large to be scrambling about under beds and dressers and cricket tables, which is, I assure you, necessary."

"An' firs' thin' in the mornin' I mus' bwing you your fob," declared Ethan, petting the ferret.

"Your fob?" asked Anne with a lift of an eyebrow.

"Indeed. That task he made for himself. I think because he is entranced with the fobs. We played with them last evening and this morning he ordained himself my fob selector."

"Yes, 'cause I am being your lion," murmured Ethan with a determined nod from the window seat.

"Your lion, my lord?"

"Well, Carley would boast to Ethan of being my tiger. And Ethan did so want to be something equally as ferocious, so—"

"You made him your lion," grinned Anne.

"Exactly so. Ought we to be sitting here without a chaperon, Miss Fairfax?"

"Oh, what am I thinking?" murmured Anne. "I shall send someone to fetch Constance at once. But I do wish to thank you, my lord, for taking Ethan and for the lovely— tree."

"Why must you send for Miss Constance?" Wheldon asked, puzzled. "I was thinking perhaps Dashell or, no, actually I was thinking of Mrs. Danson, because if she came to chaperone us, she might bring a bit of pastry with her."

"But it is Constance you have come to visit."

"No, it is you I have come to visit, Miss Fairfax."

"Well, yes, I realize that you did come to put my mind at ease concerning Ethan, but did you not—not wish to spend some time with my sister?"

"Not particularly, unless you think that for some reason I must, Miss Fairfax."

Anne's great brown eyes opened wider than ever they had done before. Her lips rounded into a perfect O. Her hands went to cover her reddening cheeks. "You have— have come to see *me*?" she asked in a whisper.

* * *

Lady Fairfax hastily wiped her hands upon the apron she had borrowed from Mrs. Danson and urged Constance to rush down to her chambers and don her terry poplin at once. "Because Dashell says that the Earl of Wheldon has arrived to pay a morning call and Anne cannot like to be entertaining the gentleman on her own. He has come, after all, to see you, my dear."

Constance, her eyes alight with laughter, thought better of explaining to her mama that the earl could not possibly care whether she made an appearance or not. I am correct, she told herself as she hurried down from the attics. The gentleman has developed a *tendre* for Annie. To think, she now has two beaux and one of them an earl! Well, and she is most deserving of them, too. She is the sweetest, kindest, most gentle person in all the world. I cannot think why Mama must assume that all gentlemen are interested in me.

Lady Fairfax, however, was complacent in her belief that Wheldon's interest lay in the younger of her daughters and that Anne would marry the Reverend Mr. Cranshaw who was not, after all, some poor parson like to spend his days in genteel poverty, but a refined gentleman with powerful political affiliations within the Church of England and like to be a rich and successful bishop one day. And I, of course, thought Lady Fairfax, will do all in my power to make that match. The Reverend Mr. Cranshaw does not require his wife to be beautiful, merely competent and charitable and virtuous and Anne most certainly is all those things. Though why she had to spill tea upon Lord Wheldon in the Reverend Mr. Cranshaw's presence, I cannot understand. She is not generally clumsy. I only hope it did not give Mr. Cranshaw a disgust of her. Straightening her skirts and pausing before the bevelled mirror to repin a few strands of hair that had been disturbed, Lady Fairfax made her way to the morning room only to find it empty of company.

"Well, where on earth?" she muttered, retracing her steps back into the hall. "I am certain Dashell said the morning room."

"Look out! Look out!" shrilled a little voice as she made her way toward the Gold Saloon. And in a moment a most hideous rat came scurrying as bold as you please toward her and darted under the skirts of her gown.

"Oh!" Lady Fairfax shrieked. "Help me! Help!" and she lifted her skirts and danced about, attempting to dislodge the rodent.

In answer to her cries a tiny, dusky-haired urchin popped out of the Gold Saloon and launched himself in her direction, diving under her skirts and shouting, "I founded 'er, lor'ship! I founded 'er!"

Lady Fairfax's arm went to her brow, all color faded from her face and she tumbled forward in a dead faint on top of both little Ethan and Fearless before either Anne or Wheldon could scramble into the corridor to catch her.

"Ow! Ow!" cried Ethan and burst into tears while attempting to make his way out from under Lady Fairfax. He was literally pinned in place by the lady and could not free himself.

Fearless had no such problem. The frisky ferret rushed out from the heap of fabric and humanity and turning to chuckle at the chaos, headed confidently toward the servants' staircase, her nose wriggling and sniffing excitedly at the air.

Lady Fairfax regained her senses to find herself prostrate upon the wine-colored fainting couch in the Gold Saloon with Anne waving a vinaigrette beneath her nose and the Earl of Wheldon standing above her, a sobbing child in his arms.

"Enough, now, Ethan," murmured the earl encouragingly. "Look around for just a moment and you will see right off that Lady Fairfax is not dead."

"She is," sobbed the child loudly. "I have killed a lady an' Mr. Wevewend Cwanshaw will send me to the giblet!"

A wonderful light lit the earl's eyes and his lips curved upward despite all his attempts to keep them straight and sober looking. And regardless that Annie was truly concerned for her mama, she could not help but grin herself.

Lady Fairfax, pushing the vinaigrette not indelicately away, peered up at Anne and then at the earl and the most inappropriate giggle emanated from between her lips.

"Oh, Mama, are you all right?" asked Anne. "Do you know who I am and where you are?"

"I must only assume," responded Lady Fairfax in an attempt at a most languid tone, "that I am in Lord Wheldon's kitchen and the Reverend Mr. Cranshaw is preparing giblets for dinner." She then giggled again and hiccoughed besides.

"What has happened to Mama?" Constance asked from the doorway, her chestnut curls brushed to a shining glow and her terry poplin gown displaying her neat little figure to perfection. "Good morning, my lord," she added with a smile.

"Good morning, Miss Constance," Lord Wheldon replied, turning to greet her. "Your mama fainted, but she is recovering nicely now."

"I killed her!" sobbed Ethan, attempting to burrow between his lordship's coat and cravat.

"You did no such thing, dearest," offered Anne reassuringly as she rose from beside the couch. "It was simply an accident and my mama will be perfectly fine, Ethan."

"Ethan?" asked Constance crossing the room toward them. "Is it little Ethan from the asylum? Whatever are you doing with Ethan in your arms, my lord?"

"I am attempting to get him to look and see that your mama is not dead, Miss Constance, but he will not do it."

"Oh, oh, there was a rat!" cried Lady Fairfax quite suddenly. "Quickly, Annie, we must get Morgan to come in from the stables and chase the thing off. I had almost forgotten. It was the most hideous, monstrous rat and it attacked me! Why if that child had not come and chased it off, I might have been bitten!"

"It—it—was not a rat, Mama," replied Anne, striving for a most serious demeanor. "It was a ferret."

"A ferret?"

"Yes, my lady," offered Wheldon, "though if one is not quite accustomed to seeing rats or ferrets, I expect one might be mistaken for the other."

"Lord Wheldon," sighed Lady Fairfax rising to a more upright position, "am I to assume that this—ferret—scampering recklessly and unattended about my house belongs to you? How does your mama do it?" she added with a groan.

"Do what, ma'am?"

"Carry on without going entirely mad, sir."

"But Mama likes Fearless," smiled Wheldon as ingenuously as he could manage over the sobbing Ethan.

"Fearless?"

"The ferret, Mama," explained Anne. "She is named Fearless because she is afraid of nothing, not even Lord Wheldon's dogs or his horses."

"Well, and I expect she was not afraid of Mama either," offered Constance.

"Wheldon, give me that child and go find this ferret of yours before my servants are driven into a panic," ordered Lady Fairfax. "And Anne and Constance, you will help him, please. Come, Ethan," she continued, putting her arms gently about the child, "you are not to cry any longer, my dear, because I am not in the least dead and no one is going to send you to the giblet. Uh, gibbet."

* * *

"Oh, deuce take it," mumbled Wheldon as he followed Anne and Constance down the first floor corridor, "I have left my whistle with Ethan."

"Your whistle, my lord?" asked Constance.

"Yes. It is a penny whistle. Generally Fearless will come when you blow it. If you will excuse me, I shall go fetch it."

"Generally Fearless will come?" laughed Constance once his lordship had departed. "Oh, Annie, he is the most charming gentleman. I do so like him, do not you?"

"Oh, yes," Anne replied with a swift nod of her head. "But whatever is he doing with Ethan?"

"Well—well—I explained to him, you know, how the Reverend Mr. Cranshaw meant to indenture the tyke to the undertaker and I—well—I expect I said certain things that made him think I could not bear the thought of it. And—and—"

"And he went off the very next day and took Ethan into his own charge," finished Constance succinctly. "How proud you must be to wield such influence over an earl. Why, your slightest wish is his command."

"Oh, never," giggled Anne nervously. "He merely felt as I did about the matter, I think. I am not one to be wielding influence, Constance, and well you know it. But— but he did come to visit me," she added rather breathlessly.

"I knew it," declared Constance with a wide smile. "Mama would have it that it was I he came to see, but I knew it could not be because I have seen the way he looks at you."

"Have it," interrupted the earl, strolling back to them with a tiny whistle near to buried in his large palm. "Now we must only decide where is the most likely room to find her and go there and whistle. We could whistle from here, but she does tend to take her own sweet time in coming and it will be better if we are as close to her as possible."

"Can we not simply walk about the house blowing the

whistle every now and then?" asked Anne. "Then perhaps we will ferret her out faster."

"You said that on purpose," chuckled Wheldon while Constance fell into gales of laughter.

"Yes, I did," nodded Anne smugly. "I rather like the thought of ferreting out a ferret."

Fearless, however, paid not the least attention to the three human beings wandering about Fairfax House pausing to blow upon a tin whistle every now and then. She was well and happily occupied in Mrs. Danson's kitchen snacking upon a small plate of turbot and not inclined to be distracted from it.

"Oh no," groaned Wheldon as the search party entered that chamber and spied the animal as comfortable as you please upon the kitchen table. "She is gobbling up your dinner."

"Last evening's dinner," offered Mrs. Danson from beside the sink. "I have not yet begun to cook this evening's dinner. So, she is yours, my lord. I thought that must be the case."

"You did, Mrs. Danson?" Anne could not believe how calm the cook seemed.

"Indeed, Miss Anne. See how she cleans her plate—quite as slick as his lordship. And now she must have this bowl of water, I think. And then she will be satisfied."

"Oh, she is a darling," whispered Constance, coming up beside the table. "However could Mama think her to be a rat?"

"A good many people mistake them for rats, Miss Constance, but I, myself, could never see the resemblance," declared Mrs. Danson, setting the bowl of water before her furry guest. "My own papa was used to hunt rabbits with ferrets."

"Thank goodness," grinned Wheldon, "or else you might have brought a meat cleaver down upon Fearless's head rather than having served her the leftover turbot."

The fond look Wheldon bestowed upon Miss Anne as

she joined Miss Constance at the table and ran one long finger down the animal's back was not lost upon Mrs. Danson. Why, his lordship has tossed his cap over the windmill for our Annie, she thought, a very special happiness rising to glow in her eyes. Just look how the gentleman smiles upon her.

The gentleman was not smiling, however, once he had settled the ferret back into his pocket, retrieved Ethan and made his farewells to the ladies. He frowned for the entire carriage ride back to Hunkapillar. And he frowned all the way up the staircase to his chambers. And he frowned all the while Tucker helped him to change his damp cravat and equally damp coat for dry ones.

"What is it, my lord?" asked that worthy as the earl stood before his looking glass tying his gleaming neckcloth into a fashionable Mailcoach. "May I be of assistance somehow?"

"What? Oh, no, Tuck, I shouldn't think so. I have just made a fool of myself again I fear."

"Never, sir," protested Tucker vehemently. He had a great dislike of hearing his lordship refer to himself in such derogatory terms. "You may, perchance, be a bit whimsical from time to time, but you are never a fool, my lord."

"I am a great gawking clunch and well you know it too, Tuck! I went to pay a call upon Miss Fairfax and somehow, though I swore to be on my best behavior, I managed to upset the entire household and cause Lady Fairfax to faint dead away as well."

"Oh, sir!"

"Yes, well you may stare, Tucker. It is because I am a Rayne, is it not? I have inherited all of my papa's tendencies and grandpapa's too. I am mad as a hatter just like the rest of them. I cannot even pay a call upon the woman I love without tossing her household into chaos. I do wish Simms were here."

"The lady you love, my lord? Simms, my lord?"

"Yes, Miss Fairfax, the lady I love. And I wish Simms were here because he might know how Papa won Mama's hand. There must be some secret to it, some way to avoid acting like a Rayne when the necessity arises."

"There is nothing wrong, my lord," declared Tucker heartily, "with acting like a Rayne when that is precisely what one is. Your mama knew exactly what your papa was like before they married. Mr. Simms has told me as much. And she loved your papa because of his—ebullience—not in spite of it. I, myself, have heard her say so time and again to your lordship's sisters."

Seven

Anne stared at herself in the looking glass. The gown did not fit at all. Constance had discovered it in one of the trunks in the attic and seized upon it as a perfect costume for Anne, but there was no way that Anne would be able to wear it. A shimmering gold brocade from the last century, it sported wide panniers, a tightly fitted bodice, and a square-cut neckline edged with filet lace. The color gave a warm glow to Anne's deep brown eyes and highlighted strands of gold in her dark brown tresses, but no matter how much Anne inhaled, Constance could not close the back nor make the waist stay down where it belonged nor tug the quaintly fitted sleeves down around Annie's wrists where they really ought to be.

"And unless I am to walk about in a most awkward squatting position," Anne lamented, "it will never reach my ankles, much less the floor, Constance."

"Well, but we can add to the hem, Annie. There is a length of brocade just matches this in the trunk. And with Mama's tiara and amber necklace, you will look like a queen."

"Yes," sighed Anne, exhaling and popping open the tabs at the back, "a fat queen who cannot afford a gown that fits. Constance, the panniers make me look a veritable mountain."

There was a bleakness and a cracking in her sister's voice that decided Constance on the spot. "You are absolutely correct," she announced abruptly. "This gown will not do at all. Come, I shall help you out of it and into your morning dress." And then, thought Constance, I shall go downstairs and speak to Thomas.

The day had dawned wet and miserable and even as Annie struggled out of the gown a great clap of thunder shuddered through the house. "I shall just pin some patches upon my old wool round gown, wrap Mama's ugly purple shawl about my shoulders, let my hair hang any which way and go as a beggar woman," muttered Anne. "It is a costume party after all, and there will likely be gypsies and the like. A beggar woman will fit in amongst them very well."

"Perhaps," agreed Constance distractedly. "Do not give up hope, my dear. It is only that most of the ladies in our family have been tiny, insignificant little things like myself. But that is not to say that we will find nothing that fits you."

Lord Wheldon will be having a miserable time of it as well, Constance thought, helping her sister to don her grey wool. There cannot be much, not even in the attics of Hunkapillar, that will fit so large a gentleman as his lordship. "Is Thomas in his study do you think, Annie? They will not be hunting today."

"Yes, I think he is going over accounts with Mr. Farmer."

"Good. There is something I mean to ask him." Constance took herself off directly to her brother's study.

"It was a decidedly stupid idea," drawled Averdon peering down with some consideration at the alignment of balls upon the billiard table. "And I am sorry for it, Aubrey. If Mama and Catherine had paused to give it the slightest consideration, they would have tipped to how stupid it was too."

"Actually, it should be quite entertaining, Averdon," offered Lord Desmond, who waited patiently with stick in hand for the duke to take his shot. "At this very moment your attics are overflowing with highly excited ladies and gentlemen."

"Yes, but you will notice, Desmond, that my cousin is not one of the gentlemen. Are you, Aubrey?"

"No," sighed Wheldon, standing with his hands behind his back staring bleakly out at the wildly blowing rain.

"No, and that, Desmond, is because there is no possible way that anything in our attics will fit my cuz, so there is no hope for him to make a costume from that source."

"Wheldon may come in his own rig and announce that he is a modern Gulliver amongst us Lilliputians."

"Cruel, Desmond," droned the duke, taking his shot and missing every single ball on the table. "Thunderation! I swear, Wheldon, I cannot concentrate knowing you are behind me pouting!"

"Shall I leave then?"

"No, ninny, that's not the answer. We shall cease this insipid game and put our heads together and come up with a costume for you. What say you, Desmond?"

"Good idea. You and I, Duke, know what we will wear so we've time enough to lend Wheldon a hand."

"What will you wear?" asked Wheldon, turning to face the gentlemen.

"We shall both be judges, Wheldon, wigs, robes and all," grinned Averdon. "And Catherine has discovered the makings for a most enchanting ensemble which she claims to be representative of the court of Queen Elizabeth, though I beg to doubt it."

"And my Cordelia goes as a shepherdess with crook

and all," laughed Desmond. "Though how she intends to dance with that wicked stick in her hand I cannot guess."

"Come, Aubrey," urged Averdon, giving his cousin an encouraging pat on the shoulder. "We shall all three of us go up into the attics and search every corner. Perhaps we shall discover something that may be added to the clothes you already possess and contrive a costume that way."

The attics of Hunkapillar stretched the entire length and breadth of the mansion. Separated by walls and half-walls, with numerous nooks and crannies, they seemed a giant maze as likely to swallow up the burrowers amongst the treasures as to present them with untold glories. A number of footmen stood in attendance with branches of candles to add to the dismal illumination which filtered through the windows. Countless laughs and giggles and chuckles and cries of delight filled the air. Even Wheldon's countenance gained a bit of brightness as he watched the eager searches and discoveries going on about him.

"We have been through everything in these first two rooms," announced Averdon. "Let us proceed in a westerly direction, eh?"

With immense patience Averdon, Wheldon and Desmond scrambled amongst the remnants of previous generations but there was nothing. Wheldon tried on waistcoats that would not reach from his shoulders to his waist, coats that threatened to split at the seams when he had gotten but one shoulder into them, and numerous hats and wigs and periwigs that merely sat atop his curls without so much as touching his head. They were all of them near to giving it up when the dowager duchess appeared beside them, her arm tucked quite protectively through that of Miss Fairfax.

"Wheldon," she laughed, "dispose of that cocked hat immediately and come here, sir. I have something to show you and this young lady."

"What Mama?" asked Averdon, curiosity shining in his eyes.

"Never you mind, or you either, Desmond. The two of you are well taken care of I believe. What I have to show these two young people is a secret."

Anne could not for a moment believe that Thomas had ordered up the coach and conveyed her to Hunkapillar himself without the slightest protest. Nor could she believe the welcome she had received from the dowager duchess the moment she had stepped inside. And now, most overwhelming of all, she and the Earl of Wheldon were being escorted by that formidable matron down the entire length of the attic followed by a tall footman in livery carrying the most gigantic branch of candles.

"Now, let me see," murmured the dowager releasing her hold on them both and gazing steadily at a blank wall. "It is one of the knotholes, but which one? La, it is so very long since I have come here. I ought to have begun in the king's suite, for that entrance I know."

"Entrance, Aunt? What entrance? This is the wall at the far end of the house."

"No, it is not," mumbled the dowager. "You only think it is, Aubrey, because you lack the suitable imagination. No, that is unfair. Your imagination would quite likely have matched his—everyone thought his head filled with windmills too."

"Whose head, Aunt?" asked Wheldon, excessively curious.

"The Duke of Buckingham, my dear. Ah, of course, it is this one," murmured the dowager, striking a knothole in the wood which looked quite like every other knothole as far as Wheldon could discern. His surprise when a door abruptly sprang inward was surpassed only by that of Miss Fairfax.

"They were all of them terrible scamps, you know. And the then Duke of Averdon and his duchess adored them," she smiled, escorting Wheldon and Anne into a room of quite odd dimensions, being extremely long and narrow. "Grissom, set the candles upon that table, if you please. We shall not need you any longer."

"Yes, your grace," murmured the footman, doing as he was instructed and departing.

"Wheldon, do me the favor to close that door. You need simply give it a shove. Now, we shall see if we cannot do something for you, Miss Fairfax. I was hoping you would think to take advantage of our attics, you know, from the first. I have never actually seen any of these gowns upon a young lady, but I long to do so." With that, the dowager made her way to an ornate armoire and swung open its doors eagerly. "Come closer, my dear, and have a look."

Anne still gazing about, distracted, at the quaint but lovely room which boasted a tremendous canopied bed covered in hangings of red and white and walls painted by a most artistic hand to resemble a pleasant bower, had to be urged again to join the dowager before she crossed the room to peer into the cabinet. "Oh!" she exclaimed then, quite taken by surprise. "Oh, your grace, they are so beautiful!"

"Indeed," nodded the dowager, "and most wonderfully preserved. The armoire is fully lined with cedar, you see, and seals completely when closed. And aside from that, I and all the duchesses before me since the Restoration have seen to it that the clothes are competently cared for. I have not yet shown them to my son's wife, but I shall soon. They are a legacy to be treasured, do you not agree?"

"But, to whom did they belong, your grace?"

"To a most audacious young woman. An actress she was, by the name of Nell Gwynn."

"Nell Gwynn?" gasped Wheldon taking long strides toward the armoire.

"Hush, my dear, they are not the sort of clothes you imagine them to be. They are quite proper, I assure you, and exquisitely sewn, and quite likely to be just Miss Fairfax's size because Nell was no insignificant, diminutive creature."

"No, I should think not," agreed Wheldon nervously running his fingers through his golden curls. "I have seen paintings of her, your grace."

"Yes," laughed the dowager, "and I can imagine what she was wearing in those, Aubrey, but I assure you that she did ofttimes dress like a perfect lady of the court. Miss Fairfax, you shall look through these and select any of them you wish, and then we shall take them down to my chambers and try them on and decide which best suits you and call upon my dresser to make any necessary adjustments, though I doubt there will be much to be done. Nephew, come. There is another armoire at the far end that you, I think, will find even more intriguing."

"Do not tell me, Aunt," grinned Wheldon, "that it is filled with Buckingham's things because even he was not so tall as I."

"No, no, not the Buck's, Aubrey, the king's."

"King Charlie's?"

"Indeed. Buckingham designed the room and painted the walls and ceiling, and supplied the furniture, but it was all for Charles' pleasure. And if I am at all correct, the king was quite near you in size. And if he was not quite so powerfully built about the shoulders, the coats then were not fitted so snugly and there will be room enough to stuff you into them."

The dowager made her way back and forth between the two young people giving her considered opinion on their excited discoveries and once they had both made their final selections, she took the branch of candles in her own hand and led them through a nearly invisible door at the south end of the chamber, down a narrow staircase and through a second door which opened into what had long been known at Hunkapillar as the king's suite.

"Does Lynn know this passage exists?" asked Wheldon

in some awe. "He has never mentioned it, not even when we were boys."

"He has not the least idea," chuckled the dowager. "See how the door disappears. When one does not know of it, it is invisible. But I shall tell him one day," she said with a lift of her finger, "when I am ready. And you, Aubrey, are not to precede me in the matter. Now, off with you to your own chamber. Put yourself in your valet's hands, and see what can be done with you. And you, my dear Miss Fairfax, attend me to my chambers."

Anne could not believe her good fortune. All the way home through the rain and wind she sat tucked up in the old traveling coach, her eyes sparkling and her lips set into a most winsome smile. On the box Fairfax, swathed in a great coat, a wide-brimmed hat and a layer of scarves, drove his bays carefully through the growing mire, a smile upon his countenance as well. His mama would never believe it, so he would not tell her, but Averdon, himself, had confided in him that the Earl of Wheldon had developed a decided *tendre* for Annie. Not Constance—Annie!

Not that Constance was not a dear. It had been she, after all, who had fairly ordered him to drive Annie to Hunkapillar to take advantage of the duchesses' offer to prowl their attics in search of costumes. And that, from the look he had seen on Annie's face, had been a most fortunate idea. Constance was an amazingly good sister and cared as much for Annie as he cared himself. It was just that he was a brother and had but the barest idea of what could be done for the girl. But now, now Annie had prospects! Now, at last, he could pick up that sanctimonious Cranshaw by the seat of his breeches and toss him out through the front door. Well, no, he wouldn't do that. His mama would have palpitations. But at least he need not worry any longer that Annie would never have another beau but Cranshaw, and that was beyond all things encour-

aging. Because, and he must face it, Annie would marry
Cranshaw if no other gentleman took an interest in her.
She would marry him and she would strive to make him
a good wife, because a wife and a mother was exactly what
she wished to be. But how much better if she could marry
a great gun like the earl!

He bought The Valentine and rescued Ethan and
brought me a pear tree, mused Anne, her smile still lingering as the coach jolted over the road. Mrs. Danson is correct. Lord Wheldon is truly a gentleman to be admired.
And Mama is wrong to think him a madman and a bumbler.
He is kind and gentle and funny and must be a blessing
to his mama and his sisters. And the dowager duchess is
most fond of him. Why, she spent all the time while I tried
on those wonderful gowns singing her nephew's praises.
How very lucky I am to have such a gentleman to be my
friend! For that is exactly what he is, she told herself silently, else he would not have come to pay me a morning
call nor have concerned himself with Ethan's fate. Well,
and I shall be a good and faithful friend to him, too.

Oh, if only, she thought then, I could somehow bring
Lord Wheldon to—love me. But that is nonsense, she told
herself. I am not a woman inspires love in a gentleman. I
am much too large and plain. "But I shall strive to be
someone he can respect," she whispered into the emptiness of the coach. "I cannot be a beauty, or a belle, or a
toast, but I can be a trustworthy friend to him and perhaps,
someday, a miracle will occur." Though how any miracle
as great as the most handsome and dynamic gentleman in
all of England suddenly wishing to marry a plain country
girl like herself could possibly happen, she dared not con-
template.

They arrived home safely to the crashing of thunder
amongst the clouds and Anne hurried inside to be met by
a most bemused Dashell. "There are visitors in the drawing
room, miss, and her ladyship hopes you will join them as
quickly as possible."

"Visitors? But who, Dashell? Oh, dear, one of them is not the Reverend Mr. Cranshaw, is it?"

"No, miss. They are the dowager Countess of Wheldon and Lady Cecily and Lady Charlotte Rayne."

"So, this is your eldest daughter, Ermentrude," smiled the dowager countess broadly. She was a woman of commanding presence, with the exact angelic features that made her son so instantly appealing and golden hair that was rapidly changing to silver. "I am so very pleased to meet you, Miss Fairfax. Cecily, Charlotte, come here at once and make Miss Fairfax's acquaintance. We were on our way to Hunkapillar, you see, and one of the horses lost a shoe. So I said to the girls, why do we not stop at the Fairfax's. It has been so very long since I have visited with Ermentrude. Of course," she chuckled, "it has been simply ages since I visited with anyone not a near neighbor. But I did think that this was the perfect opportunity, and so we stopped and sent one of the grooms into Tilby with the horse to have it shod. They will return sooner or later I have no doubt. If they do not drown along the way," she added with a gleam of good humor in her eyes. "We have decided to surprise Aubrey. He will be surprised, I guarantee it."

The two young ladies who presented themselves to Anne with glowing smiles and led her off to the other side of the room where they and Constance had been having the most delightful chat were as similar as any two sisters might be and both possessed of their brother's good looks, though in a much more delicate fashion. Lady Cecily was nearly eighteen and quite looking forward to her promised Season in London and Lady Charlotte, Anne was surprised to discover, a mere twelve years and most excited to be included in this little journey of theirs. For that is precisely what Cecily called it—a little journey—though it had taken them all of two and a half days to travel down from Yorkshire. "And you had to come, of course, Charlotte," Cecily nodded. "Mama expects you to take charge of Aubrey's foxes and carry them back to Brookhaven. Aunt Theo wrote in her letter that he rescued them because of you."

"Yes, indeed he did," acknowledged Anne, grinning at the youngest of the young ladies. "He said just that when he was tucking them into his waistcoat."

"Were you with him?" asked Cecily.

"Constance and I both. We rode out to search for him."

"And we found him upon an outcropping tucking tiny foxes into his coat," giggled Constance. "He said he could not let them there to starve because his Charlotte would never forgive him."

"No, I shouldn't have, either," declared Charlotte with a stubborn cast to her cherubic countenance. "I do not in the least understand how anyone can go about killing foxes and pheasants and innocent little rabbits."

"You will one day, when you marry a gentleman who has fields and crops of his own that he must protect," murmured Anne.

"No, she will not," giggled Cecily, giving her sister's hand a pat. "Charlotte will refuse to understand and the gentleman will be obliged to plant a field solely for the convenience and support of the wild animals."

"Which he will do," spoke up Charlotte confidently, "because he will be my husband and love me and wish to put my mind at ease on the matter just as Aubrey does."

"Your brother plants a field just for the use of the animals?" asked Anne in wonder.

"Indeed, and he does not hunt either."

"But he does hunt," replied Constance. "We have seen him behind the Duke of Averdon's pack. He is the most amazing rider."

Cecily and Charlotte both fell into gales of sweet laughter. "My brother is most exceptional when it comes to hunting," explained Lady Cecily when they had quietened. "He is well-known as a bruising rider, pluck to the backbone, but he has never, I think, been anywhere near a treeing.''

"What, never?" exclaimed Anne.

"Never. Cousin Lynn says he has become famous for always finding somewhere else to be at the close of a hunt. Usually, it is in some tenant's kitchen eating bread and cheese. The gentlemen are forever quizzing him about it, Lynn says, but Aubrey does not care. He would not kill a mouse if it jumped into his lap and spit in his eye. He says it is because of Charlotte, but I rather think Aubrey cannot bear to kill anything.''

"He killed a dog once," offered Charlotte. "I saw him do't.''

"Yes, you were very small. Papa was gone and the dog plagued the tenants. It was rabid. Aubrey took Papa's long gun and shot the beast dead. But that is an entirely different thing, Charlotte. A gentleman must protect his people from such dreadful harm. It is expected of him.''

Eight

"Wheldon rode The Valentine in the hunt this morning," Thomas Fairfax announced excitedly. "Annie, he has got the rascal to do his bidding. They were up and over every rasper and never once did The Valentine attempt to unseat him!" Fairfax's pure exhaltation pulsed nearly visible as he paced the library. "By Jupiter, but Wheldon is a great gun, Annie!"

"And did he take the brush?" asked Anne, her brother's enthusiasm bringing a smile to her countenance.

"Well, no, but that is of no account because he never has been present at a treeing, Annie, much less a brushing. It is one of his eccentricities. All of the gentlemen know so, and they jest about it too. They say he is obliged to turn off near the end of every hunt to forage for food amongst the cottagers."

Anne gazed out the window and reflected with considerable tenderness on Lady Cecily's statement that her brother could not kill so much as a mouse. What a compassionate gentleman he was. Even his actions upon the hunting field spoke of it. "And The Valentine—he obeyed the earl's commands?"

"On the instant."

"Drat!" exclaimed Anne abruptly.

"Drat? But I thought you wished for them to hit it off."

"No, not drat about that, Thomas. It is the Reverend Mr. Cranshaw tooling up the drive in his gig."

"Demme! That gentleman drives me quite mad with all his sermonizing. You are not going to marry him, are you? Please say you do not intend to marry the man, Annie."

"But he is the only gentleman has ever thought to broach the subject to you, Thomas," murmured Anne, moving away from the window. "And though you put him off, I do believe he will bring it up again."

"Well, but you need not accept him. Perhaps some other gentleman will discover he loves you," Thomas replied, his mind awhirl with thoughts of Wheldon. "One never knows."

"I doubt that will happen, Thomas."

"Well but then you shall remain here, Annie. I shall love to have you always with me."

"I have no wish to become a burden to you, Thomas. One day you will marry and set up your nursery and neither you nor your wife will want a spinster sister about to interfere. And besides, my dear, I do want to be married. It is my fondest wish to have a home and babes of my own. But I did think that perhaps, if we were both to accompany Mama and Constance to London in the spring—so that we might rent out Fairfax House, you see, and have a bit of extra money that way—if we were both to accompany them, perhaps I might meet someone—some other gentleman—who could bring himself to offer for me."

"That," cried Fairfax exuberantly, "is an excellent idea!"

"Yes, and it is not as though you must expend a great deal of money to dress me, Thomas, because I shall simply chaperone Constance and no one will expect a chaperon to be all the crack. But do, please, be patient with the Reverend Mr. Cranshaw, because so far he is my only hope for a family of my own and Mama quite expects me to marry him."

Miss Fairfax's only hope was at that very moment being escorted to the drawing room on the first floor and into Lady Fairfax's presence. "I shall fetch Miss Anne," Dashell assured the young lady's mama. He had just descended the staircase and turned in the direction of the library when a knock came upon the door.

The knock sounded again, louder, in a rapid staccato. Dashell turned back toward the front entrance.

The knock grew heavier and more insistent. "Hurry!" a voice called. "Hurry!" A most amazing clattering and clunking and thumping on the opposite side of the door followed this call and Dashell, mystified, hesitated as he put his hand to the latch.

"Whatever is going on?" cried Anne, rushing into the hall followed closely by her brother.

"No, no, cease and desist, you ninny!" exclaimed the voice on the other side of the door. "Get back, do you hear me?"

Anne, eyeing Dashell in wonder, reached for the latch and tugged the door open wide.

Lord Wheldon fairly fell in upon her and would have knocked her to the floor had not Thomas and Dashell both reached out to support them. Attempting to stomp in behind Wheldon, thrusting at him with his great snout, was The Valentine.

"I'm comin', m'lord!" yelled a voice from behind the gelding. "I'm comin'!"

"What is happening?" giggled Anne, attempting to hide Wheldon behind her. "What is The Valentine trying to do?"

"Eat my hair!" Wheldon laughed. "He attempts to munch on my curls whenever I saddle him but apparently his craving has now reached overwhelming proportions. Here, let me," he added, coming out from behind Anne to shove at The Valentine. But no sooner did he draw within reach than the gelding surged forward, stretching his neck and pressing into the opening.

"Lord Wheldon, do go and hide," commanded Annie, still giggling as The Valentine tried for Wheldon's curls. "Thomas, stop whooping. All this laughter is encouraging the wretched beast. Morgan, are you still there?"

"Aye, miss, but I cannot get by the horse to reach 'is bridle. Oren couldn't hold 'im, miss, which was how he got to come af'er his lor'ship in the firs' place."

Anne, tears of laughter now rolling down her cheeks, took hold of The Valentine's bridle, and speaking to him between chuckles, backed the horse out of the doorway and down the steps.

"He actually listens to her," whispered Wheldon as he peered out from behind Fairfax.

"Yes," Fairfax nodded. "He likes Annie very well."

"I do not believe I have ever heard of such a thing," declared the Reverend Mr. Cranshaw eyeing the Earl of Wheldon askance. "What did you do, sir, to entice the monster?"

Wheldon, who now sat sipping at a glass of claret in the Fairfax's drawing room, was still hard-pressed to keep from bursting into laughter. Anne could tell by the way his lips quivered and the muscles in his cheeks twitched.

"I am quite certain that Lord Wheldon did nothing whatsoever," Anne offered in his defense. "The Valentine is a villainous beast and lives to torture all of mankind."

"No, not all of mankind," snickered Wheldon. "Only myself of late. He has forsaken all others to plague me."

"Nonsense," sniffed Lady Fairfax.

"Truth, ma'am," replied Wheldon. "Now I've bought

the beast he has decided to save all of his nonsense for myself alone."

"You have purchased The Valentine?" asked Lady Fairfax, her gaze going immediately to her son.

"Yes, ma'am."

"Why was I not told, Thomas?"

"I thought it best to wait a bit, Mama, because—well—Lord Wheldon might return him, you see."

"Never," drawled Wheldon with a shake of his golden curls. "We are exceedingly fond of each other. I, of his ability on the field and he, of my hair."

"Why that is perfectly wonderful," cried Lady Fairfax. "How much did you pay, my lord, for the beast?"

Thomas's gaze sought Wheldon's and then Anne's found him as well. Something odd was going on. The earl wanted less than anything to cause more ruckus, especially in the presence of the Reverend Mr. Cranshaw, but he could not read from their glances what the two wished of him. "Fifteen hundred, ma'am."

"Fifteen hundred pounds?" gasped Lady Fairfax. "But this is wonderful! My dear," she added, her smile beaming in Anne's direction, "do you not understand what this means? Why you now have a most respectable dowry!"

The Reverend Mr. Cranshaw's eyes sparked at the words. The Earl of Wheldon choked on a swallow of wine and succumbed to a spasm of coughing. When the coughing did not cease, Anne rose and went to clap the earl on the back between his broad shoulders.

"I think—I—need some air," gasped Wheldon. "Will you—excuse me, please?"

"I'll come with you, Wheldon," offered Thomas, and together the two gentlemen left the room.

Anne was distraught. "Perhaps I had better go with them, Mama," she breathed. "The earl is truly choking."

"Nonsense, Wheldon will recover without your assistance, my dear," protested the Reverend Mr. Cranshaw. "Wine in his windpipe is all. No need to put oneself out.

Come sit here by me and we shall discuss the Duchess of Averdon's ball.''

"Do you attend?" asked Lady Fairfax, urging her daughter to a seat beside the reverend with a wave of her hand and a glower.

"Most certainly, my lady. And I have already devised a most intriguing costume. I shall go as a buccaneer."

"A b-buccaneer?" asked Anne, her eyes widening in surprise.

The Reverend Mr. Cranshaw lifted an eyebrow. "It is a costume ball, my dear. You did not expect me to appear in my church robes I hope?"

"Oh, no! But I never thought—wherever did you discover clothes to turn you into a buccaneer?"

"In Lady Fallingham's attic. Lady Margaret Fallingham was so kind as to invite me to join her in a search of their trunks."

The Reverend Mr. Cranshaw bestowed such a look upon her that Anne was quite sure he had expected all along to be invited to search through the Fairfax's attic at her side and she was much relieved that that idea had not occurred to her mama.

And such a thing to think, she scolded herself silently. Here I sit contemplating marriage to this gentleman and I do not even wish him beside me in an attic. Whatever is wrong with me? I know perfectly well what is wrong with me, she sighed inwardly. I am in love with Lord Wheldon. Aubrey, she thought tenderly. Aubrey Edward Rayne. But that is a dream, and nothing more.

"You want to offer for my sister?" gasped Fairfax. "You truly do?" His heart soared as he strolled beside Wheldon through what remained of the garden in winter.

The earl, who had at last ceased his coughing, halted and met Fairfax's gaze. "Say yes or no, Fairfax. I assure you if she accepts you'll not be disappointed in the marriage settlements. I have lost my heart to her, you see. I lost it the moment we met.''

"She slammed the door on you and nearly broke your nose.''

"She has a *tendre* for that blasted vicar, don't she?'' muttered Wheldon. ''That's why you hesitate.''

"Cranshaw?''

"He is everything a gentleman ought to be and not a great clunch like myself. He does not suffer from a plague of whimsicalities. And he ain't poor either, is he? No, I thought not, because his clothes are all the crack, you know. Well, but I am an earl, Fairfax. An earl ought to have some standing with her—though I expect not, if she is already in love.''

"But she is not in love,'' offered Fairfax finding it incredibly hard to keep from laughing.

"She ain't?''

"Not with the Reverend Mr. Cranshaw.''

"Who then? How many suitors has your sister? Numerous, I expect. She is, after all, a veritable Juno. But I do wish I had not been the one to provide her with a respectable dowry, Fairfax. Unfair, I think, to make the least likely of her beaux provide more incentive for the others. Did you see the Reverend Mr. Cranshaw's eyes light up when your mama mentioned it?''

"Yes,'' groaned Fairfax between laughter and pain. ''As if a fire had just been lit in the pit of his belly. Are you certain you have feelings for Annie, my lord?''

"I—every tender feeling ever conceived.''

"Then you have my permission to pay your addresses to her. When did you plan on doing so?''

Fairfax watched a variety of emotions flicker across the earl's countenance, not the least of which was pure joy.

"At the ball,'' replied Wheldon with a grin. ''I thought that would be romantic. My sisters always long for things to be romantic and I expect Anne does as well. You will not warn her of it, will you? Because it will not be nearly so romantic if you do. And perhaps if she does not accept at once, she will think it over just because I have tried to do the thing up proper."

"She does like you, you know," Fairfax said encouragingly. "If The Valentine had attempted to follow me in through the front door, Annie would not have found it the least bit amusing."

"No, but I do not want her to find me amusing, Fairfax. I want her to marry me."

The earl sent his excuses and his farewells by way of Fairfax and did not return to the drawing room. He went instead directly back to Hunkapillar.

"How beautiful," chirped Lady Fairfax as Dashell entered the drawing room just before dinner that evening with a bouquet of snowdrops, jonquils and one red rose in hand. "Look, Constance, what someone has sent you. Is there a card, Dashell?"

"Indeed, my lady," murmured that worthy, "but they are not for Miss Constance."

"Not for Miss Constance?"

"No, my lady. They are for Miss Anne."

"For me?" asked Anne surprised.

"They must be from the Reverend Mr. Cranshaw," nodded her Mama knowingly. "Though how he has managed to procure such lovely blooms in the dead of winter I cannot imagine. Annie, how blessed you are to have attracted such a respectable gentleman."

"Yes, Mama," sighed Anne, taking the bouquet already arranged in a fine Venetian glass vase and setting it upon the table beside her.

"Are you not going to read the card, Annie?" asked Fairfax, confident that he knew who had sent the flowers and that Cranshaw had had no part in it.

Anne, knowing full well that the flowers could only have

come from the Reverend Mr. Cranshaw—most likely an extra attention on his part in respect for her sudden acquisition of a dowry—nodded dumbly. She did not care if they were beautiful and, likely, dreadfully expensive. Her heart did not leap at the sight of them, nor did her pulses race with excitement.

I cannot think why I am so dull, she thought to herself, taking the card into her hand. Yes, I can, she amended. It is because Lord Wheldon left us without a word. He was most terribly embarrassed, of course, first by that awful horse and then by Mama's announcing that his money was to become my dowry. He will never wish to see me again, much less speak with me, and I must give up any hope of his asking me to dance at the Averdon's ball.

Anne glanced down at the card in her hand. It had all been some unattainable dream from the very first. She had known as much. Why had she let herself hope that someone as handsome and sweet and wonderful as the Earl of Wheldon could come to see beyond her plain face and unfashionable figure and find her agreeable? The Earl of Wheldon was—the Earl of Wheldon? Anne's great brown eyes blinked unbelievingly and she held the card farther away to read it more clearly. Imprinted on the tiny square in finely engraved letters was his name: Aubrey Edward Rayne, Earl of Wheldon. And beneath the letters a scribbled line: *May I have the first waltz on St. Valentine's Day, Miss Fairfax, in honor of The Valentine who made us known to each other?* And below that an erratically scribbled signature: *Wheldon.*

"Are they from the Reverend Mr. Cranshaw, Annie?" asked Constance crossing the room to stand behind her sister's chair and peering over Anne's shoulder. "Oh, Annie," she whispered bending nearer her sister's ear. "Oh, Annie, I knew! I knew from the very first when he could not keep his eyes from you and did not see me at all!"

"What?" asked Lady Fairfax. "What is it you say, Constance? Whatever are you about whispering like that?"

"I think the flowers are not from Cranshaw, Mama," grinned Fairfax, watching the blush rise to Anne's cheeks.

"Not from the Reverend Mr. Cranshaw? But of course they are. Who else would they be from, Thomas? It is not as though Anne has a plethora of suitors."

"They are from Lord Wheldon, Mama," murmured Anne, stunned. "He asks me to grant him the first waltz at the ball."

"Wheldon? Oh, my!" exclaimed Lady Fairfax, one hand fluttering to her breast. "Oh, my goodness!"

"Mama, what is it?" asked Constance. "Shall I fetch your vinaigrette?"

"Wheldon," mumbled Lady Fairfax distractedly. "The man has windmills in his head!"

"Yes, but he is an earl, Mama," chuckled Fairfax. "And I should think it an honor that he requests Anne to partner him in advance of the occasion. This may bespeak a certain partiality for Annie on the earl's part, might it not?"

"Yes, it very well might," gasped Lady Fairfax. "But he is a Rayne! Our lives will be Bedlam from morning to night if he has developed a *tendre* for your sister!"

To Lady Fairfax's amazement, however, the Earl of Wheldon did not turn her household into Bedlam for the remainder of the week. True, he did arrive upon her doorstep four days out of five, twice bringing his mama and his sisters with him, but calamity did not dog his heels. He drank his tea instead of having it spilled upon him, made polite conversation, and did not loose any urchins or small animals upon her. And Lady Wheldon and the girls were determined to be most pleasant company.

"Because we know how Aubrey is," giggled Cecily beside Constance on the window seat in the Gold Saloon the afternoon of the day before the Averdon's ball. "Aunt Theo wrote us immediately when Cousin Lynn divined that Aubrey was in love. And once she had read the letter nothing could have kept Mama home."

"She wished to inspect my sister?" asked Constance, a slight frown creasing her brow.

"Oh, no! She wished to keep Aubrey from making a tremendous bumblebath of everything. He has never courted anyone before, you see, and he is always so— exuberant. He is a great deal like Papa was used to be," smiled Cecily. "And Mama says that she remembers exactly what it was like to be courted by Papa and that no young lady ought to face such an onslaught of goodwill without competent advice from one who has suffered through the thing."

Constance's trill of laughter, united with Cecily's, drew Anne's attention as she entered the room on Wheldon's arm, her cheeks pink from the wind and her eyes glowing with merriment.

"How was your drive, my dear?" asked Lady Wheldon with a smile. "It is always an experience to be up beside Aubrey in his curricle, with Carley at the rear. Carley is such an upstart."

"Not anymore, my lady," grinned Anne. "Carley has learned a lesson in respect, I think."

"Never!" interjected Wheldon. "Merely silenced for a brief time. He will find his tongue again shortly."

"Whatever happened?" asked Cecily, tugging Constance with her to the sopha and beckoning Anne to join them. "Aubrey, do go away. You have had Anne all to yourself for most of the afternoon. Now it is our turn to have her."

Wheldon, with a nod of his head, escorted Anne to the sopha and then wandered off at his mama's direction to locate Fairfax.

"What did he do?" asked Cecily quietly. "He did not overturn you, I know, because Aubrey is a regular Jehu."

"Oh, yes, indeed he is," replied Anne, her eyes aglow with good humour. "He must be the finest whip in all of England."

"Yes, but what did he do to set Carley down?"

"Well, it was the most amazing thing. We were on the High Road, you see, between here and Tilby, just before the curve that leads to the bridge across Tasbury Ripple. And I said," Anne's lips quivered upward into the broadest smile. "I said, 'Do you know, my lord, I have never ridden behind a team at more than a sedate trot. I do wonder how it feels when gentlemen like yourself race.' And in an instant Lord Wheldon gave his horses their heads and we sped over the road at such a pace! I thought we would take to the skies! It was the most exhilarating thing!"

"But that would not at all bother Carley."

"Oh, no, it was not the speed, though he and I both clung tightly so we should not be blown away. It was passing the Reverend Mr. Cranshaw's gig on the curve going down on to the bridge. It is very narrow and because of the curve we did not see the gig until we were upon it."

"Mercy!" breathed Constance.

"Yes, exactly," laughed Anne breathlessly. "I thought certainly one or the other vehicle must be overturned. But no! Lord Wheldon slipped by on the inside leaving but a hair's breadth between the wheel hubs. It was so very thrilling. I positively shouted in triumph which I should not have done had I realized how pale and shaking poor Carley had grown. His teeth were still chattering when we reached home and Lord Wheldon had to lift him down and commend him to Morgan's care."

"But you were not afraid, were you?" asked Cecily hopefully.

"Well, your brother did not seem unduly upset and so I trusted he knew what must be done."

"Yes, that is exactly what one must do with Aubrey,"

nodded Cecily. "Trust him. He always knows what must be done. Though at times his method of doing it appears extraordinary. But so it was with Papa and Grandpapa too. Mama will have it that all of the Rayne gentlemen have had an odd kick to their gallop."

Nine

Dark clouds seethed across the moon and lightning speared the skies the evening of the costume ball, but the stable yard at Hunkapillar swelled with coaches and the stables with cattle as the Averdons' neighbors ignored the likelihood of a storm. In the ballroom five chandeliers illuminated the exquisite and often ingenious costumes as the guests gathered amidst an indoor bower created by the female members of the house party.

Anne gazed about her, enthralled. Hothouse roses and snowdrops and jonquils blossomed amidst ferns and mosses attached to every conceivable space. Even pine branches and holly contributed to the decorations, laced and braided into long strands and fastened in some unfathomable way to the ceiling to provide the true feeling of an arbor above one's head. The only thing missing, she thought, was the grass at one's feet. But, of course, one could not possibly lay grass upon a ballroom floor. It would prove wretched for dancing.

In a small recess at the far end of the ballroom a group of musicians from the village of Tilby nervously toodled

and plucked upon their instruments and hoped for the receiving line to dissolve itself and flow into the chamber. And then, thought Anne, the ball will truly begin. How magical it all is! And for the moment it did not matter at all that she would spend most of her time on one of the delicate white chairs or benches sprinkled along the walls in little garden-like groupings. For the moment it was enough to be a part of the wonderful fantasy surrounding her.

And she was a part of it! In Nell Gwynn's flowing robe of red velvet piped with gold, slit at sleeves and shoulders to reveal an inset of golden silk and open down the front to reveal an undergown of the same shining fabric, with her hair fashioned into a crown bedecked with rosebuds and snowdrops by the duchess' own hairdresser, and with a strand of blood red rubies—loaned to her by the dowager duchess herself—fastened 'round her neck and setting off the low bodice of Nell's robe, Anne felt more alive and glowing than ever in her life. She had stepped back through time into another world, where the king himself could love a woman of large proportions and had.

"Oh, Constance, look at him!" Anne whispered excitedly as her gaze fell upon Wheldon entering the room. "He is exquisite! There is not another gentleman equal to him."

And that was no more than truth. With his mother on one arm and his sister Cecily on the other, Wheldon's appearance caused a stir amongst the satrys and the shepherdesses, the gypsies and the courtiers. Even Lady Fairfax gave a gasp as she spied him.

In a long coat of royal blue velvet with silver trim on pockets and cuffs, the sleeves and shoulders slit and inset with sky-blue satin, lace rioting down his shirtfront and foaming from his sleeves, his long legs encased in matching royal blue velvet knee-breeches and white silk stockings ending in coal-black shoes with wide silver buckles, Wheldon caught and held the attention of every lady in the room. His golden curls sparkled. His eyes glistened like sapphires in the glow of a thousand candles. The supple grace of his tall, powerful form was emphasized to such a degree that he made even the Duke of Averdon appear a mere mortal in the presence of a Zeus.

When he led the duchess out on to the floor to open the ball Anne could not keep her eyes from him. And when he danced next with his mother and then with his sister, she felt her heart beating in time with his every step. And when at last he came to claim his waltz and led her to the floor she was overcome by the nearness of him and her face flushed and her heart panicked and her senses seemed to go all awry,

"How lovely you look," Wheldon murmured as he placed one gloved hand firmly at the small of her back and took her hand with the other. "You are perfection, Miss Fairfax. Nell could not have been more beautiful than you are at this very moment."

The music began and he swept her into a wide circle, the smile on his face and the glow in his eyes bringing even more of a blush to Anne's cheeks. To dance with him was sheer wonder. She floated over the floor in his arms as if she weighed not one ounce more than Constance or Cecily or any of the other young ladies of dainty and demure proportions. Nor did her height at all occur to her, except for the novelty of needing to look upward to meet Wheldon's bemused glance. And his glance was bemused. So much so, in fact, that it brought a wide grin to Anne's countenance. "What is it?" she asked. "You look so—"

"Entranced?"

"Well, I was going to say bewildered," chuckled Anne.

"That, too," agreed Wheldon with a nod. "Do you know that your voice is like the lazy drone of bees in my summer garden and that your eyes glow with the warmth and comfort of my hearth on a frigid winter's night? And when you blush, as you are now and very prettily too, I see all the innocence of my youth."

"My lord," murmured Anne, "such fustian!"

"No, Miss Fairfax, it is not fustian."

"Spanish coin, then."

"Good, solid, English gold. You are the most exquisite woman I have ever known."

A frown replaced Anne's smile. "I am not a gudgeon, Lord Wheldon. I do have a looking glass. I know I am an enormous woman with a plain face and cow eyes and hands the size of omlette pans. It is unkind in you to make sport of me."

"Make sport of you?"

"Yes," replied Anne, tears starting to her eyes. "I have had to watch myself grow taller and larger and more unattractive my entire life and I have accepted it. And I do not appreciate your spewing such nonsense at me."

"But Anne—"

"I thought—I dreamed—" stuttered Anne, fighting to hold back the tears that threatened, "that someday some gentleman might—*like* me for what I am. But—but—"

She seemed about to tug free of his arms and run from the floor in the midst of the waltz, and Wheldon, confused and fearing to lose her, pulled her more closely to himself, overwhelming her with the sudden power of his embrace.

"Do not. Oh, please, do not," sobbed Anne. "Let me go, my lord, before I embarrass you no end."

"No," replied Wheldon in an urgent whisper. "You do not embarrass me, Anne, nor can you ever do so. Whatever I have said to discompose you, I beg you to forgive it. I am a great gawking clunch and I knew I should make a mess of it. But—I have spoken nothing but the truth. I do love your voice and your eyes. I love everything about you, Anne. I love your aplomb when faced with ferrets and foxes and your compassion and your sense of humor. And I love your strength and your fortitude, for I have seen that too, blind though you undoubtedly think me. And I love the way you fit in my arms, as though God created you particularly to fit there. Look at me, Anne, please. You are the woman I have yearned for forever. Do not tell me I have lost you only because I cannot find you less than what you are.''

The waltz came to an end just there and Anne, tears streaming down her cheeks, spun from his arms and rushed through the open French windows and out on to the balcony leaving Wheldon staring helplessly after her.

"Darling," murmured a pleasant voice as two firm hands grasped Wheldon's arm, "you cannot remain standing in the middle of the floor."

"Mama," Wheldon acknowledged, looking down, "I have said something very wrong."

"Come and sit with me a moment, Aubrey."

"No, but, Anne is gone out on to the balcony. And I know I ought to follow her, but she don't want me."

"Her brother will go after her, Aubrey. See, there is Fairfax stepping out to the balcony just now. Your Anne will be perfectly safe in his care."

"But, Mama," murmured Wheldon, allowing Lady Wheldon to lead him to one of the groupings of chairs, "I have made her cry. I ought to go to her but she does not want me, I think."

"What did you say to her, Aubrey?"

"I have no idea. I mean, I only said how beautiful she was and she called me a liar and said I was making sport of her."

"And did you tell her that you are not a liar and would never think to make sport of her?"

"I told her I loved her, Mama. And that I could not help how I saw her. She is beautiful and she is wonderful. Is it because I am such a great gawking clunch she wants nothing to do with me?"

Lady Wheldon attempted unsuccessfully to hide a smile. "You are not a great gawking clunch, dearest."

"Yes, I am."

"Why do you think so?"

"I am not blind, madam, or stupid. I need only recall my general experience—oh!" exclaimed Wheldon softly.

"Oh?"

"*You* think that I am handsome, do you not, Mama?"

"Extremely. A vision of style and symmetry and extremely intelligent to boot."

"And that is just the thing, is it not? Yes, that is exactly the thing!"

"Good. Now you may go out on to the balcony and explain it to Miss Fairfax. And do not harrass her, Aubrey. She may require more time than you to understand, because she has not had the advantage of ten sisters and a papa with windmills in his head."

The Reverend Mr. Cranshaw, dashing in his buccaneer garb, had not missed a moment of the argument that had gone forward upon the dance floor. And when Wheldon had pulled Miss Fairfax closer within his arms and tears had begun to streak Anne's cheeks, the Reverend Mr. Cranshaw's heart had soared.

For over a year Cranshaw had taken for granted that sooner or later Miss Anne Fairfax would be his. He did not credit Fairfax's opposition to him. The young woman would be of age in a matter of months and Fairfax's consent would no longer be necessary. Cranshaw had been certain of Miss Fairfax. Who else, after all, was there to offer for her? Why she was a travesty—but exactly the kind of travesty Cranshaw craved. She was a Fairfax, an ancient and honored name that would add much to his esteem. And yet she would be grateful to him for marrying her and therefore satisfied with whatever he chose to give her. She would be eager to do his bidding and to make him comfortable. And she would certainly never be demanding. No, a woman of Miss Fairfax's unfortunate size and obvious unattractiveness would know better than to be demanding of her husband.

And then that insufferable Wheldon had appeared and posed a serious threat to his plans. At least, Cranshaw had thought the gentleman might prove a threat, for Wheldon had looked upon Miss Fairfax with a particularly suspect gleam in his eye. But now everything would be as it should be. He need only go to her and provide Miss Fairfax a word of comfort, declaiming against the ungainly giant and taking Miss Fairfax's side in the argument. And that was precisely what he would do.

His back straight, his head cocked, proud of his appearance in the swashbuckling outfit which became him admirably, the Reverend Mr. Cranshaw made his way to the balcony.

"Now, now, Anne, my dear," he declared, coming up behind the young woman who was crying upon her brother's shoulder and placing a hand upon her back. "What has that great oaf said to you to make you so unhappy?"

"Go away, Cranshaw," muttered Fairfax. "It is none of it your concern."

"Oh, but it is, Thomas. This is the woman I wish to marry, you know, and all that gives her pain concerns me most dearly."

"Balderdash," grumbled Fairfax. "It is none of your affair."

"I beg to differ with you, Fairfax, but all that happens to dear Anne is my affair. Do you go away and let me comfort her."

"Not on your life," declared Fairfax. "She don't want any of your comfort, do you, Annie?"

"N-no," replied Anne with a muffled sob. "I only w-want to go home, Thomas."

"Yes, and so we shall, sweetling. Very soon."

"Come, Anne, tell me what he said to you," urged Cranshaw. "If he has offended you to such a degree as it seems, I shall take the great clunch aside and deal him a sermon he will not like forget for a thousand years. Yes, and I shall see to it that the others at this party discover how despicable he is, too."

"He is not a great clunch!" exclaimed Anne, turning about in her brother's arms to face the Reverend Mr. Cranshaw. "He is not despicable! Do not you dare to call him so! It is people like you make him think himself less than he is!"

"Indeed, and who make you think yourself less than you are, too, Miss Fairfax," Wheldon's voice rumbled before him as he came across the balcony. "I believe Miss Fairfax has expressed a wish to be relieved of your company, Cranshaw."

"Pah! It is you she has no wish to see."

"That is between Anne and myself and I shall deal with it. Will you leave, or must I toss you over the rail? I will and with the greatest good will, I assure you."

"Yes, and I shall help him," muttered Fairfax.

The Reverend Mr. Cranshaw looked from one to the other of them, his lips drawn into a most unbecoming sneer. He then bowed regally to Anne. "I know you are most distraught, my dear, and so I shall not take offense at your wishing me gone. You must only summon me and I shall be back at your side within moments." He then departed without a backward glance.

"And now you, my lord," Thomas Fairfax murmured. "Annie does not want to speak to you either."

"Y-yes, I d-do, Thomas."

"You do?"

"Uh-huh, but do not go away."

"No, I shan't, Annie."

"No, because I want you to hear everything."

"But why?"

"Because—I depend upon you, Thomas, to tell me what is true. You have never lied to me. You will not lie to me now."

Lord Wheldon's eyes in the light of the Chinese lanterns now swinging in an undecided wind, caught at Thomas's and Fairfax was surprised to discern an amused glint in them.

"Yes, you are her brother and she will believe what you tell her," Wheldon said solemnly but with a hint of a smile. "Tell her she is beautiful, Fairfax."

"You are beautiful, Anne," murmured Fairfax. "Most especially tonight. That gown becomes you so."

"I am—beautiful?"

"To me, dearest sister and to Constance as well, you have always been exceedingly beautiful."

"There, you see, it is just what my mama said. And what you said too, Annie," roared Wheldon ecstatically.

"What *I* said?"

"You said it was people like Cranshaw made me think myself less than I am. And do you know, that is exactly it. When *you* look at me, Miss Fairfax, do you see a great gawking clunch? Because that frightened me, you know. I thought you might. I thought sure you did when you stormed away."

"Oh, no. Do never think such an ugly thing, my lord," replied Anne moving out of her brother's arms to take Wheldon's hands in her own. "You are handsome and strong and funny and most, most kind. You are like a Greek god come down to stroll amongst the mortals. So, too, must King Charles have looked amidst the puny macaronis of his court."

"And as you look, so must Nell have looked amidst such puling maids as were hailed by his macaronis," responded Wheldon, grinning and pulling her closer. "Can you not understand, my dearest Anne? What you have seen all these years in your looking glass is not what I see. It is a vision of yourself colored by the comments of people who do not look upon you with the eyes of uncompromising love. But Fairfax loves you beyond anything, and to him you are beautiful. And your sister loves you without condition, and to her you are beautiful. And I have loved you, Anne, with my whole heart and with my whole soul, from the first moment I laid eyes upon you, and to me you are the most beautiful woman in all the world.''

"Hear! Hear!" concurred Fairfax. "May I go now, Annie?" he asked, with an embarrassed smile. "I rather think there are things Wheldon means to say that would be better said in my absence. Deuce take it, it's beginning to rain!"

"Beginning? It's coming in buckets. Inside before we drown!" roared Wheldon as the storm crashed over them. Lightning sparked and crackled across the park. Thunder rattled the windows as the three hurried back into the ballroom.

"They are waltzing again, Anne," Wheldon grinned as he took a handkerchief from his pocket and gently wiped the tears, which had mixed with raindrops, from her cheeks. "Will you waltz with me one more time? The breeze we shall make will dry us off," he added teasingly.

"I am not so very wet, my lord," Anne replied, her mind reeling and at the same time numb as she puzzled over his words upon the balcony.

"Then waltz with me because you are compassionate, Miss Fairfax," murmured Wheldon.

"Because I am compassionate?"

"Yes, I am desolate that I made you cry and I long to be forgiven for it."

"I do forgive you."

"Then waltz with me, Annie, to prove that you forgive me."

Anne nodded solemnly and Wheldon swept her on to the floor and into the waltz. For the longest time he stared down at her saying nothing and Anne was most uncomfortably aware of his silence. Then as they dipped into a wide turn, the earl chuckled.

"What?" asked Anne. "Why do you laugh, my lord?"

"Aubrey. My name is Aubrey, and I should be thankful were you to call me by it. And I must beg your pardon for making free of your name without your permission, should I not? May I call you Anne?"

"Y-yes," nodded Anne. "But you did not tell me why you laughed, my lo—Aubrey."

"Because you are being so solemn. And because I am such a failure at being romantic. I meant to sweep you off your feet and into my arms this night, you see. And instead I sent you weeping into your brother's arms."

"Which was not romantic at all," Anne replied, a smile trembling to her lips.

"Not at all. Shall I tell you something else that is not romantic, Annie?"

"What?"

"These shoes are too small and at this very moment my toe is poking out the left one."

Anne glanced down at the offending toe and giggled.

"That, my dear, is much better," murmured Wheldon. "I have said that I love you, Anne. Might you—do you think you could possibly come to love me? No, do not grow solemn and thoughtful and do not let that somber look which I can see dawning take residence upon your countenance. I have your brother's permission to pay my addresses to you, my dear Miss Fairfax, and I wish to marry you and share my life with you to my dying day, but I do not wish to have you doubting my words and my intentions and speaking badly of yourself again. So I shall only ask you now to consider my suit and when you have done so to your own satisfaction, you will give me your answer. You may take hours or days or weeks or months, Anne. I vow I will wait for however long it takes you to decide."

A crash of thunder so close that it actually sent the chandeliers to quaking above their heads punctuated this speech. The musicians faltered and somewhere below stairs shouting could be heard. In a moment a footman in full livery came rushing into the room calling excitedly for the Duke of Averdon.

"What is it, Dale?" asked Averdon loudly, making his way through the crowd.

"Lightning has struck the stables, your grace," gasped the footman in a rush. "The stables are aflame!"

Averdon was off at a run, every other able-bodied gentleman after him, into the corridor, down the rear stairs and out into the storm.

Ten

Rain like pellets of ice sizzled across the stable yard. The wind raged. Horses screamed. Ghastly specters of courtiers, gypsies, buccaneers and country squires, drenched to the skin, struggled to pull and push coaches, to clear a wide path to the stable doors amidst scorching heat and flashes of lightning, while around and above them fire roared louder than the thunder.

Ladies in gowns and hoops and flowing robes united with serving girls, ladies' maids and even the housekeeper to discover buckets and fill them and shuttle them hand over hand down a long line toward the gentlemen and footmen and valets and grooms who rushed into the heat of the flames to toss water urgently and wildly but ineffectively upon the savagely burning building.

Blazing faggots, seized by the gale, spun upward into the night air and flared and hissed and fell back toward earth springing to flame again on coach tops and coat sleeves, on leather and lace while sickeningly sweet smoke scorched nostrils and throats and narrowed eyes and forced tears down soot stained faces.

Annie, her heart pounding, prayed as she swung bucket after bucket toward the blaze. Her eyes frantically searched the specters for a sight of Wheldon. And then she saw him, spinning away from the back of a coach and hurling himself against the wind toward the stable doors. The horses, she thought. Thank God, he is going for the horses. In a moment Averdon and her brother Thomas and Lord Fallingham in his courtier's costume were fighting their way into the stables behind the earl. And moments after that frenzied, screaming, panicked horses erupted into the yard and fled before the flames. Shouts and bellows from the gentlemen outside the doors, slapping hands and beating coats and swinging sticks forced the great beasts away from the bucket brigade and off across the yard into the park at the side of the mansion and farther into the home woods.

"Miss, miss," screeched a voice near Anne and she turned to find the little tiger, Carley, tugging at her gown. "The roof be comin' down an' Ethan be los' in there!"

"Ethan?" shouted Anne over the noise of fire and storm. She abandoned her place in the line to kneel before Carley and pull him close. "Ethan is in the stable?"

"Aye, in there!" screamed Carley back at her, tears streaming down his face, his finger pointing at the conflagration. "We was playin' wif Fearless in the hay. I done dragged Ethan out, miss, but he runned back in af'er Fearless!"

"My God, does Lord Wheldon know?"

"I couldn't fine 'im! I couldn't fine 'im," wailed Carley. "An' wouldn't none o' t'other gen'lemen lis'en ta me!"

"You stay here, Carley," Anne ordered. "Take my place in the line. And do not leave, do you hear me?"

Carley nodded and sobbed and stepped up into the bucket brigade.

Anne, her hair loosed and hanging, her lovely robe covered in mud and soot and water, lifted her skirts and ran, straining against the wind, toward the stable doors.

Smoke burned her nostrils and the heat nearly over-whelmed her as she struggled inside the burning building, but she refused to be turned back. Thomas and Lord Fallingham and Averdon met her just inside the door, and she was nearly trampled beneath the hooves of lunging horses. Thomas grabbed at her skirt and pulled her aside.

"What are you doing here?" he shouted.

"Aubrey! Where is Aubrey?"

"Gone to the box stalls at the rear. We have got them all out but The Valentine," bellowed Fairfax. "Go back, Annie, now!"

"No! No! Ethan is in here, Thomas! Little Ethan is in here!"

"Damnation!" exclaimed Fairfax, spinning away from Anne to catch Fallingham just before he hit the floor.

"Help me get him out!" Averdon yelled over the constant howling of the flames. "He cannot breathe, Fairfax. Help me get him out and away from the smoke!"

Annie left her brother and Averdon bending over Fallingham and ran deeper into the building, the heat searing her face and forcing her to a slower stumble the farther in she went. Around her burning beams shuddered and swung loose, smoke bellowed and the wind and the fire roared. "Aubrey!" she shrieked. "Aubrey! Ethan, where are you! Answer me!"

Coughing, slowing to a teetering walk, Annie grabbed at her hanging locks and brought her drenched, waist-length hair over her shoulder and up to cover her mouth and nose. "Aubrey!" she screamed through the wet mask. "Ethan! Aubrey!"

Just as she thought she could stumble forward no longer a strong hand grabbed at her arm and jerked her to the right. Wheldon hauled her into his arms and pulled her along with him to the floor of a partially destroyed box stall. "Easier to breathe down here," he gasped, shoving her to the side to avoid The Valentine's nervously dancing hooves.

"Ethan is in here!" yelled Annie above the monstrous groaning and snapping and hissing of the fire. "We must find Ethan!"

"Beneath The Valentine!" Wheldon shouted back, pointing.

Annie's heat-seared glance turned to the space just beside them. Under the great horse's belly, between the carefully dancing hooves, huddled low upon the floorboards, lay Ethan.

A sharp crack shuddered the walls around them.

"The beam is giving way!" Wheldon shouted. And before Annie could understand what it was he meant to do, he reached under The Valentine and tugged Ethan recklessly to them and thrust him into Annie's arms. He tossed the coat he had already shed over the both of their heads and tore off his shirt, tying it in one urgent movement over the gelding's eyes and then, grabbing a handful of The Valentine's mane he mounted the shuddering horse's bare back and stood up upon it, stretching his arms toward the long beam that supported the ceiling above the stall.

"Hold, Val. I'll not forsake you! Steady old fellow! Take the boy and run, Annie! Go now!"

Anne choked on sobs and smoke as she rose with Ethan in her arms. The Valentine had ceased his dancing and stood motionless and silent amidst the Hades that had been a stable. Only the excited twitching of his nostrils and his shuddering betrayed his panic. Balanced precariously upon the great beast's back, the Earl of Wheldon, his gloves beginning to smoulder, held the thick, long beam that supported what remained of the ceiling above the stall, held it above his head, every muscle in his body straining to keep back the burning rubble that strove to come cascading down upon them engulfing them all in flames.

"Hold, Val! Run, Annie! Hurry!" he bellowed, and Anne, a great obstruction in her throat that had nothing to do with the smoke or the fire, pulled the coat farther over her own and Ethan's head and stumbled out of the stall. She could see nothing but smoke and flames. She could hear nothing but her own and Ethan's tortured breathing. And every ounce of her wanted to turn back into the stall and pull Wheldon down into her arms and die all four of them together, she and Wheldon and Ethan wrapped in each other's arms beside The Valentine. But she drove the thought from her mind. Wheldon had chosen to sacrifice himself for her and for a poor orphaned boy. She could not let such a noble deed be performed in vain. She put one foot doggedly in front of the other, tumbling into a rail, careering off a post, tangling one slipper in her skirts and nearly falling. And just as she thought she could never find the way out, that she had turned wrong somehow, that she could carry Ethan not one more step, hands seized her and took the child and she was lifted up into strong arms and out into the sizzling rain.

Fairfax and Averdon carried their burdens as far from the building as they could, both of them gasping for breath, Averdon stumbling once under Annie's weight. And just as Averdon set Annie upon her feet the most monstrous crash turned all their gazes to the burning building. The great obstruction in Annie's throat flew upward and out in a scream of terror and rage and unrestrained sorrow and split the air around them as the stable roof collapsed, the walls fell inward and a great ball of flame rose into the grey and black and orange night sky. And then, like Pegasus with Zeus aboard, shooting directly from the fireball, The Valentine, unblinded and with Wheldon astride, leapt fallen rafters and buttresses and spiked and burning boards into the relative safety of the stable yard. As the gelding stumbled to an unsteady halt Annie tore off her thoroughly drenched robe and rushed forward. She grabbed Wheldon's arm, jerked him from the horse's back and shoved him to the ground, throwing the heavy, wet velvet over him.

"The Valentine!" Wheldon yelled up at her, rolling over and over in the mud, stripping the robe from himself even as he did so. "Put it on Val!" he shouted, tossing her robe back to her. "He will let you, Annie! Do not let him burn!"

Anne seized the robe and swung about to toss it over the horse's back only to find that Averdon was already clinging to The Valentine's ears, bringing his head down to hold him still, and a number of other men were slinging wet coats and buckets of water all over the horse. She turned back to the earl then and knelt down in the muck of the stable yard. He had ceased to roll about, and she lay her ruined red velvet robe over him and placed his head in her lap, playing her fingers through his singed and soot-covered curls. Thomas, a sobbing Ethan in his arms, came to stand over them. On the ground beside Anne, where she had discarded the coat Wheldon had placed over her head, one of the coat pockets began to wiggle. Anne, dazed, stared at it uncomprehendingly. The sodden, burnt, muddy material lurched and popped upward and shuddered. And then, chattering and chuckling all unheard beneath the storm, a grimy Fearless scrambled out into the open air, scurried over Annie's knee, went to sit on Wheldon's shoulder, and set herself to licking the mud from the earl's chin.

Anne sat in silence, her hands folded in her lap, gazing out through the windows of the Gold Saloon at a sky of warm blue dotted with puffs of white cloud. It had been three weeks since the fire and though messages had been sent and received, she had not actually seen the Earl of Wheldon since three strong gentlemen had assisted him up the staircase at Hunkapillar. His mama and his sisters had come to visit and had assured her that he was recovering. Thomas had gone to see him and come back with the amused word that Lord Wheldon and The Valentine shared the same physician and that both were irascible but doing well.

But I wish to see the man for myself, thought Anne, angrily. What balderdash these customs are that forbid me entrance to his chamber. Well, I shall abide by them no longer. I do not care one fig what Mama or the dowager duchess or even Aubrey's mama says. I will see him whether they approve or not. I will see him if I must fight my way into his chambers. Surely, surely, they must understand. I love him. I love him with all my heart and I cannot bear to have him locked away from me. It is callous and unfeeling. He will think I care nothing for him, that I despise him. After all he has done, not to go to him is quite like saying I despise him.

Tears started to Anne's eyes at the thought that he should gain such an opinion of her through no fault of her own, but she dashed them away with the back of her hand. I shall don my riding habit and order one of the hacks saddled and if Mama asks where I am off to, I shall say that I am dull and long to gallop across the fields. And if I must take Morgan with me—well, he cannot betray my destination until we are returned and then it will make not the least bit of difference. "I shall sneak into Hunkapillar if I must," she declared in a stubborn whisper.

"Pardon, Miss Anne?" asked Dashell from the doorway.

"Oh, I did not see you there, Dashell. It is nothing. I was just speaking a thought aloud."

"Indeed, miss. I have been instructed to inform you, Miss, that there are a number of ladies and gentlemen wishing to see you."

"A number of ladies and gentlemen?"

"Just so, Miss."

"You must show them into the morning room then and inform Mama and Constance."

"I think not, Miss. They are in the courtyard and will not come in. Lord Fairfax has gone out to them and sent me to fetch you."

"Very well, I shall go down at once," replied Anne list-lessly. Botheration! she thought. And just when I have decided upon my course. Now I will be forced to delay until these visitors take their leave. And Thomas will be about, wanting to know where I am bound. With a sigh, Anne rose and followed Dashell back down the corridor, down the staircase and to the door which he opened for her, a most disturbing smile flickering across his counte-nance.

Anne, not stopping to so much as wrap a shawl about her, thinking that the lingering chill in the air would permit her to make her excuses quickly and send the visitors on their way, stepped out into the morning sunshine and came to a most surprised pause upon the top step.

"What? Will you not come down and greet us properly, Miss Fairfax?" asked a laughing voice that made her heart leap with joy. "And we have come all this way, and brought you posies."

"Aubrey!" Anne squeaked and in a moment she was down the steps and engulfed in his waiting arms.

"Enough," chuckled Wheldon, bestowing a kiss upon her cheek and then setting her back from him. "While I detest the necessity of loosing you from my arms for even a moment, there are two gentlemen here come most re-spectfully to give you thanks. Now, you rascals," called Wheldon over his shoulder and behind him the door of the coach before which he stood sprung open and Carley and Ethan tumbled excitedly out all clean and polished and dressed impeccably in the earl's livery, each boy with a tiny bouquet of hot-house roses and jonquils clutched in both hands.

"We picked 'em ourselfs," declared Carley proudly, thrusting his flowers up under Anne's nose.

"They is fwom all of us!" announced Ethan with a most enchanting smile.

"From *all* of you?"

"Indeed," nodded Wheldon soberly but with a most

amused gleam in his eyes. "Ethan, you have let the coach door swing shut behind you and so all of you are not quite present."

"Oh!" squeaked Ethan, and thrusting his bouquet into Annie's hands ran back to the coach, opened the door and climbed in.

The dark curls disappeared for a moment and then they were back. Little hands dangled a sleek ferret over the top step and then freed Fearless to scramble down on her own. The dark curls disappeared again and then reappeared and one after another five tiny foxes tumbled down the carriage steps into the courtyard.

"We know you did not rescue the foxes, Anne," explained the earl as he bent and scooped the ferret up and placed her in Annie's arms where Fearless immediately set about sniffing and tasting the flowers in Annie's hands, "but if you had not rescued Ethan, you see, they would have been without their official keeper and very sad."

Anne could not keep from laughing as the ferret ate a rose petal and the foxes scrambled around her skirts, Ethan and Carley both attempting to herd them one way and then the other.

"And there is one last gentleman come to call upon you," grinned the earl. "Now, Fairfax."

Anne followed the earl's gaze and sighed as her brother led The Valentine out from behind the coach. He was scrubbed and brushed and though a few tiny bald spots could be seen through his hair, he arched his neck proudly and walked with a most regal bounce in his step. Roses and jonquils and snowdrops had been braided into his mane and tail and a wreath of flowers fitted about his neck.

"You did not have such a wonderful and romantic St. Valentine's Day as I had planned for you to have, my dearest Miss Fairfax," whispered Wheldon in her ear, "so I am hoping that perhaps we can make this a second St. Valentine's Day, and who better to symbolize it than The Valentine himself?"

"He is splendid," breathed Anne.

"Indeed he is," smiled Wheldon staring down at her and not glancing at the horse at all, "but not nearly as splendid as you, my dear. You are the most splendid of all God's creatures. I know I promised to give you all the time you required, Annie, but I am hoping—I am hoping—"

Anne, her heart near to bursting with love and joy and pride and mirth at the spectacle surrounding her could wait no longer. She caught the ferret in one hand and passed her to Ethan, scooted a fox kit from between her feet and standing on tip-toe, threw her arms, posies in one hand, about his neck and drawing him down to her, pressed her lips eagerly to his.

"Does that mean you *will* marry me?" asked Wheldon breathlessly with the most innocent countenance when at last their lips had parted.

"Yes," giggled Anne. "Yes, yes, yes, most certainly, yes!"

"Yes!" shouted Wheldon. "She said yes!"

"Hurrah! Hurrah!" screeched Carley and Ethan, dancing merrily about.

"Hurrah!" shouted Fairfax, laughing quite uninhibitedly and waving upward at the house.

"Hurrah!" came Constance's voice on a charming trill of laughter. "Mama she has said yes. Annie has said yes!"

The earl folded a giggling and most starry-eyed Miss Fairfax into his arms and pressed his lips to hers once again. He kissed her so long and so passionately that Annie thought she would burn up with fever right there in the courtyard. And then most suddenly he lurched forward and their lips parted.

"I am sorry," called Fairfax. "He pulled free. I should run for the door if I were you."

"Run, Annie!" laughed Wheldon, taking her hand in his. "The Valentine is after my hair again! Run!"

"I thought—I thought you had c-conquered him," giggled Anne as a grinning Dashell, who had not left his post in the doorway, ushered the dashing, laughing pair over the threshold.

"Conquered? Conquered?" chuckled Wheldon sinking down upon the stairs and pulling Anne down atop him as Dashell closed the door with himself on the outside of it. "If I have conquered your heart, Annie, I do not care a fig for conquering The Valentine. He may eat my hair and bite my knee and send me flying over his head for the rest of our lives, and I shall smile each time he does so. That great, wretched, most noble beast has given me you. For that extraordinary gift, The Valentine shall continue victorious for the rest of his days."

ABOUT THE AUTHOR

Judith A. Lansdowne grew up in Kenosha, Wisconsin. Following graduation from high school she moved to New York City where she attended the American Academy of Dramatic Arts and spent several years acting and puppeteering. She returned to the midwest to continue her education, and after receiving her BA from the University of Wisconsin-Parkside worked as a scriptwriter, videographer, journalist and editor before turning to fiction writing full time. She and her husband recently retired to the shores of Lake Guntersville, Alabama where they are pursuing careers in fishing. They write when the weather is bad.

Judith is the author of three Zebra regency romances: *Amelia's Intrigue, The Bedeviled Duke* and *Legion's Ladies* (now on sale at bookstores everywhere). Judith loves hearing from her readers and you may write to her c/o Zebra Books. Please include a self-addressed stamped envelope if you wish a response.

The Valentine's Day Husband

Carol Quinto

One

Deborah Kensington awoke to the sound of whispers and giggles from the bedchamber adjoining hers. For a moment she wondered that Emily and Fanny were stirring on a cold February morning. Usually, she had to scold her younger sisters to roust them from their beds. Then she remembered. Today was Tuesday, the fourteenth day of February—St. Valentine's Day.

Deborah drew the quilt about her shoulders, savoring its warmth and comfort for a few more minutes. The wind whistled outside her window and she knew the floor would be like ice. She did not share her sisters' eagerness to face this morn—or their belief in foolish old legends. To her mind, St. Valentine's Day was just a pretext for merrymaking in the village, and an excuse for neglecting one's chores. But there was little she could do about the girls, not when Mama encouraged them to believe in such nonsense.

Fifteen-year-old Fanny stuck her curly red head in the door. Her large, expressive green eyes registered dismay. "Deb, why are you still abed? Oh, do hurry, or by the time we get to the village, all the good husbands will be spoken for!''

Emily, the older by one year, and newly conscious of her status as a young lady, nudged her sister. "Come along, Fanny. Deborah thinks she is too good for anyone from the village, but we shall go without her. It's what she prefers.''

Deborah heard but refrained from answering. It was not that she thought she was too good, she was . . . just different. Fully awake now, she pushed aside the muslin curtains that draped the high poster bed and reached for her wrapper. She noted gratefully that Mary had been up earlier and lit the fire, and a pitcher of water stood beside the basin on the wash stand. Probably cold by now, Deborah thought, for she had slept unaccountably late.

She washed quickly, dressed, then sat down by the window to brush out her long hair. She had braided it the night before, and now it cascaded down her back in crinkly waves. Neither blond nor brown but falling somewhere betwixt the two shades, her hair was one of the things that set her apart from her sisters. Both Emily and Fanny took after their father, their hair the same fiery red as Sir John's. The girls had also inherited his short stature and a tendency to plumpness, but Deborah was as tall and as slender as her own mother.

She picked up the miniature portrait of Lady Anne that always graced her bedside table, and wished once again that she could remember her better. Odd that she had no recollection of the face that was so like her own. Both shared the same oval shape, high brow, hazel eyes and wide mouth. Wishing she knew more about her mother, Deborah set the miniature in its customary place. Wishes were as useless as her step-mother's endless fairy stories. Papa could rarely be persuaded to speak of his first wife. Deborah had been only three when her mother died, and the following year her father had moved to the north country where he had inherited a small estate from his uncle—and a year later had married pretty Violet Cambray.

From her bedchamber, Deborah could hear the sound of her stepmother's laughter floating up the stairs. Violet was as sweet-natured as she was pretty, and her nonsensical stories of elves and fairies and the 'little' people had once enchanted Deborah. Of course, now she was too old to believe in such taradiddles, especially the folderol that surrounded St. Valentine's Day.

Deborah quickly twisted her hair into a neat chignon at the nape of her neck. Let her sisters go into Alnwick and make fools of themselves. She would spend the morning helping her father with his herbal studies, and then if time permitted, visit poor Mr. Woodworth who was suffering so dreadfully from gout. Papa had promised him a restorative three days past, but Deborah suspected it had slipped her father's mind.

Thus determined, she hurried below stairs and into the breakfast parlor. It was a cheery room to step into, particularly on a winter morn. The sun shining in the bay windows belied the crisp chilliness without, and the appetizing aromas of sausage and kippers coming from the sideboard added to the coziness of the room. Her father, sitting at the head of the table, for once did not have a journal propped in front of him, but seemed to be listening attentively to his daughters' plans for the day. He looked up, green eyes twinkling behind his spectacles, as his elder daughter took her seat.

"Deborah, my dear, as I shall not require your assistance this morning, perhaps you would like to accompany Fanny and Emily into Alnwick?"

"Thank you, Papa, but you know I do not believe in such nonsense. How absurd to imagine that the first unmarried gentleman one sees on Saint Valentine's Day is destined to become one's husband."

"I told you so," Emily muttered.

Violet, her dark auburn hair streaked with gray, looked

sadly at her step-daughter. "Of course the charm will not work if one does not believe, but if it is, as you suggest, merely a myth—which I do not for a moment admit— there can be no harm in it. And even if you do not expect to meet your husband, surely you would enjoy the booths set up in the village, and seeing all your friends. It is a lovely day for an excursion now that the weather has turned agreeable."

Fanny felt compelled to explain, "Deb's afraid she'll see someone in the village and be destined to wed him—that's why she won't come."

"For my part, I would rather wed a village lad—even someone like Harry Bittner—than be an old maid," Emily said with an arch look at her sister.

"That is quiet enough, girls," Violet scolded. "If you mean to drive in with Papa and I, you had best run up and get your hats and gloves. You both are excused." When her younger daughters had left the table, she turned to Deborah. "I know you are too sensible to pay any heed to Emily's foolishness. As for joining us in Alnwick, you must do as you please, my dear, but we should be glad to have your company. It is not often your papa can be persuaded to leave his books for an outing."

Old maid. The appellation still rang in Deborah's ears, its sting all the more potent because she knew it for the truth. At one-and-twenty she was beyond the age when most girls married. It was yet another reason why she had no desire to drive into the village. The friends her step-mother spoke of were all married. Deborah could find better ways to spend her time than enduring the pitying looks of Charlotte MacLeod or Gladys Matthews.

She managed a smile for Violet's benefit, declined the invitation, and explained she intended to visit Mr. Wood-worth.

"Excellent," Sir John approved. "You may bring him the tincture of daffodil I promised for his gout, but remember to caution him to take no more than a spoonful on rising each morn."

Deborah nodded. She was as familiar with the potions her father brewed from his herbs, and nearly as knowledgeable about their use as he was. She knew precisely where in his storeroom to find the mixture distilled in wine from the flowers of daffodils.

Violet, who had little interest in herbs, rose, saying, "Well, you should be safe enough. Mr. Woodworth is long married, so you need have no fear on seeing him this day." At a look from her husband, she hurriedly added, "If, of course, one believed in the St. Valentine's Day legend, which I know, you do not."

The legend was nonsense, Deborah told herself, as she walked along the road, carefully avoiding the puddles left from the rain the day before. And if ever she doubted it, she need only recall the morning four years ago when she had arisen early and driven the gig to Mrs. Webster's. Their neighbor had sent an urgent message pleading for Sir John's help. Willie, the lady's youngest, had been severely scalded by a pan of boiling water he'd managed to overturn, and Mrs. Webster had pleaded with Sir John for a salve to heal the wounds.

Fortunately the mixture she desired was one of the recipes Sir John kept ready for use in his storeroom. Made from the juice of leaves of the thorn apples boiled, then strained, and mixed again with rosin, wax and turpentine, the salve was well-known in Northumberland as a curative for burns and other wounds. Sir John, on one of his expeditions to gather herbs, had not been at home that morning, but Deborah had found the necessary bottle and driven at once to the Websters'. It was on her return home that she saw the gentleman who'd had such a strange effect on her nerves.

She'd paused on the hill looking down at Lion Bridge

where it crossed the river Aln. From long habit, she glanced at the parapet where the stone lion with his stiff flagpole of a tail greeted visitors to Alnwick. The lion honoured the Percys who owned the castle overlooking the village, and was depicted on their coat of arms. Unfortunately, the lion's tail, extending in a rigid, straight line, proved an irresistible temptation to certain village lads, and it was broken off at least once each year.

That morning the lion had been guarding the bridge with his tail intact. Not that Deborah had paid the beast much attention. Her gaze had focused on the lone rider crossing the bridge on a magnificent black stallion. That the gentleman was a member of the aristocracy, she did not doubt. Even from her distant post on the hill, she could see he was splendidly clad, and the horse he rode far superior to the sort of carriage animal generally seen in Alnwick.

He had halted on the bridge near the lion, and dismounted. For several long minutes he gazed at the river, then up at the hills surrounding him. Deborah knew she was visible; that she was guilty of spying on him. But she had remained motionless in the gig, unable to drive on. . . . Even then the legend of St. Valentine had been in the back of her mind, and for an instant, she'd dared to hope that this gentleman of unusual height, broad shoulders, and dark hair, might be the one destined for her.

She had watched as he suddenly turned and mounted, but when he started his horse in her direction, she'd suddenly panicked. Lifting the reins, she'd urged their old mare to hurry homeward. Within moments, she was out of sight, her heart racing faster than old Bessie's hooves. She had drawn the mare to a halt just north of the lane leading home to compose herself.

Her response to the sight of a gentleman was uncharacteristically foolish. It was not as though she'd never been courted. At seventeen, she had already declined two offers for her hand. But none of the men from the village had ever aroused in her the rather frightening anticipation evoked by just a mere glimpse of a stranger.

Such was his unsettling effect, Deborah had never mentioned seeing him, but she had listened more carefully than was her wont to the gossip of the village. She'd expected to hear that the Percys were in residence at the castle, for she was certain her gentleman must be an aristocratic visitor. But the Percys were absent and no news of a stranger came to her ears. She had even driven out very early for the next several mornings, but the stranger had disappeared into the mists rising from the river. So much for the legend of St. Valentine's Day. Far from becoming her husband, Deborah had never laid eyes on the gentleman again. Not once in four years.

She had even began to wonder if she had not imagined the entire incident. Rarely did anyone of note visit Alnwick. They were too far north for it to be a stopping place for genteel travelers, and there was nothing remarkable about the village to attract visitors. Even the roads were disgraceful, she thought, as her booted foot slipped in a muddied rut.

She had stepped into the middle of the road where it was somewhat higher—and dryer—and tried to scrape some of the mud from the soles of her boots. She was caught unaware when the sound of wheels and thud of horses' hooves warned her that a carriage was approaching at an indecently wicked pace.

Deborah dropped her skirts and made haste to move to the embankment, but she had just stepped over the broad ruts when a carriage drawn by four powerful gray horses swept round the curve of the road. She barely caught sight of the driver, but a tiger perched at the rear of the carriage let out a strangled oath as he passed less than a foot from her. The splash of the horses' hooves as they plunged into the ruts splattered her dress with mud. Deborah muttered her own, distinctly unladylike oath.

Fortunately, she'd worn a plain gray walking dress, one

sadly patched and mended, but it was warm and suitable enough for a call on Mr. Woodworth—or had been until some thoughtless, inconsiderate Corinthian had raced along the road as though it were his private drive. And what was he doing on Denwick Lane, she wondered. He had come from the direction of Alnwick, and the road ended at Floramor, her own home.

She had scant time to worry over it, for the driver had turned his carriage and was approaching again, this time at a more decorous pace. Deborah, still smarting from the indignity of being covered in mud, barely noted the number of capes falling in elegant folds from his driving coat, or the richness of the equipage. She saw only the arrogance in a pair of dark hooded eyes, the hawk-like visage of a proud face, and the disdain in lips that dared to smile at her predicament.

"Has no one told you that you should not walk in the middle of the road, my girl?" he demanded in a languid manner as his eyes raked insolently over her figure.

"There has been no need," she replied tartly. "Denwick Lane is a private road, and those who live here do not drive as though conducting a race."

"Perhaps they would if the road were kept in decent repair," he retorted, but his eyes reassessed her, and he added in a more conciliatory manner, "However, I see I must beg your pardon, Miss—?"

"Kensington," she snapped. "And well you should, sir, for by your reckless driving you have ruined a perfectly good dress."

Sudden amusement lightened his countenance and he laughed. "No, my dear, you are doing it too brown. If, in truth, that dreadful rag is your notion of a perfectly good dress, it's clear you've lived in this secluded country for too long—and you're much too pretty to be clad in so unfashionable a garment."

"I did not say it was fashionable, sir, merely serviceable and suitable for calling on the ill—or was until your recklessness ruined it. I doubt I shall ever be able to get it clean."

"Then count it a blessing," he suggested, clearly unrepentant.

Unamused, her brown eyes scorched him with contempt. "You may discard serviceable clothing without a qualm, sir, but to those in less fortunate situations, it is a dreadful waste."

"Good heavens, if that is all that is troubling you, I shall buy you another. Now then, I believe you said your name was Kensington. Is it too much to hope that you are related to the herbalist, Sir John?"

"I am his eldest daughter," Deborah replied stiffly.

"Excellent. Then you can direct me to Floramor. I have some specimens which, in a moment of weakness, I allowed myself to be persuaded to deliver to your father. With all possible haste, I might add. I am told that if these weeds do not reach him in good time, they will die."

Deborah hesitated. She did not doubt the gentlemen. Men of science from all over the British empire, and even abroad, occasionally sent specimens for study to her father. They were invaluable to his work of preparing a herbal, and if her father had known of their arrival, nothing would have induced him to leave the house today. But never before had any of his flowers been delivered by an aristocrat in such a manner.

"Come, my girl, are you struck dumb? Have you forgotten the direction to your home?"

Deborah flushed. "Perhaps, it is only that I am struck speechless by your rudeness, sir! As for Floramor, it is at the end of the lane—a dark gray stone house set well back from the road. Unfortunately, my father is away from home. If you will give me the specimens, I shall take them with me. I must return there in any event to change my dress."

He appeared more amused than insulted, and shook his head. "I should like to oblige you, Miss Kensington, but it's impossible. There are several boxes, certainly more than you can carry. I suggest you allow me to convey both the specimens, and yourself, to the house.''

"That would be most improper," she said. "We have not been properly introduced and—"

"Allow me to correct that oversight. I am Sunderland, and we are neighbors, Miss Kensington. My estate, Stoneleigh, lies just south of Alnwick. Perhaps you have heard of it?"

She had indeed. She doubted there was anyone in England who had not heard of the notorious Marquis of Sunderland. His scandalous doings had been the subject of much gossip for years, and in Northumberland he was lambasted as an absentee owner who allowed his estate to go to ruin under the auspices of an indifferent bailiff. His Christian name was Vidal, a corruption of Vitalis which she knew from her studies meant life—and if the gossips were correct, it was an appropriate name. He was reputed to have engaged in dozens of illicit affairs, leaving a score of illegitimate children in his wake.

She gazed at him with the curiosity of one observing strange animals in a menagerie. He was certainly fashionably dressed; his drab driving coat bore no less than fifteen capes, and a double row of silver buttons. A stylish beaver hat was set carefully over glossy black locks, and the elegantly arranged folds of starched white muslin beneath his chin would have made any dandy proud. She owned him a handsome creature, but disliked his air of self-consequence.

Finally, she said, "I have heard of Stoneleigh, and of you, my lord, and if it is a choice I have betwixt riding in your carriage or walking, I would infinitely prefer to walk." Having properly set the rake in his place, she turned on her heel and started down the lane, taking care to keep to the side of the road.

A low guffaw escaped from the tiger perched at the rear of Vidal's carriage, but when his master turned his head to glare at him, the boy quickly raised a hand to hide his merriment.

"Unless you have a wish to join Miss Kensington, Bat, I suggest you keep your comments to yourself," Vidal growled. He lifted the reins and with a flick of his wrist set his team to a slow walk. Observing Miss Kensington's slender figure as she marched indignantly ahead, he deduced she had a most attractive shape beneath the atrocity she deemed a dress. He thought fleetingly of his last mistress, who would have scorned to use such a garment as even a dust rag.

Deborah did her best to ignore Lord Sunderland, but when his carriage continued to plod along just behind her, she was provoked into glancing up at him. "Pray, sir, just drive straight ahead. One of the maids will receive the boxes from you."

"Since Sir John is not at home, there is no hurry, and if I follow you, I may be certain that I shall not lose the way."

Deborah could think of nothing to say, and stalked ahead, uncomfortably conscious of his gaze on her back.

"Be careful of that puddle," Vidal called, as she narrowly missed stepping in another of the deep ruts. "This excuse for a drive is an abomination. Are you quite certain I cannot give you a lift?"

Her chin lifted proudly. "I told you, my lord, I much prefer to walk, and would do so were the distance twice as far, rather than be seen driving in a carriage with a gentleman of your repute."

"That's a facer," he acknowledged, and added, "You know you really should not believe all you hear."

She heard the amusement in his voice and knew he was laughing at her. Annoyed, she replied, "I do not judge you by rumor alone, my lord. I have the evidence of my own eyes. One has only to drive past your estate to see that it has been allowed to fall into a deplorable condition. Your tenants have my sympathy."

"It appears my tenants are more fortunate, at least in some respects, than I am," he replied. His voice remained as languid as ever, but his eyes had darkened much as clouds do at the onset of a storm, and for an instant his gloved hands tightened on the reins.

Deborah made the mistake of glancing back at him as she turned in the lane. One of her boots, already muddied, slipped on a treacherous pebble and her ankle twisted. She grasped at the hedges lining the drive, but their sparse branches gave her scant support. Helplessly, she collapsed in an ignoble heap, suffering equally from pain and mortification.

Vidal halted his team and had sprung from the curricle even as he gestured for his tiger to go to their heads. In three swift steps he was at her side. It was unkind of him, but he could not resist remaking, "They do say pride goeth before a fall. Perhaps now you will allow me to assist you."

Deborah bit her lip, fought back the surge of tears which threatened to overflow, and hastily tugged at her skirt to cover her kid boots and the portion of her leg exposed to his eyes. It was not so very far to the house and she would rather limp there, even crawl if necessary, before she would accept assistance from Lord Sunderland. She glared up at him. "Please drive on, my lord."

"Certainly," he replied agreeably. And before she realized his intent, he had bent over her, picked her up easily in his arms, and carried her towards his carriage.

She should have screamed, or perhaps swooned. However, she was not at all missish, and such was her surprise at the ease with which he had lifted her, she did neither. She knew herself not to be a featherweight, and realized there must be a great deal of strength beneath that stylish coat. She inhaled the scent of him which put her in mind of Oxlips—the sort that grew in the woods—and then she was tossed without ceremony onto the box.

"You are a most stubborn young lady, Miss Kensington," he remarked as he climbed lithely up beside her and gestured to Bat to stand away from the horses. "But you must learn to choose your ground more carefully. It never answers to attack when your position is clearly indefensible."

Recovering, she lifted her chin. "What is indefensible, my lord, is your manner, or rather your lack of manners."

He returned no answer but set his team briskly prancing up the drive. In a matter of moments he drew the grays to a halt in front of the wide doors of Floramor. He descended with the same easy grace, then lifted his hands up to her. "Will you permit my assistance now, Miss Kensington?"

She had little choice and slid towards the side of the carriage. His hands encircled her waist, but instead of setting her on her feet, he again swung her easily into his arms. "Pray, put me down at once," Deborah implored, her eyes on the windows of the house.

But he ignored her entreaty and strode towards the door. Mary had heard the carriage and opened it before him. "Oh, my heavens!"

The marquis shouldered his way inside, then demanded, "Where is the nearest sofa? Unless I am much mistaken your mistress has sprained her ankle."

"This way, sir," Mary replied, hastily dipping a curtsy, then leading him to the small drawing room just off the hall.

Vidal set his burden gently on the blue and cream sofa, then drew a footstool near for her to rest her foot upon. Before the astonished Mary, he stripped off one of his gloves, withdrew an embroidered linen handkerchief, then knelt before Deborah, and gently dabbed at the tears standing on her lashes. "Does it hurt much, my dear? I fear you wrenched your ankle badly. If you wish, Bat can fetch a doctor, but like as not he'll recommend you bathe it in cold water and keep it elevated for two or three days."

I will not cry. Swallowing hard, Deborah took the handkerchief from his hands and wiped her cheeks. She wished nothing more than to get out of her disreputable dress, get the wretched boot off her foot, and be left alone. Striving to keep her voice steady, she said as civilly as possible, "My father will see to my ankle when he returns. In the meantime, my lord, please do not let me detain you. Mary will send a boy out to collect Papa's boxes, and then you may be on your way."

Vidal took his dismissal in good part. It would be unsporting to tease her further, and he knew from past experience that her ankle must hurt like the devil. He rose easily to his feet, and made her a mock bow. "As you wish, Miss Kensington. But I am not going far, and I shall look in on you in a day or two—to make certain your ankle is quite recovered. Please convey my compliments to your father."

He was gone before she could think of a suitable retort, and it was not until much later in the day, when her family had returned home and heard an abbreviated version of her adventure, that one inescapable fact was brought to her attention.

Emily, loudly lamenting her ill luck that she was not at home when Deborah returned with so notable a person as the marquis, was interrupted by Fanny who gazed at her elder sister with awe in her wide eyes. "Do you not realize what this means, Deborah? Have you forgotten it's Saint Valentine's Day? And the first gentleman you saw was Lord Sunderland!"

Two

Deborah paid scant heed to her sister's impassioned comments. Aside from the fact that she did not believe in the St. Valentine's Day legend, Lord Sunderland was hardly a candidate for marriage with her—or with any respectable lady. He was a confirmed bachelor, a rake, ill-mannered, arrogant, conceited and obviously lost to all sense of propriety. Worse, he was an absentee landlord and had shamefully neglected his tenants. Even were he inclined to look upon Deborah as a possible bride, which was highly unlikely, *she* would not consider such a connection.

"But he was the first gentleman you saw," Fanny persisted on Thursday afternoon when she came to sit with her sister. "You know what the legend says—it means he is destined to wed you."

"The legend is nonsense," Deborah responded irritably. "And you have not considered, Fanny. Lord Sunderland is a marquis and comes from an extremely wealthy family. If he ever chooses to marry, I assure you he will look higher than a mere baronet's daughter."

"Papa says our family is a very old and honourable one.

We may not rank as high as a marquis, but I think any gentleman would be most fortunate were you to have him—and even Emily said you are the prettiest girl in Northumberland."

"Did she?" Deborah asked, quietly gratified. When they were younger, Emily and Fanny used to follow her about and emulate her in all things. But lately, her sisters had seemed only to resent Deborah and find fault with all she did.

Fanny nodded solemnly. "She said yesterday that she thought the only reason so many gentlemen came up to her was because they wished to inquire of you. I do wish you had gone with us, Deb, we had ever so much fun. But then, of course, you would not have met Lord Sunderland, so I suppose it was all for the best."

Deborah sighed, laid aside the embroidery she was stitching, and asked her sister to bring in a pot of fresh tea. It was futile trying to persuade fanciful Fanny that the encounter with Lord Sunderland meant naught. Nor was her sister the only one to persist in such delusions. Their mother and Emily were both elated with the prospect of a marquis in the family, and although Deborah tried to convince them that such a notion was an impossibility, nothing she said had the least effect. And Papa had been no help at all. On returning home Tuesday, he had treated Deborah's injury then retreated immediately to the library to inspect the boxes Lord Sunderland had delivered, and remained closeted there for the rest of the evening.

On Wednesday, he had told Deborah that the specimens were in excellent condition and he owed the marquis a vast debt of gratitude for transporting them with such promptness. Much as Sir John loved his home, he owned that living in the north made it extremely difficult to collect samples of plants that were not native to the region. He had overcome the problem of growing the more tender flowers and herbs by building an elaborate glass-house beyond the stables—but getting the specimens from London to Alnwick had always posed problems. More often than not, flowers painstakingly gathered and carefully boxed arrived in such sad condition that few of them survived.

When Sir John came in to inspect his daughter's ankle on Thursday, the problem was still much on his mind, and he remarked that he must inquire of Lord Sunderland precisely how long it took him to journey north from London. "I am of the opinion he must have made wonderful speed."

"I am not surprised," Deborah answered her father. "If the wicked pace at which the marquis travelled down Denwick Lane is usual with him, he no doubt set a new record!"

Sir John peered over his spectacles, a bit surprised by the vehemence with which his daughter spoke. "I am sure it was most unfortunate that Lord Sunderland startled you, but—"

"Startled me? Papa, he nearly ran me down, not to mention that he quite ruined my dress."

"Yes, well, that is certainly regrettable, but Deborah, my dear, only consider—six boxes of specimens, and not one of them beyond revival! 'Tis quite remarkable. I am much beholden to him. I only wish you had invited him to dine, or at least offered him a cup of tea."

"I was hardly in a position to do so, Papa," she pointed out, but her father had picked up one of his journals, and was quickly lost in his studies. His head bent over the book, he wandered from the room, leaving his daughter to fume silently. Nothing was as important to her papa as his precious plants. In all probability, if she *had* been run down, he would have only remarked it was most unfortunate and began the task of unpacking his boxes.

Deborah knew she was doing her parent an injustice. In truth, her father was extremely kind and deeply attached to all his family, even if he sometimes forgot their existence in the pursuit of his studies—but she was in a wretched mood. Her foot, despite her father wrapping it and dosing her with one of his curatives, still ached painfully, and all the attention focused on Lord Sunderland had given her an irritable headache. She shifted position again, wondered what had happened to Fanny with the tea, and was about to call for Mary, when the drawing room door opened.

Fanny danced into the room carrying a large parcel heavily wrapped in paper and tied securely. "This was just delivered, Deb—for you, with Lord Sunderland's compliments."

Deborah stared at the package as Fanny laid it beside her on the sofa. "Are you certain it is for me, and not for Papa?"

"Goose, how can you be so silly? Does it look as though it contains plants? Oh, do open it. Are you not curious?"

Deborah gingerly fingered the wrappings. She suspected what the parcel contained, and if she were correct, it was not at all an appropriate gift. Another example of Lord Sunderland's high-handedness, and lack of scruples, she told herself. But deep inside, she could not quite suppress a small quiver of pleasure.

Fanny fetched a pair of scissors and the binding cords were quickly cut, the paper wrappings laid open. Nestled in the tissue below, was a billow of muslin whitework. Carefully, Deborah drew the garment out, and spread it across her lap. The stylish walking dress had a high waistline, long sleeves, puffed at the shoulder, and a border of tiny flowers—and it was exquisitely made. Whatever his faults, the marquis had excellent taste, and if her eyes did not deceive her, he had judged her size perfectly. A sudden warmth flushed her cheeks as she remembered the feel of his hands about her waist.

"Oh, Deb, it's beautiful," Fanny squealed.

"Gracious, girls, what is all the commotion?" Lady Kensington asked as she stepped into the room. "Fanny, I could hear you in the library. Pray, remember that you are a young lady now. Only a hoyden would raise her voice in such an unbecoming manner."

"Yes, Mama," Fanny answered dutifully. "But do come see what Lord Sunderland has sent to Deborah."

Violet's brows rose as she approached the sofa and observed the walking dress spread across her elder daughter's lap. "My dear! I gather his lordship means to make amends for splattering your old gown with mud—but to send you a new dress—well, I confess I hardly know what to say."

"I do. It is most inappropriate," Deborah replied, even while she fingered the satin ribbon woven through the sleeves and across the bodice. "I shall send it back at once."

"Let us not be hasty," Violet counseled. "Perhaps we should see what your papa thinks. After all, we do not wish to offend Lord Sunderland when he has been so kind."

Emily came into the room, putting off her pelisse and gloves, and, immediately exclaimed over the gown. After she had examined it, she sat down heavily in one of the wing chairs near the fireplace, lamenting, "I wish I had a handsome marquis sending me presents. Deborah has all the luck."

"I do not call it luck when one is nearly run down by a carriage, and one's ankle is sprained—and how do you know Lord Sunderland is handsome?"

Emily smiled smugly. "I called on Charlotte MacLeod this morning, and I vow it was all she could talk about. Lord Sunderland visited Alnwick yesterday, and it appears he means to set his estate in order. He purchased all manner of supplies, and engaged a score of workmen. There has not been so much excitement in the village since the Earl of Northumberland's last visit. It's plain he means to abide here awhile, so perhaps, dear Deborah, you will have opportunity to see him again."

"She will if this is any indication," Fanny announced, waving aloft a white visiting card which she had unearthed from the tissue. On the back, in a bold sprawling hand was a message from Sunderland.

"Oh, what does it say?" Emily demanded, her eyes alight with excitement.

"Give me that," Deborah scolded, snatching the card from her sister's hand. She silently read the words: *Pray, accept my apologies and my hope that the enclosed garment will serve to make amends. I shall give myself the pleasure of calling on you tomorrow to see for myself that you have suffered no lasting harm.*

A blush suffusing her face, Deborah passed the card to her mother as she silently wished that Lord Sunderland had not promised to call. Now nothing would convince Violet, Emily, or Fanny, that the legend of St. Valentine was mere nonsense. Which, of course, it was, she told herself firmly.

At breakfast Friday morning, Deborah announced her decision not to receive Lord Sunderland when he called. Her decision caused consternation among the feminine members of her family, and she knew it was likely her father would be disappointed as well. Fortunately, he was already at work in the library.

Violet sighed. "I do not know what your papa will say. Only last evening he remarked that we owe extraordinary civility to Lord Sunderland."

"I am sure his lordship will understand," Deborah replied calmly. "I shall retire to the small parlor at the rear of the house, and you may tell him that I do not feel well enough to receive guests."

"Well, for my part," Emily declared, "I think you are extremely selfish! If you would only make a push to encourage Lord Sunderland, you could marry well enough to benefit us all. I'll wager he has a house in London. Oh, Deb, only think of it. Fanny and I could have a Season in Town."

"Emily, please try to understand. There is no question of marriage. The Marquis is merely amusing himself at my expense. If you had met him! I will only say that he is arrogant, self-centered—"

"Oh, Deb, how can you say so when he sent you that lovely dress?" Fanny demanded. "It was most thoughtful of him, and generous, too, since the dress he ruined was only one of your old ones."

"Generous? I suspect he spends more on his cravats in a month then he did on my dress. To a person of Sunderland's wealth, it was a mere trifle, and I intend to return it to him."

Violet quelled her younger girls with a look, and lightly patted her elder daughter's hand. "My dear, I think you do the gentleman an injustice. For some reason, you seem to have taken him into dislike, but he appears to have behaved very properly."

Deborah bit her lip to refrain from blurting out how that very proper gentleman had ruthlessly swept her into his arms, or how he had taunted her about her dress being little better than a rag, which, while true, was not something any person with the smallest degree of civility would have mentioned. However, it seemed impossible to convince the rest of the family that the marquis was not the gentleman they imagined him to be. Her stepmother and sisters would have to learn for themselves what Lord Sunderland was truly like. Deborah quietly begged leave to be excused, and using the cane her father had provided, limped into the small parlor.

Although her ankle was much recovered, she did not wish to let his lordship off the hook so easily. Let him think he had injured her most grievously! Perhaps that would penetrate his smug air of superiority, Deborah thought as she settled herself on the sofa and picked up her needlepoint. The others could make a fuss over him when he called; she would occupy herself with something useful.

But Deborah had not set many stitches before there was

a tap on the door and her father looked in. "My dear, may I speak with you for a moment?"

"Of course, Papa. Do you need help with cataloguing the new specimens? I promise you I am sufficiently recovered to be of assistance."

"Perhaps tomorrow," he replied with an air of vagueness. "I own I have missed your help these last two days, but I wish to speak with you about something else." He hesitated then seated himself in one of the wing chairs facing the sofa, and said in his gentle voice, "Your mama tells me that it is your intention not to receive Lord Sunderland when he calls this afternoon. I should like you to reconsider."

"But Papa, I—"

"Pray, hear me out, Deborah. If you have taken his lordship into dislike, I will not dispute with you, nor encourage him to call on you again. However, he has done me a signal service, and I would not have him meet with discourtesy in this house." He paused, looking down at his hands, then cleared his throat and continued. "I have never pressed you to wed, although you have received several offers. Perhaps that is due to my own disinclination to lose a valuable assistant, or just my own dislike for Mr. Bittner, but I prefer to believe it is because I have respect for your judgment. You are possessed with remarkable intelligence and, I believe, must be the best judge of your own happiness."

"Thank you," she replied softly, much touched by his faith in her.

Sir John nodded. "Nor shall I press you now, my child, to receive a gentleman you have taken into dislike. Much as I may regret it, I do not question your reasons or your judgment. I know you to be sufficiently sensible not to act out of mere caprice or frivolity. Nevertheless, I hope that you will oblige me by receiving Lord Sunderland when he calls today. I am under an obligation to the gentleman, and it would . . . sadden me were he to receive less than the courtesy due him in this house.''

"But if Mama and the girls receive him in my stead, surely that would suffice?''

Her father rose, adjusted his spectacles, then smiled down at her. "I believe you know the answer.''

Left alone, Deborah fumed. Her father was the kindest of men, and for all that he spent so much of his time immersed in his books, he had an innate sense of courtesy. He had not spoken idly when he said her failure to receive Lord Sunderland would sadden him. Papa held the notion that a guest in his home must be treated with the utmost consideration. No matter his own feelings, a visitor at Floramor—whether it was one of Emily's silly beaus, or the parson whose tongue ran on greased wheels—was always treated politely.

Deborah sighed, knowing she had no choice. She would have to receive Lord Sunderland, and do so with every appearance of pleasure.

His lordship called at four that afternoon, and was shown into the drawing room. Sir John rose to make him welcome, and while the marquis was made known to Lady Kensington, Deborah had ample time to observe him.

Emily would certainly dub him handsome, she thought. His olive green riding coat, superbly cut, fit snugly over his broad shoulders—as snugly as the buff doeskin trousers hugging his lordship's muscular thighs, or the black leather Hessian boots expertly fitted from knee to toe. His collar was not particularly high, but it framed a beautifully tied cravat of starched white lawn. His mode of dress was neither as stylish as a dandy, nor as careless as a sportsman—but of a certainty, it flattered the gentleman.

He moved with an easy grace and spoke in a pleasantly low voice that had Emily blushing, and Fanny grinning at him in an idiotish manner.

"And, of course, you have met my eldest daughter, Miss Kensington," Sir John said as they paused in front of Deborah's chair.

"In a most unfortunate manner," Sunderland replied, smiling down at Deborah. "May I dare to hope that you have forgiven me, and that your ankle is quite recovered?"

"It is mending very fast," she answered coolly while ignoring the first part of his question.

"You relieve me greatly," he replied, and if he was put off by her lack of warmth, he did not show it. Instead, he turned to her father, remarking, "I expect Miss Kensington's speedy recovery is due to your excellent care, sir. Everyone I met in Alnwick spoke most highly of the work you do. Tell me, is it true that you have devised a cure for arthritis?"

"Not a cure, my lord, merely a potion that eases inflammation of the joints. I find that if a decoction of the roots of Madder is mixed with a preparation of sea Holly it is most effective. Of course one must first—" he stopped abruptly, noticing his wife, seated behind Lord Sunderland, shaking her head in an admonitory manner. He understood and continued, "I must apologize, my lord. I fear I tend to monopolize the conversation when it comes to my plants. Pray be seated. I promise not to bore you further."

The marquis took the side chair opposite the sofa where Sir John's three daughters reposed. A round table stood next to him, and on the other side, Lady Kensington presided over the tea preparations. She enquired if Lord Sunderland preferred cream, lemon or sugar while she poured him a cup.

"One lump of sugar if you will," he replied, then assured his host, "Far from being bored, I am keenly interested in your work, particularly that relating to arthritis. My aunt, who is rather elderly, suffers dreadfully from the malady. There are days when she cannot move about without the aid of a cane. If you could provide her something to ease her pain, we would both be exceedingly grateful."

"Then you must allow me to supply you with a bottle of my potion. Instruct your aunt to take a spoonful on rising, after which she must abstain from either eating or drinking for at least an hour. If it proves helpful, I could provide her with the recipe. It's a fairly simple process provided she is the sort of lady who is accustomed to preparing restoratives."

Vidal smiled charmingly. "She is. I spent much of my childhood in her house and she was always dosing my brother and I with one curative or another."

"They must have been most effective," Emily said boldly. "You appear very . . . healthy, my lord."

"Thank you," he said with a chuckle, "but I fear I cannot give my aunt the credit. More often than not, we hid—or poured her concoctions into the garden just outside the window. I will say the roses which grew there seemed to find it beneficial. They are reputed to be the finest in London."

Deborah smiled, as did the others, but it did not reach her eyes. Inside she was seething. Lord Sunderland sat in the drawing room quite as though he were in the custom of spending his afternoons in such a tame manner. He conversed warmly, without the least pretention in his voice or manner. He was deferential to her father, attentive to Violet, and clearly amused by both Fanny and Emily. Deborah remained the only one of the family not to be charmed. But then she had seen another side of Lord Sunderland—when he had behaved with arrogance and blithe unconcern for ought save his own convenience. She was also mindful of the tales she heard of his lordship's licentious behavior, and the shameful way he had neglected his estate and tenants.

She continued to study him as he regaled the family with tales of his boyhood exploits with his younger brother, Philip. The dark hooded eyes glinted with laughter, the thin lips so capable of sneering curved becomingly upwards, and not once did that strong chin lift in an imperious manner. Deborah owned that, had she not met him previously, she, too, would be beguiled by his manner.

"Will your brother be coming to Alnwick to visit, my lord?" Fanny asked with undisguised interest.

"Eventually, perhaps, but Philip married last spring and is presently occupied with making improvements to an estate he purchased." He nearly laughed aloud as he saw the disappointment on the young girl's face. He could not resist teasing her a little, saying, "However, if all goes well, I plan to have my sisters join me this summer. I hope I may depend on you, Miss Fanny, and you, Miss Emily, to make them feel welcome."

"Of course, my lord," Fanny answered without noticeable enthusiasm.

"I am certain your sisters must be delightful young ladies," Lady Kensington said in an effort to atone for her daughters' lackadaisical response.

Vidal thanked her, then, mischief lurking in his eyes, added, "I would solicit your kindness for my younger brothers as well. Neither Octavius nor Sebastian are enthused with the notion of living so far north. However, I think once they make the acquaintance of such lovely young ladies as your daughters, it will do much to reconcile them."

While Emily and Fanny assured him of their willingness to be of assistance, and plied him with dozens of questions, Deborah covertly watched the marquis, a puzzled look in her eyes. She'd heard scores of tales about Sunderland, but she could not recall anyone ever mentioning his brothers. Somehow, she'd had the distinct impression that his lordship possessed no other family. Instead, it appeared he had three younger brothers and two sisters, and as the eldest of the clan, took a patriarchal interest in his siblings.

Finally, unable to contain her curiosity, she asked, "But

surely, your sisters have not been left in your charge, my lord?''

The dark eyes flickered in her direction. "You sound surprised, Miss Kensington, but I promise you I am a very strict guardian.''

Rakes often are, she thought, unimpressed.

"Your parents?'' Lady Kensington inquired in her gentle voice, ready sympathy in her warm eyes.

The marquis explained he had lost both his parents several years before when they had succumbed to a fever. It was clear he did not wish to speak of the details, and Violet did not press him, but it was also obvious that he had won her complete approval. Her maternal instincts springing to the fore, she was ready to take him to her heart. Deborah almost laughed aloud. She had never seen anyone look less in need of mothering than Lord Sunderland.

The marquis suddenly looked in her direction and smiled with singular sweetness. "I fear it is time I took my leave. Amazing, is it not, how quickly time passes when one is with pleasant company?''

"I had not noticed,'' Deborah answered pointedly. If he thought she would be as easily duped as the rest of her family, he had a great deal to learn.

Her sisters, however, were loud in their protests and Lady Kensington did her best to persuade Lord Sunderland to remain for dinner. Even Sir John added his entreaty.

"You tempt me greatly,'' his lordship replied, "but I fear I have been too long away from Stoneleigh as it is. I've employed a very good bailiff to oversee the renovations— there is a great deal which must be done to the house before my sisters and brothers arrive—but the work seems to go much faster when I am present.''

"And speed is always an object with you, is it not, my lord?'' Deborah taunted.

"Not always, Miss Kensington. I suspect you have not entirely forgiven me for racing my curricle in a private lane, but if you will allow it, I should like to prove I can drive at a most sober pace."

"That is hardly necessary, Lord Sunderland."

"Indeed it is. I should hate to think you might become fearful of strolling in your own lane merely because I am residing in the neighborhood. Permit me to take you for a drive on the morrow, and demonstrate what a sober and prodigiously slow whip I can be."

She could not help smiling slightly, but answered primly, "I am not in the least fearful, my lord, and I must resume my duties with my father—"

"Not at once, my dear," Sir John interrupted, his eyes twinkling behind his spectacles. "We shall wait a few more days, I think, until your ankle is completely mended. In the meantime, I believe it might be quite beneficial for you to drive out with Lord Sunderland. I am certain the fresh air and a bit of sun will do much to hasten your recovery. If you wish, you may go with my blessing."

She was left with nothing to say, and Lord Sunderland was quick to take advantage of her position. "Splendid, it's settled then. I shall call for you at three, if that is agreeable?"

She reluctantly gave her consent, managed to bid him a good day in a civil tone, then sighed with relief as he left the room with her father.

As soon as the gentlemen were beyond the door, Lady Kensington beamed at her eldest daughter, and hugged her warmly. "Deborah, my dearest girl, he is charming, utterly charming, and it is plain he is quite taken with you. Nothing could be more providential—a Marquis, and with two younger brothers! My stars, but we are indeed fortunate."

Three

Deborah was ready when Lord Sunderland called the following day. Despite the protests of her sisters, she had chosen to wear a simple blue silk walking dress. It was not even the best she owned, but she said she was saving her green for church on Sunday, and nothing would induce her to wear the white muslin that Lord Sunderland had sent. She tried to explain to her mother that to be forced to spend above an hour in his lordship's company, wearing a dress which he had purchased, would place her in an intolerable position.

Violet scoffed at such a notion, told her daughter she had too much sensibility, but did not press the issue. She was too gratified at seeing Deborah driving out with a marquis to quibble over minor points. And if her daughter's dress was not particularly stylish, at least it was covered by a new cloak—a very stylish garment, trimmed as it was with swansdown. She also had a new bonnet and a large muff, the total effect of which Violet declared to be very pretty.

Lord Sunderland apparently approved as well, for he

complimented her as he handed her into his carriage. She was surprised to see that he was driving a trim little carriage harnessed to a pair of well-formed chestnuts. The tiger he'd referred to as Bat stood at the horses's head.

The marquis saw her assessing glance and smiled. "I thought you would feel safer with only one team, and it's such a pretty day, I put the top down. However, if you think it too cold?"

"Not at all," she replied politely. "As long as the sun is shining, I much prefer to be in the open. But I am surprised you brought more than one carriage with you to Alnwick. I gather you intend a long stay?"

"Would you be pleased if I answered yes?" he asked as he gathered up the reins and motioned to his tiger to stand away. The boy let go, then scurried round to climb up on the platform at the back.

Her brows rose slightly, and she replied coolly. "I have not given the matter any thought, and cannot conceive that my opinion could make the slightest difference to you."

"But it does," he said with a rather strange smile. Then, without giving her opportunity to comment, he continued, "I see I am still in your black books. Tell me, Miss Kensington, do you ride?"

"When I have the opportunity."

"I mean really ride, not merely canter once round the park, then sedately return to the stables."

"I am not in the habit of riding in a park, my lord," she retorted, nettled that he thought her so unsporting. "I would wager I ride as well as you."

"That is a wager I will gladly accept," he declared, setting his team to a brisk trot. "What shall we name as stakes?"

She flushed. "I did not mean we should actually conduct a contest, my lord. It was merely a manner of speaking."

He turned and grinned at her. "Afraid, Miss Kensington?"

"Certainly not. I have ridden all my life but, setting aside the impropriety of participating in such a race, it would be a most unequal contest. The livestock at Floramor can hardly compare with your own stable."

He turned the carriage off Denwick Lane, taking the old road towards Alnwick. "You have made two objections, Miss Kensington. Which shall I answer first? The impropriety? You seem to hold a poor opinion of me, though I suspect I am no worse than any other gentleman of your acquaintance—"

"That is open to debate," she muttered, but very low.

Pretending not to have heard, he continued, "However, I am not proposing that we invite the village as witnesses. I was suggesting a private race, the sort two friends might indulge in when out riding. As for your horse, you may choose from any in my stables."

She heard the strangled oath from the tiger perched behind them, but like his lordship, ignored the diminutive groom. She eyed the chestnuts in front of them, and recalled the splendid grays she'd seen on his arrival. The two horses stabled at Floramor were adequate for their needs, but hardly of the same calibre. Old Bessie was used whenever they took the gig out, and her sister, Tessie, was occasionally ridden, but she seldom moved faster than a trot. Deborah thought fleetingly of how wonderful it would be to ride a horse capable of moving faster than a brisk trot—but she could not give into the temptation. Reluctantly, she said, "That is most generous of you, my lord, but I must decline."

"Then I shall not press you," he replied. "Of course, I am disappointed. I had thought you more—well, it does not matter." He slowed the carriage and gestured towards Lion Bridge. "A magnificent view from here, is it not?"

It was, but she was more interested in what Lord Sunderland had been about to say. "You had thought me what, sir?"

"Nothing, Miss Kensington, nothing at all. Pray forget

I mentioned the matter," he said earnestly, looking a trifle abashed.

"I insist on knowing what you meant, my lord."

He shrugged. "I only . . . well, I confess I thought you more pluck to the backbone. But backing down from a race is really nothing to be ashamed of, and I assure you, I quite understand."

The struggle within was brief; her pride won easily over her good sense. Deborah lifted her chin in a determined manner. "We will race when and where you please, my lord."

"No, I was foolish to suggest it. You were quite right to—"

"When and where you will, my lord."

"I am reluctant to disoblige a lady. If you insist, why not tomorrow? The stretch of Denwick Lane from Floramor to end of the wood?"

"Consider it settled," she declared, a flush of excitement lending colour to her cheeks.

"And the wager?" he asked, his dark eyes suddenly glinting with mischief. "I am given to understand that there is an Assembly every Wednesday in Alnwick. If you lose, you must allow me the privilege of escorting you, and leading you out for the first dance."

"Very well," she conceded, concealing her surprise at his choice of stakes. She thought for a moment of what she could ask in return, then settled on a penalty she believed would humble his lordship. "If I win, then you must agree to come assist Papa with his cataloguing for a week—on the pretext of wishing to know more about his herbal studies."

"Agreed," he said with such enthusiasm that Deborah began to wonder if she had not been deliberately provoked into entering the race. She studied his profile, but there was nothing to give her a hint of his thoughts. Then he turned off the road, guiding the carriage up an over-grown, rutted dirt lane. Uneasily she asked, "Where are you taking me, my lord?"

"Why, to Stoneleigh. You must select the horse you wish to ride."

Having been neatly maneuvered into a position which made it impossible for her to protest, she glanced away, pretending an interest in the landscape. Although Stoneleigh was situated within easy driving distance of Floramor, she had never viewed the estate—but she had heard tales of the scandalous revels hosted there by the Earl of Sunderland. It had been several years, but she could still recall coming into the still room one morning, and overhearing Mary talking to another of the maids. Debauchery was mentioned, and women who were no better than they should be, staying at Stoneleigh without benefit of chaperons. But of course Mary would say no more once she realized Deborah had come into the room.

"You are very quiet, Miss Kensington."

"I was just . . . just thinking how odd it is that I have never before seen Stoneleigh."

"No? I confess I am glad. I should like to be the one to show it to you. The house is nearly as old as Northumberland's castle, though of course much smaller. The family always considered the holding a minor one."

She nodded. "I have heard of Sunderland House outside of London. It is your county seat, I believe?"

"No longer," he replied, narrowly missing a deep rut in the road. "Apparently rumor does not travel as swiftly as I believed or you would know that Sunderland House has been let. Once the necessary renovations have been completed, I intend to make Stoneleigh my home. And at the top of the list is improvement to this excuse for a road. It's in lamentable condition."

"It has been long neglected," she commented with only the slightest touch of censure in her voice. Her thoughts were on his remarkable statement. In all her years of living in Alnwick, she could not recall the marquis ever residing at Stoneleigh for more than a fortnight or so, and that but infrequently. It was rumored that Sunderland only came north when outrage over his disreputable behavior drove him from London. Even then, he had never made the slightest effort to endear himself to his neighbours. Far from it, his licentious behaviour had shocked the country-side.

"How very somber you look, Miss Kensington. Dare I ask what you are thinking?"

"I was wondering why you should suddenly choose to live in a remote part of the country, my lord," she replied frankly. "Alnwick has little to offer a gentleman of your . . . your reputation."

"One day we shall discuss my reputation in great detail. I have warned you not to believe all you hear. But for now, come and see if you approve of the stables."

They had driven into the courtyard. Here, too, were signs of neglect and decay, but dozens of workmen were in evidence, and the clatter they set up with their hammer and saws, and calling out to one another, was near deafening. She saw several men on the roof of the stone house; another was measuring a shattered window, and everywhere she looked, stone masons were busily at work. She allowed Lord Sunderland to hand her down without comment.

"I hope one day I will be able to invite your family to dine here—at present it is hardly habitable, but we are making progress. Yes, Geoff, what is it?" he asked as an earnest young man, a sheaf of paper in his hand, a worried frown on his brow, approached.

Deborah recognized tall, dour, Geoffrey Lodestock from Alnwick. They were not well acquainted for he was several years older, but she knew his ambition was to be an architect. Unfortunately, there were few commissions in the county, especially for one lacking experience, and he had not the wherewithal to travel south and set up business. She smiled cordially as he doffed his hat.

"My lord, it's fortunate you returned. We discovered massive dryrot in the north wing, and two of the great chandeliers are completely rusted through. I have closed the entrance off until we can determine the extent of the damage. I must warn you, sir, 'tis not safe. Also, the lumber delivered this morning is not what I specified. It will have to go back . . ."

Deborah wandered away, allowing the marquis a few moments of privacy. She idly watched the gardeners at work on the east side of the house, clearing away the tangle of shrubs and weeds that were choking what was left of a formal garden. Then a small waif of a boy careened round the corner of the house, nearly knocking her off her feet.

"Pardon, miss," he muttered and would have taken flight, but she caught hold of his arm.

"Whoa, my lad. Where are you off to in such a hurry? Do you not realize it is dangerous to run pell-mell through here with so much work at hand?"

With a frightened look behind him, he muttered that he was sorry and tried to squirm free again as one of the gardeners came round the house. "Let me go!"

"Hold 'im, miss," the gardener ordered as he strode towards them brandishing a sturdy switch. "I'll teach the little beggar to steal!"

"Not with that you won't," she replied staunchly, and to the boy whispered reassuringly, "Stand still. I will not allow anyone to hurt you."

"You don't understand, miss," the gardener protested. "This here whelp is a thief. He's been stealing from all the workmen, but today we set a trap for 'im. I woulda' had 'im but he's quicker than a greased pig." The workman's hat came off and he nodded deferentially as the marquis approached. "My lord, we caught the thief I told you about. Bold as brass he was, going right into the gazebo."

"I see," Sunderland replied gravely. "You may leave him to me."

It was clear the gardener would prefer to exact his own vengeance, but after a brief hesitation, he nodded again, and reluctantly left the trio. The marquis ruffled the boy's hair. "What have you to say for yourself, my lad?"

The boy, possibly ten or eleven, shrugged, pretending a nonchalance he was far from feeling. But Deborah, standing behind him her hands resting on his shoulders, felt the thinness of his bones, and the shiver that shook them. She turned him around, taking his hands in her own, and knelt in front of him so her eyes were on a level with his. "You need not be afraid," she said gently.

"I only snatched a sandwich or two," the boy complained. "It weren't much."

"Perhaps not, but you must know stealing is wrong. What would your parents say?"

A disdainful shrug answered her. "Ain't got none. My pa loped off last spring and then Ma took sick and died."

"But—but who is taking care of you?"

"Don't need nobody," he replied and kicked at the dirt with his toe. "I kin take care of myself."

Deborah looked helplessly up at Sunderland. "I suppose we could take him to the parsonage—"

The waif squirmed beneath her hands. "Just let me go, lady. I ain't going back to no orphanage."

"I can see that will not answer," his lordship said with a smile. "Tell me lad, what are you called?"

"Toby," he muttered, as if defying the marquis to find fault with it.

"An excellent name," Lord Sunderland said, suppressing a grin. "Tell me, Toby, how would like to work in my stables? It just so happens my head groom mentioned we could use another lad."

The round eyes widened. "Do you mean it, sir?"

"If you are willing to abide my rules, I am willing to give you a chance. But it will mean hard work," Vidal warned, "and Williams's word in the stables is law. You disobey him, and he will toss you out on your heels. Is that understood?"

When the boy nodded eagerly, he smiled. "Come with me, then, and I'll introduce you to Williams. He'll show you about and explain your duties."

When they reached the stables and the situation was explained to the head groom, Deborah noticed the man did not seem the least surprised at being saddled with an urchin. She watched Williams lead the now docile boy away, then remarked, "That was well done of you, my lord."

"You need not sound so astonished, Miss Kensington. Did you truly expect me to have the lad arrested?"

"No, of course not, but you might have turned him over to the poor house, or the parson, rather than employing him yourself. I rather suspect he will be a difficult charge."

"You forget I have several younger brothers. I doubt young Toby will be as much trouble. But come, let me show you the horses."

The afternoon spent in Lord Sunderland's company gave Deborah much to think about. She had found it difficult to maintain an air of reserve with him after he had behaved so well with young Toby, and the marquis had treated her with so much deference, such thoughtfulness, she was very near to revising her first disastrous opinion of him. She sternly reminded herself that any gentleman who enjoyed Sunderland's reputation would naturally have to be possessed of a certain degree of charm; otherwise he would hardly be successful at seducing so many ladies.

Violet, of course, was titillated to learn Deborah meant to ride out with the his lordship the following afternoon, and nothing would convince her that an invitation to go riding was not tantamount to a proposal. In a burst of generosity, she owned that she was quite mistaken in having held that Deborah was foolish to turn down Henry Bittner last year when he had offered for her for the third time, or chasing off Roger Comstock when it became clear he intended marriage. "I am sure they are both very nice gentlemen, and each has a tidy little property. Either would have been an acceptable match—but a marquis! My dear Deborah, I confess I never hoped to see you so well wed, but it is no more than you deserve for you are a very good girl, and sweet-natured."

"Thank you, Mama, but pray do not have the banns called just yet," Deborah replied with a shake of her head. "Lord Sunderland has shown he has no inclination to marriage, and even were he to suddenly change, I do not believe his lordship and I are well-suited."

Astonished, Violet stared at her. "Not well-suited? Pray do not talk to me of such foolishness. He is handsome; he is wealthy; and he is a marquis. One could not possibly wish for more."

"And you are destined for each other," Fanny added as she spread heavy cream on a scone. "Remember the Saint Valentine's Day legend."

"Which is nothing but nonsense," Deborah replied. "You know I do not believe in it. If it were true, I would have been wed years ago, and so would you and Emily. Who was the first gentleman you saw on Valentine's Day this year?"

Fanny made a face. "William Comstock," she said, mentioning the younger brother of the ill-favored Roger. She rationalized quickly and added, "But that does not count, for I am scarce old enough to marry. I think one must be seventeen."

Hoping to put an end to such speculation, Deborah said, "When I was seventeen, the first gentleman I saw on Saint Valentine's Day was a stranger who had paused to rest on Lion Bridge. I never saw him again."

Emily looked up. "Perhaps one must believe in the legend for it to be effective."

Exasperated, Deborah escaped into the library, intending to assist her father for an hour or two. She knew in that sanctuary she would not have to listen to such inane talk. Her father was an herbalist and dealt in facts and precise measurements. There would be no serious talk of superstitions, myths or legends. She settled down at her desk in the alcove by the window, and in her neat hand, began recording the description and virtues of several plants from her father's notes.

Within a few moments, she glanced up to see Sir John watching her, a pensive look in his eyes. "What is it, Papa? Why are you staring at me so strangely?"

He waved a hand as if to discount his behaviour. "Pay me no heed, my dear. I was merely thinking of how much I shall miss you when you are wed. I doubt not that it will be difficult to find another who can make sense of my hand. Your stepmother tries, but she says it's little better than a scrawl and she cannot distinguish the letters."

"I suppose it seems perfectly clear to me because I am so accustomed to it," Deborah said. "But you need not trouble yourself, Papa. I do not intend to marry soon . . . if, indeed, I ever do."

"You will, my dear, I am most certain of it, and soon, I think."

His words sounded almost like a prophesy. Startled, Deborah pleaded, "Papa, surely *you* do not believe in the Saint Valentine's Day legend?"

He laughed. "It seems most unlikely to me, and dependent on so many variables, one could possibly document the truth of it. I think it just a tale—I have encountered many such in our work. No, I was not thinking of the legend, but rather of the way Lord Sunderland looked at you when he called. It was most marked. But we waste time, my dear." He adjusted his spectacles, and bent his head once again over his books.

Unsettled by his comments, Deborah returned to her own work, and picked up the next sheet of foolscap on which Sir John had inscribed his notes. Determined to set Lord Sunderland from her mind, she studied the words written in her father's shaky, nearly illegible hand. Was it an omen or mere coincidence that the stalk-like plant he'd depicted was formally called *Poma Amoris*—the Apple of Love?

It was a beautiful afternoon for a ride. The day was exceptionally warm for the end of February, and with the sun shining benevolently, one sensed spring could not be too far distant. Deborah felt her spirits rising the instant she stepped outside with Lord Sunderland and saw the horses waiting.

The day before she had chosen a small black mare with sleek lines, velvety eyes and a proud neck. Sunderland's groom, Williams, had assured her the mare, for all her small size, possessed considerable speed. She had a excellent pedigree and would have been part of his lordship's racing stable except for her size.

Deborah had adored her on sight. The marquis told her the mare was called *Bellesoir*—his sister Katharine had named her during a period when she was studying French—and was a splendid choice. The mare was too small to carry his weight, but she was a favourite of his sisters, both of whom were neck-or-nothing riders.

Sunderland gave her a leg up, remarking that he did not know how ladies managed to ride side-saddle without falling off. Deborah, who'd been riding since she was five, laughed. She hooked her left boot in the stirrup, anchored her right leg over the horn provided for that purpose, then hurriedly arranged the voluminous skirts of her blue riding habit. After gathering the reins, she nodded to the groom to stand away. Bellesoir pranced, testing the mettle of her rider, but after a few minutes she settled down. Deborah leaned forward and caressed the silky neck while murmuring soft words of encouragement.

The marquis mounted his own horse, a handsome chestnut hunter with strength in every line of his powerful form.

Deborah thought the animal looked to be temperamental, but Sunderland had him in hand within a minute or two, and led the way down the drive. Deborah rode next to him, with the groom following a discreet distance behind.

"I am surprised to see Williams, my lord. I would have thought his duties too demanding for him to play the role of chaperon."

"How observant you are, Miss Kensington. He said much the same, which accounts for his sour expression this afternoon. However, Williams has been with me since I was a boy, and I have the utmost faith in his discretion—which, in view of our race, outweighed other considerations. We must have a care for your reputation."

He spoke quite seriously. Did he not realize the irony of his remarks, Deborah wondered. Why, just being seen in his company was probably sufficient cause to set the gossips' tongues wagging. But she supposed it was a compliment to her that he was concerned. Aloud, she said, "I believe my credit is good enough to ensure my reputation would not be damaged even were the news of our race to spread."

"Do not be too certain," he replied with unaccustomed grimness. "I thought much the same once, but I quickly learned that people are apt to believe the worst of one, and scandalous tidbits have a way of spreading much more rapidly than the truth ever did."

He sounded like a man who had been unjustly slandered, and for a moment she felt almost sorry for him, which was absurd. He would probably laugh if he knew, and, indeed, the notion was ridiculous. He was, after all, the marquis of Sunderland, and his black reputation was known the length of England. Even if one were inclined to be charitable and discount the tales of all the illegitimate children he'd fathered, the hundreds of ladies he was said to have seduced—which she thought must be quite exaggerated—one could not turn a blind eye to the way he had neglected

Stoneleigh and his tenants. To her, that was a grave crime and quite unforgivable.

Her family, however, did not share her convictions. Fanny and Emily were willing to pardon the marquis anything, blinded as they were by his title and wealth. Violet would overlook his past conduct for she was too kindhearted to ever think ill of anyone. And Papa, who seemed disposed to like the marquis, never listened to gossip. Deborah liked to think she did not either, but she had seen for herself the disreputable state of Stoneleigh ... and loath though she was to admit it, she knew she was not completely unsusceptible to his lordship's considerable charm.

Rather than feeling sorry for him, she would do well to be on her guard.

With that in mind, she said, "I dislike tattle-mongers as much as you, my lord. But do you not believe in the old adage that there is no fire without some smoke? I think that a gentleman—or lady—who has led a blameless life is unlikely to suddenly find that he or she is the subject of malicious gossip."

"Once I might have agreed with you, but—well, you are still very young," he said, an odd expression in his dark eyes. However, the grim lines she'd noted about his mouth had disappeared and his mood seemed lighter. He grinned at her, suddenly looking very boyish. "Let us speak of something else. It's too fair a day to waste on idle speculation. Shall we quicken the pace? I would have you become accustomed to Bellesoir before our race."

She was more than willing and the black mare responded beautifully to her commands. They cantered to the end of the drive, then turned on Denwick Lane.

"From here to the woods?" he asked as he reined in his horse. "Is that not what we agreed upon?"

Deborah nodded mutely and prayed no carriage would appear. Rarely, did they have visitors, but it was just her luck that Mrs. MacLeod or Mrs. Comstock would choose this of all days to call on Mama.

"Of course if you have reconsidered—"

"Not at all, my lord." It may have been foolish of her to agree to such a race, but she had, and she would not go back on her word now.

He nodded, then gestured to his groom. "Is Williams acceptable to you as a judge?"

"Certainly, but I hardly think it will be difficult to decide who won."

"One never knows." He turned and instructed Williams to ride to the far end of the trees and wait there for them. When he was in place, he was to lift his hand and wave a handkerchief, then drop it, signalling the start of the race.

It was obvious from the groom's frown as he accepted the handkerchief, and his reluctant manner, that he disapproved of the affair. He glanced once at Deborah, sighed, then rode ahead.

The horses seemed to sense the excitement of their owners. Deborah held the reins tautly. She knew Sunderland had a slight advantage. His chestnut, so much larger than the mare, would have a longer stride, but she hoped that would be offset by her own lighter weight.

She saw Williams take his position, and an instant later his arm lifted. She tensed as the handkerchief fell. The chestnut, with his awesome power and long legs, lunged ahead by half-a-length. Using the pressure of her left knee and the reins, Deborah urged her mare forward. She had raced frequently when she was younger, and the old exhilaration returned. Leaning forward over Bellesoir's neck, she coaxed the tiny black to exert all of her strength. The ground flew beneath their feet, and the wind fanned Deborah's face. She felt her riding hat loosen and fall, but she was too intent on the race to care. Inch by inch, she closed the gap between the mare and the chestnut. She was nearly abreast of him when they passed Williams.

She reined in, slowly drawing Bellesoir to a halt, then

patted her neck, murmuring soft words of praise. Deborah glanced up as Sunderland, having turned his horse, cantered towards her.

"Well done, Miss Kensington. A longer course and you might have won your race."

Deborah, her cheeks flushed, her eyes bright, long blond hair tumbled about her shoulders, laughed. She'd lost, but it had been such a good race, she could not regret it. "I think you are being kind, my lord, but I will not complain. Bellesoir is truly a beauty and a delight to ride."

"A beauty," he echoed, but his eyes were on Deborah, not the mare. "It appears you lost more than the race. Williams, will you fetch Miss Kensington's hat?"

Abruptly aware of how she must appear, Deborah lifted a hand and tried vainly to tidy her hair. She avoided his eyes and said, "Well, sir, you have won your wager. I shall expect to see you Wednesday, next."

"If by that you mean I shall not see you before the Assembly, I shall regret our wager, but I hope that is not your intent. Bellesoir and half a dozen other horses at Stoneleigh need exercising. I should be vastly indebted to you, Miss Kensington, if you would ride them for me as often as possible."

"Surely, there are other people who could oblige you," she demurred.

"None who handle Bellesoir as well as you. She's too small to carry my weight or Williams. Bat could perhaps handle her, but he has not your light hand on the reins— and I would not trust her to just anyone. However, if you are worried about the propriety of riding at Stoneleigh, you may bring one or both your sisters with you."

Leaning forward, Deborah caressed the mare's neck. She felt oddly flattered, and tempted . . . much too tempted.

Four

Deborah's decision to oblige Lord Sunderland by riding Bellesoir may have troubled her, but it delighted the rest of her family. She took both Fanny and Emily with her the next afternoon for she was determined not to be caught alone with his lordship. But her precautions proved unnecessary. The marquis was not at home, nor was he present on any of the succeeding afternoons when they called. However, Williams had standing orders to allow Miss Kensington and her sisters to take out whatever horses they wished, and his housekeeper, Mrs. Painwick, always left word that the young ladies should come up to the house for a cup of tea before leaving.

None of the sisters could resist the temptation to see the inside of Stoneleigh, and so it was that in a very short time they were on terms with the housekeeper who delighted in showing them the newest renovations. Deborah learned Mrs. Painwick had been with his lordship since he was in petticoats, and she plainly idolized him. It surprised Deborah for she had not thought a man of Lord Sunderland's reputation the sort to inspire loyalty or devotion in his servants. But apparently he did, and not with just the housekeeper. From Williams to Bat and Toby in the stables, to the head gardener, it was plain his lordship was not only respected, but well-liked.

Nor was the house what she expected from a gentleman reputed to host drunken revels. Of course, he was expecting his sisters, but all the same Deborah was impressed with the appointments and the quiet elegance of the renovated rooms. She puzzled over the apparent contradictions of his nature—and his continued absence.

She had thought he would be present when she rode Bellesoir, perhaps would even force his company on her, and she had been quite prepared to behave in a cool but dignified manner designed to put Lord Sunderland in his place. But far from pressing his attentions on her, he appeared to have lost interest, and could not be troubled to be at hand when she rode. Strangely enough, Deborah discovered she felt something very much like disappointment. Which was absurd, she told herself, since it was a matter of indifference to her whether she saw him or not.

Nevertheless, when Wednesday arrived and a billet from Lord Sunderland was delivered to Violet at Floramor, Deborah watched her open it with a sinking heart, fearing that his lordship meant to cry off from attending the Assembly. Her stepmother, however, seemed pleased at what she read, and passed the letter to Deborah. It took only a few seconds to skim the few lines. Deborah smiled, but not for the world would she admit the relief she'd felt when she'd read in his bold hand that he would call for the ladies at eight, and looked forward to the pleasure of their company.

Emily looked over her shoulder, squealed happily, and could barely contain her excitement over attending her first assembly. Sir John's dislike of such gatherings and his preference for spending his evenings in the library meant he could seldom be persuaded to accompany the ladies of the house, and Violet would not consider attending without a gentleman to lend them escort.

Deborah had cared little. At sixteen, she had attended the assemblies with eagerness, at seventeen with the optimism born of youth that she might meet an eligible suitor. At eighteen, she went with reluctance and only at her stepmother's insistence, and for the last two years, she had not attended above four or five times. This year, however, Emily was old enough to go, and if her older sister lacked enthusiasm, she more than made up for it with her excited chatter and predictions of a splendid evening. Fanny, at fifteen, was considered still too young by her mother, and sulked until Sir John told her that if her attitude did not improve, she would not be permitted to attend an Assembly until she was eighteen.

Finding Fanny unsympathetic, Emily conferred with her elder sister, asking her advice on what gown to wear and how she should dress her hair, then changed her mind a dozen times. Deborah affected an air of resignation, but she accepted her stepmother's help in entwining a sheath of artificial pink roses in her hair, which was pulled to the back of her head, and fell in a shimmering cascade of curls. Violet, stepping back to admire her handiwork, declared there was not a prettier girl in all of Northumberland.

Deborah discounted her stepmother's remarks knowing her to be biased, but a few moments before the hour of eight, standing alone in her room in front of the looking glass, she decided she looked very well. She had chosen an evening dress consisting of a blush pink satin slip worn beneath an overdress of white net. The delicate coloring of the gown complemented her own fair coloring; the low cut bodice and short sleeves showed her shoulders to advantage and set off the single strand of pearls she wore.

Lord Sunderland would not dare describe this dress as a rag or dreadfully unstylish, she thought with satisfaction as she picked up her gloves and the tiny matching pink reticule.

"Deb, what is keeping you?" Fanny called out as she scurried up the stairs, having been sent to fetch her sister. It lacked only a minute or two before eight. "Mama said to tell you to hurry—" she was saying as she stepped into the room, but stopped abruptly, as she gazed in awe at her sister. "Oh, how beautiful you look!"

Whether it was the novelty of having a strange gentleman escort the ladies—and Deborah owned Lord Sunderland looked uncommonly handsome in his black dress coat— or the infectious gaiety of Emily, Deborah entered the Northumberland Hall Assembly Rooms on Market Street that evening with an unexpected sense of anticipation.

Their party was immediately greeted by Mr. Phineas Filbert, the Master of Ceremonies, who expressed at some length, and in the most embarrassingly fawning manner, his gratification at having the marquis visit the rooms. *Toadeater*, Deborah thought uncharitably. Fortunately, Lord Sunderland seemed to have as little patience as she with the profuse flattery and deftly cut Mr. Filbert off. Nor were the services of the Master needed.

Emily, far from lacking partners, was immediately surrounded by several young men from the village, all clamouring for the privilege of leading her out for the opening minuet. She used her fan to good effect, fluttering her eyelashes as she peered over it, teasing her various beaus before allowing George Rowley to pencil in his name beside the first set on her dance card.

Deborah, too, was surrounded—by a bevy of females who expressed their pleasure at seeing her, but whose eyes kept wandering towards the marquis. More amused than annoyed, she obligingly introduced him to several of her friends. She was quite prepared to see Lord Sunderland exert the charm with which he was reputed to have seduced so many females. But although he spoke civilly to each young lady, there was not the least appearance in his manner or his words of the philanderer—and he solicited none of her friends for a dance. After a very few moments, he begged leave to be excused on the pretext of finding Lady Kensington a chair.

"Thank you, my lord but pray do not trouble yourself on my account," Violet said. "I shall simply join the other ladies." She gestured towards the far wall where a long row of chairs had been arranged for the convenience of the dowagers, anxious mothers and those unfortunate young ladies not solicited to dance.

"And I shall bear you company until I see you comfortably settled," he replied with a small bow. To Deborah, he added, "Miss Kensington, do you join us or would you prefer to remain with your friends?"

Electing to accompany her stepmother, the trio strolled slowly across the room. Endeavoring to make polite conversation, she remarked, "I fear you will find our assemblies very dull, my lord."

"Do you? What a very odd opinion you must have of me. The gentleman who could not find considerable pleasure in this company must be exacting to a fault."

"Very prettily said, my lord. However, I only meant that after all the glittering balls you must have attended in London, Alnwick will seem rather tame by comparison."

"Miss Kensington! Oh, Miss Kensington!" Harry Bittner called as he crossed the room in mincing steps, moving as rapidly as his black patent shoes with the raised heels would permit.

With an inward sigh, Deborah paused and waited for him to approach. Harry fancied himself a dandy. His collars were easily the highest in the room, and so heavily starched he had difficulty in turning his head. His coat was a deep burgundy which would have been unexceptional had he not paired it with a garish yellow waistcoat, and tried to fill out the shoulders with buckram padding.

"A friend of yours?" Sunderland asked, *sotto voce,* as the gentleman approached.

"Lady Kensington, Miss Kensington, your servant," Harry said, bowing as deeply as his corset would permit.

When the ladies had acknowledged him, Deborah made him known to Lord Sunderland. Bows were exchanged, but it was clear Mr. Bittner was not one of his lordship's admirers. At the first opportunity, he turned and with the air of one conveying a great favor, informed Deborah that he would be pleased to have the honor of leading her out for the opening minuet.

"I am sorry, Mr. Bittner," she replied, "but I am promised to Lord Sunderland."

"I see," he said, a frown of disapproval creasing his brow. "Then will you not walk a little way with me? There is something of a private nature I particularly wish to say to you."

"Oh, I—perhaps, we could speak later?" she said, trying desperately to think of an adequate excuse. "At present, I must help Mama find a seat."

"Allow me to perform that service for you," Sunderland said, a look of devilment in his dark eyes. "You may safely entrust Lady Kensington to my care since I apprehend that Mr. Bittner wishes to speak to you on a matter of some urgency."

"Thank you, my lord," she returned, her tone polite but a look of fury in her hazel eyes. She reluctantly accepted Harry's proffered arm and strolled a few paces with him, but her thoughts were on Lord Sunderland. She had almost revised her opinion of him, but here was the rake of the black reputation. The gentleman with no principles. Deborah had no doubt he was laughing at her expense, laughing at Harry, and at all the provincials in this room. She had seen again the sort of crude humour that had annoyed her so on their first meeting. The sheer arrogance of the man, the—

"My dear Miss Kensington, I cannot tell you of my emotions on seeing you enter this room with Lord Sunderland."

"I beg your pardon?" Deborah said, only half-listening to Harry.

"Of course, I was delighted to see *you*, but when I realized with whom you had arrived—my dear, I must speak frankly. To see a lady of your innocence, your gentle nature, consorting with a man like Sunderland, tears my heart asunder. You have been sheltered much of your life, so I have no doubt you are unaware of the vile deeds laid at his door—too vile, my dear, to so much as hint at in your presence. But his sins are many and well known. Indeed, I cannot imagine what Sir John was thinking of to allow you to be seen in such company!"

They had paused and Harry was speaking with passionate intensity. His voice was low at the moment, but heads were starting to turn in their direction. Deborah loosened his hold on her arm. Not stopping to consider that the sentiments he expressed were almost an echo of her own, she felt an unreasonable irritation and replied coolly, "I should tell you, sir, that Papa is most fond of Lord Sunderland. As for his reputation—you must know that neither Papa nor I listen to idle gossip. Now, sir, pray allow me to return to my mother."

"Ah, you are angry with me," he said with a waggish wave of his gloved hand as he blocked her path. "Of course I quite understand. I know that you are too kind-hearted, too generous to readily think ill of others. But my dear Miss Kensington, in this instance, you must allow me to be the better judge. *I* have been to London."

Deborah sighed as he embarked on what was certain to be a lengthy monologue. Ever since he had visited what he called The Metropolis two years ago, he considered himself an expert on fashion, an arbitrator of taste, and a sophisticated man of the world. She glanced over his shoulder to see Sunderland bend attentively to speak to Violet, and her stepmother laugh at whatever he'd said. The marquis might well be an unscrupulous rake, she thought. He might amuse himself at her expense, and provoke her beyond bearing—but at least he never bored her.

". . . and I assure you, Miss Kensington, nothing, save my continuing regard for your well-being, would have induced me to speak so plainly. Of course, if I had but known that you wished to attend the assembly, I would have gladly provided you escort myself, and I can certainly arrange to drive you home."

"You are most kind, Mr. Bittner, but that is hardly necessary. Pray give me leave," Deborah said as she moved to step around him.

He reached for her hand. "My dear, I do not believe you quite understand. Mother has already commented on the odd appearance you present, arriving here with Lord Sunderland when it is well-known that you and I have nearly reached an understanding."

Deborah sighed. He had proposed to her on three separate occasions, and each time she had firmly declined his offer, but Harry Bittner was so certain of his own worth that he refused to believe she meant it. She had learned there was nothing she could say to persuade him otherwise. Aware that she was the focus of many eyes, she managed a smile and replied sweetly, "You are mistaken, sir. There is no understanding between us, but do give your mother my regards. Indeed, I believe she is signalling to you."

Harry turned to search the area near the door where he had left his mother, and in that instant, Deborah slipped past him and hurried towards her own party.

Lord Sunderland met her halfway, an odd smile on his lips. "I was beginning to wonder if you meant to recant on our wager. I gather your friend was warning you away from my company."

Her chin lifted. "I always keep my word. I might add that I am not in the habit of choosing my friends based on the recommendations—or warnings—of others."

"I am pleased to hear you say so," he replied as he

offered her his arm. The sets were just forming and he led her forward to take their position. "I thought perhaps that your—shall we say hostility?—on our first meeting was perhaps due to rumours you had heard regarding my reputation."

"My hostility, my lord, was due to your regrettable lack of manners, your arrogance and your lack of consideration for anyone other than yourself. Your reputation had nought to do with it."

"And yet . . . I do seem to recall that you said you would rather walk twice as far than to be seen driving with a gentleman of my ill repute."

Her color heightened, Deborah released his arm, took her place in the set forming, and curtsied gracefully as the music began. Opposite her, Lord Sunderland bowed. Fuming silently, she waited until the steps brought them together, then murmured, "Naturally, I had heard of your reputation, my lord, but I would not have believed it did not your boorish conduct confirm the ill opinion you enjoy among the populace."

Far from being insulted, Sunderland laughed aloud and with such unalloyed amusement, several ladies and gentlemen turned to stare, but he ignored them. He lifted his hand, entwined with Deborah's, above his shoulder, turned her neatly beneath his arm, then looked down at her.

She could not quite fathom the odd look in his eyes, but it sent a shiver racing down her spine.

"My little innocent," he whispered so softly only she could hear. "If you think my behavior on meeting you exemplifies the sort of conduct which has earned the name of Sunderland so black a reputation, you are even more naive than I had imagined."

She glanced away, unable to bear the intensity of his gaze.

"Speechless, my dear?" he asked after a moment. "Now it's my turn to be astonished. I thought nothing I could say would ever have the power to unsettle you."

"Is that your desire, my lord? To . . . to unsettle me?" she asked, her voice pitched as low as his.

"Why, no, Miss Kensington, but I hardly think the middle of the Assembly Room is the place to tell you what I do desire—but you may believe that it is a great deal more than a mere wish to see you discomposed."

The minuet ended with a flourish. The marquis bowed, then drew her gloved hand through the crook of his elbow. He said nothing further, but escorted her across the room to where Violet waited. He bowed again, and as though they had merely been discussing the weather or some innocuous topic, remarked, "Perhaps we may continue our conversation later?" Then he was gone.

Deborah spent the next morning working diligently in the library with her father, but it was hardly a productive session. Several times, she made mistakes in recording the attributes and virtues of certain specimens. Sir John, after noting that his daughter had misnamed Goat's Beard, a rather common garden flower which he had grown successfully in the glass house for years, recommended Deborah go for a drive, or—if she were so inclined—visit Stoneleigh and exercise his lordship's horses.

She apologized for her inability to concentrate, blamed it on the late hour they had returned the previous night, and agreed that fresh air might prove beneficial. She slipped out of the house without telling Emily or Fanny where she was going. At breakfast, both girls could speak of little but the Assembly. Fanny demanded every detail, and Emily was not loath to oblige her. She recounted all the particulars—including the fact that Lord Sunderland had stood up with no one except Deborah, and only for the opening minuet. The rest of the evening he had spent at Lady Kensington's side, amusing her with anecdotes about London. Her younger daughters speculated on what such conduct might mean until Deborah thought she must go mad.

She had sought refuge in the library, but thoughts of the Assembly—of Lord Sunderland especially—distracted her. Why had he wished to attend if he had no inclination to dance? And what was his purpose in signalling her out? His peculiar behaviour had provided fodder for the gossips. Deborah knew the conversation at breakfast that morning would be much the same in dozens of homes in Alnwick. *She* would be talked about, though she had done nothing to warrant it.

Considering the matter dispassionately as she drove the gig towards Stoneleigh, Deborah owned that merely allowing Lord Sunderland to escort her to the Assembly was sufficient to set tongues wagging. She had known that, of course, but the marquis had made it much worse by not soliciting any other young lady to stand up with him. Was it his intention to make her the brunt of gossip, to have her named linked with his by the villagers?

Deborah arrived at Stoneleigh with no answers to her troubling questions. Toby came running from the barn as she drove into the courtyard, and went at once to her mare's head while she dismounted. It was hardly necessary. Old Bess had to be prodded to move at all, but Deborah was pleased to see the boy attending to his duties with such promptness, and greeted him warmly.

"You riding today, Miss Kensington? Williams says Bellesoir is in need of an outing. He was hoping you'd come."

"Then we must not disappoint him," she replied with a smile. "You may tell Williams to saddle her up, Toby."

"Yes, ma'am," the boy said as he deftly unhitched Old Bessie, then led her towards the paddock.

Deborah glanced idly round the courtyard while she waited for one of the grooms to bring out Bellesoir. She noted the vast improvement of the yard in the last fortnight. The stables and fences had been given a fresh coat of paint, and the surrounding lawn neatly trimmed. Weeds which had choked the flower beds and drive were no longer in evidence. Stoneleigh was beginning to look prosperous.

A horse nickered behind her. She turned, expecting to see Williams or Bat leading out Bellesoir, but her gaze encountered Lord Sunderland's. She thought fleetingly that he looked as handsome in riding clothes as he did in formal evening attire. Then she realized he was leading two horses. Flustered, she sought for something to say and remarked inanely, "My lord, I had not expected to see you here."

The corners of his wide mouth tugged upwards though he tried to suppress an outright grin. "I do live here, Miss Kensington."

She blushed. "Yes, of course."

"I hope my presence won't cause you to change your mind about riding today. Bellesoir needs a good run, and I've been neglecting Jupiter here," he said, gesturing to the chestnut hunter nudging his shoulder.

"I do not think it would be proper, my lord. If I had known you wished to ride, I would have brought one of my sisters, but for us to go out alone—"

"Surely you do not think I would suggest anything so improper?" he interrupted, his dark eyes mocking her. "A groom will naturally accompany us."

"I should dislike to take Williams from his work, my lord."

"Oh, not Williams. I promised young Toby he could ride with us as groom. I think it would fair break his heart if you refuse—he's saddling a horse now and is so full of pride, his shirt buttons are likely to pop."

As he spoke, the boy emerged from the stables, leading a dappled gray mare. He swaggered a bit as he strode towards them, grinning all the while.

Had it been Williams, or Bat, or one of the other undergrooms, Deborah might have made her excuses, but she had not the heart to disappoint Toby. She allowed the marquis to give her a leg up, then warned him, "It will have to be a brief ride, my lord. I promised Papa I would not be long."

"As you wish," he replied, mounting his own horse. "I thought we might cut across the meadow where we can give the horses a gallop, then canter back through the woods. The gardeners have cleared a decent bridal path as far down as the stream."

She nodded her agreement and gestured for him to lead the way.

Sunderland hesitated. "We can go round by the road and have Toby open the gate, or cut across the lawn here and jump the fence. Which would you prefer?"

"The fence by all means," Deborah replied. Did he think her too faint-hearted to jump?

They kept the horses to a brisk trot as they cut across the lawn. The sun was warm on her back, the air crisp and fresh and she began to relax a little. Lord Sunderland seemed disinclined for conversation, which suited her mood. She glanced back once or twice and saw Toby about fifteen paces back, very conscious of his new duties.

"The fence is just ahead," Sunderland said, interrupting her pleasant reverie. "Shall we give the horses their heads?"

She nodded and nudged Bellesoir with her knee while subtly shifting her weight. The small mare responded at once and with such a sudden surge of power, Deborah was almost caught unaware. She tightened the reins slightly, but Bellesoir had been penned up too long, and was determined to run. Deborah drew back on the reins, but the mare ignored her, plunging straight ahead.

Deborah flew past his lordship, her heart in her mouth. She felt the ribbons of her hat loosen, then the rush of air lifted it from her head, but that was the least of her worries. Once before a horse had bolted with her and she knew she had little chance of controlling Bellesoir. It was one of the disadvantages of riding sidesaddle. She braced herself, praying the mare would take the fence without mishap.

The marquis realized a second too late that Deborah was not challenging him to another race. He caught a glimpse of her chalk-white face, the grim way her mouth was set, then spurred Jupiter—but there wasn't enough time. Sunderland saw at once that he could not head the mare off—they were too close to the fence. He set his own horse, and took the jump almost the same instant Deborah did. Behind them, Toby raced to catch up.

Bellesoir bolted across the pasture, but she was no match for the hunter, and Sunderland gained a length on her. He turned his horse slightly, edging closer to the black mare. Another two lengths and he was near enough to lean forward and catch her bridle. He gradually forced her to slow the pace, then pulled up.

The marquis dismounted just as Toby galloped towards him. He gestured to the boy to hold the reins, then strode quickly to Deborah's side, demanding roughly, "Are you hurt?"

Too shaken too speak, her breath coming in painful gasps, she slid from the saddle into his waiting arms. Her muscles had turned to water and she knew she could not stand without his support. For a long moment, she took immense comfort from the feeling of security that engulfed her as she nestled against his broad chest.

Sunderland held her, murmuring soft endearments against her hair. His large hand slid down her back, soothing her as he would a skittish filly. "There now, my darling—it is over and you're safe . . . quite safe."

Her heart slowed its frantic beating, and a little color returned to her face. Still, she did not move from his embrace. It felt so good to be enveloped in his muscular arms, so right to rest her head against his shoulder, so comforting to feel his hand lightly stroking her back—but it was also very wrong. She tilted her head back slightly, intending to tell him she was unharmed.

As her gaze locked with his, her lips parted slightly, but she stood perfectly still, almost mesmerized by the intensity of his dark eyes.

"Deborah . . ." His voice was whisper soft, almost as soft as the kiss he bestowed on her temple. Then his lips were moving against her mouth.

She closed her eyes. Swept away by a torrent of emotion, she silenced her conscience. No kiss had ever tasted as sweet . . . or as wicked.

Five

Deborah, who had refused dinner, reclined on her bed and pressed a linen handkerchief soaked in lavender water against her brow. Every time she thought of the brazen way she had behaved with Lord Sunderland, she cringed. It was mortifying to recall that she had done nothing to prevent him from kissing her—nothing, not the least protest had escaped her lips. Still, she might be forgiven such conduct under the circumstances . . . except that she had quite enjoyed the experience.

Flushing anew with embarrassment, Deborah moaned silently. She had no clear recollection of arriving home, only that Lord Sunderland had insisted on driving her in the gig. He had made polite conversation, and she supposed she must have answered him, but she knew not what she'd said. She could not meet his eyes, not after her disgraceful conduct. If only she had objected . . . made some slight effort to free herself from his embrace—instead it was the marquis who had gently set her apart from him.

He had smiled down at her, then gently brushed an

errant curl from her brow. She recalled he'd made some inane remark about how dangerous she was. The notion of herself as dangerous was so ludicrous, she would have laughed if she did not feel so wretched. He probably meant it to be kind, in the same way he'd been kind to her friends at the Assembly—only they had not thrown themselves at his head.

She heard a tap on the door and Violet's voice asking permission to enter. Reluctantly, Deborah called for her to come in.

"Still feeling ill, my dear? Your papa believes it is just a matter of nerves and desires you take this potion. He says it will calm you and allow you to rest easy tonight."

"What is it?" Deborah asked with an apprehensive look at the glass her stepmother held out. The liquid within had a strange, greenish tint.

"I am sure I have not the least idea, but your papa says it will do you good, and you are to drink it all." Violet placed the glass on the bedside table, then sat down on the bed next to her eldest daughter. She took Deborah's hand in her own, and said gently, "My dear, I may not know much about your papa's potions, and even less about horses, but I suspect there is more to your malady than the fright you took. I am not so old that I cannot recognize the signs of a young lady sorely troubled by a gentleman. Would you like to tell me about it?"

Deborah squeezed her hand. "Thank you, Mama, but there is nothing to . . . to tell."

Violet sighed. Lord Sunderland was at the root of the problem, she was certain of it. Her stepdaughter was an intrepid rider. She had seen Deborah thrown several times, and not the worst of her falls had ever sent the girl to bed with a megrim. Unfortunately, Deborah was not like Fanny or Emily—she was very reserved, and given to keeping her thoughts to herself.

Knowing it would be useless to press her daughter, Violet rose. "Very well, but I must tell you that Lord Sunderland seemed vastly concerned. He spoke with your papa at some length, and has promised to call on the morrow to see how you do. Deborah, I realize you have reservations regarding his lordship's character, but your father and I feel that he has behaved just as he ought, particularly in this instant.''

Deborah lay still, her eyes closed, until she heard the door softly shut. She wished she had the courage to tell her stepmother the truth. Neither she nor Sunderland had behaved as they ought. The thought brought a renewed attack of misery. What had she been thinking of? Clinging to his lordship in that ridiculous fashion, utterly lost to all sense of propriety and morality . . . she supposed she was fortunate Sunderland had not taken advantage of her. Certainly, one could begin to see how he had successfully seduced so many ladies. If she, who held him in aversion, could succumb to his charm, how much more vulnerable must be other ladies.

She eyed the potion Papa had sent up to settle her nerves, but did not taste it. What she needed was a magic elixir to make her impervious to Lord Sunderland. She owned he was uncommonly handsome; she willingly admitted he had considerable charm, and his kiss . . . his kiss had, for a brief moment, lifted her to the heights of heaven. But it meant nothing. Deborah reminded herself of his scandalous reputation—the score of ladies he was rumoured to have seduced, the illegitimate children he'd sired.

And even if one were inclined to set aside his reputation, to turn a deaf ear to all the rumors, one could not forgive the disgraceful way he had let Stoneleigh go to ruin and the lack of regard for his tenants. She could not care for a man with so few principles. Or should not, she amended, remembering how it felt to be held in his arms. If her traitorous body was so weak that it craved to feel his mouth on hers again, then she must stay away from Lord Sunderland—as far away as possible. Her decision should have brought her comfort, but instead another tear crept from beneath her lashes.

For ten days, Deborah kept her vow, deftly avoiding the marquis. He called the day after Bellesoir bolted, but she was not at home. He called again two days later, but Deborah had seen his carriage from the library window, and she slipped out the terrace doors, much to her stepmother's distress. Violet tried to persuade her to accompany Emily and Fanny to Stoneleigh, but Deborah refused. And when her sisters went without her, and returned with messages from Lord Sunderland, she turned a deaf ear.

Sir John worried over her.

He watched as his daughter immersed herself in work on the herbal, spending her days cataloguing the specimens, diligently recording his observations, or nurturing tender new shoots in the glass house. But there was only so much that could be accomplished at a time, and when the records were all brought up to date, Sir John suggested she take the air, or visit with her friends. Deborah refused to do either, and instead occupied herself with answering his correspondence.

Had her absorption in his work sprung from a true interest, or given her the least enjoyment, Sir John would have been delighted. But there was something heart-breaking in the way Deborah bent over her desk, silent and uncommunicative. Although she had always been the most reticent of his children, she possessed an irrepressible sense of the absurd. In the past when she was working, the silence in the library was frequently broken by sudden outbursts of her clear laughter. She had found much amusement in the common names of plants like *Go-To-Bed-At-Noon* or *Jack-an-apes on Horseback*, and had taken pleasure in relating some of the more ridiculous superstitions attached to certain plants. But not this week. She spoke but seldom, and there was a marked sadness about her mouth and a grave look in her hazel eyes that he could not like.

On Monday, not knowing what else to do, Sir John declared a holiday, and ordered his daughter from the library for a week.

"But Papa, what am I to do?" she protested.

"Why, whatever you wish, my dear. Your stepmama and sisters plan to pay a call on Mrs. MacLeod this morning. You could accompany them, or if that is not to your taste, perhaps a walk would do you good—put some color back in those pretty cheeks of yours."

Deborah found none of his suggestions appealing. She had once enjoyed Charlotte MacLeod's company, but ever since she'd wed, her friend had adopted a rather condescending attitude and always enquired of Deborah if she planned to marry soon. Her teasing suggestions that Harry Bittner would not wait forever grated on Deborah's nerves.

And a walk left one with too much time to think. Deborah sought distraction with one of the novels Emily had brought back from the lending library in Alnwick. With every expectation of enjoying a diverting read, she settled in the drawing room near the windows to take advantage of the morning light. The book, written anonymously, was highly recommended, and Emily had been effusive in her praise of it. But the tale of two sisters, one with an excess of sensibility, and the other with perhaps too much practical sense, failed to hold Deborah's attention for long. With a sigh, she laid the book aside, and decided that, after all, a walk might prove invigorating, and she would take her sketching book along with her. It had been some time since she had done any drawing, and today, with the sun shining and a hint of spring in the air, might be the ideal time to renew her skills.

Thus decided, she gathered her materials, informed Mary that she would return later in the afternoon, and set off down the lane with an apple tucked in the pocket of her cottage cloak in case she became hungry. If one went round by road, it was a considerable distance to Alnwick, but Deborah knew of a shorter way through the woods, and that path would bring her out on the hill overlooking Lion Bridge. Thinking that the prospect would make a very nice sketch, she set off in that direction.

It took only twenty minutes or so, and she had found the walk through the woods peaceful. Perhaps Papa was right, she thought. She needed to get out in the fresh air, give her mind a new direction. She chose a spot in the sun where the grass had already sprouted, settled herself comfortably and opened her sketching book. The view was perfect. With deft strokes, she outlined the bridge, the parapet, and the stone lion with his ramrod stiff tail.

Surveying her work with a critical eye, Deborah realized she was in almost the exact position she'd been four years ago when she saw the stranger on St. Valentine's Day. With a wistful smile, she penciled in the lines of the black horse he'd ridden. Odd, she thought, how perfectly she remembered every detail—almost as if it had occurred yesterday. A pity she had run away. Perhaps, if she had remained and met the gentleman, he might have made the legend of St. Valentine's Day come true. Idly, she sketched what she recalled of him; his dark cloak with several capes, the beaver hat, a bit of his profile.

She sat back and critically studied the drawing. An instant later, her pencil slashed angry lines across the page. Without realizing it, she had drawn a reasonable likeness of Lord Sunderland. Furious with herself, Deborah crumpled the sheet and tucked it in her pocket as she rose to her feet. There was little point in remaining. She knew she would not be able to concentrate.

Annoyed with herself, she retraced her steps and had nearly reached Denwick Lane when she heard a carriage approaching. She recognized the equipage and the team of chestnuts at once. Sunderland! Was there no escaping the man? Luckily, he was leaving Floramor, not just arriving, so she need not see him. She waited on the wooded path for the carriage to pass. He was driving at a wicked pace. Apparently his promise to her that she need not fear to walk in the lane had meant little.

Then she realized it was not Lord Sunderland handling the reins, but Williams—and he seemed to be in the dickens of a hurry.

It was no concern of hers, she told herself. But a nagging thought that something might be amiss caused her to quicken her steps. When she reached the house, she didn't pause to put off her hat or cloak, but went immediately to the library in search of her father. The book-lined room was empty. The presentiment within her that something was dreadfully wrong grew stronger.

"Mary?" she called as she returned to the hall, and met only silence.

A few moments later, she found the maid just coming out of the stillroom.

"Lawks, Miss Deborah, it startled me, coming on you like that when I thought none of the family at home."

"That is what I wished to ask you, Mary. Where is Papa?"

"He went to Stoneleigh, Miss. There's been a dreadful accident, and with Doctor Jennings away from home, they sent for Sir John to see if he could help."

"What . . . what sort of accident?" Deborah asked, her chest tightening painfully.

"I don't know exactly, Miss Deborah. I only heard bits and pieces, but it 'pears like the ceiling collapsed in the old wing of the house. They been working on it, but that wing was closed—or supposed to be. Anyway, that groom of his lordship's came and begged your papa to—"

"Did he say who was hurt?" Deborah interrupted.

"I can't say for certain, miss. I only heard part of what was said, then Sir John sent me to fetch some of his medicines—but it sounded like it was his lordship."

A sick feeling rose in Deborah's throat. Her hands were trembled so badly, she had to clasp them together as she tried to concentrate on what Mary was saying.

"They don't know how bad it is yet, miss. One of the workmen found his lordship, but he was unconscious, and that groom said as how they weren't able to bring him around."

She opened her mouth to speak but had to swallow twice before she could force the words beyond her throat. "I will see if . . . if Papa needs my help. Tell . . . tell Mama." It was all she could manage to say. Horrible visions of Lord Sunderland lying helpless flashed before her eyes as she hurried down the hall, and out the door.

Lifting her skirts, Deborah ran towards the stables. Mama had the gig and Old Bessie, but Tessie was still in the stables. The lad who mucked out the stalls and cared for the horses was startled to see his young mistress in such a state, but he obligingly saddled the mare for her, then gave her a leg up. Moments later, Deborah turned Tessie onto Denwick Lane, and urged the mare to hurry. A fast trot was the best Tessie could do.

Deborah murmured a prayer that Lord Sunderland was not fatally hurt. Papa, she thought, must be with him by now, and he would know what to do. She held the thought as though it were a talisman to ward off harm. *Please let him be safe.*

Wretched, Deborah finally admitted to herself that she had done the unpardonable. She had fallen in love with a rake and a scoundrel. No matter what her mind told her, no matter how despicable she thought his behavior, her heart ached for the sight of him alive and well. *Please, please dear Lord, let him be safe.*

Six

The road to Stoneleigh seemed impossibly long, and with each passing moment, Deborah envisioned the worst. The notion that she might never again cross swords with the marquis, never again hear that deep voice, or see his dark eyes lighten with amusement, was almost too much to bear. He might be a scoundrel and a rake, but she loved him. Loved him as she had never thought to love any man—loved him irrevocably with every fiber of her heart and her soul. She remembered again the warmth of his kiss and the feel of his strong arms around her. It had been heaven, she thought, and she had tossed it away as though it were nothing.

She saw now with blinding clarity that she had been a fool, presuming to judge Lord Sunderland as though she herself were perfect. His behavior in the past was something she could not like, but since coming to Alnwick, he had redeemed himself. She recalled his efforts to restore the estate . . . his kindness to young Toby, his generosity to her sisters . . . and Papa and Mama liked him. Everyone liked him, she thought, remembering Mrs. Painwick and

Williams' devotion. Only she had stood apart, withholding her friendship, her approval . . . her heart.

She had been afraid to trust Lord Sunderland, afraid to risk being hurt if he were only toying with her affections. She had allowed his reputation to frighten her. Of course, it was possible she was right, possible that he was a rake merely intent on seducing her, but there was only one way to find out. She vowed silently that if she were granted a second chance, she would let him know of the affection she held for him.

Deborah saw Lord Sunderland's carriage abandoned in the drive, his team of chestnuts still in harness. Icy fingers clutched at her heart. Surely, it was an indication of how serious matters stood for Williams to leave the horses standing. She slid off Tessie's back, and tied the reins securely before nervously approaching the door.

It swung open before she could lift the knocker, and a young boy rushed out, colliding with her on the step.

He clutched at her shoulder to prevent her falling. "I beg your pardon, miss!"

Deborah had a fleeting impression of a youth, perhaps seventeen, in coloring and build much like his lordship. His hair was disordered, as though he had pushed his hands through it several times; his cravat was yanked loose, and his coat was badly stained and ripped along the sleeve. She realized at once he must be his lordship's brother, and he was obviously in a state of distress. She swallowed over the lump in her throat, and said, "I came to enquire of your brother."

"He is not well, miss. I was just on my way to see if Doctor Jennings has returned yet. There is a gentleman with him—the herbalist, Sir John—and he's doing what he can, but my brother is still unconscious."

She saw the moistness in the boy's eyes and with ready sympathy touched his hand. "I am Sir John's daughter, and I assure you that no one knows more about medicine than my father. You, I think, must be either Octavius or Sebastian?''

"Sebastian," he replied, too distracted to question how she knew of him. "Will you excuse me, miss? I promised I would go at once.''

"Of course. There is no need to stand on ceremony with me, and I will not detain you. Just tell me where I may find your brother.''

"In the north wing—but don't go in there. The ceiling caved in which is how he came to be hurt. It's all my fault. I deserve to be flogged—''

"There is little to be gained from blaming yourself," Deborah interrupted. "Go and find the doctor. I will see what I can do to assist Papa.''

The boy needed no further urging. With a nod, he dashed down the steps and ran for the carriage. Deborah stood in the doorway, watching him for a moment as she gathered her courage. Then she turned and stepped into the hall, closing the door behind her.

She crossed the marble floor, her footsteps the only sound in the vast entry hall. No sign of Mrs. Painwick or any of the maids. Despite what Sebastian had said, Deborah assumed everyone must be in the old wing. She knew from prior visits it was located on the far side of the house, and dimly recollected that there was a dark corridor leading in that direction. She found it after several false starts. As she traversed its dim, shadowy length, she caught the sound of voices. Quickening her pace, Deborah strained to catch the words, but the long hall distorted sounds. Still she could see light at the end, and the heavy door propped open.

"I believe we may safely move him now," Sir John was saying as Deborah approached. Her father's back was to the door, and so intent was he on the inert body stretched out on the floor in front of him that he did not hear her approach.

"Papa, how is he?" Deborah asked anxiously as she

stepped into the cavern of what had once been an enormous ballroom. She could not look at the still form, but her gaze took in the crumbled plaster, wood, and stone strewn round the room, and the mangled piles of metal and glass that had once been chandeliers. Despite the danger, she noted Mrs. Painwick, Williams, Toby, and several of the maids standing respectfully near the door.

"I came as soon as I heard—" she began but broke off her words abruptly, staring numbly at the sight of Lord Sunderland, kneeling on the other side of her father. Dazed, still not quite comprehending, her gaze shifted to the still body on the floor.

The marquis rose to his feet the same instant and strode to her side. "Do not come any further, Miss Kensington. It's too dangerous."

"I . . . I thought you were injured, my lord," she murmured, her eyes raking over every detail of his beloved face and body.

For a second the worry in his eyes abated and the strain about his mouth lessened. He smiled down at her. "It was kind of you to come, but it is my brother, Octavius, who is hurt."

"I am glad you are here, Deborah," her father said. "The boy's leg is broken. I've put a splint on it and treated it with a poultice of the roots of Solomon's Seale, but until he regains consciousness, we cannot tell if there are further injuries. He may require nursing—"

"I shall tend to him," the housekeeper broke in jealously. "I've looked after Master Octavius since he was an infant, sir."

"And 'tis obvious you've done an excellent job, but the poultice will need to be changed every few hours. My daughter will show you how to prepare it and apply it. Now then, while we move the lad, will you see the cook and order a tea prepared? I believe we may each benefit by taking nourishment."

The housekeeper nodded reluctantly, and Deborah,

seeing how troubled she was, moved to her side. After a last, lingering look at Lord Sunderland, she said, "I shall come with you, Mrs. Painwick, and perhaps you will tell me how . . . Octavius came to be hurt."

Late that afternoon, when Mrs. Painwick had been persuaded to take a rest, Deborah sat in the darkened room, watching for some sign of movement from Octavius. He had awakened briefly, long enough for Sir John to examine him and to be sure there was no lasting damage. The poor boy had been in a great deal of pain, and a dose of laudanum had mercifully put him to sleep again. Papa said it was best for it allowed him to escape from the pain of his leg. And as long as his breathing remained steady, there was no need to worry. Deborah sat quietly watching him. He was a handsome boy, she thought, a great deal like his lordship though considerably younger.

A light tap on the door drew her attention and she called softly for the person to enter. She glanced round, expecting to see Mrs. Painwick, who refused to leave her charge for long, but it was young Sebastian who stepped into the room.

"How is he?" he asked, his own dark eyes holding a mixture of guilt and worry. He had returned earlier with a report that the doctor had not returned, nor was expected before the morrow. He'd been despondent until Sir John told him his brother would recover, and only needed time and rest.

"He is still sleeping, but he may awake at any moment."

"Do you think . . . that is, could I sit with him for awhile?"

Deborah nodded. "Of course. Indeed, I think the sound of your voice may do him much good." He did not look much reassured as he drew up another chair and sat near the bed. Knowing something of how he must feel, she sought to distract him. "When your brother is recovered,

I hope you will both come to visit us at Floramor. My sisters will be pleased to meet you."

He smiled slightly. "Vidal told us they are both very pretty girls. We . . . we had hoped to call on you Friday."

"Do not let it trouble you. I am certain that both Emily and Fanny will come to Stoneleigh as soon as Octavius is sufficiently recovered—or perhaps before. Do you plan a long visit?" The question was a tactful one for the house-keeper had told her the boys were sent down from their school, the result of a prank gone awry.

"Until the autumn," he said miserably, thinking of the lecture Vidal had read them. The expulsion had been his fault, too.

Misunderstanding, Deborah said sympathetically, "I think you will come to like Alnwick. I know Stoneleigh is not as grand as Sunderland House, and you must miss it terribly, but there are any number of young people here who will all be anxious to make your acquaintance."

Sebastian looked at her puzzled. "Sunderland House? You must have us confused with my cousin. We are the Deveraux branch of the family. Until Vidal inherited the title last year, we lived in Appleby in a house much smaller than Stoneleigh, I can tell you! Octavius and I shared a room, as did my sisters. Living here will be grand."

Inherited the title last year? "But I have heard of Vidal, the Marquis of Sunderland for years . . ."

Sebastian sighed. "Everyone has. It has caused us no end of trouble. You see Vidal was my grandfather's name, and both my brother and his cousin were named for him in the hope that he would leave his wealth to one or the other. My cousin, Vidal Everild, was in direct line for the title, and in the end grandfather left him his fortune so he could maintain Sunderland House and his other holdings, which was a waste. He squandered most of it and let his estates go to ruin. I don't know what might have happened if he hadn't cashed in his chips last year. He was driving a stage coach, nine sheets to the wind, and overturned it.

Broke his neck," Sebastian added with a note of satisfaction.

Deborah shook her head. "I do not understand—your brother never said a word."

"He wouldn't, but he hoped that by moving so far north, he could escape all the rumours about his cousin. I can't tell you how many people shunned him, Miss Kensington, without knowing him at all. You'd think anyone could see the sort of man he is—which is nothing like his cousin."

"Yes, of course," she said, blushing slightly. "Sebastian, would you sit with Octavius until Mrs. Painwick returns? There is something I must do."

When he agreed, she hurried from the room, and went in search of Lord Sunderland. She found him in the library, but, unfortunately, her father was sitting with him. What she had to say to his lordship was not something she wished to voice in front of her father.

Both men looked up as she came in. "Sebastian? Is he awake?" Sunderland asked, rising to his feet.

Deborah saw the concern and caring in his eyes, and wondered again how she could have been so mistaken in his character. She smiled to reassure him. "He is resting yet, and Octavius is sitting with him. I only came out for a breath of air. I . . . I thought I might walk in the garden."

As she hoped he would, Lord Sunderland crossed to her side. "Will you allow me to accompany you? It's growing dark out, and you should not wander about alone."

"Thank you, my lord. I would be grateful for your company."

"Sir John? Do you care to come with us?"

"Thank you, no. I shall remain here in case the boy awakens, and perhaps close my own eyes for a few moments."

Prayers were answered, Deborah thought, as she stepped into the hall. Lord Sunderland found her cloak for her and placed it gently about her shoulders. She nearly forgot everything else, reveling in the feel of his strong hand against her arm as he guided her down the hall and through the tall windows that opened onto the garden.

"I must thank you, Miss Kensington, for coming to our assistance. I am very grateful, especially since I know you had . . . reason not to visit this house."

She could not bear the cool politeness of his voice, or that he should yet think she still held him in aversion. She said urgently, "My lord, please do not be kind to me—I feel I do not deserve it. The truth is I misjudged you terribly, and I owe you an apology."

He paused to glance down at her, and in the fading rays of the afternoon sun she saw the question in his eyes, and then the quick comprehension.

"I see. I gather Sebastian has been talking to you."

"He told me about your cousin, if that is what you mean," she replied. "My lord, I wish you would have told me yourself. You must have known that I mistook you for him."

He shrugged lightly. "You are the not the first to do so, my dear, nor likely the last. I suppose I should have set you straight, but I had foolishly hoped that you might come to like me despite what you had heard—but let us speak of something else. Once Octavius recovers—"

"No," she protested swiftly, laying a hand on his arm. She'd heard the underlying note of wistfulness in his voice. She could not allow him to continue to think she'd been indifferent. Swallowing her pride, she said quietly, "My lord, I was not as impervious to your charm as you seem to think. Surely that day when Bellesoir bolted with me, you must have realized I was . . . attracted to you. I allowed you to kiss me—"

"You are very sweet, Miss Kensington, but there is no need to dissemble," he interrupted. He took both her hands in his and gazed down into her eyes. "I remember every detail of that day. I remember that the liberty I took shocked you so much that you were near speechless, and

I remember that you took pains to avoid me the next day when I called, and each day since.''

"You don't understand! True, I avoided you, but I did so because I feared you were merely toying with my affections. I knew of your reputation, or thought I did. I knew about the countless women you were reputed to have seduced, but even so I was afraid I could not resist you. I wanted nothing so much as to be held in your arms again—"

Her words moved him as nothing else could. Unable to resist, he bent his head, silencing her explanation with his lips. His hands released hers, but only to draw her closer. He held her pinioned in his arms, so close he could feel the frantic beating of her heart.

Frightened by her own audacity, Deborah trembled in his arms, but she would not draw back. Boldly, she lifted her hands to encircle his shoulders, and allowed her fingers to caress the silky tendrils of his hair. Her conduct was brazen but she worried over it for only an instant. Then she gave herself up to the sweet ecstasy of his kisses. Her lips moved willingly beneath his, welcoming him with a warmth and desire that surprised them both.

Vidal lifted his head and gazed wonderingly into her hazel eyes. He was deeply touched that she had come to him in this manner, that she now trusted him . . . and if a small part of his heart regretted that she had not done so before, it was, after all, unimportant. He kissed her lightly on the brow, then stepped back. He lifted his hand and gently stroked her cheek. "I am . . . honored, my dear, but I beg you not to trust me too far. You cannot begin to imagine how much I desire you. Indeed, I have done so since the first time I saw you."

She clasped his hand in hers and bent her head to kiss his fingers. "I have been such a fool—can you forgive me?"

"There is nothing to forgive—unless you refuse to wed me."

Relieved, her heart nearly bursting with joy, she laughed softly. "Is that a proposal, my lord? I vow I would expect better of a gentleman of your reputed address."

He smiled, then before she realized his intent, he knelt before her. On bended knee, his voice low and husky, he declared, "You have captured my heart, Deborah Kensington. I doubt that I am worthy of you, but I vow to love you, to cherish you always. Without you by my side, I am less than nothing. Will you, my darling, give me your hand in marriage?"

Thrilled by his words, Deborah looked tenderly down at him. It was she, this time, who reached out and gently stroked his cheek. "You have my hand, my lord, and I believe you have always possessed my heart."

He rose then, and to her intense delight, took her in his arms once again, sealing their betrothal with a long and loving kiss. When he reluctantly released her, he took her hands in his. Abruptly, he realized how cold she must be. "Your hands are like ice, Deborah. Did you leave your gloves inside?"

She shook her head. In truth, she'd been unaware of the cold, and she was in no hurry to return to the house and the propriety that must prevail within. "I think they are in my cloak," she said, as she searched the pockets. She found them, but as she pulled out her gloves, a crumpled sheet of paper fluttered to the ground.

Vidal quickly bent and retrieved it.

Deborah reached for it at the same time, embarrassed that he might see her sketch of him. "I was drawing this afternoon. I am afraid it is not very good. I shall put it in the fire."

"Are you saying my wife-to-be has no talent as an artist?" he teased. "I do not believe it!" He unfolded the paper, and smoothed it out. He recognized Lion Bridge at once, and then saw his own likeness. *She had been thinking of him— before she learned of his cousin!* The knowledge pleased him beyond reason. He looked down at her and said softly, "I would say you have considerable talent, my dear. May I keep this?"

"If you wish, my lord—"

"Vidal," he corrected.

"Vidal," she amended, savouring the sound of his name on her lips. "But I must confess it was not you I wished to draw. Only you were so much on my mind, I could not concentrate . . ."

"Then I am even more flattered. But tell me, my love, who was it you were trying to sketch? Have I a rival?"

She shook her head, blushing. "You must know that would be impossible, sir! As for the gentleman, I know not his name."

His brows lifted in astonishment. "How intriguing. I would hear more."

"There is not much to tell. It is mere foolishness. Do you know the legend of Saint Valentine's Day?"

"I do and pray you will not refer to it as foolishness. Lest you have forgotten, it was on that day I first saw you."

"So my sisters have often reminded me, but I place no stock in such nonsense. If there were any truth to the legend, I would have wed the gentleman I was trying to draw. He was a stranger to Alnwick, and I saw him on Saint Valentine's Day morn four years ago. He rode a beautiful black stallion and had paused on Lion Bridge, I suppose, to admire the view. But I never saw him again, and instead, blessedly so, fate brought you to me."

Vidal looked stunned for a moment, then threw his head back and laughed aloud.

Deborah stared at him. Aloud, she said, "I do not see cause for such amusement."

He hugged her to him. "If I am not much mistaken, my sweet, I am the gentleman you saw that day. I visited Alnwick four years ago in February, and I was much struck by the view from Lion Bridge. It's one of the reasons I chose to make my home at Stoneleigh."

"But . . . but how can that be?" she questioned. "Surely,

had you visited, I would have heard. Strangers are much remarked on in the village."

"I doubt my visit was noticed. I was here only a day or two, and camped out at Stoneleigh. I saw no one except for a few of my cousin's servants. And do not forget that I was not the marquis then, but simply Mr. Deveraux. I had heard reports that the estate been abandoned, and came to see for myself. This house has been in the family for above a hundred years, and I had some notion that my cousin might be willing to sell it to me, rather than see it go to ruin. He would not agree, of course, but I never forgot it."

"And when you inherited the title, you came back to restore the house. Do you know I hated you for neglecting it and forsaking the tenants?"

"Understandably. I felt much the same about my cousin, but it was not in my power to do ought until he died suddenly."

Dazed, Deborah murmured, "Do you see what this means, Vidal?"

"That we were destined for each other? I never doubted it, my sweet," he replied, dropping a light kiss on her brow.

But she was not to be distracted, and said somberly, "Vidal, you must promise me something."

"Anything, my darling . . ."

"Never, never tell my sisters or my mama that you were the gentleman on the bridge!"

"If you wish, but why?"

"Oh, they would be convinced beyond doubt that the legend is true, and I should never hear the end of it. You and I know that it must be only coincidence that you were here four years ago, and I chanced to see you. It can have nothing to do with the legend, can it?"

He laughed, but not unkindly, and enfolded her in his arms. "Perhaps not, but then again . . . as Lord Byron wrote, ''Tis strange—but true; for truth is always strange.'

Believe what you will, my dear. For myself, I shall always be grateful to that I found you, whatever the reason that brought me here.''

As the sun began to sink beyond the hills, and the dusk drew in about them, their silhouettes merged into one long shadow. Quiet reigned in the peaceful garden save for the soft sigh of the young lady nestled in the arms of the gentleman whom fate had destined her to wed.

Fate . . . or St. Valentine.

ABOUT THE AUTHOR

Carol Quinto lives with her family in Deltona, Florida. Her previous Zebra regency romance, *The Duke Who Came To Visit*, is available at bookstores everywhere. She is currently working on her next Zebra regency romance, *Sister Of The Bride*, which will be published in June 1997. Carol loves hearing from readers and you may write to her c/o Zebra Books. Please include a self-addressed stamped envelope if you wish a response.

ROMANCE FROM JANELLE TAYLOR

ANYTHING FOR LOVE   (0-8217-4992-7, $5.99)

DESTINY MINE   (0-8217-5185-9, $5.99)

CHASE THE WIND   (0-8217-4740-1, $5.99)

MIDNIGHT SECRETS   (0-8217-5280-4, $5.99)

MOONBEAMS AND MAGIC   (0-8217-0184-4, $5.99)

SWEET SAVAGE HEART   (0-8217-5276-6, $5.99)

ROMANCE FROM JO BEVERLY

DANGEROUS JOY   (0-8217-5129-8, $5.99)

FORBIDDEN   (0-8217-4488-7, $4.99)

THE SHATTERED ROSE   (0-8217-5310-X, $5.99)

TEMPTING FORTUNE   (0-8217-4858-0, $4.99)